**Suzanne Wright** lives in England with her husband and two children. When she's not spending time with her family, she's writing, reading or doing her version of housework – sweeping the house with a look.

She's worked in a pharmaceutical company, at a Disney store, at a primary school as a voluntary teaching assistant, at the RSCPA, and has a First Class Honours degree in Psychology and Identity Studies.

As to her interests, she enjoys reading, writing, reading, writing (sort of eat, sleep, write, repeat), spending time with her family, movie nights with her sisters and playing with her two Bengal kittens.

**To connect with Suzanne online:**

Website: http://www.suzannewright.co.uk
Facebook: https://www.facebook.com/suzannewrightfanpage
Instagram: instagram.com/suzanne_wright_author

The Dark in You series

*Burn*
*Blaze*
*Ashes*
*Embers*
*Shadows*
*Omens*
*Fallen*

# REAPER

## *Suzanne Wright*

PIATKUS

PIATKUS

First published in Great Britain in 2022 by Piatkus

3 5 7 9 10 8 6 4



*All characters and events in this publication, other than those clearly in the public domain, are fictitious and any resemblance to real persons, living or dead, is purely coincidental.*



A CIP catalogue record for this book is available from the British Library.

ISBN 978-0-349-42847-5

Printed and bound in Great Britain by Clays Ltd, Elcograf S.p.A.

Papers used by Piatkus are from well-managed forests and other responsible sources.

Piatkus
An imprint of
Little, Brown Book Group
Carmelite House
50 Victoria Embankment
London EC4Y 0DZ

An Hachette UK Company
www.hachette.co.uk
www.littlebrown.co.uk

*For Jimmy and Mike*

# CHAPTER ONE

Someone *really* needed to remind this guy that it was universally considered rude to stare.

Piper Winslow didn't judge those who gave social etiquette the cold shoulder. She'd been known to snub it herself on occasion. Life was more interesting that way. But there was an essential difference between ignoring social customs and point-blank failing to exercise common decency.

She was pretty sure that this particular reaper was very aware that it was downright disrespectful to oh so blatantly stare at people. And yet, the big bold bastard—who hadn't said so much as a brief hello to Piper—kept his gaze fixed firmly on her like it was his right. And her middle finger was beginning to twitch.

Flexing her hand around the handles of her shopping bags, Piper did her best to appear unaffected. She strived to instead focus on the other three demons in front of her and drown out the sounds echoing throughout the mall—the mish-mash of voices, the slapping of shoes on tile, the ringing of cell phones, the music playing low.

But an internal voice just kept whispering . . . *he's* still *staring at you.*

What, did she have something on her face? It didn't seem likely. Levi's companions weren't slanting her weird glances as they chatted with her. Plus, this wasn't the first time she'd caught him watching her so intently. He'd done it a few times, actually.

If he meant to simply rattle her he was wasting his time. Few things made Piper nervous. Namely wasps, her mother's driving skills, and sticking a foot out of her bedcovers at night since she'd be irrationally tormented by the thought of Annabelle grabbing it.

Piper might have wondered if she was on the receiving end of an eye-fuck. She knew better, though. Knew for a fact that Levi Cutler wasn't remotely attracted to her. Piper wasn't his type—his words, not hers. Words he'd spoken to her stepsister back when he and Celeste had dated six years ago.

It was the first time Piper had ever begrudged the woman anything. Levi . . . he was a man who made an impact on every level, and he'd for sure made an impact on Piper back then. It really had sucked large to have a thing for her stepsister's boyfriend, of all people. But Piper couldn't be faulted for that—she was just an innocent bystander. Mother Nature was to blame for shaping him the way she had.

Tall and unabashedly male, Levi had the powerful build of an MMA fighter. Broad, solid shoulders. Superbly toned arms. A hard, defined chest. Just so much lean muscle that her poor hormones didn't know what to do with themselves. Every part of him was a weapon, and it showed.

Normally, the whole 'dangerous and dominant' thing didn't really do it for her. Hell, 'dominant' seemed too tame a word for

Levi. He was an alpha to the core—it came across in everything about him. His unflinching gaze. His self-assuredness. His coolly calm, in-command air. The menacing, animal grace with which he walked. How he stood like a sentry—his head up, his back straight, his feet wide apart.

His voice was a lure all on its own—deep, smoky, compelling. His short hair was a rich dark espresso brown, and those steely gunmetal gray eyes . . . well, they were *still* locked on her.

An itch built between her shoulder blades. If they'd been alone, she would have demanded to know what the hell his problem was. But speak to him that way in front of the Primes of their lair? Nah, that wasn't an option.

Levi was not only a sentinel, he was the personal bodyguard of the male Prime. Knox Thorne expected the demons of his lair to respect all four of his sentinels. The merciless Prime didn't tolerate any bullshit so, yeah, she'd swerve pissing him off. Even her inner demon—a psychopathic entity that didn't find fear unpleasant enough to heed it—wouldn't want to get on the wrong side of him.

Her demon nonetheless would have surfaced to warn off Levi if it felt that he meant to make Piper feel threatened. But it never got that sense from him whenever he watched her this way. Neither did she but, ugh, she didn't know.

"I heard you quit your job recently," said Harper, Knox's mate and anchor. All demons had predestined psychic mates to whom they formed a bond that prevented them from turning rogue. Anchors looked out for each other and could be incredibly possessive, so sometimes the line between friend and lover blurred, but not all became mates.

Piper nodded and said, "Last week." Which was why she was here at the mall indulging in some retail therapy. Well, it was good for the soul. And stuff.

Absentmindedly toying with the gold tips of her dark hair, Harper twisted her mouth. "Tell me to butt out of your business if you want, but I was wondering why you quit."

Well it really came down to the fact that the man who was both Piper's ex-boss and ex-boyfriend was something of a dick. But she didn't want to get into all that. "I felt like a change," she fudged. When Harper lifted a 'please expand' brow, Piper sighed and added, "I don't like to badmouth previous employers."

Harper's lips quirked. "I like that response." The pale blue color of her eyes swirled like liquid, their shade deepening as they became the color of warm honey—her eyes routinely changed in such a way, and there was no predicting what shade they'd be next. "I'm only asking because I'm looking to hire another tattoo artist. I know you're good. I've seen your work. So if you're interested, give me a call and we'll set up an interview."

Piper blinked, perking up. "I'd definitely be interested."

Urban Ink was a highly popular tattoo studio here at the Underground—aptly named due to the massive demonic paradise being located below ground. It was kind of like the Las Vegas Strip, only way more eccentric with its combat ring, hellhound racetracks, and all manner of shit you simply would not expect to see. Demons were easily bored and liked cheap thrills, so it was a busy place.

"Good," said Harper, handing her a business card. "My number's on here. Be sure to call me." Her polite smile dimmed. "On another—and seriously dreary—note, we should probably let you know that Sefton's free." She was referring to a member of their lair who, in Piper's humble opinion, needed a lobotomy.

"We released him yesterday," Knox added, his ebony eyes sharp. The dude was hot as hell—tall and dark and confident. "He was . . . appropriately punished."

Piper would bet that was something of an understatement. Sefton had been held in the lair's prison for the past two months, and she didn't doubt that he'd been taken to Knox's Chamber, where lots of delightful forms of torture allegedly took place.

Well, that was what happened when you put a pregnant woman asleep and trapped her in her worst nightmare, forcing her to re-experience it over and over—which, in this particular woman's case, had been delivering a stillborn baby. To her, it had felt very real every time.

As a breed of demon known as a nightmare, Sefton could do that shit to people.

As a fellow nightmare, so could Piper.

She could also bring people out of such unnatural sleeps. So she'd woken the woman, who'd then fingered Sefton—a rejected suitor—as the culprit. Apparently, he'd cried his innocence when detained and had insisted that Piper convinced the pregnant woman to lyingly accuse him. No one other than his family, who now harbored a massive grudge against Piper, actually believed him.

"I highly doubt he will give you any trouble," Knox continued. "But if he does, be sure to report it."

"Is Sefton's brother still bothering you?" asked Tanner, another sentinel. The hellhound was also Harper's bodyguard.

Piper shook her head. "Whatever you said to Jasper worked a treat. He backed off. I've had no more calls from their father either."

Making enemies was nothing new for Piper, courtesy of one of her preternatural abilities. It was exclusive to her kind, but not very common. She could delve into a person's memories, though not *any* memory—only those that were nightmarish in nature, such as attacks and near-death experiences. As she sank into the memory, she could slow down the incident, study each scene, and search for clues.

In doing so, Piper had helped identify many offenders within her lair over the years. She'd occasionally had to subsequently deal with verbal abuse from them or their loved ones. It was absolutely tedious, but she was used to it at this point.

What was *more* than tedious was Levi staring at her with such mind-melting intensity. So if he could just tone it down, that would be great. But he didn't seem inclined to.

Eager to head home, Piper wrapped up the conversation and said her goodbyes to Tanner and the Primes. Keeping her expression friendly by sheer force of will, she met Levi's gaze once more. Going for breezy, she said, "See you around, take care." *And may the chocolate chips in your muffins continually turn out to be raisins*, she barely refrained from adding.

"You too," was his only reply. But then his psyche boldly gave her own a featherlight stroke in what felt like a goodbye, she wasn't sure—

A magnetic force viciously yanked at her mind, attempting to bond her psyche with his, causing an alien pressure to build in her head. Disorientation struck Piper first, but that was quickly buried under shock as realization slammed into her.

Holy hell, they were anchors.

That knowledge now glimmered in Levi's eyes, along with an emotion she would never have expected to see in his gaze as he looked at her: Possession.

Piper's heart went into overdrive. She didn't move. Neither did he. Nor did either of them give in to the pull of the bond.

Her inner demon didn't like his lack of action. It felt rejected. Piper, too, felt the sting of it. And yet, she continued to simply stand there, gaping at him.

*Abort. Abort.*

She mumbled more goodbyes and walked away. Her pulse still going haywire, she stepped onto an escalator, half expecting him to come after her. He didn't, though. And maybe that was for the best. Because accepting Levi as her anchor would lead to a shitshow of epic proportions.

Seriously. Celeste. Would. *Flip*.

The banshee might have dumped him, but she hadn't stopped caring about him. She'd hate that Piper had any claim to him, and that would spur Celeste into attempting to seduce him. The banshee might even succeed.

Celeste was good at drawing men back to her. Piper had seen it happen time and time again with other males. And now, with the new thread of possessiveness worming its way through her, Piper knew it would pain her to watch Levi and Celeste make their way back to each other.

Reaching the first floor of the mall, Piper hurried outside and onto the Underground's Vegas-like strip. She walked fast as she shouldered through crowds, passed venue after venue—bars, clubs, casinos, hotels, stores, restaurants—and headed to the elevator that would take her back to the surface. The whole time, her heart kept pounding in her chest.

As she began her upward journey in the elevator, Piper rubbed at her temple, feeling a headache coming on as the anchor bond continued to pull at her psyche. Her inner demon was officially in a snit. It wanted to return to Levi but was torn on whether it wanted to claim him on the spot or quite simply throat-punch him.

Piper doubted the entity's indignation would last long, or that—despite his inaction—it would easily let him go. The demon firmly believed that he belonged to it. It didn't care that he was Celeste's ex, though it did hate that he'd been intimate with the banshee.

So did Piper.

And that galled her.

Generally, she didn't do 'jealousy.' Which was a good thing, really, or she'd have been devastated when her ex, Kelvin, began banging the tattoo studio's receptionist a mere week after he and Piper agreed to separate.

The elevator finally slowed to a stop. Stepping out of it, she nodded at the demons guarding it and then crossed the basement of the club which concealed the Underground's entrance. Outside the building, she headed to the Charger she'd parked in the lot and dumped her bags in the trunk.

Driving home, she thought back on how stupid she'd been to get involved with Kelvin. Piper knew better than to mix business with pleasure. Especially when the 'business' in this case was also her boss. The relationship hadn't worked out, but there'd been no hard feelings between them. Still, it had been a kick to the gut that he'd moved on so fast. The kick might not have packed the same, for lack of a better word, punch if the receptionist wasn't someone who'd—as he knew perfectly well—always been a bitch to Piper.

More, the couple didn't confine their relationship to after-work hours. No, it had all happened right under Piper's nose. He and Trinity had repeatedly snuck off throughout the day to have sex at the studio. The office, the stockroom, the break room, the restroom—anywhere and everywhere.

Piper had done her best to ignore it. Until last week. Realizing she'd left her cell at the studio after closing time, she'd hurried back to grab it . . . and found him fucking Trinity on the chair at Piper's station. So she'd quit and then ignored all his subsequent attempts to contact her. No way was she going to work for a man who quite clearly had so little respect for her and so little regard for their friendship.

If Piper formed the anchor bond with Levi and was later forced to watch as he and Celeste became sexually reacquainted, it would be like tuning into the Kelvin show all over again, but far worse. She'd been able to walk away from Kelvin; she could move on with her life and never see him again. But there would be no walking away from Levi if they were bonded. Piper wouldn't even be able to keep a huge distance from him, since it would be mentally uncomfortable for them to be apart for long periods of time.

Knowing she had zero chance of calming the organ in her chest if she kept reflecting on everything, Piper forced herself to concentrate on the road; to simply focus on turning, switching gears, and upping or slowing her speed. But the moment she arrived at her house and parked at the curb in her usual spot, all the thoughts she'd shoved aside fought for headspace.

Sighing, Piper closed her eyes. She'd never thought that her anchor might be someone who she couldn't have in her life. She'd always imagined that she'd be thrilled to find them. Not simply because her psi-mate could strengthen her and stabilize her demon, but because she'd liked the thought of having someone who'd always have her back.

Oh, her mom and stepdad loved and supported her, but their dynamics were a little complicated. Whitney and Joe had met when Piper was just five and Celeste was eleven. The two girls . . . It wasn't that they clashed. Celeste—angry at her parents' separation and her mother's abandonment—had simply been determined to dislike both Piper and Whitney, and that had never changed.

Piper felt sorry for Celeste in many ways. The woman had a right to her anger and hurt. But constantly and unfairly venting those emotions on Piper? No, that wasn't cool.

Whitney and Joe never took sides. Piper understood why. But

their inaction was part of the problem. Celeste knew she could pull all kinds of stunts but then escape any censure by crying "*You love Piper more than me, you always take her side.*"

The tears worked every time, especially since Joe was so busy trying to compensate for how her mother had up and left her.

For Piper, it would have been nice to have someone who wouldn't be concerned with placating Celeste. Someone who would back Piper in every instance, no matter how many tears her stepsister shed.

There were downsides of having anchors, of course. Psi-mates could be as meddlesome and hyper-protective as they were territorial. But she'd have happily taken the bad along with the good, because the first could never outweigh the latter, in her opinion.

Thinking on how drawn she'd felt to Levi on sight years ago, Piper wondered if she'd subconsciously sensed he was her psi-mate. Back then, she'd done her best to hide her attraction to him. And she'd thought she'd been successful at it. Until she'd overheard a conversation between him and Celeste . . .

*"Have you noticed that my stepsister has a crush on you?" Celeste laughed, as if it were sad and pathetic. "Not that I blame her or anything." A pause. "You're not interested in her, are you?"*

*"She's not my type," said Levi.*

*"You like curves and boobs and ass. She's too thin." Celeste sniffed in disdain. "Sometimes, I wonder if maybe she has an eating disorder. It's possible, right?"*

*"Possible," he agreed.*

*"Some girls can really work a size zero. Not her. She just looks sickly. She needs some damn meat on her bones for certain. Well, if she's going for the 'I'm dying a slow but certain death' look, she totally has it down, right?"*

*"Hmm."*

*"And she wonders why she doesn't have a boyfriend."* A snort. *"Well the rest of us don't wonder, that's for sure."*

*"Hmm."*

Piper hadn't waited around to hear more. She'd rushed off before anyone could notice she'd overheard them.

She hadn't been hurt by Celeste's words. She was used to the banshee criticizing her delicate build—a build that ran in Piper's maternal family and was not at all the product of an eating disorder. But it had stung that Levi hadn't disagreed with any of the bitchy crap the banshee spouted.

It was irrational of Piper, yes. She and Levi had spoken on several occasions before that day, but they were never anything close to friends. He didn't *know* her. Plus, Celeste was his girlfriend. So there had been no reason for him to speak up in Piper's defense. Yet, his failure to do so had nonetheless stabbed her in the gut.

Likewise, it had burned that he'd no doubt been as amused by the crush as Celeste. His 'She's not my type' comment had rankled too, though it had come as absolutely no surprise to Piper.

All in all, it hadn't been a pleasant moment. But it hadn't ranked as highly on the unpleasant scale as when he didn't even acknowledge her as his anchor earlier.

Crossing to her house with her bags in hand, Piper reached back to rub at her nape. Her demon believed he'd come to them at some point—it kept sending her mental pictures of the proprietary look he'd worn when their psyches tried fusing together.

The entity had seemingly decided to ignore that there'd been no other emotion on his face. There'd been no apparent pleasure at finding his psi-mate, no resolve to form the bond, no interest in even *talking* to her.

As such, Piper felt she could safely conclude that he wouldn't be coming after her. His rejection of the bond was a good thing. Really. Seriously. Truly. Because forming an irrevocable psychic bond with a man she was not only begrudgingly attracted to but who was her stepsister's ex-boyfriend? That was just asking for trouble.

Looking down at her doorstep, Piper double-blinked, her nose twitching. Was that . . . was that a bag of dogshit? Ah, hell, it was.

She swore beneath her breath.

Man, this was *so* not her day.

Levi Cutler watched as Piper made a mad yet graceful dash for the escalator. If it wasn't for the glint of panic in her eyes, he'd have followed. Chasing down a predator who felt mentally cornered would never end well. He could give her a little time alone to get past her shock and to process their discovery. A discovery he had not at all seen coming.

One minute, he'd been staring at her, wondering if she had any clue of the many filthy things he wanted to do to her. The next moment, he'd psychically touched her without thought . . . and his world had upended. All of a sudden, she was right there at the center of it. His priorities had shifted in an instant. Nothing had changed, and yet everything felt different.

His demon had all but lunged for her, determined to claim what belonged to it. But Levi had been too taken off-guard to do anything other than stand there, at a complete loss for words.

The entity wasn't unhappy that she'd fled. On the contrary, it was amused that she thought there was anywhere she could run to escape it. The demon liked a good chase, and what better prize to receive at the end of a hunt than an anchor bond?

And there *would* be a bond.

Neither Levi nor his inner entity would settle for anything else.

Tanner looked at him, his brow wrinkled. "Is she your—"

"Don't." Levi wasn't going to have this conversation in public.

"Okay." Tanner pointed at the escalator. "But don't you think you should—"

"Don't."

The hellhound raised his hands in surrender.

Knox went to speak but then instead pursed his lips.

"Where to next?" Levi asked Harper, who studied him for a long moment but then rolled with it and mentioned a clothing store.

Over the next hour, Levi kept his senses on high alert as they wandered around the mall. He usually found no issue with keeping his mind focused on his job. But right then, it wasn't working so well. All he wanted was to be with Piper.

He couldn't stop obsessing over if she was all right, what she was doing, where her head was at. Like she'd taken over some corner of his mind. He suspected she'd permanently reside there from here on out. And he found himself okay with it, even if it was such an odd sensation.

He was more than relieved when Harper finally declared she was ready to leave. Later, as Levi parked the Primes' Bentley outside the entrance of their grand home, Harper and Tanner slid out of the vehicle.

Knox lingered. "I'm guessing you're not coming with us to Raini and Maddox's party tonight," he said, referring to an anchored pair who had also taken each other as mates.

"I have to see Piper," said Levi. They had much to talk about, not to mention an anchor bond to form.

"I thought as much. This situation may not be easy for you to navigate, what with her being the sister of an ex-bed buddy."

"Stepsister," Levi automatically corrected.

Knox inclined his head. "Whitney and Joe only ever refer to them as sisters, so I'm accustomed to doing the same."

"In many families, the 'step' part wouldn't be considered significant. But it is to Celeste—she never lets Piper forget they're not blood relatives. I don't yet know if their poor relationship will make the anchor situation easier or harder on Piper." He'd claim her either way.

"One would think that Celeste would cease immaturely resenting Piper and Whitney."

"She's a bitch toward both women, most especially Piper." Levi felt his jaw harden. "That ends now that I'm around. I won't allow it to continue."

"Sadly, I doubt it will go as smoothly as you're hoping. If you need to take some time off to get this situation sorted so you can claim Piper as your anchor, do so. This is important. Larkin can take over for you as my personal bodyguard until then."

Levi gave him a nod of thanks. "I'll call you tomorrow."

After parking the Bentley in the garage, Levi switched to his own car and drove en route to Piper's home. He knew where she lived. He knew plenty about her. He'd kept a subtle eye on her over the past six years.

Essentially, he'd channeled his attraction to her into looking out for her, since he hadn't been able to act on what he wanted.

He'd officially met her for the first time when—only two weeks before he and Celeste went their separate ways—she'd reluctantly introduced Piper to him . . . and he'd found himself caught up in pale green eyes so striking they could steal the breath from a man's lungs. She'd been barely eighteen at the time. Just a baby. And the mere thought of touching her had made him feel like a cradle-robbing bastard. But that hadn't stopped him from *looking*.

Slender with soft, subtle curves, Piper had legs up to her shoulders. Her long dark hair was thick and glossy as a panther's coat. He loved her voice—it was velvet and whiskey and pure sin. Her high, perky breasts made him think of apples. He liked apples.

She had strong cheekbones and slightly tanned skin that looked smooth as silk. He thought she might have some Romanian in her heritage, but he wasn't sure.

Back then, he'd ignored his attraction to her. He'd blocked it out. Or tried. He'd so spectacularly failed that he hadn't been able to bring himself to even *touch* Celeste. He would have ended things with the banshee if she hadn't beat him to the punch.

Despite Piper's age—he'd *tried* to let it matter but he'd failed with that as well—he might have made a move on her. It wasn't like he'd been in a serious relationship with Celeste. It had been short and shallow and non-exclusive, and they hadn't seen much of each other due to his work commitments.

However, the aftermath of their split had been far from plain sailing. And there was already so much bad blood between the two women . . . He hadn't wanted to make it worse, so he'd stayed away. And whenever they'd come across each other, he'd taken the opportunity to drink in every inch of her.

He thought of Piper from time to time. She simply *popped* into his thoughts. Some women did that. They gripped you somehow and never let go. They slipped into your mind, made a place for themselves there, and brought on the 'what ifs.'

It wasn't purely about her appearance, it was the sheer guts she showed, over and over. Whenever she used her ability to walk through a person's nightmarish memory, Piper experienced it through their senses . . . as if it were happening to her. She had to block out the victim's fear and pain to break down what happened and identify the culprit. It left her wiped, but she never hesitated to help if called upon, despite that she often had to deal with bullshit from said culprits or their families. Levi had personally intercepted many times on her behalf, though she didn't know that.

Finally arriving at her house, Levi cut the engine and headed up the narrow path that slunk through her front lawn. He knocked on her door, which opened mere moments later. Piper stood there, a glass of red wine in hand. Her gut-grabbing eyes fixed on his, making his body tighten.

"We need to talk," he said.

She muttered what sounded like, "Fuck my life," and then walked inside, leaving the door open in a reluctant invitation.

He bit back a smile and followed her into the living room. Moving to stand in front of the fireplace, she observed him closely as she sipped her wine, saying nothing. His demon returned her scrutiny, perversely pleased by how prickly she was right then.

Levi planted his feet. "You ran from me. Actually, that's not right. You ran from what you learned."

"You didn't exactly jump for joy yourself."

He flexed his fingers as her molten-sex voice slid down his spine. "I think it's safe to say it came as a shock to both of us, and neither reacted as we should have. I saw you needed time to process it, so I didn't follow you. Was that the wrong call?" He didn't believe so.

Sighing, she rubbed at her brow. "Forming the bond would be a real bad idea."

He tensed. "Don't fight this, Piper."

"Celeste—"

"Has nothing to do with this situation," he finished.

"But she'll shove her way into it. You know that. Ignoring the facts doesn't negate them."

"The only facts that matter are pretty simple. You're my anchor. You belong to me." Which gave him more satisfaction than he suspected she'd be comfortable with. "I'm yours just the same. I'm not walking away from you, so don't think to ask it of me."

"Put aside the anchor possessiveness for one minute and look at the bigger picture. Celeste thinks of you as the one that got away. So you and me having *any* kind of connection? No, she'd never take it well. Add in that she was recently dumped by her boyfriend, and she isn't in a good place right now."

"All that is sad for Celeste." Not that he actually gave much of a shit. "But how *she* feels isn't what's important to me."

"You're not at all reluctant to form the bond?" Piper asked, clearly skeptical. "You and Celeste didn't exactly part on good terms. The aftermath was ugly. Drama galore. You really want to put yourself back in her path?"

"I don't care about her path, I care about *ours*. I'm not going to let her get in the way. Nothing ever gets between me and what's mine. And you, Piper . . . you're mine."

Something he couldn't quite name flared in her eyes. She tipped her head back and drained her glass. The sight of her throat working as she swallowed the wine made his blood heat. She only made it worse by swiping her tongue over her lips, utterly oblivious to the effect she had on him.

As she placed her empty glass on the fire mantel, Levi took slow, easy steps toward her and said, "What you and I discovered today is a *good* thing, Piper. Something that should be celebrated. You can't tell me you weren't looking forward to finding your psi-mate. The vast majority of demons are. I sure as shit wanted to find mine, and here you are."

Here she'd been for *six years*, and he hadn't known who she was to him and his demon. He hadn't at all sensed it. That galled Levi big time.

He reached out and briefly gave her hand a light squeeze. A mistake, really, because the feel of her skin beneath his own only ramped up his arousal. He'd apparently made the unconscious decision to torture himself. Hunger briefly flamed to life in her eyes, making his stomach clench.

Ignoring the demands of his body, he said, "I'm not going anywhere. Especially not to placate someone who has no relevance to the situation. You're what matters to me. You're my priority." He saw that that got to her. That she wanted to reach for what he was offering. He also saw that she wasn't done hesitating.

She folded her arms. "And what if you and Celeste get back together? She'd be your priority then, she'd—Why is that funny?"

He tried dimming his amused smile with little success. "Because the idea of it is laughable. I have no interest in her, Piper. We ended for a reason. A good one."

"She dumped you."

Why Piper seemed to be under the impression that Levi was cut up about it, he had no clue. "She did it to spur me into not only fully committing to her but also agreeing to give up both my sentinel position and my role as Knox's bodyguard. She didn't like that I kept things casual, or that so much of my time and attention was taken up by my positions. Her plan had no prayer of working. I'd already decided by then that I wanted out anyway."

"I didn't know she asked you to give up your roles. It doesn't surprise me, though. She likes to be the center of all things." Piper nibbled on her lower lip. "You know, even if she doesn't want you anymore, she'll try to win you back."

"Try to pull me away from you, you mean? Maybe, but . . . I don't want her. I don't feel anything for her. That won't change."

Piper exhaled heavily, her gaze filled with so much uncertainty.

"The problem is you're used to tiptoeing around her feelings and triggers. I noticed that when I was involved with her. Your mother does it, too. So does Joe. Maybe they actively encourage you to do it, or maybe it's a case of learned behavior. Either way, it's automatic for you."

Piper double-blinked, seemingly taken off-guard. "Well . . . she's had it hard."

"You think that means her feelings hold more importance than yours?" Levi shook his head. "People like Celeste make everyone around them feel like they're walking on a minefield. How many times have you vetoed something on the basis that she'll pitch a fit? You've done it to keep the peace, but in doing so, you've also gone without." That wouldn't be happening anymore. Levi would nip that shit in the bud.

Some of the starch slipped from Piper's shoulders. She looked away, pensive. He wondered if this was the first time she'd realized how often she considered Celeste's feelings before making decisions.

"Look at me." He waited until her gaze leapt to his before he went on, "We *are* going to claim each other as anchors. I'm not asking you to agree to do it straight away, though I'd be up for it if you were. We'll take the time to get to know each other, if that's what you need. But understand this. I won't walk away. Not for you. Not for anyone. My demon wouldn't stand for it if I tried. And neither would yours."

"Quite the bossy bitch, aren't you?" There was no heat in her words.

He felt his mouth cant up. Oh, she really had no idea just how domineering he could be. He highly suspected he'd drive her crazy, but he had no intention of warning her.

She thrust her hands into her hair and puffed out a breath. "I need you to give me some time. Space."

He shrugged. "Sure, if that's what you need."

She squinted, suspicious. She should be. Because his idea of 'time and space' meant he'd be back in, oh, about twelve hours.

Levi grabbed her phone from the coffee table and punched in his number, pleased she didn't object. He then called himself using her cell so he could store her own number. He pinned her with a look. "You need anything, anything at all, you call me."

She lazily saluted him, her expression all 'Whatever.'

He didn't want to leave her. Not yet. But he'd be back soon enough, and then they could begin the whole 'getting to know each other' stage.

Needing to touch her one last time, he tucked her hair behind her ear. "Sleep well, Piper."

And then his demon abruptly *shoved* its way to the surface, taking the wheel.

Piper froze as Levi's eyes bled to black and the temperature dropped slightly. His inner entity stared at her, its gaze cold, cunning, and gleaming with possession.

Her own demon stirred in response, eyeing it boldly; sensing that it would—like Levi—steamroll both Piper and her inner entity if they allowed it. Which they wouldn't. It seemed best to communicate that now.

Forcing her muscles to untense, Piper flicked up an imperious brow. "What?"

The corner of its mouth kicked up slightly. "Hold back from us if you must, little nightmare," it said, its voice toneless. "But it will change nothing. We have waited a very, very long time to find you. We will not walk away." It gently tapped her chin. "You belong to us. With us. That is pure fact. We would not change it even if we could. So do not request that we wait too long to claim what is ours. Why bother anyway? You will still be mine. Still be his. I suggest you hurry and get used to it." The demon retreated.

*Well, now.* That fucker was intense, wasn't it?

Levi gave her a look that said he was totally behind his ever so arrogant demon on this. "I'll be seeing you soon, Piper." With that, he left.

Setting her hands on her hips, she blew out a long-ass breath. Christ, she was way too sober to deal with this right now. Well that, at least, was something she could fix.

# CHAPTER TWO

Sitting at her kitchen table the next morning, Piper waited for her best friend to answer the video call. She needed to talk about the anchor situation with someone. Olive had always been her main confidante. Although she'd relocated to Washington eight months ago to be near her newly discovered anchor, she and Piper video-called each other several times a week.

Olive answered after only a few rings, a bright smile on her elfin face. "Hey, Winslow."

Piper felt her mouth weakly quirk. "Hey, yourself."

Olive's smile faltered. "Uh-oh. What's wrong? That rat bastard Kelvin pulled another stunt, didn't he? Tell me you stabbed him at least *once*."

"I already hurled a hellfire orb at his chest."

"That's so impersonal, though. Thrusting a knife into someone is truly much more satisfying. Euphoric, even."

Piper snorted. "So your psychosis is showing no signs of retreat, I see. To answer your question, no, he's pulled no other stunts. I haven't seen him since the day I quit. He's tried calling me a few times, but I let the calls go to voicemail. I've received plenty of texts as well."

The last had read something like: *We've been friends and colleagues for years, Piper, let's not throw that away just because I fucked up.*

Their friendship hadn't meant much to him if he'd been disrespectful enough to fuck another woman on Piper's chair.

She flapped a hand. "The asshole is easy to ignore."

"So what's wrong, then?"

"Nothing should be wrong, really. In fact, the whole thing should feel 'right.' And it does. Kinda. To a degree."

Olive's eyes lit up. "You're babbling. Interesting. Ooh, I feel some intriguing news coming on."

Piper took a swig of her grapefruit juice and then set the glass back on the table. "Okay, so, you remember Levi Cutler, right? The sentinel who Celeste loosely and briefly dated years ago?"

"The one you not so secretly wanted to ride like Seabiscuit?"

"Well . . . yeah."

"Of course. That hottie is not a man who will be easily forgotten by any woman. What about him?" Olive suddenly perked up. "*Wait, you screwed him?*"

"No, nothing like that." Unfortunately. "It's, well, it turns out that he's my anchor."

Olive's brows shot up. "Whoa, you serious?"

"Ultra-serious."

"Well ain't that a kick in the boob. Have you two formed the bond yet?"

Piper shook her head. Now that the shock-induced panic had faded from her system and she'd had time to properly consider everything—including all that Levi had said during his impromptu visit last night—she was no longer in the 'it can never happen' zone. Mostly because he'd pointed something out that made her mentally come at the situation from a different angle.

"At first, I didn't intend to at all. But then Levi said something, and he's right."

"What'd he say?"

"That I often give Celeste's feelings *way* too much consideration when I make decisions. I didn't realize before now how much I do it. And I don't like that I didn't realize it." Piper had always considered herself a self-aware person. She'd evidently been wrong.

"No one pays much attention to things that they do reflexively. Your mom and Joe got you into the habit of tiptoeing around Celeste like that when you were *five*. It became the norm for you. Which is messed up. I doubt she gives a single fuck what you feel about anything. She doesn't concern herself with what goes on in your life. She will if you claim Levi as your anchor, though. I take it you haven't told her he's your psi-mate."

"Not yet." Piper rubbed her thigh. "I'm not looking forward to that conversation." It wouldn't go well, and drama really wasn't her thing.

"She'll expect you to give him up," said Olive, conjuring a nailfile out of thin air. "You know that, right?"

"Yup."

"And will you do it?"

"Only if I feel that it's the right decision *for me*." The way Piper saw it, if there was anything that she had a right to stand up and fight to keep regardless of Celeste's feelings, it was her anchor. "If I thought there was a chance he might get cozy with Celeste again, I definitely wouldn't have any interest in forming the bond."

Olive nodded. "You don't need another person in your life who's going to expect you to always be mindful of her thoughts, opinions, and reactions."

"Exactly."

Olive peeked up from the nail she was filing. "Plus, seeing them together would have made the whole thing harder due to how possessive of him you'll no doubt be feeling—it comes with the anchor package, sad to say. Added to that, if all went tits up between them, *you'd* be the one caught in the middle. You don't need that."

"No, I don't. But he swore he was done with her and that there'd be no reconciliation."

"Do you believe him?"

"Yes." Piper had heard the ring of truth in his voice. "She wanted him to give up his positions within the lair so she'd have more of his time and attention. He'll never do that, so there's nowhere for them to go, relationship-wise. Plus, going by the things Levi said to me, it wasn't more than a casual fling. Either she exaggerated things to others or she ignored his intention to keep things simple because it suited her. Whatever the case, I don't foresee them starting things up again."

"Then why are you hesitating to accept him as your anchor? If it's because you want to jump his bones, don't let that be a factor. Hormones calm down, and attractions flame out eventually. Your little thing for him will wear off in time."

Piper was counting on it. "This isn't about that. I'm hesitating because I don't want to rush into things. I want to get to know him a little first." More, Piper wanted to feel she could trust him before fully bringing him into her world. After all, he'd expect to be at the damn center of it.

"That's reasonable. I asked the same of Daniel. He wasn't happy about it, but he agreed."

"Levi wasn't pleased either, but he lied that he'd be good with it. And he agreed to give me some time and space."

Olive snorted and blew on her nails.

"What?"

"Tell me, do you really think an alpha male demon being ridden hard by anchor-level possessiveness would stay away from his newly discovered psi-mate for any real length of time?"

Piper considered that for a moment and sighed. "I suppose not."

"Why do you even want space? It seems a little counterproductive, since you can't exactly get to know him if he's not around or . . ." Olive broke off and pointed the nailfile at Piper. "I see it now. You're dragging your feet because you dread having to tell your mom and Joe about the whole thing."

"I wouldn't say I dread it, but I'm certainly not eager to have the conversation. I don't know how it's going to go. I *think* they'll be supportive of me in this, regardless of whatever scene Celeste might cause. But every time I convince myself of that, I remember the many things I wasn't allowed to do because it upset her."

"Like call Joe 'Dad' or take his surname."

"Yes. Then I start second-guessing myself. It's simply second nature for Joe and my mom to do whatever's necessary to keep the peace. Not that I think they'd ask me to forsake Levi or anything, but it will absolutely gut me if they can't be happy for me about *this one thing.* I mean, it's no small matter to find your anchor, is it? And I know it's a delicate situation, but I want this to be an occasion where they don't expect me to placate Celeste. If it isn't, I know in my bones that it will change things between me, my mom, and Joe forever."

"I understand." Olive placed down the nailfile. "I'd have my worries too, in your shoes. But they love you, Piper. They want what's best for you. They will definitely want you to have your anchor. And I actually think they'll find it a plus that it's Levi. I saw how dedicated he was to his positions when I was part of the lair. This is a man who's loyal, protective, and dependable. Not everyone has that kind of luck when it comes to psi-mates."

"He's also a bossy bastard," Piper grumbled.

"Alphas usually are. Fully expect him to meddle in your life and do what he can to improve it. Like try to help you find another job, for starters."

"Harper Thorne said I could apply to work at Urban Ink, but I'm not sure if she'd be good with it now."

Olive frowned. "Why not?"

"She might not take too kindly to me not immediately bonding with Levi—he's pretty much family to her. She might even be offended on his behalf."

"I doubt it."

"Are you forgetting how badly Daniel's mom reacted when you didn't accept him as your anchor straight off the bat? She proclaimed that you didn't deserve him. That was mere moments before she threw a mug at your head. You almost bitch-slapped her at one point."

Olive lifted her index finger. "Okay, first of all, don't let it be overlooked that Tyra's an absolute crank. Second, Harper's not Levi's mom. Will she be annoyed with you for having reservations? Maybe. But, as I recall, she didn't form the anchor bond with Knox straight away."

Piper felt her brows inch up. "That's true."

"She'd be in no position to judge you and, in fact, is more likely to understand why you want to take this slow."

"Yeah, I guess." Piper tapped her fingers on the table. "I'll call her about the job in a little while. If she's changed her mind, well, she's changed her mind."

"Levi would either change it right back or rip her a new one.

All alphas are *crazy* protective—from what I observed, he didn't seem to be an exception to that. His protective streak is going to be electric where his anchor is concerned. That's quite simply how it goes." Olive's face softened. "I'm really happy you've found your psi-mate, even if the situation isn't as simple as you'd like. I'll bet your demon's glad."

"Glad. Territorial. Antsy."

"Why antsy?"

"Because the bond hasn't been formed." The entity was currently indulging in a good ole sulk about it.

"I'm guessing it doesn't like that its anchor was involved with Celeste."

"Oh, it definitely doesn't. It still wants to claim him, though."

"So do you. And you will at some point—we both know that. It's only a matter of time." Olive twisted her mouth. "So, who are you going to tell first? Your mom and Joe, or Celeste herself?"

Piper let out a long breath and then shrugged. "I don't know. I really, really don't know."

Levi was rinsing his coffee mug when he heard a knock on the front door. He padded through his apartment and over to the door. Opening it, he found Larkin stood there wearing a shit-eating grin.

"Morning," she said. "Congrats on finding your anchor. I'm *so* fucking pleased for you."

He stepped aside to let the harpy pass. "Thanks." The other sentinels had telepathically congratulated him. Considering Larkin only lived a few doors away, it didn't surprise Levi that she'd instead come to speak with him face to face about it. "You want coffee?"

"I'm good, thanks. It must have been a shock for you to learn that Piper—someone you've not only known for years but who's the stepsister of one of your old bed-buddies—is actually your anchor," said Larkin as she followed him into the spacious living area. "Tanner said you pretty much gawked at her in silence like a moron."

Feeling his lips thin, Levi sank onto the leather sofa. "There was no gawking. I did, however, stare at her without saying a word. Little surprises me, but realizing she was my anchor took me off-guard."

"Understandable," said Larkin, taking the armchair. "You didn't go to the party last night, so I'm guessing you went to see her."

"I did."

"How'd it go? Did you claim her?"

Really, he was surprised he hadn't received a call from Harper with the same questions—the sphinx liked to be in the know. He didn't doubt she'd contact him soon. "It could have gone better, but it also could have gone worse. And no, I didn't claim her."

"Why not?"

"At first, Piper was against the idea. Gradually, the more we talked, she went from being against it to simply being reluctant. I told her that we didn't need to form the bond straight away but that I *would* claim her in the near future. She requested some time and space. I agreed."

"But, of course, you're not going to actually give her either of those things."

Feeling his mouth cant up, he gave an unapologetic shrug. "I won't rush her, but I won't keep my distance either." He splayed his hands on the armrests. "Her hesitancy seems to stem from two things—her awareness that Celeste will kick up a fuss, and some unnecessary reservations she harbors that I'll start up another fling with Celeste."

"It's natural that Piper wouldn't want an anchor who'd give less of a shit about her than about the stepsister who's a total bitch to her," Larkin pointed out, flicking her long braid over her shoulder.

"Absolutely. But I assured her I have no interest in Celeste, and I sensed that she believed me. Still, she's leery. Which amuses my demon almost as much as it frustrates it."

"To be fair, a lot of people hesitate to claim their anchor on the spot. Let her get to know you."

"I plan to. I just don't like having to wait."

"And it offends you a little that she feels the need to know you better," Larkin sensed.

"Yeah, it does. I mean, I'm not exactly a stranger to her, am I?"

"No. But at the moment, she only knows Levi the sentinel—that's one part of you, not the whole. She needs to truly know *all* of you before she can fully trust you. Which means you need to be open with her. I know that being open with people isn't really your strong point, but you're gonna have to push past that. And you're going to need to remain open with her over time, not later pull back. Unless, of course, you'll both be content with a weak anchor friendship."

Levi would be far from content with that. He wanted Piper to trust, depend on, and feel safe with him. Wanted her to feel more comfortable around him than she did with anyone else.

"I didn't expect to be this affected by finding my psi-mate," he said. "Intellectually, I knew she'd be important to me. I knew I'd be protective and possessive. I knew I'd feel driven to form the bond. But I didn't anticipate how intense those feelings would be, even though I witnessed how much of an impact finding Harper had on Knox."

"I think it's one thing to *see* how it affects others. It's another thing to truly understand."

Levi nodded. "I get now why Knox was so determined to improve Harper's personal situation and bring her into our lair. I want to make Piper's life better. I want to be someone she relies on. I want us to be tied so she'll be stronger and I can feel certain she'll never turn rogue. Like I said, it's intense. And yet, it doesn't bother me. It feels too natural to be uncomfortable."

Larkin studied his face closely. "You're worried that it isn't feeling so natural and comfortable for her."

"It can't be if she's set on making me wait, can it?"

"Yes, it can. Like I already pointed out, she doesn't know you well enough to feel at ease with you having such a massive role in her life. But she'll be in the same boat as you. She'll want for and from you all the things that you want for and from her. She won't be able to help it. It's too instinctive."

He grunted. "I suppose."

"And you can find comfort in knowing that her demon won't let her hold back for long. It'll take the matter into its own hands if it deems it necessary. I doubt the situation will reach that point, though. It's not easy to stay away from your anchor once you've touched their psyche," she added, her eyes dulling.

Knowing where the harpy's mind had gone, Levi said, "You're better off without him, Lark."

"I know." She gave her head a fast shake. "We're not talking about me and my anchor, though. We're talking about you and Piper." Her tone warned him not to press her.

Levi inwardly sighed, aware that pushing the harpy on this would get him nowhere. She rarely spoke of her anchor, and he couldn't say he blamed her.

"Piper will come round," Larkin went on. "You'll allow nothing less."

"True. My only real concern is that Whitney and Joe might not back her on this. They love her, but they let her down sometimes. Not necessarily on purpose. They're so focused on keeping the peace that they tiptoe around Celeste's feelings, inadvertently making Piper feel that hers come second to them. Though I don't think they even see it."

Larkin gave him a pointed look. "You need to be prepared for how badly Celeste is going to take that you're Piper's anchor."

Annoyance fluttered through him. "I don't care how Celeste will feel about it."

"I don't mean prepare yourself for *her* sake, idiot, I mean for *Piper's*. You can't properly support your anchor through this if you're not prepared for what's coming. Celeste is going to freak. That's what she does when things don't go her way—and they won't, because you'll refuse to abandon Piper."

Too fucking right he would.

"How you handle Celeste is important. It has to break Whitney and Joe's hearts that their girls don't get along. It's highly unlikely that they'll welcome anyone into their family—and that's what you're meant to be from here on out, a part of the family—who makes that worse."

Levi tensed. "They won't keep me out of Piper's life."

"I doubt they'd try. But you'd be at odds with them. Sides could form. They may not invite you to parties or other events. Piper will be the one who suffers for that. Like it or not, you're going to need to be tactful in dealing with Celeste. Let her be the bad guy in front of others. Let her be seen as unreasonable and selfish. Be the rational and fair one. Defend Piper, but don't let Celeste draw you into pointless arguments."

He felt his jaw tighten. "You're essentially asking me to dance around Celeste's feelings and what she'll do."

"No, I'm asking you to consider how everything will affect *Piper*, and then tailor your reactions to suit *her*—no one else. But, Levi, don't wangle your way into Piper's life unless you're absolutely certain right down to your bones that no amount of drama will make you decide to walk away from her."

Anger spiked through him. "You really think I'd abandon my own anchor?"

"Hey, it happens sometimes—I know that from personal experience. And although I don't believe *you* would do that, I'm saying it anyway, because I like Piper. I wouldn't want to see her hurt."

His anger drained away. Of course Larkin would worry about that, given her own circumstances. Really, he *liked* that she was looking out for Piper. Larkin was family to him, just as Knox and the other sentinels were. They'd formed a family of sorts when they met in an orphanage for demonic children centuries ago.

"Neither would I," he told Larkin. "I appreciate you being protective of her. I hope you'll welcome her into our circle just as easily as you did Harper."

Larkin frowned, as if he was dumb for assuming differently. "Of course I will. We all will. If she's important to you, she's important to all of us. That's how we roll."

"I know. But, to paraphrase you, I'm saying it anyway because I don't want to see her hurt."

"And with you as her anchor, I'm quite certain she won't often be—you'll do your level best to make sure her life runs smoothly from now on. I'm glad of that. She needs someone who's all about her." Larkin gave him a supportive smile. "Good luck with everything. I don't doubt that you'll succeed in making her accept you and the bond sometime soon. I know exactly what a stubborn, perseverant bastard you can be. She'll see it for herself in due time."

That she would.

He and Larkin talked a little while longer, and then she

headed off to Knox and Harper's home, since she would temporarily act as the male Prime's personal bodyguard.

Intending to drop in on Piper, Levi headed out. He'd just slid into his car when Knox's mind brushed against his.

*I know I said you should take time off, but this is something you'd want to know*, the Prime telepathed, his tone dark and laced with warning. *Possibly even something you might want to involve yourself in. If so, I'll respect that.*

Levi felt his brows dip. *All right.*

*Diem Cartwright was murdered in her home*, Knox revealed, referring to a member of their lair.

Levi felt his brows snap together. *Murdered? By who?*

*We're not sure yet. Tanner only knew to check on her because someone left her eighteen-month-old son in the front yard of our lair's foster home this morning. We sent some Force members to Diem's house. They reported that she's been dead for approximately five days.* Knox paused. *Someone snapped her neck and carved an X into her forehead.*

Levi went very still, his insides seizing painfully. His inner demon slunk close to the surface, alert and somber.

*The boy wasn't dirty or hungry*, Knox went on. *Someone took care of him during the five days she was dead. They fed him, changed his diaper, combed his hair, everything. He suffered no injuries whatsoever, and there are no signs of other abuse.*

Levi closed his eyes, swallowing hard as the past swarmed him. *It has to be a coincidence*, he said, his voice like gravel.

*You don't believe in coincidences.*

*It can't be the same person.*

*I wouldn't say it can't be. It probably isn't. But we're still alive all these years later, Levi. What's to say your aunt's killer isn't still alive as well?*

# CHAPTER THREE

Walking through the small gate, Levi looked up at the detached, two-story house. It was nothing fancy. It was simple. Pleasant. Well-kept.

And the scene of a murder.

There were other reapers who could have done a walk-through of the house and examined it, but Levi needed to do this. Needed to see and sense for himself what happened here.

The person who took Diem's life couldn't be the same man who killed Levi's aunt. Not unless Levi had been wrong in believing that person was dead. Levi hoped to fuck he hadn't been wrong, because it otherwise meant that the bastard had been out there all this time. Alive. Free. *Unpunished*. And heaven only knew what he'd been up to.

Levi had been two years old when his aunt, Moira, was killed. She and his mother had been stray demons, and Moira had cared for him after his mother died in childbirth. He had no memories of anything that occurred in those two years, let alone of Moira's death.

But as an adult, he'd looked into his past. By all accounts, Moira had been a bitter, self-centered woman. There had been little evidence to suggest that she'd been an attentive guardian. He'd often been left with neighbors or home alone, even as a baby. Still, she'd kept him when she could have dumped him elsewhere.

As a reaper, he could pick up left-over emotional vibes from death scenes. But by the time he'd been old enough to return to his childhood home, any emotional echoes had long since faded. And if her soul had lingered a while, it had passed on way before then.

He'd looked into her death, determined to unearth what happened. There hadn't been much to go on, though. It was a time before forensics and CCTV. Moira's neighbors had reported seeing a man enter the house—something that apparently wasn't uncommon—but none were able to give a good description of him.

As Levi had been so well taken care of before being left at the orphanage, the police had suspected the killer could be one of his other relatives. But there had been no way to interview any of them, because no one seemed to know if Moira had any family or who his father was.

Levi might have considered that the police's theory was correct, but he'd discovered that three other women had died in similar circumstances before his aunt. It seemed more likely that they had all been targeted by the same killer with a weird-as-fuck MO. But as time went on and no other similar cases cropped up, Levi assumed the killer had somehow died. After all, the world of demons was brutal, and deaths weren't uncommon. Plus, the culprit could even be a breed of preternatural that didn't have longevity like most demons.

Levi snapped out of his memories when he sensed movement

behind him. Glancing over his shoulder, he found Tanner coming toward him, his expression grim.

"I figured you'd want to examine the scene," said the hellhound, sidling up to him. "But I was kind of hoping you'd leave others to handle it."

Hearing grass rustle, Levi looked to see one of the neighbors—who was also a member of his lair—and her partner standing on the edge of her lawn.

"Please tell me you know who hurt Diem," said Janelle, clearly distraught.

"You were friends with her?" Tanner asked.

"Not close friends, but we'd talk sometimes over coffee. She was a sweet woman. Real quiet and private, but talkative once she got going." Janelle briefly peered up at her partner and said, "Clyde and I watched over little Toby a few times while she went here or there."

"Is he all right?" Clyde asked, scratching at his sideburns. "We heard he'd been taken to the foster home."

"You heard right," Tanner told him. "He's fine. His grandparents are traveling down from Germany, he'll be going home with them."

"Do you know if she had a boyfriend?" Levi asked the couple.

"When I last spoke to her just over a week ago, she was single, and happy to be," said Janelle. "If she'd met anyone within that small timeframe, she wouldn't have brought him home. Not so soon. She didn't introduce her partners to Toby until she was positive the relationship was serious. She put her boy first."

"Did you notice anyone come or go at any point over the past five days?" asked Tanner.

Janelle's brow pinched. "No. No one at all."

Clyde pursed his lips and shook his head. "Not that I saw. But then, I don't live with Janelle, so I'm not here every day."

"Did either of you hear any noises?" asked Levi. "See any cars parked outside?"

Again, the couple answered in the negative.

"Whoever took her from Toby needs to pay for it," said Janelle, her eyes welling up. "I-I—" She promptly burst into tears.

Clyde held her close as he led her back into her house.

Tanner's gold eyes drifted over Levi's face. "You sure you want to do this?"

"I wouldn't be here if I wasn't," said Levi. He followed Tanner into the hallway, where two of the lair's Force, Enzo and Dez, stood holding a stretcher on which a long, black body bag lay. A bag that clearly wasn't empty.

Both Force members nodded at Levi and Tanner.

"Knox is waiting for you in the living room," Enzo told them. "He asked us to wait here so Levi could examine the body."

Having an affinity for the dead, Levi didn't need to open the bag and take a look at Diem to know how she died. He rested his hand on her head, and instantly he simply *knew* the cause of death and exactly how long she'd been gone. Dropping his hand, he glanced from Enzo to Dez. "You can take her now."

Enzo slid his gaze toward the living room. "I don't need to tell you to brace yourself, because it's not like your typical scene. There's no mess at all. There are no traces of blood. Nothing's been broken—"

"Other than her neck," said Levi, surprised by the flatness of his tone.

Enzo winced. "Yeah, other than that." He and Dez then left the house.

Levi walked into the living area . . . where he came to an abrupt halt as emotions slammed into him so hard they almost stole his breath. The dominant one was terror. So much paralyzing, gut-wrenching, heart-twisting terror. It permeated and pulsed through the air in waves.

More, snatches of a woman's disembodied voice reached him.

. . . *Toby, where are* . . .

. . . *answer me* . . .

. . . *don't hide from* . . .

In the center of the room, Knox looked his way. "I'd ask if you're all right, but that would be a stupid question."

Refusing to think about his aunt and if she'd been wracked by that same debilitating fear, Levi forced himself to box up his past so he could concentrate on the present. Diem and Toby needed that from him. "Diem's soul is still here, but she doesn't seem to see us. She's only concerned for Toby. She's searching for him."

Knox's brows dipped. "She doesn't know she's dead?"

"She knows, but she's refusing to acknowledge it." Levi had found that it often happened that way with parents. They didn't want to accept that they'd been forced to leave their children behind, and so they simply didn't face it.

Still, Levi repeatedly tried snaring Diem's attention by psychically reaching out to her. It would be difficult to have an *actual* conversation with her—souls didn't usually answer or even pose questions. They yelled or whined or cried, battering you with information in the hope of getting justice, but properly converse? Have a clear, two-way psychic conversation with you? That hardly ever happened.

However, he could get some information from Diem if only she'd yell details at him or something . . . except she refused to acknowledge his presence. He sighed. "I can't make her see us."

"Did you touch her body?" asked Knox.

"Yes. The break to her neck killed her. She's been dead just over five days, much like the Force members estimated."

"What are your reaper senses picking up?"

"Blind terror. Helplessness. Fury. Despair." The emotions all held a feminine vibe, which meant . . . "They were Diem's emotions."

"And whoever killed her?"

Levi frowned. "It's strange. There's satisfaction. Not a bloodthirsty kind. It's more like genuine contentment. But other emotions override it. A building frustration. Disappointment. Anger. And then a sort of bleakness. Loneliness, even."

Tanner's brow furrowed. "So . . . it's as if everything was fine at first. At least for him, anyway, since you don't sense any contentment coming from Diem. I'm guessing it was a 'him'?"

Levi nodded. "The emotions have a masculine feel to them. And something made him increasingly irritated until—finally—he felt 'done' with Diem and killed her. But then he felt lonely."

"Essentially," began Knox, "he was pleased with his chosen victim but it didn't last and so he killed her."

Levi nodded. "That's how it seems." He scraped his hand over his jaw. "There are no echoes of physical pain. She was terrified, but I don't think he physically harmed her. At least not until he killed her."

"She didn't appear to have suffered any wounds other than the broken neck and the X on her forehead," said Knox. "It's true demons heal relatively fast, so I didn't rule out that he might have hurt her. You really don't think he did?"

"No. Pain, fear, and anger are always the most dominant and easiest to sense emotions. There's no pain. She went through emotional agony—there's no doubt about that. Not physical agony, though. The mark was carved into her forehead after death."

As they walked through the house, searching each room for

clues, Levi repeatedly tried connecting with Diem. His every attempt failed. He simply couldn't reach her.

Frustrated, he flexed his fingers. "Diem's lost to us." He had enough experience with these situations to know when he was fighting a losing battle.

Knox looked from Levi to Tanner. "Speak with the neighbors. See if they have anything to say that can help."

Most of the nearby residents were stood in their front yards, so it was simple enough to question each of them. Only one claimed to have seen anyone enter Diem's property.

"It was about four or five days ago," Edith told them. "It was a man, but I didn't get a good look at him."

"What do you remember about him?" Levi asked her.

"Not much," she replied. "Nothing about him stood out to me, I suppose."

Levi kept his tone patient as he asked, "Was he tall? Short? Thin? Bulky?"

"I truly can't recall, I'm sorry."

"That's all right," Tanner assured her. "Can you remember what he was wearing?"

She squeezed her eyes shut. "White cap. Blue jeans. Black jacket . . . or maybe gray . . . It could have even been tank green, come to think of it." She tutted, opening her eyes. "I wish I'd paid more attention, but I didn't think much of it. Plus, it was raining and I was trying to hurry to get inside the house."

Disappointment simmered in Levi's gut as he and Tanner returned to Diem's living area and reported the information to their Prime.

"Only a few of the neighbors have CCTV cameras," Levi added. "And none of those cameras have a good view of this house. In other words, we have no idea who could have done this."

Knox twisted his mouth. "I know you don't want to believe it's the same person who killed your aunt and those other women many years ago, because then it would mean we were all wrong in assuming the killer was dead—meaning he not only escaped justice and you weren't able to avenge Moira, but that he could have killed many other women since. But this isn't what anyone would call a typical MO. All victims were single mothers—or, in your aunt's case, a single guardian. All had their necks snapped. All had an X carved into their forehead. And all the children were left at a safe location.

"More, those children weren't immediately dumped somewhere. The mothers, much like your aunt, were deceased for days before the children appeared outside children's homes . . . as if the sick bastard essentially parented them alone for a short while."

"It's either the same person, or a copycat," said Tanner. "Whatever the case, this has to be linked to you, Levi. The killer is either someone who thought it'd be fun to fuck with your head by replicating your aunt's death—though they'd have had to search *real* deeply into your past to unearth any of this information—or they're the person who killed her, they know who you are, and they want you to know they're around. It'd be a hell of a coincidence for them to otherwise do this to someone in *your* lair."

Levi frowned. "So, what, you think this person has kept track of the kids they dumped at orphanages and foster homes?"

Tanner shrugged his broad shoulders. "Maybe. Or maybe they found you accidentally. It could be that they somehow recognized you—or your aura or energy signature or something. Look, we know this person is fucked up. Might they be pleased to run into a kid they once 'parented' for a few days? Possibly. Might they want to announce their presence in a really messed up way of saying hi? Again, maybe."

His heart beating a little too fast, Levi scrubbed a hand down his face. "If he's not dead, if he's been free as a goddamn bird all these years, then I fucked up majorly."

"We *all* concluded that he was dead," Knox reminded him. "Serial killers don't just stop. It seemed reasonable to assume that he died. I don't know why else he *would* have stopped, but we have to consider that he isn't buried six feet under after all."

Levi ground his back teeth. "If it is him, he made a huge fucking mistake by letting me know he was alive. Because I'll make it my personal mission to ensure he doesn't stay alive for long."

Scanning the many contents of her fridge, Piper hummed to herself. She liked to cook. It relaxed her. But as ideas for various meals sprang to her mind, none gripped her. She was in one of those weird moods where she was hungry but didn't feel like eating any of the meals she usually favored. Ugh.

She closed the refrigerator and began browsing through her cupboards, hoping inspiration would strike her. That turned out to be a pointless hope.

A knock came at the front door.

Piper felt her brows flit together. It would be fair to say she wasn't the most social of beings, so there weren't a lot of people who'd generally stop by.

Suspecting it might be Levi, she puffed out a long breath as she strode down the hallway, totally ignoring the fluttering in her stomach. She glanced through the door's peephole. Her face hardened. Not Levi. Not anyone she'd want to see.

Piper pulled open the door. "This seemed like a good idea to you? Honestly?" Did he *want* her to throw another hellfire orb at him? Because she wouldn't be opposed to that.

Kelvin flapped his arms. "I didn't know what else to do. You wouldn't take my calls. You wouldn't reply to my texts. I don't know if you've even listened to any of my voicemails. At least hear me out, Piper."

She itched to slam the door in his face, but that would be awarding him the sort of emotional reaction he simply wasn't worthy of. Plus, indifference would piss him off far more anyway. So she gave a bored shrug and said, "Fine. Say what you want to say and then go."

The corners of his eyes tightened at her dismissive tone. "We're really going to do this? Throw away our friendship?"

"Well you shit all over it, so . . ."

He cringed. "What I did was in poor taste, for sure. Okay, that's an understatement. But I didn't purposely set out to have sex with Trinity on your chair. The moment was intense, there was a lot of stumbling and turning, and then suddenly she was sitting on your chair."

Folding her arms, Piper propped her hip against the doorjamb. "And you didn't ask her to move?"

His mouth opened and closed. "I was caught up in the moment."

"Ah, I see." She skimmed her finger along the underside of her chin. "Tell me, Kelvin. If you'd walked into the studio and found me lying on your chair while a guy drilled his dick into me, how would you have felt?"

He grimaced. "Disrespected. Pissed. Hurt that you'd even think to do that." He heaved a sigh. "I'm sorry, Piper. Really. I'm not gonna ask you to forgive me any time soon—I know I don't deserve to be let off with it so easily. But at least come back to work."

"I'm no longer one of your employees. I quit, remember?"

His face softened slightly. "You didn't really mean that." He looked amused that she'd believe he'd think differently. "You only said it because you were angry."

"Oh, I was angry. I was also completely serious."

He studied her for a long moment, and then his cheeks began to redden. "Piper, you can't leave the studio."

"Sure I can. Already did."

"You have clients! You're fully booked for the next few months!"

"Someone else can take them on. Including you."

He shook his head, a beseeching look on his face. "Piper, don't do this."

"It's done."

Noting movement in her peripheral vision, she glanced to her left . . . and her stomach hardened as she noticed Sefton and his brother, Jasper, striding down the sidewalk. Knowing her history with them, Kelvin quieted and watched the two males closely.

As the brothers passed her house, Sefton made a point of not looking at her. Jasper, however, tossed her a vicious snarl. A snarl she'd seen the day he yelled in her face and raised his fist to her after storming into her previous place of work. It was Kelvin who jumped between them, shoved Jasper away from her, and then slammed his fist into Jasper's nose. See, Kelvin wasn't a *complete* asshole, but he was a man she no longer trusted.

Once the siblings were a fair distance away, he turned back to her. "Has Sefton given you any problems?"

She shook her head. "And no, Jasper hasn't confronted me again, before you ask."

"Well the last one earned him a broken nose, so maybe that's why. You know you can call on me if he gives you any more problems."

"And we both know I won't."

He sighed. "We agreed that if our relationship didn't work out we wouldn't let it come between us."

"And we didn't. But look at the shit you pulled afterward. Within days, you were fucking someone else. A woman who's a twat to me, no less. And you did it under my nose. Like . . . I could actually *hear* you two going at it most of the time."

He shrugged. "I didn't think you'd care."

"And if I'd been sneaking off to various rooms within the studio to have sex with one of our colleagues, you'd have been fine with that?"

Kelvin pulled a face. "No. No, I wouldn't have." He let out a long breath. "How can I make it up to you? You want Trinity fired? Because I'll fire her if it's the only way you'll feel comfortable coming back to work. She's replaceable. You're not."

"There are plenty of other tattooists."

"But there's only one of you, and I don't want to lose you. You want a raise, I'll give you a raise. Whatever it takes."

"I'm not coming back, Kelvin."

A muscle in his cheek flexed. "I admitted I fucked up, I apologized, I gave you time, I'm—"

"Not the person I thought you were," she finished. "I don't think you realize how much respect I lost for you when I saw that, hey, you have absolutely none for me or my feelings. I would *never* have done what you did. Never. And you know what, I don't think you *were* caught up in the damn moment. Not at all. She asked you to fuck her right there, and you did."

His eyes flickered. Yeah, she was right.

"I'll bet a part of you even got a kick out of screwing her on your oblivious ex's chair."

"Not in a malicious way. I mean, it wasn't a dig at *you* personally," he added, like she therefore shouldn't be so offended.

"I can just imagine how things would have gone if I hadn't walked in on you two. I'd have remained oblivious, and you and Trinity would have been exchanging secret little smiles behind my back at work. Hell, you probably would have even made use of my chair again."

Groaning, he thrust a hand through his hair. "I know I'm an asshole, but don't make the shop and our clients pay for that."

"*Your* clients, Kelvin. I'm out."

"Come on, Piper, I said I was sorry. It was a fucked up thing to do. *Beyond* fucked up. I will make it up to you, I swear, just . . ." He trailed off on hearing a car pull up. "Hey, is that Levi Cutler?"

# CHAPTER FOUR

Why yes, yes it was Levi.

Her inner demon smiled, satisfied. It had been sure that he'd return soon. It was pleased that he hadn't allowed Piper to keep him at bay. Pleased that he wanted the anchor bond enough to insist on having her time and attention.

Watching as Levi slid out of his vehicle, Piper felt a frown pull at her brow. The reaper seemed to have a default serious expression. Not quite a glare, but certainly not a welcoming look. Right now, his face was utterly blank in a way that made her scalp prickle.

He was also holding a pizza box.

Stalking up her path, he pinned Kelvin with a vacant stare. Her ex didn't move other than to swallow hard.

Levi settled his gaze on her, dismissing the other male the way he would a gnat. If it wasn't for the fact that there was clearly something very wrong, she might have pointed out that he was supposed to be giving her time or space and then turned the reaper away. Might have. Probably not.

She wondered if his blank look had something to do with Diem's death. News spread fast around their lair, so Piper had heard about the murder, though she didn't know any specific details. If Levi had been the reaper to examine the scene, it would explain his mood. Either way, as Knox's sentinel, he no doubt played some part in investigating the crime, so he'd probably had a super shit day.

Her heart squeezed. Yeah, she wouldn't be turning him away.

"So you've come bearing gifts," she said, eyeing the very large pizza box. "Or one, anyway."

He climbed onto her front step and ate up her personal space, making her pulse jump. And now her hormones were doing the conga, and her stomach began doing forward flips like it was aiming for an Olympic medal.

"Figured we could eat while we talked," he said.

Translation: They weren't done discussing the anchor matter.

"Are there anchovies on the pizza?" she asked.

"No."

"Then you may enter."

Humor flickered in his eyes. "Appreciated."

She stepped back, opening the door wider, and he shouldered past her . . . casually walking into her home like he did it every day.

Kelvin blinked at her. "So you and he . . .?"

"No, we're not dating," said Piper. "Now I really have to go."

"Fine." Kelvin rolled his shoulders. "Call me when you're ready to come back to work." He appeared to truly think she would, despite all she'd said.

Before Piper had the chance to correct his assumption, he turned and headed for his vehicle. Inwardly sighing, she closed the door. Hearing noises coming from the kitchen, she padded into the room, drawing in the smells of melted cheese, hot peppers, and pepperoni. Her stomach rumbled. Her fussy appetite had no issue with pizza, apparently.

Stood at the island, Levi looked up from where he was opening the square box. "I thought you quit your job."

So he'd been eavesdropping. "I did. Kelvin's not taking my resignation seriously."

"He will once you're working at Urban Ink. Have you called Harper yet?"

Piper snorted. "Like you don't already know the answer to that."

One corner of his mouth lifted. "She *may* have called to ask me some nosy-ass questions, and she *may* have also mentioned that she arranged for you to have an official interview tomorrow."

"Drink?" Piper offered as she grabbed herself a bottle of water.

He perched his epic ass on a stool. "Water is fine."

She set both bottles on the island, nabbed a slice of pizza, and then settled on the seat opposite him. Had she ever envisioned a scenario in which she'd be sharing a pizza with Levi Cutler in her kitchen? Nope. Not ever.

Deciding not to pry about whatever was bugging him until after they'd eaten, she instead asked, "Is Harper pissed on your behalf that I didn't jump at forming the bond?" It would be better for Piper to know that before the interview.

His brow furrowed. "No. She wasn't surprised, and she understands. She's also confident you'll come round." He bit into his pizza. "After all, she knows from personal experience how hard it is to fight the pull of a psi-mate bond."

It really *was* a pull. Piper felt it even now. It had been a background 'pulse' in her head all day. But now that he was here, the pull was stronger. Gah. "This isn't you giving me time and space."

"I gave you some." He removed the cap from his water bottle.

"Did you really think I'd stay away? That I'd be good with setting aside every right I have to you?" He gave a slow shake of his head. "I can agree to wait a little before we form the bond, but I won't keep my distance. I won't act like you're anything other than my anchor."

"You know, I'm surprised by how much you want this."

"Why?"

She took a bite out of her pizza. "You've always seemed so self-sufficient to me. Like you don't need anything or anyone."

"You're not 'anyone.' You're my psi-mate. Maybe that doesn't mean much to you, but it does to me."

She gave him a look of disgust. "Quit with the emotional blackmail, that won't work on me."

His mouth curved. "It was worth a shot."

God, he was going to be a handful. If she accepted the bond. Which she would eventually. It would be dumb to kid herself about that.

Between bites of pizza, they discussed mundane, everyday topics. Once the box was finally empty, she closed it and pushed it aside before asking, "Are you going to tell me what's wrong?"

He sighed. "It was a shitty day. You heard about Diem, I'm sure."

"I did. Should I take it that you examined the scene?"

He nodded, his eyes wary.

"Don't worry, I wasn't going to try pumping you for details that I'm not privy to. I was just, you know, showing concern."

"See, you're good at this anchor stuff already."

Set on avoiding *that* subject for now, she tilted her head. "I have a question, but I won't be offended if you don't want to answer."

"Hit me with it."

"Is it true that you were gifted with the death touch?" The

ability was exclusive to reapers but could only be used once in their entire lives.

He drummed his fingers on the island. "Yes. And if your next question is have I ever used the ability, the answer is no."

In his position, she wouldn't use it either. Not that being able to take a life with a mere touch wouldn't be seriously helpful in a dangerous situation. There was a massive cost, though—somewhere in the world, an innocent would die. Said innocent could be a stranger, a friend, a relative, anyone. They could be young, old, or even an unborn child. The death touch did not discriminate.

"I could never envision a situation in which I ever would use the ability," said Levi. "But now that I have you in my life, well, I'm not so sure anymore."

She tensed. "I wouldn't want you to use it in my defense. You'd never forgive yourself for condemning an innocent to death."

"There's nothing I wouldn't do to keep you safe. To hesitate to use the ability in an emergency would be to trade another person's life for yours. That's not something I'd do. I would never feel guilty for doing whatever it took to keep you alive. If that makes me selfish, it makes me selfish. I don't much care. I figure if there's anything I have the right to be selfish about, it's my anchor."

She narrowed her eyes. "You're just going to keep spinning the conversation back to the matter of us being anchors, aren't you?"

He shrugged. "That elephant's not exactly gonna leave the room, is it?" He lifted his bottle and took a long swig.

Her lower stomach clenched when he swiped his tongue over his wet lips. Ugh, did she really have to be so attracted to him? Wasn't the situation complicated enough? *She* thought so.

Piper would have felt a little better about it if she'd thought the attraction was mutual.

*"She's not my type."*

Piper almost flinched at the memory. Which was stupid. It wasn't like she'd been in love with him back then, or that she'd thought she had a chance with him anyway. And yet, the offhand, dismissive way he'd spoken those words—as if Piper didn't even register on his radar—had seriously stung.

She wasn't going to hold it against him, though. It wasn't like she could blame him for her not being his type—that was out of his control. And she wouldn't expect someone to be attracted to her just because *she* was drawn to *them*. That would be plain narcissistic, and there were bigger things in the world to concern herself with.

Like how her mother and stepfather might not take the identity of her anchor well, for instance.

"What's wrong?" he asked, his gaze steady on hers.

"I was just thinking."

"About what?"

"About how my family will react to us being anchors."

"If you want them to hear it from you, it would be best for you to tell them soon. People are going to see me coming and going from here. It'll get back to your family. They might not conclude that we're anchors, they might instead assume we're . . . involved. You'd then have to explain the situation, and they'd be disappointed that you weren't upfront about this. You might as well get it over and done with."

"It's easy for you to say that. You won't have to deal with the aftermath."

Surprised she'd say that, Levi leaned forward and rested his forearms on the island, liking how her pupils dilated. "Now that's where you're wrong. For one thing, I'll always be here for you when you need someone. For another, I have every intention of being present when you tell your family."

Her brows drew together. "You want to be there?"

"Of course."

"It could get ugly. Like *really* ugly. Why put yourself through it?"

Levi's chest squeezed. He didn't like that Piper expected so little from people, from *him*. "I get that you're not used to having someone at your back, but that changed for you the moment I realized you're my anchor. No matter who or what shit you're dealing with in the future, you won't be dealing with it alone. I'll be in front of you, next to you, behind you—whatever you need. And I will *always* be on your side. I will always back you in whatever you want or need to do." That got to her, he sensed. That touched her where it counted.

She swallowed, eyeing him closely. "And you're truly okay with us taking the time to get to know each other before we form the bond?"

"I'm not thrilled about it, and I can't promise I won't pester you to give in—that would be a vow I'd break for sure. But if it's important to you to wait, I'll deal." For now. "It's not as if my claim to you doesn't count as things stand. You and I are tied by fate with or without the bond. Demons come in pairs. You know, part of me feels sorry for you."

"Why?"

"I'm going to drive you nuts. I will want your trust. I will want you to turn to me. I will want you to rely on me. But you already know that, don't you? It makes you uncomfortable, because you're not used to depending on people."

"Well give the reaper a cookie."

His mouth twitched. Being around her . . . he liked it. Liked just looking at her. Liked knowing that this woman belonged to him. It satisfied him on a visceral level. Even steadied him.

Mentally, he'd been in a bad place all day. Examining Diem's death scene, feeling what she felt, experiencing what her killer felt, having to accept that the killer could well be the same person who murdered his aunt . . . All in all, it had been a mind fuck.

Not wanting to come to Piper in a black mood, he'd tried shoving it all aside, but it had repeatedly crept into his thoughts. As he now sat opposite his anchor, though, the shit fest had no hold on him. Her hold was simply that much stronger.

Recalling Larkin encouraging him to be open with Piper, he thought about raising the subject of his aunt; thought about running some theories by her. But that would be lumbering a lot of heavy shit on her, and they didn't know each other well enough for her to feel comfortable with that.

Plus, the last thing he wanted was to taint the evening. He wanted her to be relaxed and at ease in his company—something she currently seemed to be, which pleased both him and his demon.

"Being mine won't be so terrible, you know," he told her. "You'll see that soon. But only if you don't hold me at arm's length. We can't truly otherwise get to know each other. So, can you agree not to insist on my giving you space the same way I'm agreeing not to insist that I don't have to give you time?"

She licked her lips, and fuck if his gut didn't clench. An image of that tongue licking its way up his cock flashed in his mind's eye. He inwardly cursed.

He really shouldn't be letting his thoughts turn X-rated around her. But, honestly, he didn't see that stopping anytime soon. Discovering Piper was his anchor, that he had such singular rights to her, had only intensified his need for her.

Would he be able to keep his hands off her? In the short-term, maybe. But in the long run? Probably not.

He definitely couldn't afford to act on what he wanted now. She was skittish enough as it was. She needed time to adjust to him being her anchor before she could even *think* of letting him touch her that way.

The problem was . . . Levi wasn't confident that his demon would care to bear that in mind. It was too focused on her. Too determined to find out how her mouth tasted. Too intent on knowing just exactly how hot and tight she'd feel around—

*Fuck*, now his cock was twitching to life. Levi subtly drew in a steadying breath through his nose, willing his body to calm the hell down. His demon chuckled, the bastard.

"Yeah, I can do that," she finally said, snapping Levi out of his private struggle.

At her agreement, something in him settled, making a knot in his gut unravel. "Good. Now tell me . . . just how much of a problem is Kelvin making of himself?"

She flicked up a brow. "Is this how things are going to be? You'll see I might have some issue, and you'll want to take care of it yourself?"

"Yes. You can handle your own problems, I know. I simply don't intend for you to have to. And you won't make that difficult for me, will you?" It was a firm suggestion.

She didn't bristle as he'd expected. She instead said, "Of course I won't."

He narrowed his eyes. "I want your word that you won't be stubborn and surly when I step in to fix your problems for you."

She held up a hand. "I swear it on my dead canary's ashes."

He blinked. "You had a canary?"

"Yeah. Paulie. He died of scabies. Very sad."

Both he and his demon frowned, not entirely sure they believed her. Deciding to let it go for now, Levi prompted, "So, Kelvin?"

"He's not an 'issue,' just a minor annoyance. But if that changes, I'll let you know."

"Does he want you back?" Levi asked, managing to keep his voice casual. "I know you two dated for a short while." His demon tensed as it awaited her answer.

"He's not interested in anything other than keeping me as an employee."

"You sound very sure of that."

"I am."

Levi wasn't. There'd been something in the other male's eyes earlier. Something dark and resentful. As if seeing another man near her had made Kelvin feel threatened on some level. "Who dumped who?"

"It was a mutual agreement to part ways."

"That doesn't mean he was happy about it."

"No, he was fine with it. Seriously. He moved on very fast. Like *uber* fast."

"He might have been hoping to make you jealous. Or he could have been trying to prove to himself that he *was* okay with the separation by fucking other women."

Piper shook her head. "Kelvin doesn't want us to get back together."

Levi felt his insides seize as he asked, "And if he did?"

"He'd be awfully disappointed. I'm not interested in giving things another shot."

Like that, Levi's system relaxed. He might not be planning to put any moves on her anytime soon, but he wouldn't be able to stand back while Kelvin or other males made a play. Levi's demon would warn them off if he didn't do it himself. "On another note, what time is your job interview tomorrow?"

"Ten thirty a.m.," she replied, her shoulders stiffening slightly with what appeared to be nerves.

"I'll pick you up and take you." He raised his hand before she could object. "You have your own car, I know. I'll leave my car here and ride shotgun if you're intent on driving yourself there. Either way, I'm going with you."

Her eyes flashed. "Are you now?"

"As I've already pointed out, we can't get to know each other if we don't spend time together. Besides, I don't want you going alone. Job interviews can be nerve-wracking, and being under the same roof as Khloë Wallis for any length of time can give anyone a case of anxiety."

Piper snickered. "I like Khloë. I mean, I don't know her well, but I've spoken with her a few times. I got the impression she's a riot."

"Yeah, 'riot' works." He slanted his head. "When do you want to speak to your family about us?"

She pulled a face. "I'd rather tell them all at once. My mom called an hour ago and invited me to her house tomorrow to have dinner with her, Joe, and Celeste. I could maybe tell them then, but Celeste's reaction will spoil the evening. It doesn't seem fair to do that to my mom and Joe."

"Could you eat a meal with them guilt-free knowing you were holding back news that they'd want to know?"

She grimaced. "No."

"Then it would be best to tell them when you first arrive. When *we* first arrive. Don't feel bad that it might taint their evening, because the fact is that it *shouldn't*. This is good news for you. They should see it that way. If they don't, that won't be on you."

"I know. My mom and Joe *will* be pleased that I've found my psi-mate."

"They'll just wish it wasn't me."

"I suspect it will be more that they'll wish you hadn't once been involved with Celeste."

Well, he harbored that same wish, so he wouldn't blame them for that. "And what about you? Do you regret that I'm your anchor?" He hadn't meant to ask that, but there was no taking the words back.

"No."

"Just no?"

"Just no."

Oddly enough, the simple answer appeased him and his demon more than a paragraph of placatory words would have done. "Before you ask, no, I don't regret that you're mine."

"I wasn't going to ask that."

"You weren't?"

"No. You'd have no reason to regret it. As anchors go, I'm a winner."

He chuckled. "And so humble."

The conversation turned lighter after that. Spending time with her was . . . easy. That was Piper, though. She might not be bubbly or cheery, but she was an easy person to be around.

Part of it was that there was a calmness to her—possibly something that came from the quiet strength she emanated. The other part of it was that she didn't simply listen to what you said, she paid attention with her entire being. Her eyes never wandered, her focus never shifted, her body language remained open.

She left a person feeling well-rested. As if they'd woken from a long, deep, dreamless sleep. Which was ironic, really, considering she was a nightmare.

By the time Levi rose from the stool to leave her house, there was a peaceful stillness inside him. A steady calm. That lasted right up until he walked outside and saw that someone had slashed her tires.

A growl built in his chest. "What the fuck?"

"Little bastards," she muttered, her face tight.

"You know who did this?"

"Apparently there's a group of human kids going around pulling all kinds of crap. They left a bag of dogshit on my doorstep last night."

"Dogshit?"

She shrugged. "At least it was in a bag."

Levi didn't care if it was in a fucking decontamination device, it shouldn't have been on her goddamn doorstep. Also . . . "You should have told me."

"Why?"

"What do you mean, why?"

"It's not like they placed a bomb on the step. And they're only kids. Now if they'd thrown clumps of shit at my front door or something, yeah, you'd have received a call. What good is an anchor to a girl if they won't come wash canine waste off her house? Or get rid of wasps?"

Shaking his head, Levi looked at her wheels once more. "I'll have someone come and replace your tires."

"That's okay, I can—"

"I'll have someone come and replace your tires," he repeated. "I told you, there'll be no more of you dealing with things alone. Never again, Piper. Let me fix this for you." *Trust me to be someone who won't let you down.*

She sighed and then gave him a 'have at it' shrug. "All right."

His insides relaxing, Levi nodded. He felt bad for her. Really. Because he'd be highly overprotective where she was concerned, and he had the distinct feeling she'd feel smothered in no time at all. "I'll pick you up tomorrow morning at ten. Be ready."

# CHAPTER FIVE

Riding shotgun the next morning, Piper slid Levi a sideways look. This couldn't possibly last. It couldn't.

She'd seen plenty of anchored pairs in their 'honeymoon stage.' They were both on their best behavior, showed each other their best sides, and generally got caught up in the novelty of finding and bonding with their anchor.

As time went on and anchored pairs became relaxed around each other, their behavior kind of 'slipped.' Oh, they were still fully invested in their anchors—that never changed. But they spent less time together and ceased trying to impress each other.

Levi . . . he'd so far been a model anchor. Showing up with pizza might have been a small thing, but it was still thoughtful. He could have come empty-handed. The same applied to this morning. She'd expected him to merely beep the horn or text her when he arrived, but he'd showed up with coffee and pastries. How he knew what her favorites were, she wasn't sure. He'd simply said, "I have my sources."

Coming outside to realize all her tires had indeed been replaced while she slept had been another *tick* in his column. Then, all the while assuring her that the interview would go well and she had no need to feel nervous, he'd ever so courteously escorted her to his car and insisted on opening the front passenger door for her.

Okay, they were little things. But little things mattered. And they added up.

A downside of having Levi as her anchor was that he played havoc with her hormones. Like Olive said, though, the attraction would fade.

Piper simply needed to 'friend zone' him. She'd done it with other guys. She could do it with Levi as they got to know each other.

She'd need to do it fast, because she couldn't afford to be uncomfortable around her own anchor . . . the way she was at this very moment.

Right now, the air was thick with the tension thrumming through her. Mostly because of the dream she'd had last night. She couldn't recall all of it. But she remembered kissing him, remembered him gently pushing her away, remembered his pitying 'I don't think of you that way' smile.

She'd woken with a renewed determination to ensure she never did anything—let alone stupidly kiss him—that would reveal that her attraction to him hadn't yet given up the ghost. She *never* wanted to receive that pitying smile in real life. Ever. But being so careful and second-guessing her words and actions had left her strung tight.

Piper strived to breathe away her tension, silently ordering her feminine parts to pull themselves together. But it wasn't happening. Then again, when you were in a small, confined space with over six feet of dark power and raw sexuality, the odds were low that you'd be anything close to relaxed anyway.

"You don't need to be so nervous, it'll be fine," said Levi. "Harper won't bite you. That's more my thing."

Oh, he thought Piper was so tense because of her upcoming interview with . . . She frowned as the latter words sank in. "Biting is your thing?"

His mouth curved into a panty-dropping smile that made her stomach flutter.

"Funny. I'm kind of partial to it, too." Shit, had she really just said that? God, she had. The words simply popped out. Piper faced forward, ignoring the weight of his gaze.

"That so?" he asked, a gritty quality to his voice.

She didn't respond. She wasn't going to allow even the most harmless bit of flirting to go on between them. That would just be stupid.

Nothing more was said as they drove to the club that concealed the entrance to the Underground. Levi parked the car and skirted the hood, frowning when she opened her door and slid out.

"You don't need to act all courteous and stuff," she said. "Except when there are wasps in my house. You can come to my rescue then."

"First of all, it's not an act. Second of all, what's your beef with wasps?"

"They buzz and chase and sting you for shits and giggles."

A smile plucked at one corner of his mouth. "You've been chased by a wasp?"

"Multiple times. No provocation is required. They seem to hate me on sight."

His smile kicked up a little more. Oh, he thought she was joking? Yeah, no.

Levi stayed at her side yet ever so slightly in front of her as they walked to the club. Well, it was more like he prowled, his eyes sweeping his surroundings in a very predatory way that appealed to her demon.

He was one big enticement to her inner entity. It wasn't a simple case of the psychopathic shit finding his power a total turn-on. Levi was so very controlled and self-possessed, but there was an undercurrent of something wild that was barely leashed. That intrigued her demon big time.

In the basement of the club, he remained just as close as they headed to the elevator. They stepped inside, he pressed the down button, the doors slid closed . . . and her muscles again stiffened as she once more found herself alone with him in such close quarters. The atmosphere quickly turned thick, and she swallowed hard around a throat gone dry.

"Relax," he coaxed, which might have helped if he hadn't leaned into her. "You'll be fine."

Yeah, *if* he gave her some physical space. Which he didn't. And so the wicked tension inside her remained.

Finally, the shiny doors opened. She took a long, relieved breath as they stepped out of the elevator.

Again, he prowled at her side but slightly in front, radiating protective energy. She knew he'd block any threat that might come her way. It was new and strange but not necessarily in a bad way. Still, it would take some getting used to. *If*, in fact, they spent much time together after the bond was formed. She highly doubted they would.

Levi had his own life—a busy one at that. You couldn't be a sentinel *and* a personal bodyguard to a Prime while still having a lot of free time. And he'd likely want to spend much of that time with friends or running errands.

She believed he *would* make an effort to be a strong presence in her life and that she *would* be his priority. But she couldn't see how his responsibilities wouldn't get in the way of him acting on that. If Piper ever asked for his help, she'd no doubt get it. But he might not always be able to break away from his commitments, so she might find that he'd send others in his place. Particularly since he often traveled with Knox.

It wouldn't mean that she and Levi would have a *bad* anchor relationship. It simply meant that it would resemble a long-distance one. He might not live far away, but he wouldn't always be close or available.

Piper wouldn't blame or resent Levi for that. She respected how devoted he was to his positions within the lair. And really, them spending so much time apart wouldn't be a negative thing. It wasn't always good for anchors to be in each other's pockets. Especially since jealousy and possessiveness often came into play and made it difficult for the pair to have relationships with others.

It hadn't escaped her attention last night that Levi hadn't seemed to like the thought of her with Kelvin. She hadn't read anything into it. Levi wouldn't *want* to feel that way. It would be instinctive. Piper could have been *anyone* and he'd have still felt that way if they were his anchor.

Similarly, she'd find it difficult to see him with others. Even when she managed to stick him in a 'friend' box, her anchor instincts would be an issue. As such, it would be better for them to have space from each other and be able to keep some aspects of their personal lives private.

Levi came to a stop outside a glass door and looked her way. "Ready?"

She peered up at the huge sign above it that read, *Urban Ink*. Ah, they'd arrived. And the sign was seriously cool. The font was a sort of graffitied calligraphy.

Piper straightened her shoulders. "Ready."

He pushed open the door and waved her inside, surprising her by sticking very close as they both entered. The front of his body was almost literally plastered against her back. He probably thought she'd find the contact reassuring. Well, he was mistaken.

Piper glanced around, taking it all in. *Nice.* And very spacious. The white walls and ceiling boasted tattoo flash and gorgeous metal art such as Chinese dragons and tribal swirls.

Four stations were situated behind the reception area, which was uber tidy. The cushions on the sofa were perfectly placed, the portfolios on the super clean coffee table were neatly stacked, and everything on the chrome reception desk that doubled as a jewelry display cabinet seemed to have its very own place.

Behind the desk stood Khloë, a bright yet mischievous smile on her face. The small, olive-skinned imp was mated to another of Knox's sentinels, Keenan, and also happened to be Harper's cousin.

"Hey, Piper," Khloë greeted. "Why are you all but wearing Levi?" She looked at him. "Dude, do you have no concept of personal space?"

"Could you tell Harper that Piper's arrived for her interview?" Levi asked.

"Sure," replied Khloë. "*Harper!*" she yelled without turning. "*Piper's here!*"

Leaning over a woman sprawled on a chair, the female Prime lifted her head and met Piper's gaze. "Two minutes," she mouthed.

Piper nodded and took a seat on the sofa. Levi sat beside her, the side of his body pressed to hers. She thought about scooting over, but that might reveal just how uncomfortable she found it to be so close to him. He might realize that—

And *there* she was, second-guessing her behavior around him again. Ugh.

Piper cast him a quick look, noticing that his eyes were on the nearby wall-mounted TV. "I appreciate you coming with me. You don't have to stay, though. I know you must be busy."

He met her gaze. "Not too busy to be here when you need me."

"But you're Knox's bodyguard."

"I'm taking some time off."

"Oh." That surprised her, given how seriously he took his roles—she wouldn't have thought he'd be comfortable with temporarily setting his responsibilities aside. "Still, you don't have to stay and—Wait, I get it. You're here to *make sure* I get the job. You're gonna freak if I don't, and you'll push Harper to change her mind."

He frowned. "I don't 'freak.' But will I be pissed if Harper doesn't employ you? Absolutely. And she'd be a fool not to hire you. I've seen your work. The back tattoo you did for Larkin is seriously impressive."

"Uh, thanks. But I wouldn't want a job because my anchor intimidated someone into giving it to me."

"Would I do that?"

"Yes. Yes, you absolutely would."

His mouth quirking, he gave an unapologetic shrug. "I'm very protective of who matters to me. I like to make sure their life is running smoothly and that they have what they need. And what you currently need is a job."

"Raini co-owns this place, right?" The beautiful demon was also a succubus and fellow tattooist. "Will she sit in on the interview?"

"As I understand it, she prefers to leave that to Harper. They've had many applicants, but the sphinx vetoed them all."

No pressure, then.

Shortly after that, Harper crossed to the reception area with a professional smile. "Hi, Piper, sorry for the wait."

"No problem." Piper rose to her feet and shook the hand Harper held out. "However this goes, I appreciate you considering me. And no, Levi, you can't come along to the interview."

Harper chuckled. "He was totally gonna ask to be present."

Standing, Levi grunted, not bothering to deny it. His hand settled on Piper's shoulder—warm, supportive, and strong. "I'll be here when you're done."

She nodded and then walked behind Harper as they passed the stations that were separated with black-and-white checkered partitions. The other tattooists, Raini and Devon, both offered her friendly smiles.

Inside the office, Piper took the seat Harper indicated, metaphorically crossing her fingers and toes that all would go well.

Levi sank back onto the sofa, not at all impressed that he'd been told to wait here. It wasn't as if he would have interrupted the interview. Much.

His demon cricked its neck, wound tight. It would no doubt feel edgy right up until Piper was claimed and wore the anchor mark, declaring she was under the protection of both Levi and his demon.

Levi felt just as tightly wound. Not simply due to the absence of the anchor bond, but because his mind was a place of chaos right now. The thought that his aunt's killer could be not only alive but close by . . . it fucked with him. And when he was alone, there was no powering down his brain. His thoughts repeatedly circled back to the matter, sifting through the facts, pondering the many possibilities, driving him nuts.

Right now, Piper was his bright spot. She gave him something else to think about. Something else to focus on. She kept his mind solidly on the present rather than the past.

She also repeatedly caused his cock to stir in his jeans. It didn't take much. A flash of her dimples. A whiff of her floral scent. A glimpse of her cleavage. The sight of her teeth digging into her lower lip.

The woman really had no idea how fiercely tempting she was to him.

Levi narrowed his eyes as Khloë hurried over and sat beside him, a huge grin on her face. "What?" he asked.

"So," she began casually, "you've found your anchor. What a fun development. I'll bet your demon's psyched."

"What do you want?"

"A lotto win. A villa in Italy. A rocket launcher. A Bull Shit. A rollercoaster in my backyard."

Wrong question. You had to be a little more specific when dealing with imps, especially *this* particular one. Levi sighed. "I meant, what do you want *from me*?"

"Not sex, if that's what you're worried about."

"My mind honestly didn't go there. Now ask whatever you want to ask."

"Okay, okay." Khloë clasped her hands together. "Can I be there when you tell Celeste the good news?"

"No."

Her hands flopped to her lap. "Ah, come on."

"What's your problem with Celeste?"

"She came on to Keenan."

Levi felt his brows draw together. "She did? When?"

"Oh, uh . . . about four years ago."

Levi blinked. "A period when you and him weren't even seeing each other, let alone mated?"

"Yes."

"Then I'm not understanding why you have an issue with her."

"She came on to Keenan," Khloë repeated, enunciating every word. "Dude, are you not listening to me or something?"

"I'm listening, I'm just confused."

"What's there to be confused about? She's hot for Keenan. She keeps smiling at him. I don't like it. Or how she looks at me all judgy. I'd enjoy seeing her have a total meltdown, so can I be there when you tell her that Piper's your anchor?"

"No."

Khloë pouted. "Why are you always so *mean* to me? Don't you like me? Is that what it is? God, it is, isn't it? I'll bet you think Keenan can do better than me. You do, don't you? You think—"

"Khloë," he interrupted with a sigh.

"Yup?"

"Be quiet."

She slanted her head. "Have you changed your mind?"

"No."

The pout came back. "You are so unfair! Why are you being like this? Why can't you—" She cut off when Devon splayed her hand over Khloë's face.

"Stop tormenting Levi," said Devon.

Khloë laughed, batting away the hellcat's hand.

"I'm surprised Tanner's not here," Levi said to Devon. The hellhound had been hovering around his mate since learning she was pregnant.

She flicked her ultraviolet ringlets over her shoulder. "He and I have an agreement. I'll go on maternity leave *slightly* earlier than I'd originally planned if he doesn't insist on smothering me."

Levi felt his brow crease. "That doesn't seem enough to keep him from sitting on this sofa throughout your entire shift."

"Ah, well, my seriously frustrated hellcat *may* have surfaced and clawed at his face earlier."

Levi winced. "Yeah, that'd do it."

Just then, Raini made her way over to them, beaming. "Congrats on finding your anchor, Levi. We're all so pleased for you. And we're all totally planning to big you up so she'll cave and form the bond fast."

"We call it Operation Break Piper," Khloë chipped in.

Raini frowned. "No, *you* call it that."

Devon nodded. "The rest of us simply call it helping Levi out."

Khloë let out a tired sigh. "And you wonder why I think you're all boring."

Devon pursed her lips. "I don't wonder that. I don't wonder why you do or think half the things you do." She gave the imp a condescending pat on the head. "I've given up on trying to understand you, sweetie. It's a pointless endeavor."

"Only for those who are weak of mind and will," said Khloë.

Devon rolled her cat-green eyes. "Just go answer the phone."

"It's not ringing."

"Pretend it is."

"Like we're pretending you're not constipated?"

"*Khloë*."

The little imp raised her shoulders. "What? It's nothing to be ashamed about. We all struggle to drop the Lincoln log from time to time."

Devon squeezed her eyes shut. "Stop."

"Especially pregnant women. A lot of them get sewer capped."

"Seriously, *stop*."

"Don't worry, you'll release the kraken sooner or later." Khloë patted her arm. "This poo shall pass."

Raini swore. "Dev, you can't keep grabbing her by the throat!"

*

Later that day, Piper blew out a breath as Levi pulled up outside the bungalow that Whitney and Joe shared. Celeste was already here—her car was parked nearby. Awesome.

Piper was tempted to delay passing on her news. Not for the sake of procrastinating, but because she didn't want to spoil what had otherwise been a good day. She'd gotten a job, which she'd officially start tomorrow. Levi had taken her to one of her favorite Underground restaurants to celebrate, so that had been a bonus. They'd talked for hours, exchanging funny stories, not touching on anything *too* serious or personal. It seemed a shame to shit all over the day.

But backing out wasn't really an option. She and Levi had been seen together by many people in the Underground. Someone would pass on that little nugget of info to her family, who'd then for sure ask her about it. And if she had to be all, "Well we're anchors but I didn't get around to telling you," it would look like she'd been hiding it. It would look like she'd *felt* that she had to hide it. Which would only feed Celeste's belief that it was wrong for Piper and Levi to bond—that was how the woman would see it.

"It'll be all right, Piper," said Levi, resting his hand on her knee.

He really needed to stop touching her, because it wasn't helping her friend-zone the holy hell out of him. "You sure you want to come with me?"

He snorted and slid out of the car.

She'd take that as a yes.

Piper edged out of the vehicle and took a steadying breath, her inner demon very still and serious. With him behind her, she walked up the path, used her key to let herself into the house, and then followed the sounds of voices into the kitchen. Whitney was plating up food while Joe and Celeste stood near the open back door, talking to each other.

Whitney looked Piper's way and smiled, but that smile wavered when she spotted Levi. Just the same, Joe's warm look faltered at the sight of the reaper. And Celeste? She went utterly rigid.

Her hands clasped, Whitney came forward. "Hello, sweetheart." She kissed Piper's cheek. "Levi, I wasn't expecting you."

Joe sidled up to his mate and gave Piper a gentle smile before offering his hand to Levi, who then shook it. "Always good to see you, Levi. Is everything all right?" Ah, Joe had assumed he was here to discuss a lair issue of some sort.

"Everything is fine," said Levi. He gave Piper a 'the floor is yours' look.

She turned to the others. "I came to tell you . . . well, *we* came to tell you . . . that we recently discovered we're anchors."

Delight lit up Whitney's face. "Oh, that's wonderful news."

Just like that, the hard lump in Piper's stomach fell away.

"Well damn," said Joe, his lips curling. "Congratulations. It was the last thing I was expecting—"

"You are kidding me," Celeste blurted out, her voice dead.

*And here we go.*

Celeste strode forward, her hard gaze bouncing from Piper to Levi. "Anchors?" She might as well have said the word 'cannibals' it came out ringing with so much disgust.

"Anchors," Piper confirmed.

A humorless chuckle bubbled out of the banshee. "This is a joke, right? A *bad* one."

"No joke."

Poking the inside of her cheek with her tongue, Celeste folded her arms. "And have you formed the bond?"

"No, but—"

"Good. At least you've got the sense to realize it can't happen."

"Do you really think I'd have come here and made this announcement if I meant to forsake Levi and the bond?"

Her eyes hard and gleaming like chips of ice, Celeste said, "I won't allow it."

Whitney whirled to face the banshee, her expression a mask of horror. "You can't expect Piper to give up her psi-mate."

"Oh, I can and I do," said Celeste.

Whitney spluttered. "Having an anchor is vital to every demon. It's the only way to be sure she'll never turn rogue. She needs the bond."

"*I won't allow it.*"

"It's not for you to allow or disallow," Levi told Celeste, the epitome of calm. "It has nothing to do with you."

"Nothing to do with me," the banshee echoed quietly, a note of disbelief in her tone. It was really never a good sign when one of her kind lowered their voice like that.

"This is about me and Piper, no one else," Levi stated.

Celeste sucked in a breath. "Are you forgetting we were once together?"

Joe raised a calming hand toward his daughter. "Let's not—"

"Well, are you?" she pushed, glaring at Levi.

"It's completely irrelevant here," said the reaper, still remarkably calm.

"Oh, I'm *irrelevant*? We were together for four months!"

"Six years ago. Not that that matters. It's in the past, and that past has no bearing on—"

"Don't you try to dismiss what we had!"

Piper lifted her hands. "Okay, enough. You're making this whole thing about you, Celeste. It's not."

Joe turned to his daughter again. "Honey, there's no sense in being angry with Piper or Levi for this. No one here is out to hurt you. People can't choose who their anchors are. This is out of their hands."

Celeste's fingers curled like claws. "But they can choose

whether or not they form the bond! They're *choosing* to do it! I'm not having it, Dad. I'm not."

Good Lord, the woman was a trial. "It isn't your decision to make."

Celeste snarled. "What if it was the other way around? Huh? What if you found out Kelvin is my anchor?"

"Then I'd feel sorry for you." He was a freaking tool.

"You'd really bond with my ex? A man I slept with? A man I cared for? A man who loved me?"

Levi coughed to hide a snicker. He'd never once implied that he cared for her, let alone professed to love her. She'd complained about it often.

Although he'd known she'd take his and Piper's announcement badly, the whole 'I won't allow it' had still taken him by surprise. Was she really so used to getting her own way that she thought she could dictate how this situation would go?

There were so many things he wanted to say to Celeste right now. Starting with how utterly self-absorbed and childish she was acting. But Larkin's warning played on loop in his mind . . .

*Let her be the bad guy in front of others. Let her be seen as unreasonable and selfish. Be the rational and fair one. Defend Piper, but don't let Celeste draw you into pointless arguments.*

So he'd bitten back most of what he'd love to say, knowing that this was the right way to deal with the situation for Piper's sake. But right now, to be blunt, being tactful sucked.

"None of that is important here, Celeste," said Piper. "I'm sorry if that hurts you, but it's not. And the fact that you'd begrudge me an anchor bond, *knowing* how important it is for me to have one . . . well, what does that say about you?"

"No one will expect you to be happy for them, Celeste, but at least let it lie," Joe said to her.

The banshee glared at him. "Let it lie? Are you not getting how fucked up this is?"

"Perhaps Levi and Piper being anchors might be awkward for you at first, but it's not as if they're in a relationship," said Joe.

"It's close enough to count." Celeste whirled on Levi. "This isn't even a little bit weird for you? Finding out that your psi-mate is actually the stepsister of your ex?"

"No," Levi replied simply.

"Well it *should* be."

"I don't think of Piper in terms of who she is to you," he went on. "I think of her in terms of who she is to me."

"Who she is to you? She's not going to be *anyone* to you. I won't fucking have it!"

"Celeste, try to calm down," Whitney cut in. "Yelling isn't helping. And you can't really want Piper to walk away from the very person that will keep her and her demon stable."

The banshee sneered at Whitney. "Well of course you'd take *her* side."

Joe closed his eyes. "There are no sides."

Celeste planted her hands on her hips. "So you're not all banding together against me?"

"We're not against you, we merely don't feel the same way about this situation as you do," said Joe.

"Because Piper's happiness is more important than mine, right?" Her voice broke.

Levi telepathically reached out to Piper. *She's good at manipulating them, isn't she?*

*She does it subconsciously at this point*, his anchor said. *Stay tuned for the 'You love Piper more than me' part of the segment.*

"That's not what I said, Celeste," Joe told her patiently.

"You don't need to say it," the banshee clipped. "Your actions are *screaming* it. I'm supposed to accept my own ex as *family*? I'm supposed to be happy that he'll now be all about my stepsister?"

"No one is saying that," said Joe.

"But you don't care how hard this is for me. No, don't say you do. Don't lie. If you really cared, your first reaction wouldn't have been to congratulate them. You'd have at least been sensitive to how this would affect me."

Joe flapped his arms in a helpless gesture. "What would you have us do, Celeste? Really? We can't change this situation. We can't make someone else be Piper's anchor. Nor can we erase your past with Levi. We can only move forward."

"As one big, happy family?" Celeste snorted. "You wouldn't expect that of *her* if the situation was reversed. You always put her feelings before mine, and then you're always so surprised when I point out that you love her more than you do me."

*Told you it would come*, said Piper, her mind gently bumping Levi's. The psychic contact eased his entity's tension slightly. The demon found the banshee pathetic, but it worried her dramatics would eventually cause Whitney and Joe to back her.

Celeste's eyes welled up, and she wrapped her arms around her body. "You always plead with me to try and get along with her. Do you really see that ever happening now?"

As the room temperature abruptly cooled, Levi looked to see that Piper's eyes had bled to black.

Her demon glared at Celeste, who froze. "I cannot begin to tell you how much dealing with you bores me," it told the banshee, making Levi's demon chuckle. "I will say this only once. No machinations on your part will prevent the forming of the anchor bond. I would not allow it. *She* would not allow it. And as much as you wish to ignore it, he would not allow it. Throw petty tantrums if you must, but know they will achieve nothing."

Pleased with the entity's statement and the assertiveness with which it had spoken, Levi's own demon lost every bit of its tension.

The moment Piper's entity subsided, Levi announced, "Piper and I are leaving now." Eating a meal with these people . . . yeah, that wouldn't happen this evening. "We have somewhere to be."

Celeste swiped at her tears and turned to her father. "Well you should go and again shake the hand of the man who doesn't at all care how his selfish actions are going to affect the people in this room."

"Selfish," Levi echoed. "Hmm." *So she still does a lot of projecting?*

*Yep*, Piper replied. "I'll speak to you again soon," she told her mother and Joe, who looked as though they'd prefer to ask her to stay but thought better of it.

In the car, Piper clicked on her seatbelt and said to Levi, "Well, welcome to the family. I'll bet you're so excited to be part of it."

He switched on the engine and pulled out onto the road. "I like your mom and Joe. Celeste might think that acting like a drama queen makes this difficult for me, but it doesn't. She's easy to dismiss. Just a brat throwing a tantrum. It took me a while to see the real her, because we didn't spend much time together, and she's good at showing people what she thinks they want to see. I didn't care enough to look any deeper or I would have seen how much more there was to her."

"You didn't care for her as deeply as she believes?"

"I didn't care for her at all, Piper. I barely knew her."

"The way she tells it, you were serious about her but struggle too much with commitment and so the two of you had to part ways."

"I have no problem committing to anything. That said, I've

never been in a serious relationship. I never met anyone I was serious about. But Larkin's right when she says I walk into relationships with a closed mind and don't make an effort to build something real. If I wasn't that way, maybe I would have at some point found myself truly interested in someone. But after years and years of being given the ultimatum of 'it's me or your roles—choose,' it became instinct to keep my relationships casual and not invest anything of myself into them."

"You don't expect them to last."

"No. And they don't. It's usually me who gets dumped as opposed to doing the dumping. Can you guess why?"

"Because you don't care enough to bother doing it yourself."

He nodded. "And that was how it went down with Celeste. I don't know if she truly believes I loved her or if she simply wants to believe it."

Maybe it made Piper a bit of a bitch, but she was relieved to hear that he hadn't loved Celeste. It smoothed over the jagged edges of Piper's jealousy. Plus, she didn't have to worry that he might later change his mind about reconciling with the banshee.

"It could be the latter," said Piper. "What her mom did . . . it's like it made something in Celeste die. It left her with a void. Nothing fills it. And she seeks validation from others. I can understand why she's so angry. I mean, imagine if your mom woke from a coma and had not only forgotten you but didn't want to stick around to reconnect with you. Imagine if she then flitted off without even a goodbye, and you told yourself she'd come home once her memories returned . . . only she never did. It would wreck a child, wouldn't it?"

"Lots of people have emotional wounds, Piper. Some don't handle them well, and I don't think anyone would ever expect them to. But nothing gives them the right to project all their anger and pain onto the people who aren't responsible for those wounds."

"Well, now she's also feeling a whole heaping of jealousy sprinkled with bitterness. She's going to be a pain in our asses until she's worked it out of her system."

Switching gears, Levi went on, "That wasn't just about jealousy or bitterness. In manipulating Whitney and Joe, she also controls what *you* do to some extent. She tried controlling me with subtle techniques, but I wouldn't stand for it. So she knows I won't let her pull that shit with you; that she'll lose her favorite whipping girl. That's part of why she exploded."

Piper felt her brows knit. "Wow, you're right. I didn't see that before. I should have, because it's kind of obvious that she'd feel the need to control the people close to her—she can then ensure they don't go anywhere. She can keep them from hurting her the way her mom did. It all comes back to that."

"It would seem so." Approaching a red light, Levi slowed the vehicle. "That scene in the kitchen didn't go as badly as it could have done."

"It was one of the very few times where my mom and Joe *really* spoke up for me and refused to back down. Well, it was more that they were very strongly appealing to Celeste to accept how things are, but still. You know, there were a couple of times back there when I felt like Celeste was trying to provoke you."

"She wanted me to growl and yell and insult her so that your mother and stepfather would jump to her defense."

"I guess I should have expected that." She exhaled deeply. "Thanks again for . . . well, everything you did today."

He shot her a lopsided, sideways smile. "Like you, I'm not so bad as anchors go, am I?"

Her mouth curled. "No, not so bad at all."

# CHAPTER SIX

Leaning back against her kitchen counter the following morning, Piper absently plucked at her lower lip. She'd found a little . . . surprise when she went into her backyard a few minutes ago. A surprise that left her furious, disgusted, freaked out, and utterly confused.

The question was . . . did she tell Levi?

He'd arrive very soon, since he'd yesterday offered to drive her to work. Well, it had been more of a pressing suggestion than an offer. He'd claimed that it made sense for them to use whatever free time they both had to continue getting to know each other. It *did* make sense, so she'd agreed. And she wasn't so sure she'd be able to hide that she wanted to shit fury on someone's ass.

Really, given that he was her anchor, he'd be an obvious person to report the 'surprise' to. Particularly since he was a sentinel of their lair and would know how best to deal with the situation. So why was she hesitating? Simple. She didn't like that she was coming across as a high-maintenance anchor.

First she'd pretty much run from him and then had to be convinced not to forsake the bond. Then there were the slashed tires, which he'd had to take time out of his evening to get sorted. Also, there had been the matter of her needing a job, which he'd felt necessary to rectify if she couldn't. Celeste's outburst had come next, and that had been far from pleasant. And now there was *this* weird bullshit, which might suggest that Piper had yet another issue he'd feel compelled to handle.

The time they were spending together should be easy and fun, not peppered by crap. She wasn't worried that he'd walk away from her or anything. She simply didn't like that she was bringing drama into his world. Anchors were supposed to make each other's lives easier, not complicate them.

It already bugged her that she had nothing to offer Levi except for a bond that would prevent him from turning rogue. So many things took up his time and attention. He had so many responsibilities to juggle. But, not being a sentinel herself, she couldn't help with them. Piper had no way of improving his life or easing whatever burdens he may have. She was simply just . . . there.

Moreover, she was yet another person he felt responsible for. It made her feel like a burden. Couldn't she, at the very least, be a *subtle* addition to his life?

Not with the way things were going.

Softly cursing, Piper let her head flop forward and stared at the tiled floor. Okay, so she could keep her morning discovery to herself. But if this happened again, she'd have to report it for fear that it would otherwise continue . . . and then he'd learn that it had happened once before, and he'd no doubt be pissed that she'd kept the previous occurrence from him. How could they build a trusting friendship if she wasn't honest with him when it counted?

Piper wanted him to trust her. And, considering she had so little to offer him in anchor terms, shouldn't she at least give him *this* much? Shouldn't she give him the other things that mattered, like honesty and loyalty?

A knock at the door made her head snap up.

*Moment of truth.* Literally. Because she'd be a piss-poor anchor if she did nothing but take. There had to be some give. And if she truly wanted them to build foundations for a strong anchor relationship, she needed to do her part.

Opening the front door, she flashed him a smile.

The gorgeous bastard tipped his chin. "You ready? I would have brought you coffee and pastries again, but Harper and the girls would have had my ass, because they like to all meet in the coffeehouse next door to the studio every . . . What's wrong?"

She scratched her head. "You'd better come inside."

His eyes narrowed, he walked through the door. "What is it, Piper?"

"There's something you need to see." She padded into the kitchen, conscious of him hot on her heels, and then out into the backyard. "When I was standing at the kitchen window earlier, I noticed that one of my planters had been knocked over so I came out to fix it. When I turned around to go back inside, I found this." She turned back to face the house, he followed suit, and then his entire body went stiff as a board. "And yes, it is what you think it is. I wasn't so certain at first, but . . ."

Rage whipped through Levi like red-hot lashes—heating his blood, tightening his muscles, burning his gut. *Motherfucker.* His demon hissed, fairly vibrating with fury, as Levi crouched a few feet away from the wall, clenching his teeth so hard it sent a shooting pain along his jaw.

"At first, I thought someone had actually jerked off right here," said Piper. "But it doesn't look like they came all over the wall. There's *way* too much of it, for starters. And the . . . blobs, for lack of a better word, are too thin and stringy. It seems more like it was squirted on the wall; like someone jerked off into a container—possibly a few times—and then sprayed the contents here."

Breathing through his anger so he could speak without growling, he said, "You're right." Fuck, he could practically taste his fury. Someone had trespassed on her territory with the purpose of either marking or soiling it. Neither purpose would earn them anything less than the beating of their fucking life. "This wasn't done last night. The semen would be drier. I'd say someone did this at some point this morning and deliberately knocked over your planter in the hope that you'd come outside and discover what they'd done."

"That would be my guess as well."

Standing, Levi turned to her. "You said someone recently dumped a bag of dogshit on your doorstep."

"Kids—"

"Maybe not. Maybe it was the same person who did this."

"I don't think so. The dogshit stunt was childish."

"It was also something you dismissed as a prank committed by idiotic kids. That could have been the whole point. I'm thinking they intended to empty the bag all over the doorstep or maybe even sling it at your house. It could be that they saw your car coming or they were disturbed somehow and decided to toss the bag and leave."

She blinked. "I guess it's possible. I never did understand the point of dumping dogshit here if they were going to leave it nicely contained in a bag. Do you think they might have also slashed my tires?"

"I do. And I find it suspicious that this began shortly after Sefton was freed." The little fucker had looked shaky and cowed when he walked out of the prison, but that could have been an act. "Have you seen anything of him since he was released?"

"He and Jasper passed the house when I was talking to Kelvin the other day. They didn't speak to me. Sefton didn't even make eye-contact with me."

"What about Jasper?"

"He gave me a dismissive little snarl. That's it."

"And this happened the day your tires were slashed?"

She nodded. "Yes."

"And they were slashed sometime after you closed the door on Kelvin?"

Piper frowned. "You'd be wrong to think he had anything to do with it. He's an idiot at times, but he wouldn't do stuff like this. Really."

"People will do very strange out-of-character things when jealous." Levi had seen that a dozen times with the ex-bed buddies of Knox when they got all riled up by seeing him with Harper.

"Even if he wanted me back, which he doesn't, he'd have no reason to feel jealous—I told him that you and I aren't dating."

"That doesn't mean he'd have been fine with seeing another man enter your house. Maybe he felt compelled to mark what he believes is his territory."

She shook her head. "No, I can't see him doing this. Not for any reason. And I can't see it being Sefton either. I'm not saying he wouldn't make a nuisance of himself at some point, given he's angry with me. But do it so soon after being released, while he'll still be a mental wreck from his time in incarceration and surely *far* from interested in risking Knox's wrath? It seems unlikely that he would."

"Maybe. However, although the torture he endured wasn't solely about punishment but about deterring people from reoffending, not everyone learns their lesson. It works with most. Like Enzo. At one time, he and Dez's brother Marshall got up to all kinds of shit."

"Really?"

"Yeah. Enzo was a cocksure son of a bitch back then. A stay in Knox's Chamber had been the reality check he needed. He turned his life around, even though he also lost his brother and father near that time. He hated his father—and with good reason—but he loved his brother. It would have been easy for Enzo to go off the rails, but he didn't. He got his shit together. I'm not yet sure if Sefton will do the same. What I am sure of is that he's incredibly spiteful, just like Jasper, so we can't be so certain that either brother will keep their head down and leave you alone."

"True." Cursing, she rubbed at her forehead as lines of strain formed on her face. "I swear my life is usually relatively uneventful. It must seem like I'm someone who'll constantly be needing people to step in and deal with situations for them. I'm not." She dropped her hand to her side. "The occasional person gives me grief when I help identify a culprit, but this . . . no, stuff like this isn't regular."

He cocked his head. "You think I'll get tired of being here whenever you need me?"

She shrugged. "I don't know. Maybe."

He pinned her gaze with his. "That's not who I am, Piper. I'll always be here for you. And if you want the truth, although I'm pissed that someone did this, I'm also feeling pretty pleased right now."

Her head jerked back. "What?"

"You're used to dealing with things on your own. I know it's no little thing that you shared this with me, trusting me to help. Don't think I don't see that. I do. And it means something to me that you didn't choose to handle this alone."

"I thought about it," she admitted in a mumble.

"I'm sure you did. But in the end, you chose not to keep this from me. That's what matters." He spared the wall clock a quick look. "Let's get you to the studio. I'll have someone come and clean this mess. It will be gone by the time I pick you up after your shift is over. All right?"

Swallowing, she gave a curt nod. "All right."

The faith in those two words eased his demon's anger slightly. "Good. Now come on."

Once he'd escorted her into the studio and said his goodbyes, he drove to the apartment building where Sefton lived.

Levi didn't need to have anyone buzz him into the complex. He had the code for every lair-owned building logged on his phone's note-app. So he let himself inside and made his way to Sefton's apartment. The nightmare opened the door a few moments after Levi knocked.

Stood there in rumpled clothing, Sefton groggily double-blinked. And then he seemed to jolt into full alertness. "Uh . . . Levi. Hey."

Levi arched up a brow. "Aren't you going to invite me in?"

"Sorry. Yeah. Of course."

Following the nightmare into the living room, Levi glanced around, taking in the empty candy wrappers on the table and the ridiculous amount of clutter. "Not the tidiest person in the world, are you?"

Sefton shifted nervously from foot to foot. "I guess not."

"What time did you drag yourself out of bed this morning?"

"About ten minutes ago, maybe."

"Hmm." Levi tilted his head. The guy truly did look as though he hadn't long woken. Maybe he hadn't, but that didn't mean he hadn't simply been napping after paying Piper's house a visit. "And you didn't take a little trip at some point?"

Sefton's brow pinched. "Trip? No."

"So you weren't at Piper's house earlier spraying semen all over her wall?"

"*What?*"

"Answer the question."

Sefton spluttered. "Of course not. I'd never do something like that. Shit, that's just . . . fucked up."

"So is trapping a woman in her own personal nightmare."

Sefton flinched.

"You were severely punished for that. So severely, in fact, you may have been tempted to target the person who you feel is at fault for your capture."

The nightmare shook his head. "It wasn't me who went to Piper's house."

"And you didn't slash her car tires? Plant a bag of dogshit on her doorstep?"

"No, and no! I *swear* I didn't."

Levi barged into his personal space, going nose to nose with him. "If I find out you've lied to me, you'll be back in a cell so fucking fast your head will spin. And you'll pay, Sefton. You'll pay *hard*. No one gets to fuck with my anchor."

Sefton opened and closed his mouth in surprise. Clearly the news hadn't reached him before now.

"Tell me you understand."

"I-I understand."

Levi grunted, gave him one last look of warning, and then strode out of the apartment. Now it was time to pay Jasper a visit. The man in question still lived with his parents.

It was his father, Lester, who answered the front door. Levi had never liked him. Never liked his superior, blustery, misogynistic attitude. Never liked that he failed to hold his sons accountable for anything they did, on the grounds that 'boys will be boys.'

As it happened, Lester wasn't a real fan of Levi either—mostly because Levi *did* hold the man's sons accountable for their fuckups. So it was no surprise that Lester was struggling to hold back the same snarl Jasper often tossed at people.

Levi met his gaze steadily. "Where's Jasper? Don't lie, Lester. I'm really not in the fucking mood."

Lester snapped his mouth shut. The man might be an asshole, but he tended to choose the path of least resistance when it came to the sentinels. He showed very little respect toward the lair's Force, however.

"Jasper, you have a visitor!" Lester bellowed before backing up and folding his arms.

The man's eldest son soon came strolling out of the living room, his step faltering when he spotted Levi. Jasper cleared his throat. "Oh, uh . . ."

So very eloquent. "Do you remember the last time we had a conversation?"

Jasper lowered his eyes, but not in time to hide the anger that flashed in their depths. "I remember."

"And what did I warn you to do?"

"Stay clear of Piper." Jasper met Levi's gaze. "Look, I only walked past her house—"

"*Is* that all you did, though? I'd like to think so. I'd like to think our prior conversation wasn't a waste of my time. I don't like to waste my time." Though he had enjoyed landing a few punches on the nightmare's face. "What I really, really don't like . . . is anyone thinking they can target my anchor in any way, shape, or form."

Jasper poked the inside of his cheek with his tongue. "So that's why you've been hanging out with her."

Levi narrowed his eyes at the nightmare's poorly faked surprise. "Sefton called you after I left his place, did he?"

"He was freaked. He didn't do none of that shit to Piper. And if you're here because you think *I* might have done it, you're dead wrong."

"Am I?"

"Yes."

Levi took an aggressive step forward. "I'll tell you what I told your brother. If it turns out that you're the person responsible for targeting my anchor, you'll pay for what you did. Your beloved father here won't recognize you by the time I'm done with you."

Jasper's cheeks reddened. "I didn't target her."

"You heard him, Levi," Lester chipped in, belligerent. "He didn't do anything. My boys are innocent."

Levi's inner demon surfaced fast and said, "Your boys could never be described as innocent." The entity smiled when both males recoiled. "Do not tempt me to fully come out to play. You will both be writhing in pain and terror if I do. You, Jasper, know from experience that is true." The demon then withdrew. Levi glanced from father to son. "Try not to be dicks all your fucking lives." With that, he left.

Khloë pointed to the back of her shoulder as she stood at Piper's very own station, gazing into the large, wall-mounted mirror. "I was hoping to have it somewhere here. I like back-of-the-shoulder tattoos."

"Okay," said Piper. "Well I can come to your house and do it there if you'd like, since I can't exactly do it during work hours."

Khloë's eyes lit up. "That would be *awesome*."

"What would?" asked Devon, materializing beside the imp.

"Piper's going to come to my house and tattoo the back of my shoulder for me."

"Really?" Devon glanced at Piper. "That is awesome of you."

Piper shrugged. "I doubt it will take long. She only wants a hippo."

Devon sighed long and loud. "Would it be a *baby* hippo, by any chance?"

Piper felt her brow furrow. "Yes. I feel like I'm missing something. What am I missing?"

"The pure idiocy that runs in her veins." Folding her arms, Devon turned to Khloë. "You know Keenan will kill you if you get a tattoo of a cock, right?"

Piper drew back. "Whoa, a cock?"

Khloë raised her shoulders. "Fritz looks different than the average baby hippo—"

"Because it's not a hippo," said Devon.

Khloë's lips flattened. "Not an 'it,' a 'he.'"

"And a symptom of your insanity."

Piper looked at the imp. "Did you really think I'd tattoo a dick on you?"

"Well, you do cute, whimsical, funny stuff," said Khloë. "As for Keenan, he wouldn't mind."

"Uh, *yeah*, he would," Devon insisted. "Because unlike you, he's normal."

"I'm telling you, he'd be fine with it. As long as it was a sketch of *his* cock, anyway. Although, really, I'd struggle to fit it on the back of my shoulder." The imp ran her finger along her inner forearm. "Maybe I could have it done here."

Devon looked close to pulling on her hair. "Can you *not* be a fucking weirdo?"

"Can you *not* go take a shit?"

"*Khloë*."

"Well," Raini began, fast approaching with a wide smile on her face, "we'll be closing for lunch in a minute, someone needs to go pick up our deli order."

"I'll do it," Piper volunteered.

Raini cocked her head, making her pink-streaked blonde ponytail dance to the side. "You sure?"

Piper righted her leather chair. "Yeah, I don't mind." It would be a good thing, actually. Because whenever the studio was empty of clients for even a few moments, one or all of the girls would bring up Levi and start singing his praises.

She got the message—he was the shit, and Piper should just bond with him already.

In all honesty, Piper was increasingly warming to the idea. She simply didn't feel comfortable discussing it with a bunch of people she barely knew who were also incredibly biased where he was concerned. It was sweet that they were so loyal to and supportive of him, though. She liked that.

Piper left the studio and headed to the nearby deli. Delicious scents smothered her as she walked inside. Piper bypassed the long queue and crossed to the side of the checkout counter. She smiled at the young male there. "Hi, I'm here to pick up an order for Urban Ink."

He scanned the bags on the shelf before stopping at one and peering at the receipt stapled to it. "Order's almost ready," he told her. "It'll be another two minutes. Take a seat if you like."

Deciding she might as well use the timeslot to answer the call of nature that was bugging her bladder, she headed for the restroom. Pushing open a heavy door, she entered a narrow hallway that led to her destination. Inside, she did her business and then exited—

*Knife.*

It seemed to appear out of nowhere and head right for her chest.

Piper abruptly leaned to the side, but a blazing punch of fire lanced through her shoulder. She sharply sucked in a pained breath, shock jolting her system like a bolt of electricity.

Stumbling backwards, she could only stare at the blade *sticking out of her body.* Warm blood pooled to the surface and wet her tee.

A cruel, masculine chuckle came from a few feet in front of her . . . yet there was no one in sight.

Leaping to action, Piper launched several hellfire orbs in quick succession. Two hit the fire exit door up ahead. Three crashed into what appeared to be thin air.

There was a grunt. A curse. A growl. The sizzling of blistering flesh.

*Ha.* She conjured another orb—

"Fucking bitch."

A hard impact slammed into her temple. Another landed on her jaw. She staggered, blinking hard, a ringing sound filling her ears, and the flaming orb in her hand fizzled out. Enraged, her demon hissed and spat and lost its shit.

The blade was mercilessly *yanked* out of Piper's shoulder.

She cried out, the abrupt pain snapping her out of her daze. *Son of a fucker.* Oh, she was gonna cut a bitch up.

"Bastard." Piper blindly tossed one crackling ball of hellfire after another.

More grunts. More sizzling. Even better, the knife hit the floor with a clang.

Her demon grimly smiled. Piper moved fast, slamming her foot down on the blade before an invisible hand could snatch it up.

Another masculine curse.

Ignoring the throbbing in her shoulder and the warm blood trickling down her arm, Piper emitted a haze of hellfire bullets from her hand. Some crashed into her invisible attacker, wrenching pained grunts out of him, while others whizzed by and smashed into walls.

Curses rang through the air yet again.

She dropped fast, nabbed the knife, and swiped out. A voice hissed. Cloth tore. Dots of warm blood slapped her skin.

Piper stood and darted backwards before any upcoming punches could land. Then she followed up the move with yet another scorching hot orb. There was an *oof* of pain this time, and then came the sound of feet hammering the wooden floor as the fucker fled. The fire exit door swung open, and the footfalls quickly faded.

A breath shuddered out of her. A breath filled with pain and relief and shock because, yeah, *what the hell was all that?*

Her hand spasming around the hilt of the knife, Piper glanced at her injured, still-throbbing shoulder. She winced at the wet, crimson stain on her tee. Blood also trailed down her arm in thin ribbons. Not good.

She didn't even *think* about what she did next. It was too instinctive. Too easy.

She telepathically reached out to Levi. *Don't know if you're busy or not, but I've got a story you might want to hear.*

# CHAPTER SEVEN

A cold fury simmering in his blood, Levi stalked into Urban Ink, his eyes immediately seeking out his anchor. She sat on one of the black leather chairs, several people surrounding her without standing too close. Anger wracked his gut as he noted the red dots and streaks on her skin. His demon hissed out its own rage, intending to shatter every bone in the body of whoever attacked its anchor.

Levi didn't so much as glance at anyone else as he made a beeline for her. He ignored the voices of those who tried getting his attention. He had no interest in anyone other than Piper.

Relief flickered in her eyes when she spotted him. That relief quickly gave way to concern, so she must have sensed how close to the edge he was. Using a wet cloth to wipe at the blood spatter, she assured him, "The wound's not so bad. It's already healing. Harper bandaged it up and gave me a spare tee to wear."

Levi crouched in front of her. Fuck, he needed to hold her.

But he wasn't positive he could be gentle right now, he was worried he'd hold her too tight. So he settled for leaning his forehead against hers and breathing her in, almost growling at the coppery smell of blood that lay beneath her scent. "I'll kill him."

"Be inventive about it," she said.

"I know lots of weird and wonderful ways to make someone suffer." Drawing back slightly, he took the cloth from her hand and began carefully cleaning the spots she'd missed. "You should have called out to me sooner."

"I realized that afterward. It just all happened so fast, and I was too focused on defending myself."

"Tell me again exactly what happened. Leave nothing out. Every detail matters."

She walked him through the attack, calm and thorough, before adding, "I can't tell you much about him. All I know is he has a very deep voice, can punch mega hard, and possesses the ability to somehow conceal himself."

"I don't know of anyone with that ability," began Tanner, standing beside his mate, "but most demons don't advertise what they can do. They don't like all their strengths and weaknesses to be widely known."

"We need to know what enemies you might have, Piper," Knox told her, his dark eyes sharp.

She pursed her lips. "There are people who don't like me much or are especially pissed at me, but I wouldn't say I have big, bad enemies."

"When you talk of people who are pissed at you, I'm assuming you mean those you've played a part in identifying as guilty of crimes over the years," said Knox.

"Some," she said. "Most were their friends or lovers or family members who were upset with me. No one ever attacked or threatened to kill me, though. They just ranted, accusing me of being a liar or whatever."

Finished cleaning her, Levi placed the cloth on the shelf beneath her mirror. "You reported every confrontation, right?"

She nodded. "Yes."

"Then we already have the list of their names on file," said Levi. "We'll take a look at each one of them."

Piper worried her lower lip. "I didn't recognize his voice."

"He could have disguised it," Harper cut in. "You said it was very deep. Maybe it wasn't *naturally* that deep."

"He could also have been hired by someone," said Larkin.

Levi had already considered that, which was why . . . "Kelvin should be included on our list of suspects."

Piper frowned, shaking her head. "That bastard in the deli tried to kill me. Kelvin has no reason to want me dead. He's frustrated with me right now, but not to the point of feeling murderous."

"I agree," said Levi. "I'm not going to rule him out, though. Not until I feel confident he had nothing to do with this."

"What about Celeste?" asked Devon. "I know she's your stepsister but, to be blunt, I don't think that means anything to her."

Piper tilted her head. "Do I think she'd mourn me? No. But have me killed? No, I don't see her doing that. It's a step too far for her."

"Maybe. As with Kelvin, though, I won't rule her out until I feel positive that I safely can," said Levi.

"Is there anyone else you can think of who might mean you harm, Piper?" asked Knox.

She thought about it for a long moment and then shook her head. "No. No one."

After a few more questions were asked, Levi cupped her elbow and urged her to stand as he himself pushed to his feet. "Come on, I'm taking you home."

Piper looked from Harper to Raini. “I’ll understand if you don’t want me to come back.”

Both her new bosses frowned.

“Why wouldn’t we want you to come back?” asked Raini.

“The bastard who stabbed me might come at me again,” Piper pointed out. “He could do that here.”

“That would be on him, not you,” said Raini. “You wouldn’t be the first worker here who had danger dogging them. Sad as it might be, it’s not unusual for demons to find themselves in this situation. Our world is violent.”

Harper nodded. “The people here look out for each other. Keep coming to work as usual. Don’t put your life on hold unless you absolutely have to. And if it *does* come to that, you’ll still have a job waiting for you for when you can come back.”

“So we’ll see you tomorrow, bright and early,” said Raini.

As each of the girls gave Piper a gentle hug, mindful of her wounded shoulder, Larkin held out a duffel to Levi and said, “Here.”

He took it from her, nodding his thanks. He’d telepathically asked her to pack him an overnight bag, because there wasn’t a chance he was leaving Piper alone tonight. For one thing, her attacker could strike again. For another, she had to be shaken on some level; he didn’t want her dealing with it on her own.

Once she was ready to leave, Levi led her out of the Underground and then drove her home. Inside the house, he dropped his duffel on the hallway floor.

She glanced down at it. “Do I want to know what’s in that bag?”

“Larkin packed a bunch of my stuff, knowing I wouldn’t want to leave you tonight. Don’t ask me to, Piper. Not when we both know that whoever tried to kill you could come for you here.

Besides, am I *fuck* going to leave you alone after what you just went through."

Touched, Piper swallowed hard. She didn't bother pointing out that she was mostly fine now, because she knew that wasn't the point. Knew that the 'scuffle' earlier could have ended so differently. Namely with him mourning her. Demons who lost their anchors could go off the damn rail. And if the bond was formed at the time, a mourning anchor could even turn rogue.

"I wasn't going to object," said Piper. "If the situation was reversed, I'd have been too wound up to go on home like nothing happened. I'd have wanted to stay with you." It hadn't been easy to admit that, but the hint of warmth that seeped into his gaze made it worth it. "I've got a spare room you can use."

"I won't be sleeping. I'll be standing guard down here."

Since demons could go days without sleep, it wouldn't do him any harm.

His eyes swept over her face, so fucking *intent* on her. That laser-focus was dangerously seductive. Dammit, she didn't want to be this person who pined for someone she couldn't have. It was getting old fast. But how did you switch off an attraction that felt so basic and elemental? That seemed so completely out of your control?

"I'll find out who stabbed you, Piper. They're in for a world of pain. And if they were hired by someone, said someone will suffer worse."

She believed him. "Good."

"I'll be putting guards on you. Enzo and Dez will keep a close watch when I'm not with you. Also, I want to have a security system installed here."

"I'm sensing you expect me to object to these precautions. While I'm not fond of that high-handed tone you're using, I'm not going to put up a protest when it became clear today that someone wants me dead. I'm still trying to wrap my head around that."

"They won't get what they want, I swear that to you."

Nodding, she gestured upstairs. "I'm gonna go give myself a washdown and change clothes. I can't shower or I'll get the bandage wet."

"You go do that. I'll make dinner."

She'd already known he could cook; he'd told her during one of their talks. "You sure?"

"Positive."

"Okay, thank you." She padded out of the room and up the stairs, already sensing he was totally going to baby her tonight. She wouldn't expect any different, given he had to be shook up that someone wanted her dead. She wouldn't balk at a little hovering. Temporarily.

*Someone wanted her dead.*

God, she really *was* becoming a high-maintenance anchor.

Dinner was a quiet affair. Levi kept a close eye on Piper throughout the meal. Right then—lost in her own head, operating on autopilot—she looked so very unreachable.

He'd seen her like this each time she used her gift to help others. At first, he'd mistaken it for shock. But he'd eventually come to realize that whenever Piper felt overwhelmed, she tended to distance herself from what she was feeling. He got the sense that she preferred to wait until she was alone before she allowed herself to mentally process things.

As her anchor, he wasn't down with her dealing with anything alone. But he didn't want to push her to talk. Not now. She'd had one fuck of a night, and it was important that she get her rest so she could heal. Tomorrow, he'd do his best to make her talk. He didn't want her bottling things up.

"Did you call your mother or Joe about what happened?" he asked.

She double-blinked, snapping out of her daze. "Uh, no, they're at a party. I don't see the sense in spoiling it for them." She sighed. "They're gonna be pissed. And they're gonna expect you to magically have all the answers and ensure my safety."

He'd expect nothing less. "I *will* get answers, and I *will* keep you safe. You can count on me to do that."

"I know."

His heart squeezed. She might not be in any rush to claim him, but she did have faith in him; did seem to feel safe with him. That meant a lot, and it went a long way to soothing his demon's frustration. "I have a question for you. You seem very close to Joe, but neither you nor your mother took his surname. Why? Is it out of affection for your biological father?"

"No. Winslow is actually my mom's family name, it was never his. My father—who is convinced his calling is to be a rock star but can't sing for shit—left when I was a baby. He came back occasionally when I was little, saying he wanted to see me, but he was only really looking to borrow money from my mom. He was a total bum."

"You don't sound pissed about it." In fact, there was a note of amusement in her voice when she spoke of the male.

"He's not a bad guy. He was never mean to me or anything. He just wasn't a dad. He was too unreliable and self-centered to prioritize anyone else over himself."

"Did he at least visit you on special occasions?"

"Well he'd bring me birthday presents, but never on my actual birthday. And he only ever did it to make it *look* like he was there to see me when, really, he wanted to borrow cash from my mom again or needed a couch to sleep on for a few nights. He stopped coming back after she met Joe. And we would have taken Joe's surname if Celeste hadn't put up a stink. She did the same when he invited me to call him 'Dad.'"

*Petty bitch.* "So you don't."

"No. But Joe *is* my dad. I don't need to be biologically related to him for that to be true. Sharing DNA with someone doesn't make them your family."

"Agreed."

"On the subject of parents, you've never mentioned your own. We don't have to talk about them if it's a painful topic," she hurried to add.

His first instinct was to take the out she'd given him. When it came to his origins and childhood, there was much he didn't know. Much he didn't remember. And the memories he *did* have of that time, well, not many were fun to revisit. It was reflexive of him to balk at admitting to all that, but Larkin's assertion that he needed to be open with Piper slithered through his mind.

With a silent curse, he reluctantly confessed, "My mother, Blanche, died giving birth to me. As for my father, I don't know his identity. I'm not sure if I ever once met him as a child. It's possible he either had no clue I existed or simply didn't wish to be part of my life, because he didn't take me in after she died." Levi gave an indifferent shrug, having long ago ceased resenting it. "There really isn't much else I can tell you about them. My earliest memories are of the home for demonic orphans where I grew up."

"I don't need to ask if the home was a good place. Your flat tone says it all."

"Growing up there was no easy ride, but it could have been worse. The staff were overly strict—often to the point of being abusive. We didn't know until a couple of years ago, but some children were also sexually assaulted there. Compared to them, I didn't have it so hard."

"That doesn't detract from what you yourself went through."

Again, he shrugged. "One good thing came out of my time there. It's where I met Knox and the sentinels."

"Why didn't your lair keep you after your mom died?"

"From what I uncovered, she was a stray demon. She and her sister, Moira, left their lair together. I never did find out why, or even which lair they came from. Moira took me in after Blanche died. I don't remember her either. She allegedly wasn't very happy to have a toddler in her care, but at least she didn't give me away. After she was later murdered, I officially became an orphan."

Piper's lips parted. "Your aunt was murdered?"

Levi nodded.

"Jesus. What happened?"

He hesitated, pursing his lips. "It isn't a pretty story. *Definitely* not a good bedtime story. And you've had one hell of a day. I'd rather not add to that."

Her perceptive gaze drifted over his face. "In other words, you don't want to talk about it," she said, no judgment in her tone.

Honestly, no, he didn't. Not only because it didn't seem like the right time to pile all that crap on her, but also because it would lead to a conversation about the current murders—he *really* didn't want all that stuff circulating around her head when it was already a busy place and she needed her sleep.

And yeah, okay, he didn't want it swimming through his own mind right now either. It poked and prodded at him often, only giving him a reprieve around Piper. He wanted to enjoy that reprieve, and he certainly didn't want his attention divided tonight when he was here to keep her safe. "I'll tell you all about it one day. Just not tonight."

Seconds of silence ticked by as she stared at him. "Okay," she finally said, her voice soft and empty of reproach. She licked her lips. "I'm sorry you lost your mom and aunt, and I'm sorry you had so few people in your life who were permanent fixtures. Just so you know . . . I'm going to be one of those fixtures. I'm not going anywhere."

No, she wasn't. Because neither he nor his demon would ever let her.

A shitty dream—not quite a nightmare, just an unpleasant jumble of images and other crap—snapped Piper awake. No light was creeping around the edges of the curtains, so it was nowhere close to morning. She grabbed her cell phone and checked the time: 2:07 a.m. Fabulous.

Sitting up, she took the bottle of water from the nightstand. There wasn't much left in it, so it wasn't surprising that she was still thirsty after draining the bottle.

Piper edged out of bed and, figuring there was nothing indecent about an old baggy tee and some shorts, didn't bother slipping on a robe before leaving the room. Not wanting to startle Levi, she called out, "It's only me, don't pounce."

As she was making her way down the stairs, he moved to stand at the bottom, too fucking hot for words. It really wasn't fair.

His eyes did a slow sweep of her bare legs before lifting to meet her gaze. Stark need flickered across his face. For all of two seconds. Or maybe she'd imagined it. Yep, that was probably it. Nonetheless, her pulse jumped and her stomach twisted.

"Something wrong?" he asked, not stepping back to give her space.

Piper shook her head. "Just thirsty." She was also feeling seriously hungry. For him. For his mouth and hands on her.

She gave herself a mental slap. Jesus, the man could sure send her hormones into a tailspin. It didn't help that all that alpha energy danced along her nerve-endings. Or that a good, fast fuck would go a long way to relaxing her.

"You should have given me a telepathic shout-out," he said. "I'd have brought you a drink."

"I'm not *that* lazy. Most of the time." Piper walked into the kitchen, conscious of him following her. "I take it there's been no sign of movement outside or anything."

"None," he confirmed. "How's your shoulder?"

"A little better. The throbbing's more like a dull ache now, and the wound's itching like crazy. Which means it's healing well and fast." Taking a bottle of water from the fridge, she studied him. "You haven't calmed down any, huh?"

"It's hard to do that knowing someone tried to kill you."

Which was why she'd earlier considered pushing him to talk of his aunt's murder; she'd thought it might help for him to concentrate on something else for a little while. Nonetheless, she'd let it go. Piper would rather he shared something with her because he wanted to, not because he felt pressured.

His eyes dropped to her legs again, bold as you please. Finally, they lifted . . . only to settle on her mouth. The atmosphere suddenly felt charged. Taut. Electric. Or maybe that was just her.

Something glowed in the depths of his gray eyes. Something she couldn't quite name but that caused little bumps to sweep over her skin.

Clearing his throat, he took a step back and tipped his chin toward the doorway. "Go on up," he said, his voice thick. "Get some more sleep."

She probably wouldn't manage to doze off again. She felt wide awake, and her brain seemingly wanted to obsess over what happened at the deli. Still, she'd head on up to bed and have some 'alone time.' She couldn't risk digging out her vibrator—he'd hear that baby for sure. But her fingers would do the job just fine.

Halfway to the door, she turned to him. "By the way, um, thank you. For staying. I don't think I'd have slept at all if I'd been alone."

A line dented his brow. "I'd never have left you on your own." Crossing to her, he palmed the side of her neck, staring hard into her eyes. "I told you before, I'll always be here when you need me. You might not believe that so easily now, but you will in time."

His thumb swept over her chin and grazed her lower lip—such a simple thing, but her flesh felt so sensitized she inhaled sharply and then swallowed hard.

His pupils dilated. His grip on her neck tightened. His thumb traced the corner of her mouth.

Sexual tension sparked in the air. Hot. Dazing. Completely unexpected.

"You shouldn't have worn shorts," he said.

She blinked. "What?"

He pounced, slanting his mouth over hers. No hesitance, no tentativeness. He dived right in, plunging his tongue deep; shocking her with a bruising, unrestrained kiss that obliterated her control.

She clung to him, excitement building inside her as his hands greedily roamed over her—shaping, palming, squeezing. One hand delved into her shorts and panties to cup her ass, and the hard dig of his fingertips wrenched a moan out of her.

Something hit the floor. Her bottle. The sound penetrated her haze and made her good sense snap awake, but it was overruled by the burn of his mouth, the possessiveness in his touch, and the hotly sexual need that flamed through her system.

God, she needed this, needed him, needed—

Pain lanced through her injured shoulder, and she hissed through her teeth.

Levi jerked back, breathing hard. "Shit, you all right?"

Panting, she gave a jerky nod. "Fine." But she'd messed up. Big time.

That kiss had been thrilling. Scorching. Intoxicating. Everything she'd imagined it would be.

The bitch of it was . . . the kiss also wouldn't have happened if he hadn't been so tightly wound due to all that was going on. That stolen moment hadn't been about *her*. No, his system had needed to channel his anger into something; had needed to give the emotion an *out*.

She was the out.

Well at least they'd stopped before things went too far. One-night stands were fun and all, but this was *Levi*. Her anchor. A man she'd wanted for too long. There was nothing smart about letting a guy you badly wanted quite simply use you for a night—even if there would have been nothing disrespectful about it on his part. And so she needed to backtrack now and pretend the kiss never happened.

His cock hard and throbbing like a motherfucker, Levi watched as her dazed eyes shuttered and her body straightened. She shifted away from him, putting a respectable distance between them. He had no clue what was going on in her head, but it was clearly making her pull back. His demon narrowed its eyes at her withdrawal, not liking it.

"I'll go upstairs." She coughed to clear her throat. "Yeah, I'll go." She snatched her bottle from the floor and headed for the door.

"Running again?"

She slowly spun on her heel. "Excuse me?"

"You learned we were anchors. You fled. I kissed you. You decided to flee again. Seems this is a thing with you." Yes, he was deliberately goading her. He wanted that mask of indifference *gone*. He wanted to smash through the wall she'd thrown up between them.

He expected her to bristle and go on the defensive. He wasn't expecting the tired sigh she let out.

"You don't really want me," she said.

He winged up a brow. "I don't?"

"No. You're angry and restless and looking to give those emotions an outlet," she told him, all reasonable.

"You know what I want better than I do, do you?"

Her eyes flared. "I know I'm not your type."

"I have a type?" That was new to him.

"Apparently. And I'm not it."

Levi tilted his head. She'd said it with so much authority, so much certainty. All right, now he was just confused. "Who told you that?"

"Nobody, but . . ."

"But, what?" he pushed, his scalp prickling with unease.

Sighing again, she thrust a hand through her hair. "Let's not do this. We'll just forget—"

"Finish what you were going to say, Piper."

She weakly flapped her arms. "Does it really matter?"

"If something is related to you, yeah, it absolutely matters to me. Why do you have it in your head that you're not my type? Who put that thought there?"

She shrugged. "*You* did."

He felt his brows dart together. "What?"

"You said those very words."

Did he *fuck*.

"When Celeste talked to you about my crush on you—a

crush she found highly amusing—you told her I wasn't your type. Yeah, I overheard that conversation."

He exhaled heavily as realization settled over him. *Shit.*

"I also heard what you *didn't* say—like 'Celeste, you're being a bitch.' But would I have expected you to defend me? No. You had no reason to, and she was your girlfriend. But don't try to now make out like I'm 'fleeing' when all I'm really doing is stopping us both from doing something you'd later regret."

Raking his eyes over her face, Levi closed the distance between them. "You might say you wouldn't have expected me to defend you, but it still rankles that I didn't."

"Yes. I realize it's irrational, but yes."

Not irrational at all. He wouldn't have felt any happier about it, in her shoes. "What was I supposed to say to her, Piper? '*Actually, Celeste, I can't stop wondering what it'd feel like to have your stepsister sucking my cock*'?"

Piper's lips parted, red and swollen. His dick predictably twitched. She blinked hard. "Sorry, what?"

"A man does not tell a woman he's involved with that he finds her stepsister attractive. I didn't speak up for you, because I didn't trust that my words wouldn't reveal what I really wanted: *You*. Under me. As many times as I could have you."

She gave her head a little shake. "No, seriously, what?"

"I tried shoving all that aside. It didn't work. Not when I was with Celeste, and not after we ended things. Even the fact that you were eighteen back then ceased to mean anything to me. But I still couldn't act on what I wanted, because she isn't the kind of person who'd have paved the way for me to make a move on you, and I didn't want to make things worse between the two of you than they already were." Levi edged into her personal space. "To put it simply, I wanted you then. I still want you now."

"But you . . ."

"I told her what she needed to hear. That's all."

"And how do I know you're not doing the same to me right now?"

"You think I'm lying to you?"

She pressed the heel of her palm to her forehead. "I don't know, Levi. I never thought you'd ever say any of this to me. And I mean *ever.* It's hard to take it in. Hard to believe it. Especially when my mind is also busy working through the ton of crap that's currently going on around us."

"This wasn't the right time for me to lay this on you, I know. But I wasn't going to let you walk away thinking I meant what I said to Celeste all those years ago. I lied to her then. I'm *not* lying to *you* now."

Her arm flopped to her side. She looked so lost and overwhelmed, an ache struck his chest.

He stroked his hand over her hair. "Go to bed," he said softly.

Blinking, she gave a distracted nod.

As she padded out of the room, he scrubbed a hand down his face. His blood was still hot, his cock was still hard, her taste was still in his mouth . . . and Levi knew he wouldn't be able to wait until after they'd bonded before he made a move. Knew, too, that his demon wouldn't wait.

It would be interesting to see how long he and the entity lasted before the urge to take what they wanted became too much. Probably not more than twenty-four hours. They'd spent too many years craving her to hold back for very long.

The next time she went to bed, he'd be right there with her. And neither of them would get much sleep.

# CHAPTER EIGHT

Her phone to her ear, Piper descended the stairs the next morning. "I'm fine, Mom."

"So I heard," said Whitney, a note of anxiety in her voice. "And, like the attack itself, I should have heard that *from you.*"

"I knew you and Joe were at a party, I didn't want to ruin it. And it wasn't like there was anything you could have done. I didn't think the news would reach you so fast."

Walking into the kitchen, Piper found Levi sat at the island, an empty bowl in front of him, a half-full cup of coffee in hand. Another steaming mug was on the opposite side of the island, along with a plate on which a toasted bagel sat. And as her gaze locked with his, her lower stomach clenched at the glitter of heat there.

Memories of their kiss crawled all over her. She'd gone to bed restless and horny and so damn disoriented. She'd had it in her head for so long that she wasn't his type that she still struggled to let the apparent truth sink in.

"Tell me your attacker has been detained," said Whitney.

Piper perched herself on a stool at the island. "He hasn't yet, but he will be. Levi is on it, as are Knox and the other sentinels."

"Good. Joe and I are counting on Levi to sort out this situation and ensure you're well-protected." Whitney paused. "I'm sorry about how badly things went with Celeste the other day—"

"It isn't you who needs to apologize."

"Maybe not, but we both know you'll hear no such apology from her. I wanted to invite you and Levi to dinner. Celeste won't be there. I won't have a repeat of what happened a few days ago. Joe and I would like to get to know your anchor better."

Piper felt her face soften. "I'm sure Levi will be up for it."

"We know how busy he is. Find out what evening would be best for him and then get back to me. Now, tell me how things are going at Urban Ink."

Piper did exactly that while eating her bagel. After ending the call a few minutes later, she looked at Levi, the impact of his piercing gaze hitting her like a fist to the solar plexus. "That was my mom. She wants us to have dinner with her and Joe at their house. Just the four of us."

He lifted his cup. "When?"

"She said to ask what would be a good evening for you. She knows you're a busy guy."

"You pick a day. I'll make it happen." He sipped at his drink. "How's your shoulder?"

"Healed."

"Fully? You won't be much good with a tattoo gun today if not."

Piper took a swig of her coffee. "There's no blemish, no pain, no nothing."

"Good."

As they went on to talk about general things, she braced herself for any mention of their kiss and the conversation that had followed it. But . . . he didn't once raise the subject. Didn't even hint at it.

It wasn't entirely surprising. She'd figured he might choose to act like it hadn't happened. It was important to Levi that nothing got in the way of them forming the anchor bond, and he might worry that acting on their attraction in any way would do exactly that.

Piper was glad he wanted to keep things platonic. She was also disappointed. The whole thing was . . . ugh, she honestly had no idea what she truly wanted here.

Her demon, on the other hand, was having no such internal crisis. It was totally up for blurring some lines, so it was annoyed with both her and him for their inaction.

"I'll walk you to the coffeehouse next to the studio," he told her as she washed the dirty dishware. "The girls will be waiting for you there. After that, I have a few things to do. Enzo and Dez will stand guard outside the studio throughout your entire shift. I'll be there to pick you up as usual at closing time. If you wish to leave the studio at any time, your guards will go with you."

She nodded. "All right." Would all this protection gall her? Not at all. Getting attacked was no fun, and she'd rather make it difficult for anyone to repeat said attack.

"If you need me for anything, reach out telepathically or call my cell."

"You said you had things to do. I don't want to bother you when you're busy."

"Piper, I'll never be too busy to answer a call from you—telepathic or otherwise. You come first. Understand?"

She nodded. "Sure."

Not so convinced she *was* sure, Levi narrowed his eyes. "Do you have it in your head that you'll come second to my positions within the lair?"

"Well, I kind of expect to. I won't be upset about it. I understand you're dedicated to your roles. I admire the level of your dedication."

That comment annoyed him as much as it warmed him. Because while he liked that she respected his commitments to their lair, he didn't like that she'd so much as *think* that those commitments came before her. It annoyed his demon just the same. "I told you, you're my priority."

"Mentally, maybe. But you won't always be able to act on that, because a lot of your time is taken up by both sentinel stuff and being Knox's bodyguard. I don't say that with resentment, I swear. That's not the sort of person I am."

"And neglecting my anchor isn't the sort of person *I* am."

"I'm not saying you'll neglect me. I'm simply saying you're a busy guy and that that will be a factor here."

Levi crossed to her, pinning her gaze with his. "Let's get a few things straight. You don't come second to my positions, Piper. You never will. Am I busy? Yes. Will we always spend as much time together as we do now? No. But you can bet your sweet little ass that I'll be checking in with you on, at the very least, a weekly basis. You can reach out to me any time. I'll always answer. I'm an 'all or nothing' person, Piper. You don't have to worry that I'll be a half-assed anchor."

She nodded again. "I believe you."

He studied her closely. "Do you? Or do you believe that this is all wishful thinking on my part?"

A sigh slipped out of her. "This is one of those situations where time will tell, isn't it? Now, are you ready to leave? Because I don't want to be late for work."

He shot her a narrow-eyed look, not liking that she meant to brush the topic aside. But as this wasn't a good time for him to push, he made a mental note to revisit the matter later. "Then let's go."

He kept the conversation light as he drove, pointedly avoiding the subject of the kiss. He hadn't initially intended to say nothing of it, but she was still as tense and unsure as she had been last night. The conversation they needed to have could wait until later. And they *would* have it.

After escorting her into the coffeehouse, he did a quick walkthrough of the studio, despite knowing Piper's attacker could conceal their presence. The one thing that brought Levi comfort was that Devon's hellcat sense of smell would pick up anyone lingering in the studio who shouldn't be there.

Back in the coffeehouse, he said his goodbyes to Piper, reminded her to contact him if there was a problem, and then—barely resisting the urge to plant a kiss on her mouth—headed to Knox's main office within the Underground. It was pretty close to the studio, so it was only a matter of minutes before Levi reached the small stairwell that led to the office. His demon squinted at the sight of Celeste leaning against the wall. *For fuck's sake.*

Levi had expected her to seek him out eventually—maybe to continue their argument, or maybe to play head games with him. She'd regret it soon enough. He'd been tactful the other night due to Whitney and Joe's presence. Now that he and Celeste were alone, he had no intention of holding his tongue.

She straightened and turned to fully face him. There was nothing confrontational about her body language today. She looked nervous. Sheepish. Awkward.

And he wasn't buying it.

"What are you doing here?" Levi asked, keeping his voice bored.

She cleared her throat. “I wanted to talk to you.”

“So talk.”

“Can we go somewhere private?”

“No.”

Her mouth briefly tightened. “Fine,” she said, her voice low. “I overreacted the other night. I know that. I was shocked, and I didn’t handle it well.”

“It’s Piper you need to have this conversation with.”

“I will apologize to her. I wanted to speak with you first.”

“Well now you have.”

She stared at him for a long moment. “You don’t have any interest in talking to me, do you?”

“No.” She was a fool if she’d thought differently.

She bit down on the inside of her cheek. “So you’re jumping on Piper’s bandwagon. I suppose I should have expected that. People always take her side.”

“You can’t play me the way you do your father and Whitney. Or have you forgotten that?”

Her eyes widened. “I never tried to play you.”

“Sure you did. But it doesn’t matter. It was a long time ago—”

“Not *that* long ago. And it wasn’t as if we simply had a one-night stand or something. We were *together*.”

He snorted. “Don’t pretend what we had was anything close to serious. You spent more time with the other men you were sleeping with than you did me during those four months.”

“Because you were always so busy! And you didn’t ask for exclusivity.”

“I’m not looking for you to justify anything. I’m simply pointing out that it wasn’t quite the cozy relationship you like to imply it was.” All of which he’d have said the other night, but he hadn’t wanted to make his and Piper’s announcement all about Celeste and their past.

"You cared for me," she insisted. "You cared for your job more, I know that. But I did mean something to you."

This time, it was his demon who snorted. "I never even really knew you. You wore a mask around me. A mask that started to slip when you couldn't find a way to control me. It just kept slipping, little by little."

Her eyes flashed. "You act like it was *you* who walked away. *I* ended things between us."

"It was yet another attempt to manipulate me, though, wasn't it? You wanted me to choose you over my positions."

She perched her hands on her hips. "It's so terrible that I wanted a real commitment from you? That I wanted more for us than a fling?" Taking a long breath, she held up her hands in surrender. "I didn't come here to fight. I don't want to rehash what happened back then. Like you said, it's in the past. I'm more interested in the future." She licked her lips. "*Our* future. I want us to try again."

Fucking hell, the woman couldn't be more predictable if she tried. "You want to pull me away from Piper," he corrected.

"No, it's not that. I reacted badly the other day, but it wasn't fair of me to ask that you both give up the anchor bond. I know that, and I'm sorry. This here and now is nothing to do with the psi-mate thing. This is about us."

"There's not going to be an 'us.'"

Celeste's lips flattened. "Just because it didn't work so well the first time round doesn't mean we can't make it work a second time."

"I'm not interested in trying again."

"Because of Piper? Because you don't think she'd handle it well? Look, I could talk to her. I could make her see—"

"I'm not interested in trying again," he repeated.

Celeste's expression soured. "You won't have time for anyone *she* doesn't like? Is that how it is?"

"I don't have time for anyone who treats my anchor like shit. That includes you. But even if you were sweet as pie to her, I wouldn't want to get involved with you again. *You're* not all that invested in the idea either. You simply don't like that the stepsister you despise has rights to someone who you once considered yours." He'd never been 'hers,' but she hadn't seen it that way. "You don't like how important Piper is to me, and you're thinking that if you can get back into my bed, you'll be front and center and she'll be pushed aside. Can you not see how fucking petty and vindictive that is?"

"You're twisting everything."

"No, I'm calling you on your bullshit. Something you're not used to people doing." He took a fluid step toward her, his face hard. "Understand something, Celeste. This little hobby you have of doing your best to fuck with Piper's life—that's over. She's under my personal protection now. Anyone who tries hurting her will have to deal with me and my demon. Stepsister or not, that will include you."

He'd expected a rant, a snarl, an insult. Instead, all the tension drained out of her. Sadness glimmered in her eyes.

"That's all I wanted from you, you know," she said. "For you to claim rights to me. For you to class me as directly under your protection. But you just never did." She opened her mouth to say more but then shook her head and walked away.

He had the distinct feeling she was hoping that he, moved by her apparent despair, would call her back to him. Instead, Levi ascended the stairwell and headed to Knox's office. It was as sleek and contemporary as it was spacious. The tall glass window overlooked the combat circle where Levi liked to blow off steam occasionally.

Both Tanner and Keenan had claimed the sofa while Larkin relaxed in a cozy armchair. Just like the desk chairs, they were cushioned with Italian leather that was soft as butter.

Seated behind the executive desk, Knox turned away from the hi-tech computer and frowned at Levi. "You all right?"

Grunting, Levi spared the wall-mounted security monitors a quick glance. There was plenty of CCTV footage of the Underground. It was important to keep an eye on their kind, since they didn't always play nicely. "I'll be fine when someone informs me that they discovered who targeted Piper," he said, taking the seat opposite Knox. "Anyone have any news?"

Knox flipped his pen upside down and began idly tapping the papers in front of him with it. "Most of the people on our list of suspects have been interviewed by members of the Force. Only a few don't have alibis for the time of her attack."

"Do Jasper and Sefton have alibis?" They were Levi's main suspects.

Knox nodded. "Their father swore they were with him."

"He would have said it even if they weren't."

"But we can't prove he lied."

Larkin shifted in her seat. "Neither Jasper nor Sefton had injuries consistent with the attack that took place at the deli. In fact, no one who was interviewed had any wounds. Which means that either the injuries were healed by the time these people were questioned—which is entirely possible—or none of those people were Piper's attacker."

"No one in our lair is down on record as having the ability to conceal their appearance, but that doesn't mean they can't," said Keenan. "Deli Guy may well have been hired by someone."

"Possibly." Levi twisted his mouth. "Has Piper's ex, Kelvin, been interviewed yet?"

"Not yet," said Knox. "He wasn't home when our Force members went to see him. They plan to catch him at his tattoo shop today."

"Leave that with me," said Levi. "I'll speak with him."

Larkin tilted her head. "How's Piper?"

"Fully healed."

"Good, though I kind of meant emotionally," said the harpy. "It's not every day someone invisible tries to kill you, even in the strange world of demons."

"She seemed in shock when I saw her at the studio after the attack," Tanner chipped in.

Levi rubbed his nape. "Piper's very good at dissociating from whatever's going on inside her. I saw it over and over when she helped victims relive their attacks. She seems to prefer to process things in the privacy of her own mind."

"Kind of like you," said Tanner.

Levi nodded. "Which is why I'd be a hypocrite if I pushed her to share the things that bug her."

"But you'll push her anyway," Larkin accused, a faint smile tugging at her mouth. "Because you'll hate the thought that she could be hurting or anxious or confused. You'll want to fix it."

Unable to deny it, Levi only shrugged.

"Is she any closer to wanting to form the anchor bond?" asked Knox.

"I believe she's warming to the idea." Levi slid his gaze to Larkin. "I took your advice and let Celeste be 'the bad guy' in front of Whitney and Joe. It worked."

"Of course it worked," said Larkin with a haughty sniff. "Celeste didn't take the news well, then?"

"No." Levi puffed out a breath. "She threw a tantrum, saying she wouldn't 'allow' me and Piper to bond. But she apologized for that just now."

Tanner's brow creased. "What? Here?"

"She was waiting at the bottom of the stairwell," said Levi. "She gave me a false apology and then tried convincing me we should give things another shot."

Keenan rolled his blue eyes. "As if you'd ever be up for that. It's like she's forgotten all the drama she caused after you two ended things."

"I've learned that Celeste has a selective memory." Levi exhaled heavily. "Piper's not going to be happy when she hears about it, but I doubt she'll be surprised."

Just then, Knox's phone began to ring. The Prime held up a finger and then answered his cell.

"On another note," began Larkin, sliding her gaze to Tanner, "have you and Devon decided on any baby names?"

Tanner's mouth thinned. "Her new favorites are Engelbert for a boy and Hallelujah for a girl. It's like she wants our kid to get bullied."

Levi exchanged a smile with Keenan. They were all pretty certain that Devon was simply messing with her mate as a punishment for how much he hovered around and fussed over her.

Knox ended his call and sighed, his face grim, his eyes glittering with anger. "There's been another murder."

As they strode up the path toward the victim's house, Tanner looked at Levi. "There are other reapers who could do this."

Levi tossed him a sideways glance. "Do you really think I'd leave this to others when it could be connected to my aunt's death?"

"No. But I do think that the killer—whether they had anything to do with her death or not—wants you to investigate these deaths. This is probably his warped way of . . . reaching out to you. Even communicating with you. After all, you feel what he feels when you use your gifts. You get a vague impression of what happened. Maybe he wants that."

"He could be right, Levi," Knox said from behind them.

Glancing over his shoulder, Levi told the Prime, "I can't walk away from this."

Covering the rear, Larkin and Keenan exchanged an unhappy look.

"All right," said Knox. "I simply want you to consider that the killer could be purposely trying to draw you into this."

Levi already had considered it. In his opinion, it didn't matter either way, because he couldn't step aside. He needed to play some part in catching this bastard.

Levi took the lead as they walked into the house and through to the living room. Waves of pulsing emotions hit him like a clap of thunder. "It's like the last scene. The feminine emotions are anger, powerlessness, and a sense of utter defeat. Above it all is a blinding, choking, all-consuming fear."

Levi noticed that the body on the rug was in the process of being bagged by some members of the Force. Her face wasn't covered, so he could see the X that had been carved into her forehead. A brief touch of her arm confirmed for him that the broken neck was the cause of death and she'd been deceased for a little over two days.

Emma's body had only been found because her one-year-old child, Charlotte, had been earlier left outside the lair's foster home—clean, healthy, and unharmed, much like Diem's son, Toby.

"What are you getting from the bastard who did this, Levi?" asked Tanner as the Force members carried the body out of the house.

"Same as last time," said Levi, scanning the room. Like at the previous murder scene, no furniture was broken or upturned. There was no blood or other mess. "Contentment, a mounting irritation, disappointment, rage, loneliness. Again, it's as if all was going good in his mind, but then he became more and more annoyed—and much more quickly than he did with Diem. Killing Emma was necessary to him, but he hated the desolation that followed."

"So she was yet another victim who didn't satisfy whatever sick needs he has," said Larkin, her face tight.

"Emma's here," Levi told them as snatches of her voice floated through the air.

*. . . couldn't scream . . . helpless . . .*

*. . . my mind . . . control . . .*

*. . . so gentle . . . Charlotte . . .*

Levi frowned. "She says she was unable to scream; that she was helpless. She said 'my mind' and then 'control.'"

Keenan pursed his lips. "You think he might have the gift of mind control? That maybe he took her over? Used her as some kind of puppet?"

"It would explain why no one reported hearing any screams or cries," said Knox. "And it would also account for why there are no signs of a struggle. The women *can't* struggle. He strips them of their will."

"Has Emma said anything else?" Larkin asked Levi.

"She seems to be saying that he was gentle with Charlotte," replied Levi. "Wait, there's more. I can't quite make out her words."

*. . . remember . . . can't . . . hates . . .*

"I don't know what she's trying to say." Levi repeated the three words she'd spoken. "Now she's sobbing and muttering her daughter's name. I can feel her presence fading." He posed a few questions at her, unsurprised when she gave no answers.

"Are there any pulses of physical pain in the air?" asked Tanner.

"No. I don't believe he hurt her until the end when he broke her neck."

Leaving the house, Levi and the other sentinels spoke with the neighbors. None reported seeing or hearing anything untoward, just as none had seen a car parked outside the house. Two people, however, claimed to have seen a man enter the house two days ago, but none could give an accurate description. They just kept using the word 'average,' but they could remember what he wore—jeans, a jacket, and a cap.

Gathering in Emma's front yard with Knox and the other sentinels, Levi sighed. "As I see it, there are only two similarities between Emma and Diem—they were single, and they had a young child. They looked nothing alike, there was an eight-year age gap between them, and they didn't have similar jobs or hobbies. Aside from being part of the same lair, they were in no way connected."

"In terms of character, they were alike in some ways," said Larkin. "Gentle. Shy. Quick to smile."

"Making them nothing like my aunt," Levi pointed out.

"Maybe his tastes in character have changed." Larkin shrugged. "Emma and Diem were also good moms. And there was some friction between them and their family members."

"In summary, then, he likes single mothers who don't have the best support network," said Keenan. "So, what, he wants a woman who he feels *needs* someone? He wants to be their savior?"

"That or he prefers victims he is fairly certain won't have constant visits from family members as he doesn't wish to be interrupted. We have to operate on the assumption that he's using our lair as his metaphorical hunting ground," Knox added, a thread of menace in his voice. "I want guards on every single mother within our lair—guards who will knock on their front door every morning, ask how they're doing, and briefly check the house."

Pausing, Knox turned to Levi. "Since a man *has* been seen at both crime scenes, I don't believe it was the same person who attacked Piper or the killer would have concealed himself on entering the houses the way he did at the deli."

"I don't consider him a suspect. Being childless, Piper's not his type. Also, I don't see any reason why he'd target my anchor." Levi looked at Emma's house. "This thing he does . . . he's trying to fulfill something inside him. He doesn't get off on causing physical pain. He even makes the deaths quick. What happened to Piper was completely different, not to mention risky and sloppy."

Knox gave a slow nod. "Whoever killed Diem and Emma likes control. Nothing about what occurred at the deli was controlled."

"The person who attacked Piper . . . my money is on Sefton or Jasper." Again, Levi slid his gaze to the house. "As for who did this, I have no fucking clue who we should be looking at. Part of me wants to go hunting, but I can't bring myself to leave Piper's side right now."

"I understand," said Knox. "Your instincts—not to mention your demon—wouldn't allow it. But I would not ask you to go hunting in any case, because I believe that that's what this killer wants: to draw you into a game of cat-and-mouse. As Tanner speculated, this person is reaching out to you. He wants your attention. So we're not going to give it to him. That's what will make him slip up. *That* and making it near impossible for him to harm other single mothers within our lair. We'll get him, Levi."

"Then he's mine."

"Oh yes, then he's yours."

# CHAPTER NINE

The first thing Levi wanted to do on leaving Emma's residence was seek out his anchor. Piper might not have been in his life long, but the urge to be around her while anger roiled in his gut was as instinctive as breathing. Seeing her, smelling her, hearing her voice—all of it would have soothed both him and his demon. But she was working, and he had a male demon to question.

Striding into her previous place of work with Larkin—who'd offered to come along, since Knox had returned home and relieved her of bodyguard duty—Levi scanned his surroundings. This studio had nothing on Urban Ink. It was too plain, and it lacked character. Aside from the equipment, nothing about it said 'tattoo shop.'

The slender blonde behind the small reception desk gave Levi a quick once-over and then smiled. "Hi, do you have an—"

"We need to speak with Kelvin." Levi flicked a look at him.

The male was hunched over a customer, a buzzing tattoo gun in hand. The mere sight of him made Levi's demon curl its upper lip.

"It's gonna be at least an hour before he's done," said the blonde.

"Then he'll need to take a break, because we won't be leaving until we've spoken with him."

"I'm sorry, it's just not—"

"Either you tell him we're here," began Larkin, "or *we'll* tell him we're here."

The blonde's lips tightened. "Fine, but he'll probably ask you to come back later." She strutted—yeah, literally strutted—over to Kelvin's station and flirtatiously danced her fingertips along the side of his arm. Whatever she said into his ear had his head whipping around to face Levi and Larkin.

Kelvin seemed to mutter something under his breath. He placed down the tattoo gun, spoke briefly with his client, and then crossed to the reception area. He wore a strained smile. "Trinity said you wanted to talk to me," he said, his voice low.

Deciding to dive straight to the point, Levi said, "I'm sure you heard Piper was attacked at the deli."

Kelvin's expression sobered. "I did. I tried calling to check she was fine, but she never answered." His gaze darted from Levi to Larkin. "She's okay, right?"

"She is," Levi confirmed. "I'm sure you're aware that she's my anchor."

Kelvin nodded.

"So then you'll also be aware that I'm not going to take kindly to the attack, or to the other things that have happened around Piper lately."

Kelvin's brows dipped. "What other things?"

"Incidences of vandalism. All four of her car tires were

slashed—and on the very same day you showed up at her house, funnily enough."

Kelvin's back snapped straight. "Wait, you're thinking *I* might be responsible?"

"He's quick," muttered Larkin.

Kelvin's mouth fell open. "You've got to be fucking kidding me."

"Where were you at lunch time yesterday?" Levi asked him.

The male did a slow blink. "You can't honestly suspect me."

"I honestly can. Prove I'm wrong to do so, and tell me where you were during the time of Piper's attack."

"I was . . ." Kelvin trailed off and cursed.

"It would have been smart of you to have your story straight on the off-chance that someone would question you," said Larkin.

"It's not a story, it's the truth," Kelvin insisted. "But if it gets out, it could cause a good woman some problems."

Larkin tilted her head. "What woman?"

"A harbinger from another lair. We've been seeing each other but keeping it quiet. She has a boyfriend. He's away on a business trip right now. I was at her house yesterday. It was my day off."

"And she'll verify that?"

"If you don't ask in front of her boyfriend, yes." He reeled off the name and address of the harbinger. "I wouldn't hurt Piper."

Levi hummed. "You must have at least liked the thought of hurting her, or you wouldn't have fucked your receptionist on Piper's chair."

Larkin's brow hiked up. "You did that? Classy."

Kelvin's face reddened.

"You know, Piper thinks you're good with the breakup," Levi told him. "I don't. I think you went along with it because your bruised ego wouldn't allow you to speak up and admit the truth. It has to be frustrating that you lost her in every sense. She has no interest in even keeping you as a friend. More, you don't even have a work relationship with her. She works at Urban Ink now."

Kelvin's jaw tightened for a mere moment. "I didn't hurt Piper. Talk to the harbinger. She'll tell you I was with her yesterday. And no, I didn't slash Piper's tires. I'm not into petty shit like that. I'll bet even she doesn't believe I did it."

"She doesn't," Levi confirmed. "But she also wouldn't have believed you'd nail your assistant on her chair, and look what happened there."

Kelvin flinched. "Point taken. But you're knocking on the wrong door. I get that you won't easily dismiss a suspect when Piper's safety is on the line, but I hope that means you'll concentrate on other suspects, too. For her sake, don't focus too much on me out of jealousy."

Levi's brow inched up. "Jealousy?"

"I'm her ex. You're her anchor. You're naturally going to dislike the idea of her with other men until your possessiveness settles. Personally, I don't think you're the type to let your emotions cloud your judgment. But all demons can be irrational when it comes to their psi-mates."

"True. But by the same token, the partners and exes of demons who've found their anchor can be jealous and irrational."

"They can, but that isn't the case with me."

Levi's demon snorted. It was more than obvious that the guy didn't like knowing Piper had another male in her life—one who had more rights to her than Kelvin ever had. "For your sake, you'd better be telling the truth." He turned, dismissing him, and walked out of the shop with Larkin. He arched a brow at her. "Your verdict?"

She pursed her lips. "I don't believe he personally attacked her. After all, he'd know we'd question him; he'd look to get himself a solid alibi in advance so he could prove he wasn't at the deli. Spending that time with a woman who may lie about his whereabouts to hide their affair from her boyfriend would therefore be stupid."

Levi gave a slow nod as they began walking along the strip. "I had the same thought. So if he *did* attack Piper, he didn't plan it well. And that doesn't fit with someone who owns a business. He could have hired someone, sure. But, much like Piper, I don't see why he'd want her dead."

"Same here," said Larkin. "He could have still been responsible for the vandalism, but my gut says that those acts were committed by the same person who tried to kill her."

"My gut agrees with yours. The only thing I believe he lied about was his claim that he's not hosting the green-eyed monster."

"He wasn't as good at hiding his jealousy as he seems to think." Larkin slid Levi a sideways glance. "You're much better at it."

Levi rolled his shoulders. "I fucking loathe feeling jealous of that pathetic little prick, but the thought of him with Piper makes my damn skin crawl."

"The intensity of your territorialism will fade over time. It might not seem like it now, but look at Teague and Khloë. He wasn't a jealous asshole when she mated Keenan."

"Yeah, but I'm pretty sure that was because he was relieved to have some help keeping Khloë out of trouble."

Larkin inclined her head. "Probably. On another note, you up for visiting the harbinger to see if Kelvin's alibi checks out just on the off-chance that our guts are wrong?"

"That was my plan."

"Do I get to play with her if she needs a little motivation to talk?"

"If you mean can you and your demon scare the living shit out of her, yes. But not to the point where she's too terrified to do anything but curl up in a ball and disappear into her own mind. We need answers."

Larkin frowned. "What do you take me for, an amateur?"

"No, but your bratty demon doesn't like to stop playing when told." He shook his head. "It's like dealing with a sadistic, psychopathic child. And its giggles creep me the fuck out."

She grinned. "Which absolutely delights it."

His demon thought her entity was a fucking blast. There was a reason the staff at the orphanage had very rarely provoked Larkin, and it wasn't solely because she'd essentially had four honorary protective brothers. It was because her inner demon was one scary, callous motherfucker that wasn't bothered by threats, punishments, or displays of authority. But if you were respectful or, at the very least, let Larkin be, it wouldn't concern itself with you. The staff had been mindful of that.

"Just don't let your demon go too far—that's all I ask," he said.

"It'll be on its best behavior."

Levi grunted, not as reassured as she seemed to think he'd be. But her entity was cooperative enough during the visit they paid to the harbinger, so they managed to make the woman part with her truths—those being that she was in fact sleeping with Kelvin and he had in fact spent the previous day with her.

Leaving the harbinger's house, Larkin said, "Well I'd say the guy's no longer a suspect. Which means you have *some* good news to give Piper. Of course, any such news you give her would be overshadowed by hearing another of our lair was murdered, but still."

Levi nodded. "It doesn't help that I'll have to tell her about Celeste's earlier stunt."

Larkin winced. "Yeah, that ain't gonna go down well."

At Levi's words, Piper jerked to a halt right in the middle of her living room. Slanting her head, she slowly turned, irritation fluttering through her. "She did *what*?"

Levi raised his hands. "It's not worth getting worked up over."

"I'll be the judge of that when I know why she was lingering near Knox's office like a weirdo. What did she say?"

"She claimed she's sorry for how she reacted to our announcement—as if I'd ever believe there was a drop of sincerity in the apology."

"And?"

He hesitated. "And that she hopes she and I can 'try again.'"

Piper felt her gut roll. "What did you tell her?"

"That her hopes will come to nothing, of course. I also made it clear that I could see through all the bullshit she was spewing, and I warned her that I wouldn't allow her to use you as her whipping girl anymore."

Piper folded her arms. "I did tell you that she'd try to win you back."

"And I knew you were probably right. Anyone else would think they didn't stand a chance, given the crap she pulled after the fling ended, but Celeste . . . she's convinced herself that I cared for her, so she therefore concludes that the post-relationship drama won't matter to me."

"I only heard the gist of said 'drama.' What exactly happened?"

He hesitated again. "I don't particularly want to talk about my history with her."

Neither did Piper, but . . . "We're not. We're talking about the aftermath."

Sighing, he shrugged. "About a week after she unceremoniously dumped me, she started sending me 'I made a mistake texts' and leaving lengthy voicemails on my cell that were pretty much elaborations of those messages. I never responded. And when her attempts to contact me nonetheless continued, I blocked her number."

Piper winced. "She will have hated that."

"A few days later, she came to me swearing she was being stalked. She looked appropriately terrified and begged to be assigned a bodyguard. I didn't buy her little tale, but I said I'd have one of the Force look into it and that he'd act as a bodyguard if necessary. She protested, saying I was the only person she'd trust to protect her so she needed *me* at her side."

Oh, the woman had no shame.

"I told her I couldn't act as her personal guard. She started crying and accused me of not believing her; of dismissing her fears because I wanted to get back at her for ending the fling. She sobbed a bunch of other things before finally realizing the emotional blackmail was having no effect. She called me cold and cruel and then marched off. I thought that would be the end of it."

Piper shot him a look of disappointment. "Such naivety."

Amusement flashed in his eyes. "I learned that the following weekend, when I was at a bar with a group of people. Some guy strode up to me and accused me of texting and calling 'his girl' all the time. He had a bunch of people at his back, including Celeste. She acted like she was trying to calm him down when, really, it was obvious to me that she'd got him all stirred up in the first place."

"I heard a little about this. A fight broke out, right?" At his nod, Piper added, "She claimed you got jealous seeing her with another guy, lost your shit, and picked a fight with him."

Levi snorted. "She lied. In truth, I tried reasoning with him. But he was too smashed, too wound up—he was looking for a fight, and the guys with him were egging him on. He jumped me. His male friends jumped mine. It got ugly fast, but he and his crew soon found themselves on their asses."

"I heard you and your friends came out on top. Celeste didn't escape unscathed." To be exact, she'd had a broken nose, a split lip, a bruised cheekbone, and scratch marks on her face. "Is it true that one of the women in your group pounced on her?"

"Yes. Paloma takes no shit. It took two of her mates to drag her away from Celeste."

Piper blinked. "Really? I don't know who this Paloma is, but I feel like we could be BFFs for life. And she has more than one mate? Lucky her."

"One of the other women, Ella, was so pissed I had to talk her down from hexing Celeste."

"Hexing?"

"Ella is an incantor, she's an expert at wielding magick. She's also very eager to meet you. She heard I'd found my psi-mate and called up to not only congratulate me but badger me to introduce you to her."

"So you two are close?"

"I wouldn't say we're close, but I consider her a good friend. And no, there's never been anything between us other than friendship."

"I wasn't going to ask if there was."

"But you were wondering."

She was, dammit. "Did Celeste pull anything else after that scene at the bar?"

"No. I suspect it's partly because she got her ass kicked, and partly because Knox paid her a visit. He gave her a verbal reaming and threatened to have her detained if she didn't back off. He didn't want me to do it myself because it would have rewarded her games with my attention. He evidently got through to her, because she barely spoke to me right up until you and I made our announcement to her, Whitney, and Joe."

Piper bit the inside of her cheek. "It must be annoying that you'll have to shake her off all over again."

Levi scoffed. "Celeste is nothing but a pesky fly." The woman wouldn't be on his radar at all if it wasn't for the mere fact that her behavior affected his anchor. "I'm done talking about her—she's not important. I want to talk about you."

"What about me?"

"You were attacked yesterday," he gently reminded her. "I didn't press you to talk about it last night because I wanted you to rest."

"What is there to say? I'm still mightily pissed and struggling to understand why I'm suddenly the target of someone with rather murderous intentions."

"And?" he prodded. "Come on, you can do better than all of *one* sentence."

She sighed. "Fine. On top of livid and confused, I'm raring to fucking kill someone. Namely him. But I don't have his name. It's seriously bugging my demon that we don't know who we're up against so can't even go hunting—"

"You won't need to, I will do the hunting for you." His demon growled its agreement. "That bastard takes up enough of your mental space as it is—that's as much as he's getting. It fucking offends me that he's on your mind at all. I hate it."

"So do I. Jesus, it was annoying enough when he was vandalizing my shit. I thought he'd get bored and back off. Even if I'd expected him to escalate, I never would have thought he'd escalate to this extent. But he did. And now we're both stuck dealing with it instead of being able to focus on getting to know each other. Add in Celeste's stunts and it's just one massive clusterfuck. *Him* I can't presently do anything about. But her? I'll call her and—"

"No. I get that you want to make it clear you won't stand for her seeking me out. But she's counting on that, Piper. She knows I'm right in that you and I being anchors has nothing to do with her. So she's trying to make herself relevant to us. She's trying to get our attention in the only way she knows how. You call or confront her, you're playing into her hands."

Piper rubbed at the back of her head. "I know. But it's grating on my last nerve that she won't just leave you alone. It *has* to be driving you nuts. A lot of your time and attention is already being taken up by all the crap going on around me. She's only going to make it worse."

"She won't run me off, Piper."

Unhappy he'd sensed the worry she'd hoped to hide, she shot him an annoyed frown.

He closed the small distance between them, loosely cuffing her arms with his hands before she could even think to take a step back. "She might think she has that power, but she doesn't. No one and nothing does. Not even you." The silken warning ghosted down her spine.

She swallowed, her mouth drying up at having him loom over her, his eyes glittering with something she couldn't quite name. The compelling bastard could fluster her without any damn effort. "I'm not trying to chase you off."

"Not anymore, no. But you're still holding back from the bond. From me."

"You said you'd give me time."

"And I am." Levi slid his hands up to settle on her shoulders, and his thumbs dug into her skin just right as he began a light massage, almost pulling a moan out of her. "That doesn't mean I like it."

She needed to pull back because, dammit, his touch felt a little *too* good, and it affected her a little *too* much. Especially now that sexual restlessness simmered low in her belly courtesy of that freaking kiss. It didn't help matters that the potent, testosterone-laden pheromones he gave off were a distinct threat to her composure. Or that her demon was ushering her to pounce on him.

"I'm supposed to strengthen you, center you, mark you as mine, but I can't do any of those things yet—that eats at me," he went on. "I'm not trying to guilt you into giving me what I want. I'm simply explaining why it's hard to grant you time."

She bit back a groan as he moved his hands a little closer to her neck, his fingers still kneading and gliding. "Are you thinking I'm doing it so you'll get fed up and walk away?" It was kind of hard to follow what he was saying when he was touching her this way.

"No." Levi dipped his head, and his warm lips grazed her cheek. "By now, you know better than to think I'd ever give you up." He left a trail of barely-there kisses along her face as he moved his mouth to her ear. "Don't you?"

She shivered, her skin prickling as goosebumps rose on her flesh at the feel of his breath whispering over her ear, stirring the little hairs there. The air became thick, hot, electric. The rising tension made her pulse quicken and her breathing speed up.

Teeth scraped her earlobe. "Don't you?" he repeated.

She squeezed her eyes shut, letting out a groan of frustration. "I'm trying to friend-zone you, Levi. You're making it hard."

A low chuckle rumbled out of him. "That doesn't have a prayer of working." He brushed his mouth over hers. "You and me . . . there's something between us. The kind of something you can't ignore. The kind that needs to be explored. So we'll do that."

She eyed him warily. "I'm not sure I want us crossing those sorts of lines."

"We've already crossed them. I know your taste now. You know mine. There's no undoing that." He splayed one hand over her throat and let out a pleased hum. "Your pupils just swallowed the color of your eyes."

"Levi—"

"I would have taken you last night in your kitchen, but I knew I'd be rough the first time. You needed to heal," he added, sliding his other hand up the back of her neck and into her hair. He caught a fistful and tugged, snatching her head back. The slight pain tightened her nipples, and there was no repressing a moan this time.

She grabbed his shoulders, her body easily curving into his like it had done it a thousand times before. "This isn't a good idea. We're anchors—"

"Which means you can trust that I'd never hurt you. Not physically, not emotionally. I'm careful with what's mine." His grip on her throat flexed. "You're safe with me on every level. I'm the one person you'll never have to worry will let you down. You know it. Your demon knows it."

Piper *did* know it. The knowledge was comforting. Steadying. Emboldening. Her resolve fractured . . . and that weakness in her defenses seemed to call to the predator in him somehow, because a low growl built in his throat and he slammed his mouth down on hers.

The kiss . . . God, it was everything she needed. Hungry. Urgent. Aggressive.

The six years of wanting and waiting and craving just *exploded* between them. They pulled and dragged at each other's clothes, skimming their hands over whatever flesh they bared. His skin was sleek and hot, and feeling it against her own sent her nerve-endings buzzing.

Piper greedily gripped, scratched, and stroked as she explored the bulk of his shoulders and the dips and curves of his solid chest. Moving her hand lower, she fisted his cock. He grunted into her mouth, digging his fingertips hard into the globes of her ass. She pumped, moaning as he kissed her harder and deeper, every slide of his tongue against her own dragging her further under his spell.

He tore his mouth from hers as he palmed her breasts. "Something about knowing I own you makes me want you even more."

Then his dick was abruptly gone from her hand . . . and she honestly wasn't sure how she ended up flat on her back on the floor—he set her down so smoothly and quickly that she didn't even feel herself tilt. She just felt the cool tiles against her back as he settled his body over hers, caging her as he kept on licking into her mouth.

His fingers plunged deep inside her, shocking a gasp from her. Piper scratched at his shoulders as those fingers worked her hard while his free hand teased her breasts and his mouth left trails of bites and kisses all over her neck. Those lips and hands knew *exactly* what they were doing, knew—

A purring wash of telekinetic power brushed over her skin and clamped down on her wrists. Piper gasped as her hands were dragged from his shoulders and pressed firmly against the floor above her head.

*The fuck?*

It wasn't like having hands hold her down. It was sheer power, but it felt almost . . . sentient in the way it pulsed and flexed and tightened. Well this was new.

"My demon wants you this way," Levi told her, withdrawing his fingers from her incredibly tight pussy—she'd truly *feel* every inch of him for sure. "It wants you spread out beneath it, helpless and under its power when it fucks you. And it *will* fuck you. We both will."

He punched his hips forward, gliding his cock over her clit, and gently bit her nipple. "There are so many things I want to do to you, but they'll have to wait." He reached down and lodged the head of his cock in her pussy. "Remember, it's going to be rough." He slowly sank inch after inch of his dick inside her, loving the sight of it disappearing into her body, loving the stretch and squeeze of her hot, slick inner walls.

Her brow furrowed in discomfort, but she didn't ask him to stop or pull back. Instead, she tried impaling herself on him, hissing in annoyance when she failed. "You said it'd be rough."

"Oh, it will. But I want to savor the first time I feel your pussy sucking my dick inside you." There *would* be other times. There was no way he'd only have her once.

Finally balls-deep in her body, Levi got to his knees and lifted her hips from the floor. "Six years I've waited for this. And now here you are. Wet and needy and helpless." He lazily reared back. "Be warned, Piper. Me and my demon . . . we're not just going to fuck you. We're going to rule you. We're going to shatter you and exhaust you and use you all up. Because you're ours, and you need to fucking *feel* ours."

Levi drilled his cock into her pussy, every forward slam of his hips unapologetically violent. Feral. Unrestrained.

He couldn't slow down. Couldn't fight the drive to take her this way. It wasn't simply about the promise he'd just made her, or even about the years of pent-up need now escaping his system. It was the frustration he felt at being held at an emotional distance.

She had too many walls between them, too many boundaries. She might have acknowledged him as her anchor, but she hadn't properly acknowledged just what place that gave him in her life. He hated not feeling as important to her as she was to him. Time he could give her. But all this distance? No, that had to go.

Her hands balled up into fists, she arched into his thrusts, letting out these smoky fucking moans that squeezed his balls. "Levi."

"You need to come already, don't you?"

Her only response was a deep groan of assent. Moments later, she fractured beneath him. The force of her orgasm seemed to wrench at her spine, making it curve like a bow. She screamed, her inner muscles clenching him so goddamn tight.

Levi didn't ease up on his thrusts. He kept on powering into her, focused on ravaging and destroying her so completely that all her barriers would drop; so completely that she'd feel mastered, owned, consumed.

She soon came again, violent tremors wracking her body. And that was when his demon decided it wanted its turn.

Piper hissed in pain as power grabbed a handful of her hair and snatched up her head just as the air cooled. *Fucking ow.* She saw then that Levi's eyes had bled to black—his entity had taken the wheel. She swallowed at the sheer coldness in that inhuman gaze.

Moments earlier, she'd felt sapped of energy. Her orgasms—so intense and devastating—had pretty much drained her. But finding herself facing his demon snapped her back to full alertness. Her own entity stirred, watching it closely, liking the power it exuded.

"Yes, take a good, long look at who you belong to, little nightmare," it said, its voice empty of emotion. "Accept that you are mine. His."

She felt her brow crease. "I already have."

"There is acknowledgment, and there is acceptance. You will give us both."

She blinked as the invisible weight lifted from her wrists. "Is—"

The demon withdrew its cock, telekinetically flipped her onto her stomach, yanked her to her knees, and slammed back inside her.

The breath gusted out of her lungs. "Fuck."

Power pressed down on the spot between her shoulder blades, holding her still. Then the demon was jackhammering into her, its thrusts so savage and animalistic and impersonal they were almost cruel. Perverse as it might be, she freaking loved it.

Levi had been rough, but there was something almost unnerving about how aggressively the demon pounded into her. Like it was poised on the brink of exploding into violence. Which her entity totally dug.

The demon's hands slid under her body and grabbed her breasts. They weren't gentle. Nor were the teeth that trailed bites along her upper back. The burning stings of pain pushed all kinds of hot buttons, and she soon came with yet another scream.

The entity didn't stop. It kept on fucking in and out of her, even as she pretty much went limp in its grip. Sometimes Levi took over, but then the demon would be back. Both boldly rammed into her body like it was there purely for their use.

She hadn't thought she could come again, but she did. The explosive orgasm wrecked her from the inside out, shattering her into a billion pieces, sending her defenses crumbling into rubble. It was only then that Levi slammed his cock home one last time and emptied himself inside her.

She slumped to the floor, shuddering and fighting for breath, her brain clapping out. She barely registered Levi rearranging them both so that he lay on his back with her inelegantly sprawled over his chest.

He traced the bumps of her spine with his fingertips. "No more distance."

Her eyelids fluttered open as she remembered his demon's words . . .

*There is acknowledgment, and there is acceptance.*

And Piper realized the entity was right. She hadn't *fully* accepted either Levi or his demon into her life. Not in an emotional sense. She'd thought she had, but she'd been wrong.

It was one thing to temporarily hold back from the bond, it was another to hold her own anchor at an emotional arm's length. "No more distance," she agreed.

His hand gave her hip a little squeeze. "Good. And no freaking out because we had sex. We're anchors, we're adults, we enjoyed each other. Nothing wrong with that."

She'd known plenty of psi-mates who'd slept together once. Sometimes only for comfort, sometimes out of an attraction they thought it dumb to spend the rest of their lives fighting when they could instead burn it out at the beginning. It hadn't ruined their anchor relationship, because they hadn't made a big deal out of it. She could be just as mature about this. She could.

Should it have felt weird that she'd slept with someone who—*gag*—had . . . known her stepsister intimately? Probably. But Levi had never belonged to Celeste. On the other hand, he'd always been Piper's, she simply hadn't always known it. And that made all the difference.

He'd once said he didn't see Piper in terms of who she was to Celeste. That worked both ways now. Piper didn't view him as her stepsister's ex anymore, she viewed him as *hers*.

"No freaking out," Piper assured him, which earned her another hip-squeeze.

Was it disappointing that this would be a one-off? Yeah. But it would also be for the best. It was a damn shame that the 'best' in this instance kind of sucked.

# CHAPTER TEN

Two weeks of peace went by. Pure and utter peace.

There were no more murders, no more attacks on Piper, no more cases of vandalism. Kelvin ceased attempting to contact her, and Celeste unexpectedly kept a low profile.

Piper and Olive both believed that there was a good chance the invisible attacker—or whoever might have hired him—had backed off completely. The guy had every reason to, considering he'd otherwise have to contend with Levi. But her reaper wasn't so certain, and so she'd promised to remain vigilant.

Piper didn't believe Celeste had chosen to back down and let everything lie. When it came to her stepsister, there was often that calm-before-the-storm period. It was a banshee thing. Like they enjoyed lulling their foes into a false sense of security or something.

In any case, the uneventful weeks had given Piper and Levi a chance to spend uninterrupted, relaxing, quality time together.

Which was exactly what they did. They talked, confided, even shared secrets.

They also had sex. A lot.

Their one-night stand had become . . . well not a fling. It was more of an agreement—one they'd made after they slept together the second time.

*"We shouldn't have done that," she said, pacing near the bed.*

*"I often do things I shouldn't." He watched her, lying in bed with his hands behind his head. "You wanted it as much as I did."*

*"Yes, but I didn't mean for it to happen. It was an accident."*

*He smiled, amused. "What, you fell on my cock?"*

*She glared at him. "I mean, I hadn't planned for us to sleep together more than once. I don't want things to get all muddled between us. A single evening of sex is one thing. But I know anchored pairs who had flings that went sour, and it tainted their bond. Not even great sex is worth that."*

*He slowly sat upright. "I get where you're coming from, but here's the thing. We* will *end up in bed together again, Piper. Neither of us are done. So I say we don't fight it. I say we let it happen. Once we're anchored, we'll stop; we'll begin the anchor relationship on a platonic note, to start as we mean to go on."*

She'd hemmed and hawed over it for a few hours, unsure what to do. The more she'd thought about it, the more she'd felt that he was right. They were nothing close to done, and she'd known that she wouldn't have the willpower to resist the temptation to fall into bed with him again. It had made more sense to get it out of their systems and let boredom settle in so that they could start things afresh when they bonded.

Since then, they'd done as he'd suggested and quite simply enjoyed each other. They didn't behave in couple-like ways. They didn't date or cuddle or even flirt. Their interactions throughout the day were pretty much as they always had been.

But when they were alone in the evenings, they'd somehow end up having sex. And they never discussed or referred to it afterwards.

They also never spent a night apart. They usually went to her place after she finished work, but occasionally she stayed over at his huge swanky apartment. They didn't always sleep since, as demons, they didn't always need to. But they'd do more talking and sharing.

Although he'd parted with many secrets, there were things he kept to himself. He told her more about his time at the orphanage, for instance, but he hadn't yet spoken of his aunt's murder. Piper hadn't pushed him to tell her. He'd either do it in his own time, or he wouldn't. And who could blame him for not wanting to tear open such a wound? She didn't want to watch him bleed.

Besides, she wouldn't expect him to share *everything* just because they were anchors. It wasn't as if he otherwise held back from her. He was all-in, and she was ready to give him that same commitment.

She was ready to form the anchor bond.

Really, she'd been ready for at least a week. She'd hesitated for two very selfish reasons.

Firstly, once he finally had what he wanted and they were bonded, the amount of time they spent together would lessen considerably. She didn't want that.

Not that she thought he'd been lying when he declared he'd make time for her no matter how busy he was with work. She'd sensed he meant it. But still, as he himself had admitted, they wouldn't see as much of each other as they did now. So she'd hesitated to reach for their bond, greedily drinking in his attention and time.

There was another reason she'd procrastinated. Piper didn't want to reverse back behind the platonic lines they'd crossed.

It would feel like losing him on some level. Losing an intimacy she'd come to cherish. But she'd have to suck it up, wouldn't she? To continue to hesitate was unfair to them and their demons.

Besides, despite that she generally didn't struggle to separate emotions from sex, she really wasn't certain she could keep her feelings out of their 'agreement' any longer. It was time to step back. She'd only get hurt if she didn't.

Piper had planned to tell Levi when he picked her up from work that she was ready to bond with him. But it would have to wait until later, since her colleagues and Larkin had dragged her out for a girls' night . . . which was how Piper found herself sitting in the Underground's Xpress bar.

Although the girls were a tight group, Piper never felt like an outsider. They'd hauled her into their circle and made her one of them. And as she watched a sober Devon and a tipsy Khloë argue like cat and dog, Piper couldn't help but smile.

Her hand flexing around her bottle of water, Devon fired an impatient look at Khloë. "You can't seriously think that will ever happen."

"Why not?" asked the imp, her head bopping to the music. "Billions of people all over the globe report being abducted by aliens."

"I'm not saying there isn't other life *out there*. I'm just saying there's no possible way you'll ever have your own personal ET. He was a fucking puppet."

Swaying slightly, Raini lifted her index finger. "Actually, I think the little UFO dude was played by people wearing suits."

"Or wearing the skins of real-life aliens," said Khloë.

Devon let her head slump forward.

"You know," began Harper, stirring her fruity drink with a mini umbrella, "I struggle with the idea that UFOs even come to this planet. I mean, why bother? Why kidnap humans, experiment on them, insert microchips in them . . . and then return them, only to go back several times to, like, check on them or whatever?"

Piper pursed her lips. "It's kind of what humans do to wild animals and sea creatures, though, right?"

Each head at the table turned her way.

"Wow," said Khloë. "Mind blown."

Raini nodded. "Yeah, I never thought of it that way. Humans pluck those poor animals out of their natural habitat for all kinds of reasons. Isn't it sad how many are on the verge of extinction? We really need to do our part."

"Too many are already extinct," said Khloë. "Like mogwai."

Harper frowned. "There has never been any such thing as mogwai."

The imp's brow furrowed. "I saw them on *Gremlins*."

"They were puppets," Devon told her.

"*Or* tiny people wearing the skins of real-life mogwai," said Khloë.

Devon shook her head. "It's impossible to have a rational conversation with you."

"You're just moody because you can't get buzzed. It's not my fault you got knocked up."

Larkin peered down at the hellcat's belly. "How is little Engelbert-or-Hallelujah?"

Devon grinned. "Tanner whined to you about the names?"

"Of course," said Larkin, her mouth curving. "Are you going to keep torturing him all the way through the pregnancy?"

"Only if he doesn't stop with the smothering at some point." Devon spared Piper a look. "Speaking of overprotective males . . . who wants to bet that Levi's somewhere close?"

Everyone at the table except for Piper raised their hand.

"He said he wouldn't hang in the bar," said Piper, though

he'd made it clear that Enzo and Dez would never be far away from her.

"Yeah, *this* bar," said Devon. "He could be next door. Or someplace across the strip. He'll be close by, trust me."

"I'd have to agree, he's probably loitering somewhere." Harper set down her drink, eyeing Piper curiously. "So . . . want to tell us why you're so nervous?" It was a gentle invitation, not a nosy question.

"We're here for you," said Khloë, forming a heart shape with her hands and pressing said shape against her chest.

"It's nothing bad." Piper straightened her shoulders. "I've decided to form the bond with Levi."

Harper's eyes lit up. "That's great news!"

Khloë fist pumped, Raini gave a little clap, and a smiling Larkin tipped her drink toward Piper.

"Does he know yet?" asked Devon, her cat-green gaze bright with excitement.

Piper shook her head. "I'm going to tell him tonight and, knowing him, he'll be all '*okay, let's do it right now.*' Hence the nerves."

Raini patted her hand. "You'll like being anchored. There's something very special about the bond. It'll center you and your demon like nothing else."

Piper noticed Larkin's smile dim as the harpy then looked down at her lap, as if to veil her expression.

Khloë jumped to her feet. "This calls for shots. *We need shots.*" Then she was making a beeline for the bar, stumbling here and there.

Harper sighed. "I'll go with her to make sure she doesn't drop any glasses." The sphinx probably thought she was much steadier on her feet than her cousin but, in actuality, she was no better.

Piper had to smile when both females got distracted by the change of song and then hit the dance floor.

Larkin gently nudged Piper with her shoulder. "Levi will be thrilled, you know. And relieved. And smug. I know why you didn't want to rush into things, but I'm glad you're finally ready to bond with him."

"Me, too," said Devon, her eyes tearing up. She flapped her hands at her face. "Ignore me, it's the hormones." She leaned into Raini, who began rubbing her back.

"It's gonna be weird not seeing him every day," said Piper. "I've gotten a little too used to having him there all the time." And spending every night with him would surely stop, since there'd no longer be any need for it. She wouldn't like that much either.

Larkin smiled. "He *made sure* you got used to it. He wanted you to feel like you couldn't imagine not having him around. He's sneaky that way."

Piper snickered. "Agreed. Just do me a solid, Larkin, and make sure he doesn't take stupid risks when doing sentinel stuff. I can't be there to watch over him, so I need you to do it."

Larkin's face went all soft. "I like that you're his anchor. He deserves someone like you, who won't resent how hard or much he works. There's never been a woman in his life who hasn't held that against him at some point."

"People suck," said Piper.

"You won't be second best to his positions." Larkin leaned in, adding in a voice not loud enough to carry over the music to the other two females, "Even if *certain things* cool between you two, he'll still be up in your space often. And no, he didn't tell me that you were getting down and dirty. I sensed it for myself."

"And you didn't mention it to him?"

"Of course I did. He told me to mind my own biz. I only

wanted to know if you guys were exclusive. He doesn't usually do exclusivity, but I think it'd be a bad idea for either of you to be expecting the other to share, given there's already a lot of possessiveness at play."

Piper puffed out a breath. "Can something be exclusive when it isn't really a thing? I mean, we're not having any kind of relationship—not even a fling. We just . . . have sex. So we're like, what, anchor bed-buddies or something? I don't know what you'd call it. But we both agreed it would end the moment we formed the bond."

Larkin twisted to better face her. "He agreed to that?"

"It was his suggestion."

"Really? I wouldn't have guessed that." Larkin pursed her lips. "How do you feel about this 'thing' between you having an expiry date? Is that really what you want?"

"It's better that way. I know some anchored pairs fall into relationships. But Levi doesn't have relationships. Not serious ones, anyway. He's given up on them. I think—" She cut off with a soft curse as someone drunkenly stumbled into the table hard enough to cause the drinks to splash onto its surface.

Said someone blinked hard, righting himself. Then his eyes settled on Piper, and he snarled. "Well, look who it is, Sefton," slurred none other than Jasper.

Oh, freaking wonderful.

Larkin stiffened beside her and then went to stand.

Piper put a hand on her arm. *Let's not scare him off. He's one of Levi's main suspects. Maybe he'll blurt out a few things while drunk.* She telepathically said the same to both Devon and Raini.

Sefton tugged on his brother's sleeve. "Come on, let's go get another drink."

Water would probably be best, given the asshole's current state.

"But don't you want to say hi?" Jasper asked him, smirking. "I want to say hi."

Sefton cringed. "Jas."

"Come on, it's rude to ignore people." Jasper slid his gaze back to Piper. "Knox tortured him. Did you know that?"

Piper shrugged one shoulder. "It was an easy enough guess." Noticing Enzo and Dez creeping close, she sent them the same telepathic message she sent the other females at the table.

Jasper jabbed a finger at her. "You convinced that bitch to fals-fals-*falsely* accuse him. You *know* he didn't do shit to her. My brother went through *hell* because of you."

Sefton pulled on his arm. "Jasper—"

"Before, he used to shout his innocence," the asshole went on. "Now? Now he won't even *talk* about what happened. Because he's too scared to be sent back to that fucking Chamber."

"I'm pretty sure that was kind of the point of Knox taking him there," said Piper. "And I don't know why you repeatedly remind me Sefton was tortured when all that does is make me feel warm inside." That bastard had trapped a pregnant woman in her personal nightmare, for Christ's sake.

"Bitch," hissed Jasper.

"With pride. You can believe your brother's innocent if you want—"

"He *is* innocent, and you know it. You condemned him!"

"In your opinion. Is that why you slashed my tires?"

His head drew back. "I didn't do shit to your car, I told Levi that already. But I'd shake the hand of whoever did it. You deserve worse."

"So you thought you'd teach me a lesson at the deli?"

He squinted. "Oh, I get it, you want to pin it on me. Yeah, because whether or not people are actually guilty doesn't fucking matter to you."

"On the contrary, it very much does. But *you*—your beliefs, your behavior, your bullshit—don't matter to me in the slightest. My care cup is all empty. These scenes you cause do nothing but bore me. Like, *to tears*."

"Is that fucking so?" He planted his hands on the table and aggressively leaned toward her . . . which was when Larkin uncoiled from her seat like a snake. He stared at the harpy, his lips parted.

"I don't know why one of your favorite pastimes is making a fool of yourself," Larkin said to him. "But you've entertained us all enough for one night."

Enzo and Dez tried coming up behind him, but Sefton and his pals blocked their path as they appealed with them to leave Jasper be, promising they'd take him out of the bar.

Jasper straightened, his gaze on Larkin. "It doesn't matter to you if she accuses innocent people? She won't be held accountable for shit because she's the anchor of a sentinel? That how it is?"

"Funny how much you whine and bitch about innocence and guilt and people needing to be held accountable . . . when your daddy never holds you responsible for any damn thing," said Larkin. "He never cares if you or your idiot brother fucks up. Neither do either of you. Too many times you've messed up, and every single time you've tried to lie your way out of trouble. So all this high and mighty crap . . . yeah, I don't get it."

"It's because I'm a woman," said Piper. "All three of them have a total hate-on for our gender, Larkin. Men are the superior species who can't do any wrong in their world."

"Misogyny at its finest," said Larkin, her glare fixed on Jasper. "I really thought I'd proven that women aren't 'weak' when you were last dragged before the sentinels to be punished, Jasper. I guess not, because here you are confronting a woman you were *ordered* to leave the fuck alone. That's okay. My demon won't mind having a little fun with you. Again."

Jasper's eyes flickered, his face losing some of its color.

"Take him," she said, and then Enzo and Dez were roughly escorting him out of the bar.

Sefton looked from Piper to Larkin, his eyes pained. "He didn't mean to upset anyone, he's—"

"Blitzed, yeah," said Larkin. "But I've never found that an excuse for anything. Now shoo."

He rushed after his brother, his friends hot on his heels.

Piper looked at the harpy. "What did your demon do to Jasper?"

Larkin grinned, retaking her seat. "Plain terrified him, of course."

Piper had heard that the harpy's demon was something to be dearly feared. She'd spoken to people who'd been disciplined by Larkin, and none were forthcoming about what happened.

"You know, Lark," Devon began, "I initially thought that the main reason Knox made you a sentinel is that you grew up together and stuff. I mean, don't get me wrong, you have 'badass' written all over you. But Knox and the other sentinels are pretty protective of you. I thought that meant they thought you *needed* to be shielded. Then I realized they just act that way because you're essentially their baby sister.

"And, on joining your lair, I also discovered that you have a reputation for being ruthless and unforgiving. Also, even the mention of your demon makes people nervous. Tanner said the entity would make even a pure psychopath uneasy. Why? What gives? Because he won't expand."

The harpy smiled. "Let's just say it has some . . . issues."

"How delightfully vague."

Larkin snickered.

Just then, Khloë and Harper returned, apparently oblivious to all they'd missed. They handed out glasses and then sat.

Devon gaped as Khloë sipped at a particular drink. "How could you?"

The imp blinked. "What?"

"That's my favorite alcoholic drink," said the hellcat.

Khloë looked from side to side, seemingly baffled by Devon's agitation. "I know."

"And you're going to drink it *in front of me*?"

"Well . . . yeah."

"*Knowing* how hard it is for me to stick to freaking water?"

Khloë cocked her head. "I don't see where you're going with this."

Snorting, Harper looked at Piper. "The empathy struggle is real."

Devon glared at the imp. "I can't *believe* you sometimes."

Khloë frowned. "Jeez, what's with the tears?"

"I'm not crying," the hellcat croaked.

"You're totally crying."

"I am *not*."

"Just like you're not constipated?" Khloë jerked back. "Stop with the hissing, you ass-clogged freak!"

Devon tried diving at the imp. Raini and Larkin held her back while Piper yanked Khloë out of the way.

Harper gave her cousin a pointed look. "Apologize."

Khloë's brow furrowed. "For stating a fact?"

"For making Devon cry," said the sphinx. "Again."

"Not my fault she's hormonal."

"*Apologize*."

Rolling her eyes, Khloë knocked back a shot and then turned to Devon with a sigh. "I am so very, very sorry for . . ." Her eyes widened. "My God, I *love* this song! This is my jam!" She all but dragged Piper out of her seat and to the dance floor. She released Piper's hand and turned to face her with a *woohoo.*

A hand snapped around Piper's arm, her surroundings flashed white . . . and then she was standing in a parking lot with some big burly bastard she didn't even know. *Shit.*

She would have struck the fucker and telepathed Levi, but the hand gripping her arm was pumping power into her system. A power that was thick and heavy and drugging. It sent her thoughts scattering, drained the strength from her body, and made it feel as though the world was spinning around her.

Her legs trembled, the muscles beginning to lose their tone. She dropped to her knees, too dazed to wince at the pain of them hitting the pavement. Only the masculine grip on her arm stopped her from face-planting into the ground.

Her vision blurred. A ringing sound filled her ears. Everything seemed so very far away—even her own body.

Voices swam into her mind, calling her name, but it was *so hard* to tune into them when the power corrupting her system was lulling her into a punch-drunk state.

Her demon slammed against her consciousness, and the short reprieve from the drugging daze was enough to make her resist the 'call' to float away. Instead, she blinked hard, forcing herself to *focus*, and reached out to Levi—

Pain reverberated around her skull. Pain so terrible it made her stomach churn, and she almost threw up. A pathetic whimper left her.

A male chuckle. "Tried telepathing someone, did you? That won't work as long as I'm touching you. And I don't plan to stop touching you."

Panic raced through her. Her demon hissed between its teeth. Piper struggled to free her arm, though she was too weak to do much other than squirm.

"No sense in fighting me, you might as well save your strength," he told her. "I already telepathed my boys to say I have you. They'll be here any second, and then we'll be . . . ah, here they are."

She heard the rumbling of an engine shortly before tires screeched to a halt. Her head felt so damn heavy, but she forced it to lift. Her vision was still blurry as hell, but she could make out a black van parked a few feet away. The side door was hauled open by whoever was inside.

Her kidnapper yanked her to her feet. "Got her, boys. That shit was too easy," he said, a cocky edge to his voice.

A man leaned out of the passenger window. "Took you long enough to grab her, though. Come on, let's go."

Dread slammed into Piper. *No.* No, she was *not* going with them.

She glanced around, and her eyes locked on the neon sign ahead of her. The colors were hazy and distorted, blending into one another. She blinked rapidly and squinted, doing her best to bring the sign into focus and—*there.*

Her heart jumped. Needing her kidnapper to release her for even just a moment, she turned to dead weight in his hold. The shock of it made him drop her. She called out, *Levi! Legacy Motel parking lot!* And then she slapped her hand on the teleporter's foot, sending a small surge of power into him.

He collapsed to the ground at her side, sound asleep.

"Shit, grab them!" the dude in the passenger seat shouted.

Another male jumped out of the van's side door and rushed her, but he skidded to a halt when two people materialized.

Her heart thudded, and relief poured through her. *Levi.* One of the Force, Armand, was with him. Neither hesitated to attack even as they moved to shield her body with theirs.

The guy who'd tried grabbing her and her kidnapper retreated into the van.

Wicked fast, Levi swept out his arm, and a telekinetic blast sent the vehicle tumbling onto its side and skidding along the ground.

Struggling to fight her way through the drug-like state, Piper awkwardly pushed herself onto her hands and knees. Her arms trembled, and sweat beaded her forehead. God, she really might be sick.

Watching the spectacle up ahead, she could make out hellfire orbs and balls of bright light sailing through the air. She could feel the slight *shift* of telekinetic power. She could hear curses and grunts, though the sounds were tinny and far-away.

She needed to help Levi and Armand. Needed to do *something*. Needed to not be a fucking weakness right now.

Equally eager to join the fight, her demon egged her on. Managing to force herself to her knees, Piper shakily raised her hand, palm out. These bastards weren't leaving this parking lot alive. No fucking way.

Levi almost jerked to the side as a hail of hellfire bullets zoomed between his body and Armand's, spraying the upended van up ahead wherein its driver and passengers were taking cover. The bullets tunneled through the metal, and some must have thudded into skin, because grunts of shock and pain rang through the air.

A spike of relief reached Levi through the anger and adrenaline—if Piper was able to hurl hellfire bullets, her state was better than simply conscious. He hadn't dared take his eyes off the bastards in front of him, so he hadn't known if she'd passed out or not.

Boxing away every thought other than to kill these sons of bitches, Levi kept on attacking them. Heads and arms peeked out of the van as they launched balls of hellfire. Levi blasted the orbs with telekinetic power, sending them right back at the demons. They ducked, but one didn't drop fast enough—an orb clipped his skull, sending his head snapping to the side.

It wouldn't be long before the shitheads needed to leave their cover. Hellfire was rapidly spreading over the van, so it was lucky for them that it didn't operate like regular fire or the vehicle might have exploded by now.

Again and again, they peeked out to attack. Levi dodged and weaved, but some orbs connected, slamming into his chest or arms. Even as hellfire ate at his flesh, he retaliated with hellfire, telekinesis, and grim waves of pure despair that struck a person's soul and could reduce them to tears.

Meanwhile, Piper kept on shooting them with hellfire bullets, and Armand threw balls of white-hot light that lit the air like torches and melted both metal and flesh.

Muffled shouts were soon exchanged, and then three demons crawled out of the melting vehicle and tried making a run for it.

*Not happening.*

Levi struck with a lashing of telekinetic power that crashed into their backs like a giant cane. They hit the ground hard, agonized grunts all but gusting out of them. One rolled onto his side, a hellfire orb in hand . . . but then Larkin dropped from the sky, her large black wings outstretched. She flapped them hard, sending out a cold blast of air. The hellfire orb winked out, cries got lost in the wind, and fallen bodies skidded along the pavement.

Levi wasted no time in advancing on the three demons. Close enough now to hit them harder, he telekinetically lifted the trio and slammed them to the ground. Bones snapped. Skulls cracked. Broken screams rang out.

Larkin pounced on one. Armand singled out another. Levi hovered his hand over the chest of the third little fucker and got a psychic grip on the organ beating there. Then he squeezed, putting more and more pressure on the heart. The demon on the ground arched and gasped and slapped his hand over his chest.

Shooting him a cold smile, Levi snapped his fist shut. And the heart burst like a bubble. He kept watching the demon until the life faded from his eyes. A deep breath left Levi, and he dropped his arm to his side.

"Motherfuckers," snarled Larkin, glowering at the corpses.

Levi clicked his fingers, and the dead bodies burst into cinders that quickly disintegrated. "Yeah. Motherfuckers all the way."

Hearing the scuff of shoes, he spun and found Piper staggering toward them, her body weak and uncooperative like she hadn't slept in years. He gave her a quick head-to-toe scan. She had some blisters and burns. He felt his mouth tighten. He'd tried blocking any orbs that sailed her way but clearly hadn't managed it every time.

Crossing to her, Levi curled his arms around her and took her weight, mindful of her wounds. "I got you, baby. I got you."

"Bastard teleporter hit me with some kind of drugging power," she virtually slurred.

Closing his eyes, Levi breathed her in. Only then did he really let himself *feel*. Only then did he lift the lid on the emotions he'd boxed up.

Shock. Fury. Panic. Terror. All of it pumped through his veins and iced his blood, just as the emotions had almost done when Larkin telepathically yelled out to him in warning.

Three words. Three words had almost shattered his world.

*Piper's been taken.*

Rage had swamped his demon in a blinding, scorching hot rush that hadn't yet left its system, even as it now had Piper right there with it.

Levi's own fury wasn't going anywhere yet either. Someone had kidnapped his anchor. Had teleported her to the exterior of a demon-owned motel. To take her inside? To haul her into the van? He didn't yet know. But he'd soon find out.

"He's alive, but he isn't waking up," said Larkin, nudging the male lying on the ground with her foot. "Did you put him asleep, Piper?"

She weakly nodded. "Trapped him in his worst nightmare."

Levi squeezed her nape. "That's my girl." He glanced at Armand. "Take us to my apartment."

"We taking sleepyhead with us?" asked Armand, tipping his chin toward the male on the ground.

Levi tightened his hold on her. "We sure the fuck are, yeah."

# CHAPTER ELEVEN

Slouched on Levi's sofa, Piper glanced down at the prickling burn on her chest. It was the worst of her wounds but, fortunately, was healing as fast as the others. She still couldn't quite believe she'd been involved in yet another mini battle. It had all happened so damn fast, and it had shattered her hopes that whoever wanted her dead had backed off.

So many emotions fought for supremacy inside her, but anger won out. Anger that someone had targeted her. Anger that Levi had been hurt defending her. Anger that she had no fucking clue who'd apparently decided she'd lived long enough, just as she had no idea *why* they'd reached such a decision.

Her demon wanted to drop-kick a fucker. In its view, their 'hater' was a goddamn coward, refusing to expose themselves. Yeah, Piper could agree with that.

Feeling the weight of someone's gaze, she looked up. Levi stood directly across from her, his arms folded, his neck corded. He'd barely taken his eyes from her since they arrived at his apartment, as if worried she'd suddenly vanish from his view . . . though it wasn't as if anyone could teleport here and snatch her. The preternatural security measures in this building were tip-top, and they'd prevent any such intrusion. Still, he watched her closely, tension in every muscle.

Her body would probably be just as stiff if she didn't feel so drained. The effects of the drugging power hadn't yet completely faded, and the psychic energy she'd expended had only worsened the fatigue that plagued her.

"When are you going to question our captive?" she asked Levi. Said captive was currently asleep in the office/library with Enzo and Dez watching over him.

"When Knox arrives," Levi replied. "Armand will teleport him here."

"I'd insist on coming along to the interrogation, but I feel like I'm going to fall asleep any second now." If Piper went with them, she'd be trembling and staggering. Looking weak in front of other predators was a no-no.

"Not a lot can take me by surprise," began Larkin, sitting beside Piper, "but seeing you abruptly disappear from the dance floor like that . . . I never would have expected anyone to snatch you out of a crowd like that."

"That was why it worked," said Piper, sounding as tired as she felt. "No one would have seen it coming. And you need to stop feeling guilty, because it's really pissing me off."

Larkin's lips twitched, though no humor lit her eyes. "Can't help it. You were right there . . . and then you weren't. All the girls freaked out. Enzo and Dez lost their minds."

"You didn't fail me. No one did. Khloë was inches away from me, and even she wasn't able to stop that bastard from taking me."

"Don't think she isn't furious about it. You don't need to

worry that she might be beating herself up about it, though. Khloë doesn't really do guilt. The only people she's blaming are the people behind the kidnapping."

"And so she should." Piper looked at Levi. "*You* need to stop feeling guilty, too."

A muscle in his cheek ticked. "It galls me that even with you surrounded by people, someone was able to get to you."

"There's no real way to ensure I'm completely safe." Piper narrowed her eyes at the shifty expression that came over his face. "Whatever idea is floating around your head, well, you can push it right back out."

"It would work," he said.

"What?" asked Larkin.

Levi rubbed at his jaw. "It's something Asher once did to Harper. He didn't want her to leave him, so he slapped what were essentially power cuffs on her. She couldn't go far from his side. I'm sure there's someone who could link me and Piper in such a way."

A snicker burst out of her. "Ha, no, not happening." The guy had to be high if he thought differently.

"If you were cuffed to me—"

"I wouldn't be able to work or shower or use the goddamn toilet without you nearby. And you wouldn't be able to do any of the sentinel stuff you never tell me about. It's not realistic, and it wouldn't guarantee my safety. It would only mean I couldn't go far from your side."

"You'd be safer, though."

"Whoever wants me dead would simply take a different approach. People can be attacked from afar, remember?"

"She's right, Levi," Larkin cut in. "You can stick that close to her without cuffs anyway."

He grunted, clearly unhappy that no one wished to support his idea.

At that moment, Armand, Knox, and Harper appeared in the doorway. The two Primes settled their gazes on Piper.

"It's good to see you're relatively unharmed," said Knox.

Levi growled low in his throat.

Knox sighed. "Yes, I'm aware that even one injury is one too many. All I mean is that things could be a lot worse."

Harper cast Piper an apologetic look, seeming a lot more sober than she had earlier. "I'm sorry I wasn't able to stop that fucker from taking you."

"It wasn't your fault," Knox told his mate. "We've been over this. Three times."

"He's right," Piper said to her. "Apologies really aren't necessary."

"I know that *intellectually*." Harper shoved a hand through her hair. "I still can't help feeling bad."

Knox turned to Piper. "I'm aware that you've already given Levi a full account of what occurred tonight, but I'd like it if you would run through it with me."

"I can do that for her," said Levi. "She needs to rest."

"It's fine, Levi," said Piper before sliding her gaze back to the Prime. She relayed the event to him, leaving out no details. A yawn cracked her jaw, which had Levi straightening his shoulders.

"You have two options," he said. "You can sleep right there on the sofa, or I can put you in bed. Either way, you need sleep. You'll be safe here. Larkin and Harper will watch over you until I get back. Enzo and Dez will stand guard outside the apartment."

"I was planning to crash right here, because I really can't be bothered to move," said Piper. The main bedroom seemed so very, very far away right now. Well, the apartment was pretty big, with its living area, kitchen, master bathroom, two en-suite bedrooms, office/library, and workout space. Every room was airy, open, and spacious.

Levi gave a satisfied nod. "First, I need you to wake up our captive. No, don't get up. I'll have Enzo and Dez bring him to you."

The Force members dragged their sleeping prisoner into the living room and over to Piper. The demon was bound by thick rope that held a slight glimmer. *Magick*. He was also a hellbull. She hadn't been able to sense it earlier—she'd been too out of it, thanks to the fucking daze he put her in.

"Is the rope enchanted?" she asked.

"Yes," replied Levi. "It'll stop him from using his abilities, so we won't need to worry he'll teleport to safety."

Wise precaution. She touched the hellbull's head, releasing him from the hold of her power.

He snapped awake, breathing hard, his eyes wide with fright . . . just as anyone would after surfacing from a horrific nightmare. Those eyes bounced from person to person, and he swallowed so hard there was an audible click of his tongue.

"I won't be long," Levi told her. Then he, Knox, Armand, and the captive were gone.

Levi dumped the hellbull onto the wooden floor of Knox's boathouse. It was a place they often took people to be interrogated. Ordinarily, Levi would stand off to the side and mostly observe while his Prime did the honors. That wouldn't be happening tonight—something he'd already telepathically made clear to Knox, who hadn't objected.

The hellbull frantically glanced around, his breathing still choppy.

"Don't bother looking for exits," said Levi, circling him. "You won't escape us. No one is coming to save you. You missed a lot while you were dozing, so you're no doubt not aware that your friends are dead."

Biting out a curse, he squeezed his eyes shut.

"I have some questions for you. I'd advise you to answer them honestly. My patience is currently at an all-time low." Levi tilted his head. "What's your name?"

"Vittorio," he gritted out.

"Why did you kidnap my anchor, Vittorio?"

"Anchor?" the hellbull echoed, apparently deciding to go for clueless. Wrong decision.

Levi began to circle him again. "You know, I was very young when I realized I had a particular ability. It took me a while to learn to call on and control it. It's not an ability that helps much during battles, because it requires a lot of concentration. But during a one-to-one duel or torture sessions, it can be quite helpful. It allows me to do something like this."

The hellbull arched with a scream as Levi put immense pressure on his brain.

"Or this," Levi added.

Vittorio started to choke as the oxygen gushed out of his lungs.

"Or even this."

An agonized cry burst out of Vittorio as an impact slammed into his kidney.

"In sum, I can psychically grip any organ in your body. I can squeeze them. Twist them. Burst them. Collapse them. Inflate them. Punch them. Any number of things, really."

Sweat beading his brow, the hellbull began to shake.

"Now, I will ask you again," said Levi, his voice low and calm. "Why did you kidnap my anchor?"

"I wasn't planning to hurt her, man," replied Vittorio. "I'm just the delivery guy."

"Explain."

"I retrieve shit for people. So do—so *did*—my boys."

"Define 'shit.'"

"Cars, jewelry, people, whatever."

He classed people, classed *Piper*, as shit? Levi's demon growled. "You're saying you were hired to 'deliver' my anchor to someone?"

He nodded. "Yes."

"I want their name."

"I don't know who it was. Some guy called Alfie's burner, just like customers always do. They didn't give their name, and Alfie didn't ask for it. They told him they wanted Piper Winslow alive, and they agreed to our fee."

"Where were you supposed to deliver her?"

"We hadn't agreed on a location. We only do that once we have what or who we've been hired to retrieve."

"I'm going to need the phone number of whoever called your friend Alfie."

"I don't know it. Alfie has it on his burner. He keeps that phone in the van."

*Fuck.* The hellfire would have consumed the cell by now.

Knox's mind touched Levi's. *I'll have Armand check the wreckage just in case the phone is intact.*

Moments later, Armand disappeared.

Vittorio licked his lips. "I'm telling you, I wouldn't have hurt her." He said it like he should therefore be spared.

Anger spiked through Levi, hardening his jaw. "But you knew that whoever hired you might hurt her. That didn't stop you, did it?"

"Alfie made it clear to him that we don't deliver people to be killed. The guy assured him that he meant Piper no harm."

"And you believed that? I doubt it. I doubt your friends did either. But you felt that having that stipulation—one you didn't attempt to enforce—meant you bore no guilt in whatever might happen to the people you retrieve for others."

Vittorio shook his head. "It's not like that."

"It very much is. And this right here is the consequence. You fuckers knew what a dangerous game you were playing. You played it anyway, and I'd say you enjoyed it. After all, you boasted to your friends that snatching Piper was 'too easy.' She said you were cocky about it." Levi crouched beside him. "Taking my anchor was the worst mistake you ever could have made. But I'm thinking you've already realized that."

A scream tore out of Vittorio as Levi squeezed, tugged, twisted, punctured, and hit the organs in his body. He didn't rush. He took his time. He made it hurt. He kept it up until the bastard was dazed and drained and weak . . . just as Piper had been. Only when Vittorio was near death from internal bleeding did Levi finally rupture his brain.

Slowly standing, Levi burst the body into cinders with a mere click of his fingers.

"Feel better?" asked Knox.

"No." Clenching his fists, Levi rolled back his shoulders. "I will once I have my hands on whoever hired the hellbull."

Knox folded his arms. "The person who wants Piper dead could have paid a teleporter to appear at her side and kill her. Instead, they wanted her taken and delivered to them. I would say that means they would prefer to do the murderous deed themselves."

"And if that's the case, it would suggest that the person who attacked Piper at the deli—who *did* try to kill her on the spot—wasn't a mercenary. She went head-to-head with whoever has her in their sights."

"I had both Tanner and Keenan do some very deep digging.

Although the ability to conceal a person's presence isn't unheard of, no one the two sentinels questioned knows of anyone in or out of our lair who can do that. Whoever is after Piper has kept their ability *very* quiet."

"Because it gives them an advantage. We all have gifts we don't boast about for that very reason." Levi scrubbed a hand down his face. "I still think Jasper and Sefton are the likeliest suspects. Especially since Jasper confronted Piper earlier at the bar shortly before she was kidnapped."

Knox lifted a brow. "Is that so? I hadn't heard that."

Levi brought him up to speed. "Considering Sefton allegedly only made a half-assed attempt to pull his brother away, I'd say he didn't really mind so much that Jasper mouthed off the way he did. It suits him to let Jasper say the shit he's too scared to voice."

Knox nodded. "I'd have to agree. Unfortunately, I can't search their minds to see if your suspicions are correct."

Levi knew that. Knew that the only thing a person would find if they entered the mind of a nightmare was their own personal nightmare.

"I can, however, thoroughly question Jasper when I punish him tomorrow," said Knox. "He was warned to leave Piper be. He knew what the consequences would be if he didn't."

"I want to be there for that. It's going to be hard to leave Piper's side, though." Levi tilted his head as he remembered, "She's off work tomorrow. I should be able to convince her to spend the day in my apartment. She might agree to wait for me there." Levi wouldn't worry so much if she was safely within his home.

Just then, Armand materialized a few feet away, his expression grim. "No cell phones escaped the fire."

Levi gritted his teeth. "Fuck."

"Whoever made the call to this Alfie person probably took precautions to ensure it couldn't be traced back to them in any case," said Armand.

"Probably," Knox agreed.

After spending a few more minutes exchanging theories that got them nowhere, they returned to Levi's apartment.

His heart squeezed when he saw Piper curled up asleep on the sofa. She was far too pale, and he hated the sight of the dark smudges under her eyes. He should have prolonged the hellbull's suffering a little more.

She didn't stir as people announced they were leaving and said their goodbyes. He was glad of it. She needed her rest.

Once they were alone, Levi crossed to the sofa and stared down at her. He'd watched her sleep many times. He liked to look at her. Smell her. Touch her. Liked knowing he had such a basic claim to her—one she'd never escape.

When he realized she was his anchor and that he'd no longer have to keep his distance, he'd known he'd one day have her in his bed—or hers. He'd known it would be good. He'd known it might take some time to work the need she roused in him out of his system.

He hadn't known that that need would intensify rather than level off. He hadn't anticipated that she'd be an itch he'd never quite scratch, a tug in his stomach that would never ease up, a hum in his blood who'd addicted him better and faster than any drug.

His demon was hooked on her. It liked everything about her. And its possessiveness of her had ballooned over the past two weeks. The territorialism was no longer purely anchor based. The entity was proprietary of her on every level, and Levi doubted she had any clue.

He carefully scooped her up and carried her through his

apartment, nuzzling her hair. In his bedroom, he flicked back his coverlet and laid her on his bed. As he slipped off her shoes, he noticed her eyelids flutter open. "Hey," he said softly.

"Hey." It was a croak. She blinked hard. "What did the hellbull say?"

Levi kicked off his own shoes. "He and his friends, who thought of themselves as mere delivery men, were hired to take you to someone. He didn't have a name or other details to help us."

She sighed. "So we have nothing."

"Knox and I do feel we can be sure that the bastard at the deli wasn't hired help. He was there to kill you, and he enjoyed causing you pain. The hellbull, on the other hand, was only asked to retrieve and deliver you."

She frowned as Levi whipped off his tee, her eyes dipping to the wound on his chest. "I hate seeing you injured."

His heart squeezed. "Right back at you." He unbuttoned his fly. "Need help getting off your dress?"

"Nah, I got it."

He shed his jeans while she awkwardly shimmied out of her ruined dress before tossing it on the floor. His jaw hardened at the sight of her burns. They'd healed a little more since he last checked them, but they still had to be sore.

Sliding into bed beside her, he said, "I have a proposition."

"You want me to temporarily move in here."

He blinked. "Am I that predictable?"

"When it comes to matters concerning my safety, yes. I'm not crazy about the idea, but I can't deny it makes sense. Your security measures far exceed mine."

He stared at her for a long moment. "You're not going to fight me on this?"

"I'm all about being sensible. No one can get to me here, which means they also can't get to *you*. If I insist on staying at my house, you'll want to stay there with me. I'd then be putting you in danger of whoever might think to come for me there. That's not good with me. You're not the only one who's protective, you know."

He swallowed. "It's easy to forget that. You don't struggle to fight the pull of the bond."

"Actually, you're wrong, I *do* struggle to fight—"

"Then stop doing it. My demon hates that you're not claimed; that you don't wear an anchor mark that proclaims you're ours and we'd fight to the death for you."

There'd be something bittersweet for Levi about finally forming the bond, because he'd lose the sexual intimacy they had. He'd always known he would have to give it up eventually. Because she'd been right—casual sex *would* muddy things between them. It already had.

As much as he didn't want things to go back to the way they initially were, what kind of person would it make him to put his libido before his anchor's safety? He was her one guarantee that she'd never turn rogue. He would strengthen her and center her demon. He had to put her first because, whether she believed it or not, she *was* his priority.

"How much longer are you going to make us wait, Piper?"

"As a matter of fact, I was going to tell you tonight that I was ready. But then this happened, and I'm thinking it would be better if we waited."

"*What?*"

"When things quietened down, I thought maybe whoever targeted me had decided I was more trouble than I was worth or something. But I was wrong, and that means someone out there still wants me dead. If I die and we're bonded—"

"You're not holding back to protect me, Piper," he told her, his face hard. "No way."

"You could turn rogue."

He gripped her chin. "You're not gonna die. I'd never fucking allow it."

"The strength of your will alone can't keep me alive. People lose others all the time. We take for granted that we'll live long lives. It doesn't always work that way."

"It doesn't, no. But certain things can tip the balance in our favor. When you and I are bonded, you'll be stronger. The power that drugged you tonight? You'd have fought through that if you were anchored to me."

"I would rather we waited until the threat has passed."

"And if it was the other way around, would you accept that shit from me?"

She hesitated. "Well no, but you'd argue that we needed to wait."

"No, I wouldn't. I'd never believe that refusing to bond with you would be some sort of safety precaution. No matter the situation, you'll have a better chance of survival if we're bonded." He tightened his grip on her nape. "Don't let this person have the power you're giving them. Don't let them act as a barrier between us and our bond."

"I doubt that's their intention."

"Probably not. But you're still allowing them that level of power over you. Over us."

She sighed, a tired groan slipping out of her. "I just don't want you to end up rogue."

"Which means you'd fight harder to live if we were bonded. Am I wrong?"

She exhaled heavily. "No. No, you're not wrong."

"Then let's do this. Let's claim each other right here, right now." A selfish part of him rose up in protest, not wanting this thing they had to end. His demon let out a low growl, pissed that Levi intended to live up to the agreement he'd made with her. The entity didn't see why sex needed to be taken off the table.

"You're *sure* you want to take the chance that—"

"Right here, right now," he repeated, even though it made his chest ache.

Piper stared into his eyes for a long moment. "Okay," she said, her voice soft.

He didn't have a second to feel any triumph, because she instantly released her hold on her psyche, and it all but barreled into his.

Levi grunted as their psyches fused together, becoming two intersecting spheres. After the brief moment of disorientation passed, he said, "I feel you." It was like she was inside him now. Her psychic presence was strong and intimate, virtually humming with her confidence, quiet strength, and unswerving loyalty. Her psychic taste was just as vivid—pumpkin pie and cinnamon spice. His demon loved it.

*Mine.* Levi snaked his hand around her throat and pressed his thumb against the hollow beneath her ear, branding her. When he removed his thumb, a small glistening infinity symbol proclaiming her anchored was stamped right there. Each person's brand held a slight difference. For Piper's, a scythe slashed through both loops.

"Your turn," he told her, self-satisfaction pouring through him.

Using her thumb, she left her own mark on the hollow beneath his ear, and the slight sting quickly faded. She narrowed her eyes as she studied it. "You have a 'P' inside one loop, and a 'W' inside the lower one. What does my symbol look like?"

He described it, adding, "The bond is so much more steadying than I'd expected." It centered his demon and bolstered their strength which, most importantly, meant it did the same for both her and her inner entity. He focused on that, on how this was best for her, wrestling back the conflicting emotions attempting to surge through him.

"It's kind of weird how our minds keep brushing and bumping each other's," she said. "Though not in a bad way."

Mindful of her injuries, he drew her close and kissed her forehead, letting himself have this last moment of closeness. Tomorrow, they'd sleep in separate beds from then on. Tonight . . . tonight, he needed to hold her. "You'll get used to it."

"Your psychic taste fits you well. Whiskey and almonds. *Good* whiskey."

He felt his mouth curve. "Yours is cinnamon spice and pumpkin pie. Makes me hungry." He splayed his hand on her back, the move a little too possessive.

"Is your demon done sulking now?"

"Oh, yeah. Totally done." Which was a lie. The demon was incredibly pleased to have the bond, but it was infuriated with Levi for being prepared to let her go on a sexual level.

Squeezing his eyes shut, he pressed another soft kiss to her forehead. "Now go back to sleep. I'll be right here. I won't leave you." Not tonight. But every other night? Yeah, that he'd have to do.

# CHAPTER TWELVE

Piper woke to the feel of warm lips pressing featherlight kisses along her chest. Now healed, the flesh didn't sting at the prick of Levi's stubble. She opened her eyes to find him draped over her, braced on his elbows. His cock throbbed against her folds, hot and hard.

His mind idly brushed hers, and the fog of sleep cleared as she remembered they'd formed the psi-mate bond. Piper tensed. Had he forgotten their agreement? Was he half asleep?

She swallowed. "Levi?"

His gaze snapped to hers, glittering with heat and something she couldn't quite name. An emotion that made her heart sink. "Need to have you one last time," he said, his voice thick.

She should say no. She should. This wasn't starting as they meant to go on. But she heard herself say, "One last time." And she didn't have it in her to take the words back.

He dipped his head further down and lashed her nipple with his tongue. Splaying her hand over the back of his head, she let her eyes fall closed, sinking into the sensations as he licked and sucked and palmed and pinched. But there was no blocking out the pain of knowing she'd never feel his mouth and hands on her like this again.

Despite the benefits of the anchor bond, her heart had broken a little when they formed the psi-connection last night, because it had been an ending just as much as it had been a beginning. She was pretty sure she'd hidden her inner turmoil well, which was a relief. She didn't want him to know how much this hurt her. He'd only feel guilty, and that would do neither of them any good.

Her demon had never been keen on this agreement they'd made. It was no happier about it now. Even at this moment, it huffed and sneered, because it knew this was the end.

Levi began to edge down her body, nipping the skin here and there, tracing her tattoos with his tongue. His hands followed, taking their time as they stroked, shaped, and teased.

It felt like a goodbye. A goodbye to what they'd had. It was in the way he touched her so carefully, so reverently, so desperately . . . like they'd run out of time.

Hot tears stung the backs of her eyes. It was better this way, she reminded herself. After all, it would be wrong to drag out what would only ever be casual. This thing between them didn't *feel* wrong, though. No, it felt a little too right. And that was exactly why they needed to stick to their agreement. So she wouldn't cry. Instead, she'd soak up every moment.

As usual, he gave a sharp bite to the ivy tattoos Kelvin had given her on her hip and navel, as if Levi didn't like that Kelvin had marked her skin. But then he paused and planted his face into her stomach, his shoulders rising slightly as he took in a long breath.

She frowned, lifting her head. "You okay?"

Levi met her gaze, his own unreadable. A purring wash of telekinetic power danced over her skin and clamped around her throat, collaring her as firmly as any hand. Her head fell back in surprise, and the power pulsed and tremored. The pressure didn't hurt, but it was intense and pushed her best buttons.

Levi positioned himself between her thighs, spread them wider, and nuzzled her folds. "I'm gonna miss your taste." Then he settled in and went to work.

Her breath hitched, and a moan crawled up her throat. Damn that mouth for being so freaking skilled. He explored . . . everywhere. Her clit, her slit, her folds, her core, the entrance of her pussy, the creases of her thighs.

She writhed and moaned as the tension built and built inside her. It was when he shoved his fingers deep while rubbing the side of her clit with his tongue that she came hard.

She felt a small waft of cool air. Looking down, she saw that his demon had surfaced.

It smoothed one hand all the way up her inner thigh while planting the other on her stomach. "Be still."

Uh, what?

"I need to send a message that both you and he will understand."

It swiped its tongue between her folds, and then the skin beneath its hands began to heat. Burn. Scorch. It was almost unbearable and . . . oh *fuck*, the demon was branding her. Her eyes widened, and she shook her head. The entity paid her no attention, eating her pussy and driving her up to another orgasm.

She choked on a loud cry as she imploded, her thighs trembling. Not even the wave of pleasure could distract her from the fact that she'd been branded, though. Demons surfaced to leave such marks if they felt possessive of a lover. But she and

Levi would no longer *be* lovers after today . . . which meant it was highly likely that he'd *freak*.

Retaking control as his demon retreated, Levi looked at the brands that now marked her body. *Hell.* He knew that the entity's intent was to make a statement that it wouldn't give her—*this*—up so easily. The demon also meant to ensure that any person who'd think to fuck her or fuck *with* her would quickly change their mind.

Levi silently cursed the psychopathic shit. Unwilling to back down, it snorted, all 'game on.' It was also exceedingly smug, because it knew that Levi liked the look of those brands on her skin far too much.

Inwardly calling himself an asshole, Levi rose above her and covered her body with his own. Glazed eyes stared up at him, fevered with need. This was the last time she'd look at him this way, he realized with a sinking sensation in his gut. She'd never again be under him. Never again take his cock inside her or come apart around him.

A growl rumbled in his chest. A chest that ached and panged and squeezed. The only comfort he had was the knowledge that she'd always belong to him. No one who walked into her life would ever have the rights to her that he did. They wouldn't be able to take her from him. Wouldn't be able to deny that, being linked to her by fate itself, she'd been his *first*.

"Never forget one thing." Levi hooked one smooth leg over his shoulder and thrust hard, burying himself deep, gritting his teeth as her pussy clenched his dick. "No matter where you are, no matter who you're with, you'll always be mine. Fucking always."

He took her slowly. Lazily. Making sure she really *felt* every inch, ridge, vein; wishing he could leave an imprint of his cock inside her, so she could never forget how it felt to have him drag along those hypersensitive nerve-endings.

He hadn't planned to take her one last time. He'd reached for her when he woke, just as he normally did. But then the presence of the psi-mate bond had rung through his very being, and he'd remembered he couldn't touch her like this anymore. But he'd needed to. Just once more.

He'd fucked up when he suggested their agreement. He'd arrogantly thought he'd be easily able to break things off. But, to be fair, why would he have thought differently? He'd never craved anyone before her, so he hadn't known exactly how difficult it would be to end those cravings. He hadn't expected to find himself addicted to her rather than free of their attraction. And now, well, now he was screwed.

He didn't believe this was any easier for her than it was for him, because she clung to him tighter than usual, scratching at him with a desperation that wasn't just sexual. At least he wasn't suffering alone.

"You feel how well your pussy fits my cock, don't you?" It was a snarl loaded with possession. "Remember it, Piper. Remember how perfectly you fit me . . . like your pussy was made to take me."

Levi slanted his mouth over hers and sank his tongue inside. She palmed the back of his head as she kissed him back. They greedily ate at each other's mouths as if they'd never feast like this again . . . because they wouldn't.

He fought the orgasm rising up inside him. He didn't want to come. Didn't want this to be over.

She seemed to be wrestling with her own release, but her little whimper told him she wouldn't hold out much longer. He didn't want the last orgasm he ever gave her to be a gentle wave of pleasure. He wanted to make her fucking scream.

She gasped into his mouth as he began pounding into her body, stuffing her pussy full again and again. He took her like an animal. Rutted on her. Savagely slammed as deep as he could possibly go, knowing the friction of his skin moving against her newly branded, super-sensitive flesh would add to the pleasure.

When her pussy heated and spasmed around him, he lightly tightened his telekinetic hold on her throat—not enough to take her breath away, but enough to shove her over the edge. She screamed as she came, her back bowing, her nails digging into his shoulders. Levi's own release swallowed him whole, dimming his vision and stealing his breath.

He let her leg slip from his shoulder and collapsed forward, catching his weight on his elbows, tucking his face into her neck. He retained enough presence of mind to release her throat from his telekinetic hold.

Tremoring beneath him, she splayed one hand on his back while her free hand lightly played her fingers through his hair. She often did that after sex, and fuck if he wasn't going to miss it.

She coughed to clear her throat. "Your demon kind of branded me."

Levi tensed. She didn't *sound* pissed, but he couldn't imagine her being blasé about it either. Especially when she saw them. He spoke against her neck, "It felt the need to communicate that it's not so happy about our agreement."

"Yeah, I got that."

"Don't worry, the brands will fade in time."

Piper inwardly flinched, because yes, they'd fade . . . when his demon's sexual interest switched to another woman. Which it inevitably would. She would actually *see* its interest in her wane as the marks gradually dimmed until they were gone.

Even with Levi's warm body covering hers, she felt cold all of a sudden. She couldn't regret their agreement. She couldn't bring herself to wish away the delicious memories she now had. But *fuck* she hated that her need for him still lived and breathed inside her.

Knowing it was time to let him go, figuratively and literally, Piper let her hands slip away from his body. He stiffened for a moment, and she felt his mouth open against her neck as if he might say something. But then he slowly slid out of her and moved to kneel between her thighs, his gaze dropping down her body, settling first on her stomach and then on her inner thigh.

*The brands.*

She glanced down, and her brows flew up. Black with a faint shimmer, the tattoo-like marks were not at all what she'd expected. Each was a music score that had tiny skeleton heads mingled in with it. They were pretty yet they inexplicably made her stomach roll and a sense of unease skitter down her spine. "What's with the music?"

He stared at her, his gaze giving nothing away. "It's the death ballad."

Piper went stiff as a board. "You're joking." It was a stunned whisper.

He shook his head and slipped off the bed. "No joke."

Her entity barked a laugh, but Piper didn't share its amusement. She snapped her legs closed and bolted upright. "Your demon made me a walking death note? Seriously?"

Levi winced, unsurprised by her anger. The ballad was no little thing. However . . . "It will only have a lethal effect on a person who means you harm and is a fully grown adult."

They would feel compelled to hum the tune. Over. And over. And over. They wouldn't pause to eat or sleep or drink. They would keep humming until they eventually died—usually of dehydration. Only reapers could snap a person out of their daze, just as only reapers could write the music score.

"That's not the point, Levi. The ballad is essentially a death curse, and it's now *imprinted on my skin.* In two places. And don't act like this is purely a protective measure. The brand on my stomach mostly is, sure, but the one on my inner thigh? No. Your entity only put it there because it wants to repel anyone who tries to get between my legs."

Well . . . yeah. Looking at the score could make a person feel nauseous and uneasy, whether or not they recognized it as the death ballad or were in any way a threat. "Like I said before, the brands will fade." His demon snorted, certain no such thing would happen; that it would never let go of her on any level. "I'm sorry, Piper. It was an asshole thing for—"

"You don't need to apologize, I'm not blaming *you.* I know you'd never do anything like this. But that damn entity of yours deserves a fucking bitch slap."

That wasn't something he could or would deny.

She let out a heavy sigh and thrust a hand through her hair. "I need to shower."

Out of habit, Levi almost proposed they shower together. He gritted his teeth as he remembered that that was one of many other things they would no longer do. "You can use that one," he said, tipping his chin toward the en suite. "I'll use the main bathroom. You have some clothes in that drawer over there from when you last slept over."

She gave a slow, awkward nod. "Okay. Thanks."

They parted, showered, dressed, and soon after sat at his breakfast bar where they chomped down some cereal and made idle conversation. It was something they did pretty much every morning. Yet, this felt . . . different. Something was missing from their dynamics. Something warm and comfortable.

It made no real sense to him. It wasn't like they usually

cuddled, constantly touched each other, or invaded the other's personal space. The only intimacy they'd lose was sexual, so everything should be as it usually was.

Only it wasn't.

"Do you still want me to stay here until the danger has passed?" she asked.

"Of course," replied Levi. "Why would you feel the need to double-check?"

She shrugged and looked down into her bowl.

"Piper, just because we're not sleeping together anymore doesn't mean I'll ever be anything other than insanely overprotective of you. I want you here, where you're safest. I've got a spare bedroom you can use."

"Okay, if you're sure."

"I am sure." He pushed his empty bowl aside. "Once you're ready, I'll drive you to your place so you can pack whatever stuff you need." He paused as the intercom beeped. "Give me a second." He left the kitchen and crossed to the small screen near his front door. Two figures waited on the doorstep of his building. "Piper, your mother and Joe are here." He pressed the button that would open the main door for them.

"Shit, I forgot to tell you they were coming," said Piper, walking up behind him. "I called them while you were interrogating the hellbull. I didn't want them to hear about the attack from anyone else. They wanted to come see me this morning, I told them I'd be here. Is that okay?"

"Of course. They're your family. They're always welcome here. I've already buzzed them up."

"Thank you."

He sighed. "Quit being so formal. You don't have to thank me. Besides, I like them." They'd invited Levi and Piper to dinner twice over the past two weeks, and they'd both been warm and welcoming toward him. As that made things easier for her, he was grateful for it.

Within minutes, Whitney and Joe were breezing into his apartment. They didn't spare their surroundings a glance. They went straight to Piper, anxious and fussing.

"I'm fine, I promise," she assured them. Several times.

Joe turned to Levi and stuck out his hand. "You're going to say that gratitude isn't warranted, but I still want to thank you for getting to our girl and bringing her to safety."

Levi shook his hand. "No thanks are necessary." He almost grunted as Whitney hugged him hard.

"We can still be grateful," she told him, pulling back. "My stomach sinks every time I think of how differently things could have ended. Please tell me you have *some* idea of who wants my daughter dead."

They gathered in the living area while Levi gave them a rundown of what the hellbull told him before stiffly adding, "Basically, I have no way of linking him to whoever hired his crew."

Whitney looked at Piper. "I heard that Jasper confronted you last night. The whole lair considers him the likeliest suspect at this point. Don't think he'd make an effort to seem innocent and be nice to you in order to cover his ass. Others might put on such an act, but not him."

Joe nodded. "He's petty and vindictive, but he has no cunning or smarts. He's also used to his father lying and covering for him."

"I'll be questioning Jasper today," said Levi. "I might not be able to brand him guilty of being the person who's targeting Piper, but I can certainly hold him responsible for confronting her. He was warned to stay clear of her."

"Don't hesitate to make him hurt," said Whitney, more bloodthirsty than he would have guessed.

"Your mother and I think it would be a good idea for you to move in with us for a while," Joe told Piper. "We don't like the thought of you alone."

"Neither do I," said Levi, "which is why I asked her to stay with me. No intruder would bypass the security measures in this building. She agreed."

Joe gave a satisfied nod. "Even better."

"I'll pack your things and bring them here," Whitney offered. She held up a hand when Piper went to protest. "Let your mom feel *useful.* There's nothing I can do to help with all that's happening. It's driving me crazy. Let me do this one thing for you."

Understanding why her mother would need this, Piper lifted her hands in surrender. "All right, if it means that much to you. On a lighter note . . . Levi and I formed the anchor bond."

Whitney beamed. "That's amazing! Congratulations to both of you."

Joe echoed her sentiments, adding, "That means you're psychically stronger. I like that. If there was ever a time you needed that sort of boost, it's now."

"You ain't wrong," said Piper.

Joe's smile dimmed. "I know Celeste won't react well and . . . I'm sorry she acts the way she does, Piper. Don't say it's not for me to apologize. It is. Because it occurred to me recently that I let you down in a very big way. I was always so careful to treat you both the same. Or I thought I was. But lately, I realized all my efforts to keep the peace actually also resulted in me putting her feelings first. For your sake, I'd placate and calm and coax her. But that gave her all the attention, didn't it?"

"It wasn't only Joe who made mistakes in that regard." Whitney bit her lip. "I'm guilty of the exact same thing. I just wanted you girls to get along. I thought if we could just make Celeste see that she was loved, she'd stop feeling threatened by you; she'd leave you be. Instead, it seemed to encourage her to act out; seemed to fill her with this sense that her wants and needs should come before yours. And it must have also filled you with that same sense. I never wanted that. Joe never wanted that."

Joe nodded. "You're not second to either of us, Piper. We love you. And we are so sorry for the ways in which we let you down. Things will be different moving forward—I promise you that."

Piper swallowed, her throat thickening. She hadn't realized just how much she'd needed to hear those words until right then. Oh, she knew they loved her; knew they didn't deliberately prioritize Celeste's feelings. But Piper had needed them to verbally acknowledge the mistakes they'd made; needed to hear that things would be different from here on out.

She cleared her throat. "Okay."

A short while later, Whitney and Joe left after once more thanking Levi for 'taking care of their girl.' He'd had to bite back the comment that she was *his* girl.

Piper folded her arms. "When are you going to question Jasper?"

"Once Harper, Raini, Devon, and Khloë get here," replied Levi. "I think they might be bringing Asher."

Her brow furrowed. "You asked them to come so I wouldn't be alone?"

"No. They wanted to see and check on you. I decided to time it for when I'd be leaving so you'd have company while I was gone."

She narrowed her eyes. "Let's be real, you wanted to be spared a morning of girl talk. Am I wrong?"

"No. No, you're not wrong."

# CHAPTER THIRTEEN

Raini shoved Khloë's feet off her lap with such force the imp almost slipped off the sofa they were sharing. "For the eighth and final time—"

"Ninth," Harper chipped in.

"—I'm not massaging your feet."

Khloë pouted. "You did it for Devon yesterday."

"She's pregnant," said Raini. "When you're knocked up, I'll . . . well, I'll light a candle for your poor unborn child."

"I would make a *wonderful* mother," declared Khloë.

Everyone simply stared at her.

The imp raised her shoulders. "What?"

Devon cleared her throat. "So, Piper, how does it feel to be anchored?" she asked, relaxing into the armchair that was a carbon copy of the one on which Piper herself sat.

Aside from the fact that being bonded to Levi this way had a sting in its tail . . . "I feel stronger. Steadier. And it's a relief to know that although my demon can still reach for supremacy sometimes, it can never have full power over me." Piper would always remain the dominant of the two. "I still can't quite get used to how my mind reaches for Levi's all the time, though."

"It'll become metaphorical white noise eventually," said Harper, sitting on the rug near the toys her son had abandoned when he raced out of the room to go exploring the apartment with Keenan close behind him. "Have you told your family yet?"

"My mom and stepfather know," said Piper. "They're pleased for me. They're actually planning to drop off some of my stuff so I can stay here until the danger passes. Which reminds me that I'll have to pick a room to sleep in."

Raini's brow furrowed. "Pick a room?"

"Yeah." Noticing the women exchange odd looks, Piper frowned. "What?"

Harper scratched her cheek. "I figured you'd be sharing Levi's room, that's all."

Ah, so they were aware that he and Piper did the dirty. Bouncing her gaze from female to female, Piper said, "I didn't think you knew."

Khloë lifted one shoulder. "We kind of guessed."

"You never mentioned it," said Piper.

"We didn't think there was any point," Devon told her. "You and Levi were never couple-y, so it was clear that you were intent on keeping the fling on the down-low."

Piper fiddled with her fingers. "It wasn't a fling. We just had sex occasionally. We're not anymore, though. We agreed beforehand that we'd stop when we bonded."

"Ah." Raini bit her lip. "I gotta admit, what with how intense he is around you, I wouldn't have thought he'd be good with that. Are you?"

"It's better this way." Piper looked from Harper to Raini. "I know you two mated with your anchors, and I know it's not really unusual. But it won't work that way for me and Levi. You can't begin a relationship with someone who isn't open to having one. He's not."

Harper inclined her head. "He does tend to keep his relationships the epitome of casual." She twisted her mouth. "I don't think he'll find it easy to stick to this agreement you two made. I've seen the way he looks at you. It totally gives me tingles."

"Attraction fades," said Piper. "Haven't we all been attracted to people who we later look at and feel absolutely nothing around?"

Harper nodded hard. "Oh, definitely."

"I'm not saying it won't take a little effort for me to view him through purely platonic lenses, but it will happen eventually." Piper would make sure of it. "It's hard right now because we take up so much of each other's time and space. It won't always be that way."

"True." Harper bit on the inside of her cheek. "How does your demon feel about all this?"

"It's happy about the bond, but it's not impressed that me and Levi are choosing to go back to the way things initially were." It was pleased about his demon's brands, but Piper saw no need to talk about those with anyone. "It'll get used to it, though."

Raini gave her a sympathetic smile. "I know things must feel a little awkward at the moment, but you two can still be tight. You were friends first. You'll get things back on the platonic track soon enough."

Just then, Asher stomped into the room, a dark scowl on his adorable face.

"Why are you sulking, little man?" Harper asked him.

Asher jabbed a finger at Keenan, who was coming up behind him. "He's a meanie-weenie."

The incubus sighed. "I made him put Levi's lamp back on

the nightstand. Asher wanted to take it home. And no, I don't have any clue why."

Harper gave her son a look that said she meant business. "You know the rules, Asher. You can't take people's things without asking first."

Asher's scowl stayed firmly in place. "Heidi duz it. Koey duz it. Grams duz—"

"We're not talking about them," Harper interrupted. "Why do you even want a lamp?"

"It's blue," he replied. "I likes blue."

As Harper went on to lecture him, Raini turned to Khloë and asked, "Remember you went through a phase of stealing anything silver? Ribbons, screws, paperclips, even hair ties?"

Khloë pursed her lips. "No, not really."

"Well it was a hell of a phase," said Raini. "No one cared much about it until you started steeling wheel trims too."

Khloë's brows inched up. "*That* I remember."

Asher sighed long and loud. "I sorry."

"Good boy." Harper held her arms out to him. "Now give Mommy a hug."

"Uh . . . no." Giggling, he hurried off on those little legs, and Keenan quickly trailed after him.

Smiling at the sight, Piper asked, "Has Keenan found his psi-mate?"

It was Khloë who answered, "No, not yet. I hope he does. Not all demons are so lucky."

Piper slanted her head. "You don't think you'll find it hard to see him bound tight to someone else?"

"Nope." Khloë tucked her hair behind her ear. "I get why some people do feel that way when their mate finds their anchor, but I don't operate like that. Not all do."

"I get along *great* with my anchor's mate," said Devon.

"Hunter's the best. He and Adam—that's my anchor—are almost as excited about my pregnancy as I am. They've proclaimed themselves the baby's honorary uncles."

Piper smiled. "Aw, how sweet." She could only pray she'd be on such good terms with whoever Levi took as his mate. As things stood, though, Piper would be more likely to set the bitch on fire.

"You're zoning out again."

Snapping out of his thoughts, Levi blinked at his Prime. "Got a lot on my mind." Or, more accurately, he was striving to ignore how his bastard of a demon kept sending him mental images of Piper naked with faceless men. It wasn't necessarily trying to provoke Levi, it mostly just wanted him to feel the bite of jealousy; wanted him to declare that he'd scrap the agreement if only to ensure that no one else would have her.

Levi rolled back his shoulders. "How much longer are Tanner and Larkin going to be?"

"Mere minutes, I'd say." Knox sank deeper into the chair behind his desk, eyeing Levi carefully. "I would have thought you'd be more relaxed today, given you and Piper officially claimed each other as anchors."

Levi felt his back teeth lock. "I'll be relaxed when I've detained whoever wants her dead."

"That's not all you're mentally chewing on. Tell me what has you so distracted."

"Someone wants to wipe my anchor from the face of the Earth. You think that isn't going to distract me?"

"I think there's more. I also think you don't want to talk to me about it."

"Then why bug me?"

Humor briefly lit Knox's eyes. "You're only ever this defensive when you feel trapped or stuck or restricted."

It was true. And right then, Levi *did* feel stuck. There was no escaping that he had to stick to his word and cease sharing a bed with Piper, because there was no other option. Not realistically. So now there were boundaries and limits that weren't there before, and he knew he'd be shit at dealing with them.

"Is there no way I can help?" asked Knox.

Levi leaned back against the wall. "No. No, there's no help for it. The situation is what it is and that's that. I don't want to talk any more about it."

"Fair enough. Come to me if you change your mind."

Levi grunted.

"You must be relieved that you were able to convince Piper to temporarily move into your apartment."

"I didn't need to convince her. She'd already anticipated that I'd ask, and she said she thought it was a smart move."

"She trusts you with her safety, then. Good. I suppose it's easier for her that she's already well-acquainted with your apartment." Knox drummed his fingers on his desk. "Just be careful, Levi."

"With what?"

"With Piper's feelings. You two are sleeping together, and it's clear you like her a great deal—I've never known you to spend as much time with anyone as you do her. Now you want her living with you. That could give her the wrong idea."

No, it couldn't, because . . . "We're both clear on how things are. We're also not fucking anymore. And no, I don't want to talk about that either."

Knuckles rapped on the office door.

"Come in," Knox called out.

Tanner strolled in first, followed closely by Jasper and Sefton.

Larkin came in behind them, closed the door, and took up position there.

"Hello, Jasper, Sefton." Knox flicked his fingers, urging them to come closer.

"We had nothing to do with whatever happened to Piper last night," said Jasper, halting in front of the desk. He was doing his best to look sure and confident, but the fine line of tension in his body gave him away.

Knox lifted a brow. "No?"

"No, nothing," Jasper stated.

Sefton swallowed. "Nothing," he reiterated.

Knox cocked his head. "You didn't confront her at the Xpress bar, Jasper?"

His brows pulling together, Jasper said, "It wasn't a confrontation."

Levi folded his arms. "Then what was it?"

"I'd had a few drinks, I sniped at her a little," replied Jasper. "It was stupid, yeah, but I didn't hurt her or anything. I *definitely* didn't teleport her out of the damn bar."

Knox hummed. "But could you or your brother here have arranged for someone else to do so? Yes, that's a definite possibility."

Sefton shook his head. "We didn't, Knox, I swear. We *wouldn't*."

"We're not fans of Piper, but we don't want her dead," said Jasper. "All I want is for her to admit that she lied about my brother—that's it."

Knox locked his gaze on Sefton. "You still insist to your family that you're innocent?"

Avoiding eye-contact, he replied, "I admitted my guilt—"

"So that I'd let it alone," began Jasper, "because you don't want me to end up in the damn Chamber."

"Blind faith can be a dangerous thing, Jasper," said Knox. "As can targeting the psi-mate of someone like Levi."

"Even if we wanted to hire a person to teleport her somewhere—which we don't—we couldn't have done it," Jasper clipped. "We don't have the cash. The way I see it, a person would charge a hell of a fee to kidnap the anchor of one of your sentinels. We'd have no way of paying that."

Valid point, but . . . "Not all fees are cash-based."

Jasper raised his shoulders. "What else could we offer someone in payment? Nothing. We don't own our homes. We have no assets. Our cars are pieces of shit. An IOU wouldn't be enough of an incentive for someone to snatch a person as well-protected as Piper."

"Maybe you never intended to pay anyone," mused Knox. "Maybe your plan was to kill your hirelings once they delivered Piper to you."

"It would have been a shit plan," said Levi, dancing his gaze from one brother to the other. "But neither of you is the brightest bulb."

Jasper's mouth tightened. "It wasn't us. The only thing I'm guilty of is acting like a dick last night at the bar and . . . fuck, I don't even remember all I said."

"I have plenty of witnesses who do," Knox told him. "The words most used to describe your manner during that encounter were 'ugly,' 'aggressive,' and 'threatening.'"

Jasper's brow pinched. "I didn't threaten her."

"How do you know?" challenged Levi. "According to you, you don't recall everything you said."

"I'd remember *that.*" Jasper softly cursed. "Look, I was rude and out of line. I wouldn't have said anything to her if I hadn't been drunk."

"And as I said to your brother last night," Larkin cut in,

"I've never considered 'drunk' a valid excuse for any form of behavior."

"Neither have I," said Knox. "Speaking of Sefton—"

"He didn't do nothing," Jasper insisted. "It was all me. He tried to pull me away."

"He made a show of it, yes," Knox agreed. "But he was also overheard by a patron telling you that someone needed to give Piper a reality check." Knox pinned the other brother with a glare. "You goaded him."

Sefton's eyes widened. "No, no, it wasn't like that. Someone said they were surprised that Celeste hadn't screamed bloody murder over Piper and Levi being anchors. I said Celeste would probably do something sooner or later; that she'd never give them her blessing and that Piper needed a reality check if she thought differently. I wasn't trying to rile my brother. I *wouldn't*."

"There was no riling," said Jasper. "He had nothing to do with this."

Ignoring him, Knox spoke again to Sefton. "I think you like that your brother insists on being so mouthy. He says all the things you're too scared to say yourself. The risk is all his. That suits you just fine."

Both Sefton and Jasper began profusely objecting.

"Quiet," clipped Knox, and the protests abruptly died. He narrowed his eyes on Jasper. "You knew what would happen if you didn't keep your distance from Piper. It doesn't matter to me what state you were in last night, you have no excuse for disobeying my orders or ignoring Levi's warnings. You will be punished."

Pausing, Knox slid his gaze to Sefton. "And you will watch. You will watch your brother suffer, and then maybe you will feel motivated to ensure he doesn't earn himself another punishment. Because we both fucking know you could have dragged him away from Piper last night if you had really wanted to. You chose not to." He looked from Tanner to Larkin. "Take them."

The two sentinels dragged the brothers out of the office.

Levi scraped his hand over his jaw. "Jasper made some good points."

"He did," said Knox.

"I'm still not ready to scrub the brothers off the suspect list. They could have loaned money from someone or offered a service of some sort in trade."

"You think they might have worked together on this?"

"If it was Jasper's idea, no. He's protective of his brother, he wouldn't ask Sefton to involve himself in anything that could put him in the line of fire. But if Sefton came up with the idea, he'd have had no problem trying to get Jasper on board. He's a self-centered prick."

Knox nodded. "Jasper's not much better, but he at least feels family loyalty. I don't think Sefton's loyal to anyone but himself."

Irritated that he still had so many unanswered questions, Levi thrust a hand through his hair as he pushed away from the wall. He needed to get back to Piper but, unwilling to leave Knox without protection, he didn't move until Larkin returned. Levi then finally left the Underground and headed straight to his complex. Entering his apartment, he was greeted by silence. Apparently Harper and the others had left.

Frustration still beating in his blood, he stalked through the place in search of Piper. He found her in his spare bedroom, setting clothes into a drawer. The sight made his stomach drop. His demon narrowed its eyes, displeased that she'd set up camp somewhere other than the master bedroom.

She peered up at Levi and blinked. "Oh, hey."

He took a few steps forward. "Everyone left, I see."

"Yep." She slipped her hands into the back pockets of her jeans and began rocking back and forth on her heels, looking awkward and uncertain. "My, uh, my mom brought my stuff about half an hour ago. I figured I'd unpack. So I am. Is that okay?"

"Of course. I wouldn't want you to live out of a suitcase."

"I was just, you know, checking." She gave him a polite smile and looked away, biting her lower lip.

He backed out of the room. "I'll leave you to it. When you're done, come find me, we'll have dinner."

She nodded. "Sure. Will do."

Dinner went exactly as breakfast had. They ate, made small-talk, and each did their best to ignore the discomfiture in the air.

He hated that she didn't feel at ease around him anymore. He understood it would only be temporary, but that didn't make it any less agitating.

Determined to get rid of the awkwardness, Levi proposed they try a TV series that Larkin recommended. He and Piper needed to spend time together as friends so they could get on the right foot.

Piper accepted his proposal, so they binge-watched the entire series in his living room while munching on snacks and, six hours later, a pizza. Well, it was a long-ass series.

His plan paid off. The weird vibe between them disappeared. Their smiles were no longer stiff. Their chuckles were no longer hollow. But the moment they halted at her bedroom door that night, all the work was undone.

She cleared her throat. "Night, Levi." She pushed open the door and padded into the room.

He wanted to follow her. He didn't know if he could sleep under the same roof as her and *not* be beside her. But like he'd told Knox, the situation was what it was. Levi needed to suck it up and deal with it. "Night, Piper."

He walked away. Not to his room, but in the direction of his home gym. There was a punchbag in there that would help him get out his frustrations. His demon rather thought sex would be the better option, and the sneaky little fucker began sending Levi mental snapshots of Piper beneath them . . . above them . . . on her hands and knees in front of them.

Levi cursed the entity to hell and back. It shrugged, unperturbed by his anger. In its opinion, Levi had no one to blame for his current mood but himself. The entity wasn't even wrong.

After his workout, Levi showered and slipped into bed. He didn't sleep, though. He simply wasn't tired. So the feel of Knox's mind brushing his didn't snap Levi out of a peaceful sleep.

*A male demon from our lair was found loitering outside Sera Browne's home*, said the Prime, referring to a single mother within their lair.

Levi tensed. *Who was it?*

*Dez's brother, Marshall.*

Levi narrowed his eyes as he remembered . . . *Sera is his ex-girlfriend.*

*Yes. He ran when one of the Force members on patrol spotted him. He didn't run fast enough. Marshall claims he was hanging near her house because he worries she'll be targeted.*

*I'd say it's suspicious that he ran, but it's not for Marshall.* The man was so used to being in trouble that he fled on instinct these days. *Do you believe him?*

*I do. Although, really, I don't think he's as concerned for Sera as he is for their son. She won't allow Marshall to stay at the house until the killer's been apprehended, so he apparently decided he'd instead monitor the place from outside. I'll be taking a dip into his mind to ensure his story checks out. I would rather Dez didn't hear of this through the grapevine, so fill him in on what happened.*

Levi flipped back the coverlet. *Will do.*

He could simply call the Force member, but Levi decided to instead speak with him face-to-face. It gave him something to do.

Opening the front door to his apartment, he nodded at both Dez and Enzo, who were on guard duty.

"Everything okay?" asked Dez.

"That depends," said Levi. "Marshall was found hanging around Sera's house tonight. He ran when a Force member came upon him but was subsequently caught."

Enzo sighed at Dez. "I told you he wouldn't listen to us. The man never does."

Grunting, Dez scrubbed a hand over his face.

"Marshall said he planned on keeping a very close watch on Sera and their boy," Enzo told Levi. "Given that she wouldn't react well—and what woman *would* be cool with a cheating ex lurking outside her home?—we recommended that he didn't. We assured him that all single mothers were being monitored."

"Does Knox think my brother's the one who killed Diem and Emma?" Dez asked.

"Not at present," Levi replied. "Knox will know for sure once he reads his mind."

Dez rubbed the back of his neck. "I know it looks bad that he fled, but my brother's not a killer. Yeah, I know Marshall's no angel. But neither was Enzo, once upon a time."

True. When it came to punishments, they only had a temporary effect on Marshall. Still, he was nowhere near as wild and rebellious as he was years ago.

"Knox's walk through Marshall's mind will hopefully confirm that he's innocent," said Levi, feeling pretty certain that would be the case. Petty crimes were the man's style, not cold-blooded murders. And, given Marshall wasn't alive when Moira was murdered, he would only be guilty of the recent killings if he was a copycat. Levi could see no reason why Marshall would bother to do any such thing.

"I'll make sure he doesn't pull a stunt like this again," said Dez. "Really, though, I can't say I blame him for wanting to protect his son."

Neither could Levi.

# CHAPTER FOURTEEN

Piper waved to her client as he headed to the reception desk to pay for his tattoo. Removing her gloves, she let out a long sigh that came from the soul. After a further seven days of she and Levi trying to *find their way* as platonic anchors, her demon was about ready to scream. It hadn't initially put up too much of a protest over the ending of the agreement, because it hadn't expected either him or Piper to hold out for more than a day or two. But they had, and so the entity was unbearably frustrated right now.

Hell, so was Piper.

It shouldn't be this hard to go back to the way things were in the beginning. She wasn't a person who struggled to walk away from a relationship that had no future, so ending what had been nothing more than a simple arrangement should be easy. It wasn't. And fuck if she didn't miss him.

She still had him in her life, of course, but it wasn't the same. She'd lost pieces of him. Lost the easiness they'd once had.

More, she'd gotten used to waking up to the warmth of his body or to the touch of his hands and mouth. She'd gotten used to spending her nights with him as they'd settled together in bed—sometimes sleeping, sometimes talking, sometimes watching TV.

She'd also gotten used to coming hard on a daily basis, so her libido was kind of like *what the fuck is happening here?*

And then there was that godforsaken awkwardness. It often dissipated after they spent several hours together. But each time they first reunited—whether it be of a morning, or when he collected her from work, or whenever he came back to his apartment after venturing out for some reason—the strange vibe returned. And it hadn't begun to ease in intensity yet.

It would eventually, though. Piper believed that. She had to. The alternative? This crap came between her and Levi little by little. The truth was . . . it was already starting to.

She now didn't like how much time they spent together. She didn't like or feel comfortable living in his home. She didn't want him touching her in even the most casual sense, because it always reminded her of how he *used* to touch her. Thankfully, it was rare that he even so much as brushed his arm against hers as they walked.

It had gotten to the point where she sought subtle ways of avoiding being alone with him. She visited her parents, retreated to his guest room often, and spent time with her co-workers who'd *uber* fast become not only her friends but saviors. Sensing she needed a buffer, they often turned up at Levi's apartment to see her or they invited her to go here or there with them.

Piper wouldn't have thought she'd ever regret agreeing to his proposal, because that would be wishing away their time together. But now that there was the uncomfortable gulf between them, she wished she'd listened to her gut and kept things platonic.

Whereas she'd once lamented that they would eventually spend much time apart, now she was glad of it. She even looked forward to it. She needed a reprieve from not only the emotional hurt but also the sexual need that gave her no quarter and relentlessly plagued her system. Distance would help with that.

Although it was plain to see that Levi's attraction to her hadn't yet passed, he didn't appear to be going through any of the emotional struggles she was dealing with. He did, however, seem aggravated by the awkwardness they couldn't quite shift. And so he should be. No one should have to feel ill at ease in their own home.

She suspected he longed for Piper to return to her house so they could have some space, but she hadn't suggested moving out of his apartment. He'd never go for it—he took the matter of protecting his psi-mate seriously. Her proposal would only lead to a pointless argument, and there was enough tension between them as it was.

Her inner demon was tired of this shit. Tired of Piper hurting, of her missing him, of both she and Levi fighting the sexual chemistry. In the entity's mind, it was all senseless and they were simply being stubborn. It saw no reason why sex would complicate things. Due to its limited emotional spectrum, it would never worry that it might *fall in love* with their anchor. It didn't feel love. Couldn't.

It could, however, form intense and lifelong attachments to people. At the moment, the entity was possessive of Levi, but there was no attachment. Which was a relief, because at this point in time—with the way things stood—that attachment wouldn't be platonic, which meant the demon would never accept him having another woman in his life. It would instead expect to have his total commitment, not caring how he felt about it.

Yeah, that would be bad.

Piper didn't need to wonder if Levi's demon had accepted the new platonic nature to their dynamics yet. Not when the brands it left on her body hadn't faded in the slightest. But there was a chance that the entity was on its way to becoming accustomed to the idea. When that eventually happened, it would hit her own demon hard.

Forcing her thoughts away from the matter, she concentrated on cleaning her station and her equipment. Her last client for the day would be arriving in half an hour, so she'd have time for a coffee break.

"Piper?" Khloë called out.

Looking up from the chair she'd been wiping down, Piper blanked her expression as she spotted Celeste at the reception desk. *Oh, Lord.*

Its tolerance level ridiculously low, her inner demon hissed out a breath. Like Piper, it had been expecting this 'visit.' The only thing that came as a surprise was that it hadn't happened sooner. But then, Celeste liked to play mind games, so perhaps she'd delayed making a move, hoping to lull Piper into believing the banshee had backed down.

Aware that her co-workers were on alert, Piper crossed to her. "Celeste," she greeted simply. "What brings you here?"

"Can we talk in private?" the banshee asked.

Since Piper would rather her personal business wasn't aired in public—particularly in front of clients—she looked at Harper. "Can I use your office?"

"Sure." The Prime shot Celeste a look of warning that the banshee would be smart to heed. Whether Celeste would or not was another thing altogether.

Piper led her stepsister into the office and then leaned back against the desk, partially propping her butt on the surface. Her inner demon kept its narrowed gaze homed in on the banshee.

"I'll get right to the point." Celeste halted a few feet away from her and briefly glanced around the room. "I heard you formed the anchor bond with Levi."

"You heard correctly."

Levi's mind slid against Piper's, and then his voice poured into her mind. *Send Celeste away. She's not worth your time.*

Apparently either Enzo or Dez had given him a heads-up that she was here. Unsurprising.

*It's best to let her purge her system of whatever she wants to say,* Piper told him.

"And how are you finding 'anchor life?'" asked Celeste.

Well that wasn't a question that Piper cared to truthfully answer. "Why are you here?"

"To laugh, really."

Piper's brows snapped together. "Laugh?"

Celeste's mouth curled into a cruel smile. "Oh yes, things went exactly as I knew they would."

Levi's mind touched Piper's again. *You don't owe it to her to hear her out.*

*Never said I did,* Piper told him as she folded her arms and waited for Celeste to expand.

"It's no secret that I didn't want you and Levi to claim each other. Even the very thought of it hurt. And I hated that it hurt . . . because it forced me to face that he still has too much of a hold over me."

Piper blinked, surprised Celeste would admit to what she evidently saw as a weakness.

*Send her out or I'm coming over,* said Levi, the imperious bastard.

Not a fan of that tone, Piper clipped, *Don't fire orders at me, Levi. If I want to talk to someone, I'll talk to someone.*

A soft male curse floated into her mind.

Celeste looked at the floor. "He was right when he accused me of only wanting him back to spite you. Well, *partially* right. I also wanted to hurt him, and that meant getting him back first. But I saw that he wasn't going to be up for revisiting the past, and I don't care to waste my time."

Funny. She was wasting it now. She *had* to know that Piper really couldn't care less what Celeste thought about anything. Then again, Piper had been dancing around her wants and moods for years until recently, so maybe not.

"I didn't bother appealing for you to reconsider accepting him as your anchor. I knew you wouldn't. You've wanted Levi for a long time, and there was no way you'd hesitate to use the bond to trap him and make it so that he can't ever leave you."

Piper's frown deepened. "That's not how it went down at all."

Ignoring that, the banshee continued, "The thing is . . . the one who was being played was actually you, not him."

Exhaling an annoyed sigh, Piper scratched her temple. "Celeste, I really need to work—"

"I heard about the agreement you two made."

Piper tensed. *The fuck?*

"Someone overheard you mention it to Larkin. Don't you see that he used your crush to get you to bond with him? Don't reject the idea, *think* about it. Levi uses whatever means necessary to get what he wants. He knew he could get close to you using sex, so he proposed that you two share a bed until the bond was formed. It didn't occur to you that *maybe* he'd be happy to stop fucking you once you were bonded because he'd only been doing it to get his way? Seriously?"

Piper's stomach bottomed out. No, she hadn't considered that at all. Until right now.

"But he didn't merely sleep with you, did he? He made the kind of mark on you that's hard to scrub away." A faraway look entered Celeste's eyes. "The thing with Levi is that he knows how to make a woman feel owned," she added, a sad note to her voice. "So then it's such a shock to the body and mind when he drops you."

Her scalp prickling, Piper swallowed. As much as she despised it, she could relate to what her stepsister had said.

"He's so intense with women in the beginning," Celeste continued. "Bombs them with attention. Drinks in their attention. Makes himself a part of their everyday life so that they can't picture one that *doesn't* include him."

Piper recalled telling Larkin that she'd gotten so used to having Levi around all the time that she couldn't imagine not seeing him each and every day. The harpy's response drifted to her . . .

"*He* made sure *you got used to it. He wanted you to feel like you couldn't imagine not having him around. He's sneaky that way.*"

"He doesn't demand exclusivity of women," Celeste went on. "He doesn't need to. They can't picture having another man touch them. I used to lie to him that I was sleeping with other guys, because I wanted him to care. He didn't. Some perverse part of him gets a kick out of knowing that whoever fucks a woman he owns will fall short; that *he* is all they can think about. And that's exactly how it goes. I mean, truly, would you want another man to touch you?"

The thought alone made Piper's skin crawl.

Clearly sensing that, Celeste nodded. "He *ensured* you couldn't stomach the idea. Don't beat yourself up about it, though. You're not alone. It's what he does to women. He burrows deep under their skin. Once he's sure they feel utterly owned, his interest begins to fade."

Pausing, Celeste took a step closer, her lips pursed. "It's kind of like a kid being so excited to finally have a toy they wanted.

But once they own it, once the novelty of playing with it has worn off, it just becomes yet another toy in the box. They don't appreciate it anymore, they're more interested in what they can buy next."

Piper wished she could snort at that, but it made her think of his collection of unusual sculptures and paintings. Whenever she asked about their history, he could never remember. He would just shrug, indifferent. There was no appreciation in his eyes when he looked at them.

"Maybe something unique might be a little more valued," began Celeste, "but it'll simply be put on a shelf rather than in the toy box. The kid might look at and even touch the unique item on the shelf from time to time, but it's still just a toy at the end of the day.

"In toy terms, you're a limited edition, Piper. A collector's item. One he'll shelve, dust, keep clean, and never give away. But you'll still only ever be one of his many possessions."

Her arms still folded, Piper flexed her fingers. Her inner demon rolled its eyes, not particularly seeing the problem with being thought of as a possession. But then, it was just as bad for collecting people.

"God help you if you meet a man you want to date. Levi won't make that easy for you. He won't like others touching or taking his collector's item from his shelf. Nu-uh. Like he said to me . . . he looks at you and sees his anchor. He doesn't see *Piper*. No. He doesn't see who you are but *what* you are."

It took a lot for Piper not to wince, because that felt a little too close to the truth.

"Oh, and you're wrong if you think he'll let you return to your house. He'll want you living somewhere in his building so he can monitor your day-to-day activities. Next he'll buy you a car, because he'll want you to drive something *he* bought you—essentially marking his territory. He'll seek to have a firm hold over your world."

No, he wouldn't go *that* far. He'd always watch over Piper, but he wouldn't try to take the reins. Even if only because he knew it wouldn't work.

Celeste sniffed. "I could have warned you about all this earlier, but you wouldn't have listened to me." She slanted her head. "You're telling yourself that I've got it all wrong; that Levi wouldn't use sex as a tool."

Actually, Piper wasn't thinking that at all. She knew how ruthless he could be, especially when it came to going after what he wanted. He'd admitted it to her several times, completely unrepentant.

"I'm not claiming he's a bad person, Piper. Just that he's a collector. He likes for things to belong to him. But they don't hold his interest for long. So many of the women in his past were hurt by his withdrawal, just as I'll bet you're hurting right now. The worst of it is . . . if he was to kiss you, you wouldn't push him away. You'll always be waiting for him to pick you back up off that shelf and play with you. *Unless* you face now what others have found so hard to confront—you're not as important to him as you think you are. Oh, you're important as his anchor. But if you weren't his psi-mate, he'd have walked away by now . . . *if* he'd have even gotten involved with you in the first place."

A hard knock came at the office door.

Celeste threw it a haughty look before settling her gaze back on Piper. "Don't worry, I'm leaving. You know, part of me pities you. Like I said, he still has some hold over me. But I can stay away from him. I don't have him constantly in my orbit making demands of me. But you? You can't say the same. You'll *never* be able to say the same. He won't ever let you go, Piper. He won't ever loosen his grip on you. And anytime he feels you straining to get a little bit of distance from him, he'll do what it takes to stop you—even if it means occasionally having sex with you to lead you to temporarily believe that you two could be more than just anchors. So good luck trying to live a life that isn't dominated by Levi. You're going to need all the luck you can get."

Celeste spun on her heel and crossed to the door. Whipping it open, she paused at the sight of Devon and Khloë—both of whom were probably eavesdropping, going by the almighty scowls on their faces. Once Celeste skirted around them and left, the two females hurried into the office.

Piper blew out a breath. "You heard all that, huh?"

"We wanted to be sure she wasn't yelling at or threatening you," said Devon. "If Harper and Raini weren't busy with clients, they'd have been lingering at the door too. And they'd be just as livid as I am right now. Just to give you a heads-up, Enzo said that Levi's on his way here."

"Great," Piper mumbled.

"Don't listen to the things that bitch spouted," advised Khloë. "She's full of shit at the best of times."

Unfolding her arms, Piper gripped the edges of the desk behind her. "As much as I hate to say it, she made some good points just now. Levi *is* a collector. He *can* get under your skin. And he *will* do what it takes to get what he wants."

"There were plenty of truths in what she said," Khloë allowed, "but she twisted them."

Devon nodded. "He didn't use sex to get close to you and win you over so he could make you accept the bond. He wouldn't do that."

Probably not, but . . . "I do feel collected, though. I can't count the amount of times he and his demon have made a point of stating I belong to them."

"As their anchor, you kind of do in a sense," Devon gently pointed out.

Well, yeah. "But they say it *a lot*."

Devon laid a hand on Piper's arm. "You're not a simple commodity to Levi."

"I know. But outside of being his psi-mate, I'm not important to him. Not that it really matters either way. I can't have him in my life in more than an anchor capacity. I've accepted that. But I hate that Celeste is right—I do feel owned, I do feel sickened by the thought of another guy touching me, and I probably wouldn't reject Levi if he made a pass at me."

"I'd like to think that—" Devon cut off, cocking her head. "The bell above the door just chimed. That's probably him."

Piper hadn't heard the bell, but she didn't have hellcat enhanced senses. "I don't want him to see that she got to me. He'll demand to know what she said, and I'd rather not get into it."

"Okay," said Khloë, "so then we stroll out of the office, casual as you please, while having an everyday conversation."

His nerves rubbed raw with anger, Levi prowled into the studio just as Piper, Devon, and Khloë walked out of the office, chatting about . . . wolf spiders?

He studied his anchor. No injuries or ruffled clothing, so it was unlikely that a fight had occurred. Her expression . . . he couldn't quite read it.

Faint lines of strain marked her face, but he couldn't figure out their source. Anger? Impatience? Confusion? He truly couldn't tell, nor could he decipher the emotion that flickered in her gaze for the briefest moment when she looked at him.

Halting in front of her, he demanded, "You okay?"

She shrugged. "I'm fine."

No, she wasn't. Not really. But it would be shitty of him to push her for an honest answer right here in front of God and everyone.

He wanted so badly to reach out and palm the side of her neck, or rub her upper arm, or give her nape a comforting little squeeze. Something. Anything. But he didn't trust that he'd be easily able to step back. He was more likely to eat up her space, snatch a fistful of her hair, and take her mouth.

He balled up his hands. "Did Celeste threaten you?"

"No. She wasn't here to bitch at me for forming the bond with you either, before you ask."

He *was* about to ask that. "Then what did she want?"

"To do what she often does: annoy me for her own entertainment. She probably also hoped to provoke me into an argument so she could run back to Whitney and Joe with little tales."

He growled. "I warned her not to use you as her punchbag anymore."

"You had to know she was unlikely to heed your warning for long."

Aware that Devon and Khloë still flanked Piper, their postures protective, he cast them both a questioning look. They floundered under his scrutiny, gave him breezy smiles that didn't quite meet their eyes, and then melted away.

"You didn't need to come here," Piper said to him, a note of irritation in her tone.

Feeling unwelcome, he bristled. "I told you I would if you didn't get rid of her."

"And I told you I can talk to whoever I want. Celeste is not a threat to me. Nor is she someone I can forever avoid and ignore, because she's family. It was better to hear her out and get it over with, so I did."

Maybe, but . . . "She had no right to come to your place of work."

"Well it's not like she could have turned up at your apartment to see me, is it? You wouldn't have let her into the complex."

Too fucking right he wouldn't have.

"It left her no choice but to seek me out elsewhere, so that was what she did." Piper let out a subtle sigh, and her composed expression cracked. The lines on her face deepened. That undefinable emotion flashed in her eyes yet again. Her mouth set into a flat line. But then her armor slammed back into place, and it was like the crack had never happened.

His brow furrowing in concern, Levi took a step closer, not liking how she stiffened. "What's going on in that head of yours? Don't say 'nothing.' Something is swirling around up there, and it's upsetting you. I don't like it."

"My head is fine. I'm just tired. It's been a long day."

It had been a long fucking week. A week of craving her, missing her, trying to adjust to their new situation. He was failing massively at the latter.

His body, wound tight with unmet needs and far too desperate for her, seemed more acutely affected by her presence than ever before. The slightest thing made his blood heat—a hint of her scent, a flash of her dimples, the sway of her hips, the curving of her mouth. And knowing she wore his demon's brands beneath those clothes only made the whole thing harder. He was pretty sure the entity had counted on that when it marked her. The little shit found Levi's struggles amusing.

His demon had by no means given up on trying to make Levi's control snap. It constantly sent him mental snapshots—some sexually explicit memories, some of Piper with faceless men. As such, a swirling brew of frustration, anger, and need sat in the pit of Levi's stomach. And now motherfucking Celeste had evidently gotten into Piper's head somehow, and God only knew what play that bitch had made.

"What did Celeste say that's messing with you right now?"

"Nothing in particular. Don't get all worked up about her visit. She's not worth the emotional energy."

"True enough. And you're good at not letting her get to you. But she's currently up there in your head, toying with your thoughts. How she wormed her way in, I can't imagine. Tell me what she said, Piper. Let me help you shove her back out of your mind."

Piper swallowed. "She didn't say anything worth repeating. Anyway, I have another client coming in soon, I can't afford to sit around chatting."

He opened his mouth to speak again, but then Knox's psyche bumped his.

*I have good news and bad news*, said the Prime. *The bad news is that our killer struck again. The good news is that he didn't kill his victim this time . . . though I have no fucking clue why.*

# CHAPTER FIFTEEN

It wasn't a single mother with a young child this time. It was a twenty-four-year-old woman and her three-year-old sister. Missy and little Kyla had been home alone for a week, since their parents were on a business trip. As the single mothers of the lair were now well-protected, it appeared that the killer had sought out an alternative.

But he'd let her live.

Levi drove to the address of Missy and Kyla's grandparents, where both girls would be staying until their parents returned. Even as he knew he needed to focus on the current matter, his mind kept drifting back to Piper; to worrying over just exactly what idea Celeste had planted in her head.

He silently cursed the banshee to hell and back. Things were already strained between him and Piper. The bitch had only made it worse, and for what? What had she hoped to achieve? What was the point when it wouldn't change that he was in Piper's life? And why wouldn't Piper just tell him what was said?

Resolved that he'd get to the bottom of the matter later, Levi cut off the car's engine as he reached his destination. Knox, Larkin, and Tanner were waiting for him in the front yard. Keenan pulled up mere moments after Levi.

As the five of them gathered on the lawn, Knox said, "I haven't interviewed Missy yet, but I spoke to her grandmother. Lois claims that Missy's holding up well under the circumstances. Missy hasn't objected to us interviewing her. She wants justice. If any of you have questions for her, telepath them to me. I don't want several people firing questions at her, it may make her overwhelmed."

Levi and the other sentinels nodded.

"Force members are examining the crime scene as we speak." Knox slid his gaze to Levi. "As no deaths occurred, there'll be nothing for you to sense. Nonetheless, you're welcome to walk through the house if you wish to. For now, though, let's concentrate on Missy."

Inside her grandparents' living room, they found her sitting on a bulky upholstered chair, her arms wrapped around the legs she'd pulled up to her chest.

Levi, Knox, and the other sentinels took seats around the room, politely declining Lois' offer of drinks. The woman stood behind Missy's chair in support.

"Can you tell us what happened?" Knox gently asked her.

Missy licked her lips. "I don't know who he was."

"That's all right."

"No, it's not. I can't see his face in my head," she explained, clearly close to freaking out. "It's just a blur. He told me I'd forget him, that I wouldn't remember what he looked like, but I didn't believe him."

Levi held back a frown.

"Talk us through what happened," Knox softly coaxed.

She rubbed her chin against her knees. "I don't know how he got into the house. I was asleep, and suddenly . . . he was just there. In my head. Telling me to wake up. I did, and he was sitting on my bed. He told me I was his now; that I didn't need to be afraid; that we'd be the most perfect family."

Levi exchanged a look with Larkin.

"I wanted to scream," Missy went on. "I wanted to fight him. I wanted to telepathically call for help. *Something.* But I felt my mouth curve into a smile, and I heard myself wish him goodnight." She coughed a bitter, humorless chuckle. "*I wished him goodnight.*"

Lois stroked her hair, and Missy let out a shuddery breath before continuing, "I wasn't in control of myself. He took me over. He didn't do it to Kyla, just me. I knew he had to be the one who'd killed Diem and Emma. I knew he'd kill me, too. But I couldn't get help. I could only say what he wanted me to say. Only do what he wanted me to do."

Which correlated with the claim that Emma's soul made that she'd had no control.

Frowning, Missy shook her head. "It all felt so scripted. Like it was based on a really cheesy movie about a big sappily happy family. He called me Rosalind. And he would call Kyla either 'Bessie' or 'Munchkin'. But although he treated me like I was his partner, he never made me . . . touch him. He never touched me *that way.* But there'd be gentle hugs or shoulder massages or foot rubs." She shuddered, repulsion rippling across her face.

"Did he hurt you physically?" asked Knox.

"No. There were times I thought he would, because he looked *so angry*. But then he'd leave the room or tell me to sleep—and I would, like a damn robot. He never hurt Kyla either. He doted on her. It creeped me out, but it was better than the alternative.

"I was always worried that he'd change toward her. Especially near the end. He was so mad, then. Mad at me because I was supposed to have learned to love him. Mad at himself because he hadn't really wanted me; that I wasn't 'right.' Like I was the wrong brand of fabric softener."

It was more like she wasn't 'right' to the killer because she was Kyla's sister, not her mother.

"In the beginning, he was always smiling and laughing and saying how lucky we were to have such a beautiful family. Even when there were tears dripping down my face. He didn't acknowledge it when I cried. It was weird, I'd be smiling and chatting merrily because he was *forcing* me to, but the tears would fall because I was sobbing inside. He pretended it away. At first, anyway."

Knox leaned forward, bracing his arms on his thighs and clasping his hands. "At what point did he stop?"

"His mood changed after a few days," replied Missy. "Sometimes, he'd sit in silence and stare at the wall. Other times, words would just spill out of him."

"What sort of things did he say?"

"That he and his demon are at war. That they've been at war for a very long time. He said one of them wants normality, and the other wants blood and death. The entity hates that no one can remember them. He said his 'curse' was to always be forgotten—whatever that means—but I didn't think I really would forget him." Tears filled Missy's eyes. "He was right, though. I don't remember his name, what he looks like, or even if he was familiar to me before that day. I can recall the stuff he said, but I can't describe his voice because I *literally* can't remember what it sounds like."

Levi's scalp prickled. Maybe that was why no one had been able to give an accurate description of the male who'd come and gone from the victims' houses. He *couldn't* be remembered.

Missy inhaled deeply. "He said he was tired. Tired of being forgotten. Tired of being alone. Tired of fighting his demon. He kept saying he wanted it all to be over." She sniffled. "I thought he'd kill me. But he said it was *his* fault that things didn't work. That he shouldn't have chosen me." Her brow creased. "He said there was another time he 'got it wrong.' A time he'd mistakenly chosen a woman who was an aunt instead of a mom. He said he regretted that."

Levi tensed. The bastard had to have meant Moira. When it seemed that the killer's MO was to go after single mothers, Levi had wondered if the killer had initially thought that Moira was his mother.

"No matter how hard I try, I can't picture him." Missy's voice broke. "I just can't."

"Would you be willing to allow Piper to try to help you?" asked Knox.

Levi inwardly recoiled at the idea, biting back a reflexive objection by sheer force of will.

"Piper might not be able to see him if he has literally vanished from even your subconscious memories, but it's not impossible," Knox added.

Licking her lips, Missy gave a slow nod. "Okay. But can we maybe do it tomorrow?"

"Of course, I'll bring her by then," Knox told her, rising to his feet.

Once again gathered in the front yard with Knox and the other sentinels, Levi said, "If I was able to read emotional vibes from her house, I would probably have picked up a lot of frustration, regret, and bitterness. He didn't like 'making do.' He couldn't keep up the fantasy as well as he usually does."

"Because it was always in the back of his mind that Missy and Kyla were sisters, not mother and daughter," said Keenan.

Tanner scratched at his jaw. "If it wasn't for the fact that he's never fussed on whether the kid of his target is a boy or girl, I'd say Rosalind and Bessie were his *real* family. A family he lost and consistently tries to recreate."

"It seems more likely he renamed Missy and Kyla because he needed to see them as other people, not their true selves," said Knox. "At least now we understand why no one can ever give us a good description of him."

Larkin cocked her head. "Imagine how hard it would be if no one ever remembered you. I mean, *think* about it. You'd have nobody, because you can't build something with someone who'll forget you if you leave their side. It would be almost like you were invisible, because you'd make no lasting impression on anyone. He said that was his 'curse.' Do you think he meant that literally?" she asked no one in particular.

"It's possible." Levi pulled out his cell phone. "An incantor will know. I'll ask Mia."

Keenan frowned. "Not Ella?"

Levi shook his head. "Ella has a wide range of knowledge, but her sister's more knowledgeable when it comes to curses and hexes."

Mia answered after three rings. "Levi, it's good to hear from you."

"How are you doing, Mia?" he asked.

"Good, good," she replied. "Congrats on finding your psi-mate—Ella told me all about it. You'd better introduce Piper to us soon or we're gonna get cranky."

"Noted."

"Excellent. Now tell me why you called."

"Can someone be cursed so that they would never be remembered by others?"

There was a short moment of silence. "Such a curse does

exist, but a person would have to be enraged to inflict it on another."

"Why?"

"The cost is more than most would bear. The caster of the spell, too, will not be remembered by anyone other than the person they cursed. And there is no way to lift that curse."

The latter was unusual, from what he knew. "Thanks, Mia." After ringing off, he relayed the information to Knox and the other sentinels.

"Maybe he pissed someone off and this is his punishment," mused Tanner.

"I'd say so," said Larkin. "I mean, he was essentially robbed of relationships—past, present, and future. His family and loved ones won't remember him, and he has no way of building new relationships to compensate for that. He'll always be alone."

Keenan hummed. "Someone definitely wanted him to suffer."

"I'd say they got what they wanted," said Tanner. "And we can't really say the cost was the lives of the women he murdered. That was all on him."

Keenan twisted his mouth. "Looking at the situation, I can see why he found it easy to let Missy live. He killed the other women because they weren't what he wanted in a partner. In his view, they'd proven to be useless. He held them at fault for how things didn't work out. But with Missy, he believed *he* was in the wrong, he believed he should have chosen someone else."

"I don't think that's the only reason he let her live," said Knox. "He told Missy that he was tired and wanted all this to be over. I believe he wants to be caught."

Levi considered that for a moment. "He knew she'd pass on whatever he told her, essentially giving us clues. You know, at first, I didn't get why he'd target Missy when she lives right next door to Sera, who's being watched over by the Force. That's risky. But maybe he was tempting fate, hoping that those patrolling the area might just see and stop him."

"I think he's hoping *you'll* be the one who stops him," Tanner said to Levi. "That's why he's striking at people in our lair. That's why he wants your attention. Maybe there's something sentimental for him about being brought down by a kid he once spared."

"Perhaps," said Knox. "It might be good to talk to Dez's brother. Marshall could have seen something from outside when he was lurking around Sera's house to watch over her and their son. Not that he'd be able to give us a description of our killer, but he may have seen or heard something helpful."

"Want me to question him?" asked Tanner.

Knox pulled out his cell phone. "I'll do it now. I'll put him on speakerphone."

"Hello?" Marshall soon answered, a nervous tremor to his voice. Well not everyone felt all warm and fuzzy on realizing they were receiving a call from their indisputably merciless Prime.

"I have a question for you," Knox told him. "When you were loitering outside Sera's house, I'm guessing—given how nosy you are—that you occasionally glanced through the neighbor's windows. I need to know if you saw or heard anything suspicious happening in Missy's house."

Dead silence. "Is Missy all right?"

"Yes, but she had an unwelcome visitor—something the entire lair will hear all about in due course, so you'll soon have the answers to the many questions that are no doubt beginning to gather in your head. Right now, I need you to answer *my* question."

A puff of breath. "I saw a guy sitting at her dinner table, but I can't picture him."

"Is there anything you *do* remember about him?"

"Uh . . . well, I heard him whistling a tune—the window was partially open. A song my great-grandmother used to hum. 'Dreamers Dream.' It's from an old musical."

"I know the song. Anything else?"

"No, sorry."

"Let me know if something else comes to mind." With that, Knox ended the call.

"I don't know that tune Marshall mentioned," said Tanner.

"Well I'm not singing it to you," said Knox, making the hellhound snort. "Google it or something." He cut his gaze to Levi. "Talk to Piper. Tell her what happened and that we'll need her help. I highly doubt she'll object." He squinted. "I do hope *you're* not about to object on her behalf."

Levi would if he thought it would do any good. "I don't like what using that ability does to her. I don't like that she'll have to see and feel what Missy went through. But I won't interfere. Piper would only get pissed at me. I don't want that." They were having enough issues as it was.

Soon, Knox dismissed all but Larkin, since she was his temporary bodyguard. Levi and the other male sentinels headed to their respective vehicles. All three then made their way to the Underground, where they began their walk along the strip to the studio. The place would be closing any moment now.

"It bothers me that the killer went off script," said Tanner. "Any woman could be next, if he's so desperate to repeat his crimes that he'll settle for others whether he enjoys it or not. Devon's pregnant, that might be close enough to a single mother for him."

"He won't get near her, Tanner."

"No, he won't," Keenan agreed. "And she'd claw off his dick if he did."

Snorting, Tanner rolled back his shoulders. "I'll be glad when she goes on maternity leave. Maybe I can convince her to do it sooner."

Levi softly snickered. "Good luck with that." Arriving at the studio, he pushed open the door. The five females paused in their cleaning, their expressions somber. Levi only had eyes for Piper.

As he crossed to her, she sighed and said, "Harper told us about Missy. She heard about it from Knox. Is Missy okay?"

"She's doing about as well as anyone could expect of her," Levi replied, resisting the urge to reach out and place a comforting hand on Piper's shoulder. Dammit, he *shouldn't* have to resist touching his own damn anchor. "I'll tell you more when we're in the car." He wanted to get her home, where she'd be safer. He was always nervous about her being out in public.

Inside his car a short while later, Piper had no sooner clicked on her seatbelt than she prodded him for the information he'd promised.

Levi told her much of Missy's ordeal, reluctantly adding, "We're going to need your help with her. She can't remember the bastard. We think he might be cursed to always be forgotten. Literally cursed."

Piper blinked. "Wow."

"Knox is hoping you might be able to help us ID him by taking a dip in her mind."

"You don't seem happy about that."

Levi switched on the engine. "I've never liked the toll that ability takes on you. I like it even less now."

"I'm used to it."

"You use that phrase too often—when you speak of this gift, when you talk of Celeste's tantrums, when you mention the shit you get from relatives of the criminals you identify. You'd be lying if you said that being accustomed to it all makes any of it easier on you."

"In any case, I'll of course do what I can to help. I can't promise I'll see his face, though. Not if Missy can't recall it. Just like I can't see events that happened at a time when a person was too young to commit it to memory. And if some curse is really at play, I doubt Missy's memory of his physical features is simply repressed."

"I understand you might not be able to help," Levi assured her. "We all do. Knox simply wants you to give it a try. That's all anyone can and will ask of you. Now, are you going to tell me what play Celeste made earlier?"

Piper did a double-take at the abrupt change of topic. "We covered this already. She was merely being her usual annoying self."

"Then why are you so reluctant to talk about it?"

"Why are you so determined to hear about it?"

"Because it's obvious that she managed to upset you. You're clearly hurting, and I'm not at all good with that. No one gets to fuck with my anchor." Her eyes flared with something that made his chest hurt, and he felt like he'd said the wrong thing. "Piper—"

"Being my psi-mate doesn't make you privy to every thought that runs through my head," she said, her voice stiff. "There are things you don't want to talk about. I accept that. Now you need to accept that there's something *I* don't want to talk about. If that changes, I'll let you know. Unless or until that happens, drop the subject. It's not in your nature, I know. But you need to give me this. I make a lot of concessions for you. Now it's your turn."

Levi inwardly cursed. He hated that she was hurting and he simply wanted to fix it. But how could he push her on this when she was absolutely right—she *did* make a lot of concessions for him. More than he deserved. And yes, there were things he hadn't yet discussed with her, such as the full truth about his aunt. Pressing her right now would make him both a hypocrite and an asshole. "Fine. But if she confronts you again—"

"Let's leave it at 'fine.'"

Silence fell between them. Thick. Heavy. Uncomfortable. At that moment, she seemed more emotionally unreachable than she ever had before, and he had no fucking clue what to do about it.

Noon the following day, Piper trailed after Levi as they entered the house of Missy's grandparents. Her stomach was heavy with dread, just as it typically was during such times. Not that Piper would even consider backing out, much to Levi's disapproval. He'd asked her four times this morning if she was certain she wanted to do this. Each time Piper had confirmed that she was up for it, he'd looked both disappointed and unsurprised.

It was kind of touching that he'd choose her emotional welfare over getting answers to a mystery he desperately needed to solve for the safety of their lair . . . because it meant he really was putting her first. Well, putting *his anchor* first. If Celeste was his psi-mate, she'd receive the same intense level of attention and protectiveness from him. It would be natural, of course. But the whole thing highlighted that Celeste had been right when she said, "*He doesn't see who you are but* what *you are*."

Maybe that was a good thing, though. Maybe Piper should try doing the same with him. It would provide some emotional distance and help her move on from him. That would sure be welcome. Because she was too aware of him now. Aware of where he stood, when he moved, what emotional vibes he gave off. Like her entire being was attempting to attune itself to his.

Walking into the living room, Piper exchanged quick greetings with Knox, Harper, Larkin, and Lois before firmly settling her attention on the female sitting gingerly on the edge of an armchair. Piper gave her a gentle smile. "Hi, Missy."

"Hi." Missy rubbed her thighs. "I know I should say thank you for coming and stuff, but part of me hates that someone else will see how helpless I was."

"That's entirely understandable, though no one would think less of you for being powerless," said Piper. "We don't have to do this if you don't want to. No one will force you."

"No, I *need* to do this. It's driving me crazy that I can't remember someone I spent five days *hating*. And . . . the truth is that I blocked him out a few times. Just curled into a mental ball in a corner of my mind. I don't know what happened during those times."

"You'll get no judgment from me or anyone else. People often disappear into their own minds to protect themselves—it's instinctive."

"I know, I do, I just . . . No offense, but can we get this over with?"

"Absolutely." Kneeling before Missy, Piper lifted a hand. "I need to touch your forehead. Is that okay?"

Missy nodded, her lips trembling. "Brace yourself, because this won't be fun for you."

No, it wouldn't. But it helped that Levi had already given Piper a bullet-point version of what occurred. It not only warned her of what was to come, it meant she knew what details they already had. Levi and the others were interested in what Missy *hadn't* passed on.

Piper closed her eyes, rested her hand on the other woman's head, and thrust her consciousness into hers. Piper 'flipped' through her worst memories until—*there*.

Taking a deep breath, she sank into the real-life nightmare. She experienced it all through Missy's senses—him sitting on her bed as he announced they'd be a family, days of watching him smile and laugh but also brood and rant, his declaration that he wouldn't kill her as he'd killed the others.

She felt Missy's fear and powerlessness and fury as if those emotions were her own. Emotions that beat at her soul, roiled her stomach, seized her lungs, and overworked her heart.

When Piper finally withdrew from the memory, she realized she was shaking. Strong hands snatched her from the floor, and then Levi was holding her tightly to him. And God help her, she didn't fight him. She leaned against him while Missy's emotions bled from her system. Fucking *hell* that had been brutal.

"Did you see his face?" asked Missy.

Finally pulling back—which wasn't easy to do, because Levi wasn't inclined to release her—Piper gave a slow shake of the head. "He was a blur the whole time, I'm sorry." Unsurprised by the disappointment thickening the air, she added, "He kept whistling a tune. I don't recognize it." Piper hummed it aloud.

"I know it," said Knox. "'Dreamers Dream.' What else can you tell us?"

"He once ranted about a witch who apparently held him responsible for a crime he didn't commit," replied Piper. "She was convinced he'd raped and murdered her sister."

Knox pursed his lips. "In that case, I wouldn't be surprised if it was she who cursed him."

A question plaguing his mind, Levi telepathically reached out to Piper and asked, *Did he rape Missy during one of the times she withdrew into her mind?*

*No*, Piper told him. *He never once touched her sexually*. "His demon surfaced at one point."

Missy jerked back. "It did?"

Piper nodded. "It laughed. Not at you, at him. It regards him as weak because he won't admit to himself that he *likes* to kill; that he *likes* the control he's able to wield over others."

"He does seem to view himself as a victim," mused Harper.

"Agreed," said Piper. "He holds the witch responsible for what he's been 'forced' to do to 'emotionally survive.'"

Missy's eyes flared. "The only person who was *forced* to do anything was *me*."

"Indeed," said Levi. "So I'd have to side with his demon on one thing—the bastard's weak."

After Piper relayed other details that Missy hadn't reported—all of which seemed inconsequential—Knox announced it was time for them all to let Missy rest more.

As they walked down the front yard toward the cars, Harper gently nudged Piper. "You okay? You don't look good."

Piper shrugged. "Comes with the territory. I'll be fine in an hour or so."

Levi felt his mouth tighten. It was one thing to accept that there was a cost to using her ability, it was another to dismiss her own emotional reaction as if it had no relevance.

She licked her lips as she ran her gaze along everyone. "There was something else he said. Something I didn't think you'd want me to say in front of Missy and Lois."

Knox's gaze sharpened. "And that is?"

Piper looked at Levi. "He mentioned you. Said you're not as worked up about the murders as he thought you'd be."

Levi went very still, his stomach dropping.

"Also . . . I'm sorry to tell you this, but . . . he killed your aunt," she went on. "He talked about her. Said her mind was very dark—something he hadn't expected—and that he doubted you'd be the man you are today if you'd grown up with her as your guardian. He seemed to take pride in who you are. As if making you an orphan means he can take the credit and . . ."

She studied his face. "You don't look surprised by any of it. You were already aware of it."

He winced and opened his mouth to speak.

Piper lifted a hand. "It was a need-to-know thing. I didn't need to know, I get it."

She didn't seem upset or offended, but Levi still felt like a sack of shit. There'd been several times when he'd come close to telling her what she'd now learned for herself, but he'd always held back. And now he wished he hadn't.

"Thank you for your help today, Piper," said Knox.

She grimaced. "I don't feel like I did help much."

"You should," Knox insisted, taking the words from Levi's mouth. "We now know he literally is cursed. We know he truly is the man who murdered Levi's aunt—we assumed he was, of course, but we couldn't be one hundred percent sure until now. And we can be positive that he is in fact a demon, since his entity surfaced."

"I wasn't able to do what I came here to do, though. I wasn't able to get a glimpse of his face."

"No one thought you would. It was a long shot." Knox dipped his chin. "Again, thank you for your assistance."

Harper gave her arm a little squeeze. "Go home, eat, rest, maybe take a bath or something so you can relax. You can't go back to work in this state. You're still trembling, and you're white as a sheet."

Piper nodded. "I'll see you tomorrow, then."

"Tomorrow," she agreed.

After goodbyes were exchanged, Levi led her to his car. Inside it, he sighed. "I was going to tell you at some point that the recent killings could be linked to my aunt's murder—"

"It's okay, Levi," Piper assured him. It hurt that he'd kept her firmly out of the loop, but he was probably only permitted to speak plainly about the killer to very few people. "It's not like I didn't already know you're holding things back that you clearly don't want to talk about."

"I kept meaning to tell you, but there never seemed to be a right time. And at the moment, my past is all tangled up in the present shit fest. You've been my only bright spot, and I wanted to enjoy that."

Oh no, her heart didn't just squeeze.

"Selfish, I know, but there it is."

"Really, I'm not angry that you didn't tell me. Especially since it's sentinel stuff, and I doubt you would have gotten permission from Knox to share it with me anyway."

"You say that, but I know you're mad."

"Yes, I'm mad. I'm mad that a serial killer apparently killed your aunt. I'm angry that he's back on the scene and seems to believe he did you a fucking favor by making you an orphan. I'm mad because I saw what that motherfucker put Missy through, and I hate that he's on the loose." It all made her blood boil.

Levi laid his hand on her thigh, and the touch was so unexpected she almost flinched. "He'll be caught and stopped, Piper. I promise you that."

She didn't doubt him for a second.

Back in his apartment, he ushered her into the kitchen. "You need to eat."

She exhaled heavily, her shoulders sagging. "I'm tired, Levi."

"I know. But we need to talk."

"We don't. Truly. I'd never expect you to rip open old wounds for me." She'd never judge or be angry with someone for not wanting to share their personal pain.

"I *want* to tell you. Also, I don't want you to be alone. You can sleep once you've eaten. No, don't argue." He set his hands on her shoulders. "I know what you did today takes a lot out of you. I also know there's *no fucking way* it wasn't hard for you to see what Missy went through. I'm not going to ignore that you're feeling raw right now.

"Yeah, as you like to remind me, you're used to it. You're also used to turning inward and not leaning on anyone. Fuck that, Piper. You're not alone anymore. I'm here now. And just as you'd want me to turn to you if I was feeling like shit, I want you to turn to me."

Her chest going tight, she bit back the urge to snark that being her anchor didn't mean he had the right to expect her to rely on him . . . because it would have been an out-and-out lie. It *did* give him that right. Psi-mates were *supposed* to be there for each other. That was how it worked.

*He doesn't see who you are but* what *you are.*

Fuck if those words wouldn't stop poking at her. Piper had earlier made the decision to establish some emotional distance between her and Levi. Confiding in him here and now wouldn't exactly help with that. But he was right, if the situation had been reversed she'd have expected him to offload on her, and she'd have been hurt if he pushed her away.

Plus, he clearly wanted to get some stuff off his chest. She'd be a total bitch if she walked away from him. That wasn't who she was. So Piper sighed and said, "All right."

He let out a long breath. "Okay."

"But my stomach won't be able to handle anything heavier than a sandwich."

"A sandwich it is." He gave her shoulders a light squeeze. "Sit."

Taking a seat at the island, she watched as he pulled out bread, meat, and various condiments. It felt . . . weird to have someone insist on being at her side when she was feeling low. Not that her mother or Olive or Joe wouldn't have been there for her if they'd thought she needed them. But she rarely allowed people to *see* when she felt low.

"I can't promise I'll always come to you," she told him. "You're right, I pull inward. It's . . . automatic. Not a habit I'll easily break out of."

"It's too ingrained in you, I see that," he said. "And I suspect you made it a habit to hold in your feelings because Celeste enjoyed trampling on them. I'll bear that in mind, and I'll ask you to bear in mind that I won't stay away if I think you shouldn't be alone."

Fair enough. "I really am okay. Missy's emotions have bled from my system."

"And what about *your* emotions?"

"It was Missy who suffered, not me. I simply saw what happened."

He planted his palms on the island and leaned forward slightly. "It isn't that simple. You effectively witnessed a brutal crime—that's hard on anyone. You also felt what she felt, which will have only made it harder on you. My guess is you play down how it affects you because you feel that you don't have the right to be upset when it didn't physically happen to you."

She looked away, not liking how well he read her. "Okay, so it's hard to experience painful things that others went through. Having those images in my head is a motherfucker. Feeling their agony makes me feel sick inside. And, yes, it makes me feel raw and vulnerable and plain drained. But that's just how it goes. I don't dwell on any of it because I *like* that I'm able to help people this way—the trade-off is worth it."

"There," he said, a note of satisfaction in his voice. "Sharing isn't so hard, is it?"

She rolled her eyes. "Your turn."

He waited until he'd placed her sandwich in front of her

before he spoke. "As I've told you before, my mother and aunt were stray demons. From what I learned, Moira did love my mother. I suspect it was for that reason alone that she took me in after Blanche died. But Moira never parented me. I was a hindrance. She often left me alone or with neighbors while she went off to do whatever she did. A few people described her as self-destructive. She had more of an addictive personality than most demons. Drugs, cheap thrills, sex—they seemed to be the only things that made her feel alive."

"I've met demons like that before." Piper bit into her sandwich. "They rarely snap out of that mental state."

Levi inclined his head. "But she deserved to have the chance to see if she could. He robbed her of that. Robbed her of her life."

"And he robbed you of the only person you had left," she said with a pointed look, letting Levi know she wouldn't let him get away with discounting his own emotions just as he hadn't allowed her to dismiss her own.

He swallowed. "Yeah. I'm guessing he did to her exactly what he did to Missy, only he didn't allow her to live. I don't know for sure, because I don't remember any of it."

"Wait, you were there?"

Levi nodded. "He had to have been the one to dump me at the orphanage—part of his MO is to parent the children alone for a short time and then place them outside somewhere that shelters demonic orphans. And yes, it sickens me to know that the bastard probably cuddled and played with me, not to mention fed me and changed my clothes."

Jesus, her heart went out to him. How much of a mind fuck would that be? He might have had centuries to get used to it, but it wouldn't make it any easier to bear.

Levi flexed his fingers. "I don't have any recollection of what happened to Moira or of him."

Piper figured that the latter wasn't such a terrible thing, because he'd have otherwise been haunted by the sort of nightmares that would forever taunt Missy. But Piper could understand why he'd lament having no memory of such a pivotal time in his life.

"From what I witnessed through Missy's memories, it's like he wants to create the perfect family for himself," said Piper before taking another bite of her sandwich. "But I don't think he truly *saw* Missy or her sister. Not as people. They were more like objects to him. Toys he moved around like it was a game that he needed to control every aspect of. But then he resented that it wasn't real, that Missy wasn't willing, that everything wasn't falling into place the way he wanted, and that she wasn't who he truly wanted."

"I agree, they're more like toys to him. Dolls, even. For him, they're there to fulfill his fantasies. They have only the personality, wants, and motivations that he assigns them. He discards them when they don't prove fun to play with anymore. But in Missy's case, he didn't blame *her* for his disappointment in the game, he blamed himself for targeting sisters instead of a mother and daughter."

"Killers tend to have pathological minds. They can be obsessive about every minute aspect of how they follow whatever compulsions they have. They generally don't like to deviate from their habits and routines, though they can evolve over time."

Levi nodded. "His tastes appear to have evolved. Personality wise, Moira was nothing like Emma, Diem, or Missy. My aunt apparently had a bad attitude and a foul temper. She bore no physical similarities to them either. All that links them is their lack of an adequate support system and that they were single mothers—or, in my aunt's case, single guardian. That could actually be all he looks for in a potential victim, I don't know."

Piper bit her lip. "There'll be more victims out there."

"Yeah," said Levi, his jaw hardening. "When I looked into Moira's death, I discovered there were three similar cases. I tried hunting him but had too little to go on. For years I kept a metaphorical eye out for repeats of such crimes but there were none. I thought he was likely dead, since killers generally don't simply stop." A muscle in his cheek flexed. "I was wrong."

Piper narrowed her eyes. "You'd better not be feeling responsible for any subsequent crimes he committed or I *will* punch you in the dick."

One corner of his mouth twitched ever so slightly. "Yeah?"

"Yeah. I would have reached the same conclusion as you. I'll bet Knox and the other sentinels did too. The only person at fault for any of the lives this killer took is *him*."

"I know. I just wish I'd continued to watch for signs he was still out there."

"In my opinion, it's unlikely he stopped killing for a long period of time. He probably just got better at hiding his kills. Probably also made a point of targeting women who wouldn't be missed. And since his pattern of leaving children outside foster homes and orphanages doesn't seem to have earned much notice, it might be that he moved around a lot."

"Probably." Levi sighed and cricked his neck. "My life is good. Despite everything, I don't wish it played out differently. But it wasn't his right to put me in a situation where it happened this way."

Piper nodded. "And you'll drive that point home when you get your hands on the bastard, which you will."

"Yeah. Yeah, I will."

Once she'd finished her sandwich, she thanked him for it

and went to wash her plate. He took it from her, insisting he'd take care of it and that she needed to go rest. He even offered to run her a bath.

Dammit, could he not be an asshole to make it easier for her to erect a barrier between them? Apparently not.

She'd slam up that barrier somehow. She would. She just wasn't yet sure how.

# CHAPTER SIXTEEN

Levi was starting to notice a pattern here. Whenever the studio was closed for the day, leaving Piper free time to spend with him, one of the other girls would propose a group outing that always included Piper—just as Harper had today. During the evenings, Devon would often turn up at Levi's apartment to 'chat' with Piper, saying she simply needed a break from Tanner's overbearing ways. After the hellcat left, Piper often retreated to her bedroom.

In other words, Levi spent very little time alone with his anchor these days. And it was starting to feel as if that was by design.

And now, despite that he was never far from her side at the Underground's small amusement park, she rarely addressed him. Rarely met his eyes. Though she did cast him a smile if their gazes clashed, and she did speak to him if he tried striking up a conversation. She wasn't ignoring his presence or snubbing him. She simply seemed to prefer talking with the others.

Yeah, that stung.

Was it surprising, though? No. Despite his attempts to improve the situation, she no longer had the same ease with Levi that she had with their group.

It wasn't merely due to the good ole discomfiting vibe. It was also courtesy of the electric sexual tension that now buzzed in the air around them—a consequence, no doubt, of their continued efforts to fight what flared between them. Instead of easing away, their hunger had only intensified until it was a palpable force that taunted them both.

Still, he gave her no distance. On the contrary, he hovered so close she had to feel his body heat—hence the tension in her neck and shoulders.

She hadn't asked him to stay out of her personal space, though. Probably because she knew he wouldn't. He didn't like her being out in the open. Especially in such a public, busy place.

He'd brought along two Force members, Vin and Mason, to play bodyguard, since Enzo and Dez were off duty. But Levi couldn't relax even a little. She was too exposed here.

It wasn't so much a theme park as a section of kids' rides, such as carousels, see-sawing pirate ships, bumper cars, and a small Ferris wheel. Music, screaming, laughing, and the whirr of machinery filled the air. The scents of hot dogs, fries, popcorn, and donuts made his stomach grumble.

Both Asher and Khloë's little sister, Heidi, were loving the park. The two children were currently climbing into an overly large teacup with Khloë and Keenan.

Harper snapped photos of them. "I'll have to send some pictures to Raini and Devon."

"It's a shame they couldn't come," said Piper, cuddling the stuffed animal Heidi had asked her to hold.

"I know, right?" Harper's mouth curved as Asher giggled at Keenan. "That boy's laugh melts my heart."

"Hopefully he and Heidi won't feel ill when the ride is over," said Knox.

Harper flicked her mate a look. "They have strong stomachs."

"Yes, but we all know Khloë's going to spin that teacup as fast as she physically can."

Harper's brow furrowed. She leaned over the bar and called out to Khloë, warning her to take it easy. The imp merely saluted her.

Larkin chuckled. "Don't know about anyone else, but I'm not feeling reassured."

"Keenan will take over if need be," said Knox.

Sure enough, Khloë *really* put her back into it as she twisted the wheel. Luckily, the ride seemed to have safety measures that ensured the cups couldn't spin too fast, because it stayed at a sedate pace. Huffing, she passed control of the wheel over to Keenan.

The kids giggled and squealed throughout the duration of the ride. When it was over, they all but staggered out of the teacups and over to the exit gate with the adults close behind them.

Khloë frowned at Harper. "Don't scowl, it doesn't become you."

"I warned you to take it easy," said the sphinx. "See, this is why I don't ever let you babysit Asher alone."

"I know how to cheer you up," Heidi chirpily announced before slapping a wad of cash into Harper's hand. "And there's plenty more where that came from," the imp added with a wink, clipping her white-blonde air behind her ear.

Levi felt his mouth kick up. The kid was the most talented pickpocket he'd ever met. And she looked like butter wouldn't melt in her mouth.

Harper's lips parted. "You stole all this?"

Heidi's brow furrowed. "Stole?" she echoed, looking appropriately confused. "Oh no, I found it."

Khloë smiled. "Well that's luck for you."

Harper shot the adult imp an annoyed glance before refocusing on Heidi. "Where did you 'find' it?"

Heidi waved a hand. "Oh, here and there."

The sphinx wiped a hand down her face and then perched it on her hip. "Did you 'find' anything else?"

Heidi shrugged. "Muh," she said, noncommittal.

"Just how much cash do you have on you?"

Khloë leaned into her sister. "Don't answer that."

Flames erupted around the wad of notes. They then disappeared from Harper's hand . . . only to reappear in Asher's hand with another spurt of fire. He offered the wad to Heidi, who took it with a smile . . . except it was almost as if the notes vanished into thin air. It was like when a magician closed his hand around a coin and made it 'disappear.'

Harper sighed. "No more 'finding' things, okay? Now, I've run out of tickets, so we need extra for the other rides."

"I got it," declared Khloë.

Harper's face softened. "Thanks, Khlo."

The imp crossed to the ticket machine, slammed her fist to the side of it, and at least twenty dollars' worth of tickets got spat out.

Harper sighed again. "Freaking imps."

The children wanted to go on the pirate ship next. This time, Khloë, Keenan, *and* Harper accompanied them.

Standing behind Piper as she leaned against the barrier to watch the others enjoy the ride, Levi put a hand on the metal bar either side of her. "You feeling all right?"

She threw him a breezy smile over her shoulder. "Yeah. Just

had a childhood flashback. Celeste once vomited on one of these rides. The puke went *everywhere*."

Levi gently turned Piper to face him. "Were you on the ship with her?"

"No, I didn't want to get on it because we'd only just eaten. I was sure I'd be sick."

"You laughed, didn't you?"

"Cackled like a witch," she admitted, unrepentant.

He chuckled. "I can't say I blame you." He swept his gaze over her face. "Now are you going to tell me what's wrong?"

"Nothing's wrong."

He dipped his face toward hers. "Liar."

"I'm not lying. I'm fine. Just tired."

He narrowed his eyes. "Tired? That's all?"

"That's all."

"You promise there's nothing else?"

She nodded. "I swear it on the life of my mother's cat."

"And she truly owns a cat?"

Piper frowned. "Cats own us, Levi. Not the other way around. Jeez, how could you not know that?"

He hummed, skeptical, and her eyes dipped to his mouth. They both tensed, because something spiked in the air—something hot, heady, and entirely sexual.

She cleared her throat. "You should, um . . . you should step back and—" Her body jerked hard as a dazed look crossed her face. Awareness slipped from her eyes as she slumped, dead weight.

Levi caught her limp form in his arms, panic flaring through him. "Fuck."

His peripheral vision screamed a warning. He turned his head to see a crackling ball of hellfire zooming their way. He swept out his arm, telekinetically deflecting it. Another came their way almost instantly, pitched by an unseen assailant. Knox whacked it with an orb of his own, sending it off course.

Everyone moved fast.

Larkin fanned out her wings to shield Knox, raised her hands, and sent out a hail of black chips of hell-ice in the direction of their invisible attacker.

Obstructed by her wings, Knox struggled to accurately launch more lethal orbs of hellfire.

Vin and Mason situated themselves in front of Levi and Piper, blindly hurling energy balls and hellfire orbs.

People screamed and ran for safety. Machinery stuttered to a stop. Music abruptly cut off.

Wanting to motherfucking kill someone, Levi carefully lowered Piper to the ground and curved his body over hers. His demon's roar of fury rattled around his head. A fury Levi could goddamn relate to. The psychic blow she'd received to the head had not only knocked her out, it meant she was utterly defenseless right now.

Before anger could take him over, Levi ground his teeth as he boxed up his every emotion. He couldn't afford to feel or lose his cool. He had to fight and defend. And he had to do it from that very spot on the ground, because there was no fucking way he was leaving Piper's side.

Stuck behind the guards, he couldn't emit a telekinetic wave—he'd knock Vin and Mason down like skittles. Just the same, he couldn't toss out waves of despair or else they'd collide with the guards.

His blood bubbling with adrenaline, Levi telepathically reached out to Keenan. *You and the others taking cover?*

*Yes*, the incubus replied. *But Harper and Khloë aren't happy about sitting out the fight, even though they'd never think of abandoning the kids.*

An orb rammed into Levi's upper arm, jolting his body hard. Hissing at the prickling burn, he was tempted to shoulder his way past the others and try to thrash the invisible bastard with hard blasts of telekinesis. But that could be what the asshole wanted—to draw Levi away from Piper so she'd be vulnerable. He wasn't taking that chance.

More and more orbs sailed through the air, coming at them from different angles . . . as if the assailant was darting around unnaturally fast, no doubt taking cover behind various rides. If he meant to find an opening that would give him a direct shot at Piper, he'd fail for sure.

Vin staggered as an orb punched his chest, almost making him topple backwards over Levi and Piper. It galled Levi's demon that they were being shielded by others. It growled and snarled, conflicted—

Heat blazed along Levi's ear as an orb narrowly missed his head. Another came at him and slammed into his shoulder. *Son of a fucker.* Unlike the others, he couldn't duck or weave—he needed to stay in position to protect Piper. Being stationary made him an easier target than the others. Hence why hellfire was currently blistering and consuming patches of his skin.

Another succession of orbs came at them. Larkin flapped her wings, sending out a gust of wind that extinguished the orbs and hopefully swept their foe off his fucking feet.

Larkin's mind touched Levi's as she sent out more chips of hell-ice. *He should have given up by now—going against so many of us is stupid, and he's been hit several times.*

He had indeed. They might not be able to see him, but they noticed each time an orb crashed into what appeared to be thin air. They'd heard grunts and curses of pain.

*Why hasn't he tucked tail and run?* asked Larkin.

That was a very good question. The man was having to

dodge all kinds of shit. He was also outnumbered, and he had no way of getting to Piper. Even his ability to remain unseen couldn't protect him forever. It made sense to quit and go lick his wounds. Yet, he hadn't made a run for it.

*He could be playing with us*, said Levi. *But I don't see why he would.* An orb whacked his injured shoulder and *fuck* that hurt.

"Lower your wings, Larkin!" Knox yelled.

The harpy hesitated for a moment before dropping them.

A stream of hellfire poured out of Knox's palm and swept outwards in an arc. An agonized male cry rang through the air. Knox appeared to home in on that sound as he struck out again.

Hearing footsteps thundering away, Levi ground his teeth. He wanted to give chase, but he wouldn't leave Piper. Couldn't. So he signaled for Vin and Mason to go in his stead.

Levi looked down at her . . . and his stomach dropped. Blood was trickling out of her ears, nose, and mouth. That wasn't a normal result of a psychic blow to the head.

He put his fingers to her pulse. It was weak and thready. "No. No, no, no, no, no."

Without even thinking about it, he telepathically called out to Raini's mate, Maddox, *I need a healer.*

*Where are you?* asked Maddox.

Levi gave him his location. Mere moments later, two male demons materialized at his side—Maddox and his sentinel, Hector. Maddox took in the scene and then, without a word to anyone, teleported Levi and Piper away.

Finding himself on his living room floor, Levi got to his knees so he was no longer curved over her. "Do something," he said, a sense of urgency beating at him.

Maddox crouched down, lifted Piper's hand, and pressed his palm to hers. A red light seemed to slick its way up the veins of her arm, shoulder, neck, and then up to her head.

*Levi, what happened?* asked Harper, frantic. *Is Piper okay?*

*Maddox is healing her*, replied Levi.

*We'll come to you once the kids are safe.*

The ability to heal generally wasn't something demons could boast having. But Maddox's kind were an exception. Descendants possessed angelic blood, since one of their earliest ancestors had been a fallen angel. What many didn't know about Maddox was that he had *arch*angelic blood—that made him more powerful than the rest of his breed, not to mention far more dangerous.

Finally, the redness faded from Piper's veins.

"She'll be fine, though she might sleep a while." Maddox gently lowered her hand to the floor. "How is it she suffered a brain hemorrhage?"

His stomach sinking, Levi swallowed. He'd suspected that was the case when he saw the blood. "I have no clue," he said, his voice thick. "I thought she'd been dealt a psychic punch at first. I didn't notice she was bleeding until just before I called out to you."

"A hemorrhage like that is typically caused by a direct strike to the brain."

A strike that would have killed her if Levi had reacted too late. She could have died on the ground beneath him . . . and he'd been so preoccupied with the assailant's movements that he wouldn't have noticed.

The thought was enough to smash open the box containing Levi's emotions. Anger raged in his blood. Fear of losing her clogged his throat. Resolve to find her attacker beat in his chest like a drum. His demon was unnaturally still and quiet, barely in control while caught up in a fury that clawed at its insides.

Levi scooped her up and stood. "Thank you for healing her."

Nuzzling her hair, he carried her to the sofa and then gently set her down.

"Raini likes her a great deal," said Maddox. The demon was cold, calculated, and not one to help out of the goodness of his heart, but there was nothing he wouldn't do for his woman.

"Raini will be pissed when she hears what happened," said Hector.

Maddox nodded and returned his vacant, vivid blue gaze to Levi. "You should let me heal you."

Now that the adrenaline was bleeding from his system, each of Levi's wounds burned, prickled, and throbbed like a bitch. Still, he waved away Maddox's offer.

"If you won't allow me to do it for you, at least do it for her. She will be upset when she wakes, because she will know that each person with her at the park got caught up in the crossfire. I expect she'll feel guilty and believe she has brought her troubles to everyone else's doorstep. If she wakes and sees you in this state, it will only upset her more."

Because it would be physical evidence that Levi *was* caught up in the crossfire and suffered several wounds protecting her. He sighed. "All right. Thank you, though I know you're mostly offering because Raini will ride your ass if you don't."

A smile briefly flickered in Maddox's eyes. "She is determined that I will get along well with the mates and anchors of her friends so, yes, she will give me grief if I fail to offer aid where it is needed." Just as he'd done with Piper, he pressed his palm to Levi's and healed him.

Knox's mind touched Levi's. *Where are you?*

*My apartment*, he replied.

Knox, Harper, and Larkin appeared a few feet away in a burst of flames. Knox's ability to travel by fire wasn't common knowledge—it was one of many secrets he kept.

Levi lifted a brow. "The kids?"

"Both are fine, albeit a little shaken," said Harper, looking down at Piper. "Khloë and Keenan are watching over them."

Brushing hair away from Piper's forehead, Larkin slid her gaze to Levi. "Why did you rush off like that?"

His gut hardened as he revisited the memory. "I realized she was bleeding out of her ears, mouth, and nose."

Knox looked at Maddox. "Brain hemorrhage?"

"Yes," replied the descendant. "She's fine now, but it was a close call."

Larkin's face tightened. "So she was dying a few feet away from us, and we had no idea?"

Harper swore. "I'm gonna kill him. Whoever he is, I'm gonna kill him."

No, she wouldn't. Levi would get there first. "I couldn't understand why he seemed to be drawing the scene out. Now, I'm thinking he hoped to distract us so we wouldn't notice she wasn't simply unconscious."

"Here's what I don't get," said Larkin. "He can evidently deliver blows to the brain itself that are strong enough to cause a hemorrhage, yet he didn't do it when he attacked her at the deli. It would have made the whole thing easier for him. But he didn't do it, just as he didn't hit anyone else psychically tonight. He could have taken us all out—or at least tried. Why didn't he?"

Well now that was an excellent question.

Maddox pursed his lips. "Perhaps it's not an ability he truly possesses. He could have purchased it."

Levi felt his brows lift. "That would make sense." Some demons stole abilities from others and sold them on the black market. The problem was that stolen gifts didn't integrate themselves into a demon's psyche unless the aforementioned psyche was built to wield and control the abilities. As such, a gift could only be transferred temporarily. Some demons only got a single use out of it, if they even got any at all.

"It would explain why he didn't deal her a lethal blow that would kill her immediately," said Knox. "He would have no idea how to properly use an ability when he hasn't spent years of his life learning to master and use it to its full potential."

"I think maybe he might also have purchased the ability to move fast or teleport from spot to spot," said Larkin. "Because he did too good a job of dodging our hits and coming at us from various angles."

Knox dipped his chin. "My thoughts exactly."

"He was ballsy to go after Piper in public like that," said Harper.

Levi glanced down at Piper. "In protecting her so well, we gave him no other choice but to launch a surprise attack and strike at her from afar." He paused. "I want to know if Sefton and Jasper have alibis."

"Tanner and I will question them," said Knox. "Have you notified Piper's parents yet?"

"No, but I will," replied Levi.

Knox raked his gaze over him. "Go do that and then take a shower and change into fresh clothes. We'll watch over Piper for you."

Levi hesitated, clenching his fists.

"You'll have no chance of playing down how bad your injuries were if she sees you in that tee and notices all the smears of blood," Maddox pointed out.

Harper frowned at the descendant. "He *shouldn't* play it down."

"But he will," Knox cut in, "because he knows she's going to pointlessly feel guilty."

Larkin nodded. "She's going to claim she shouldn't go back to work for a while. She'll probably also claim she shouldn't stay here with you, Levi. She'll want to isolate herself somewhere so that no one else can again get caught in any crossfire."

Yeah, he'd already considered that. "We don't always get what we want, do we?"

# CHAPTER SEVENTEEN

A low-grade headache woke her, throbbing in her temples. Groggy, Piper forced her eyes open. Her demon blinked in surprise at the sight of Levi sat on the coffee table in front of her, his forearms rested on his thighs, his eyes locked on his clasped hands.

Piper licked her lips. "Hey," she croaked.

His head snapped up, and relief flared in his eyes. "How're you feeling?"

"I've got a little mind fog going on and . . ." Trailing off, she grimaced. "Why can I taste blood in my mouth?" The coppery scent of it filled her nostrils. "We were in the park. Why are we not in the park anymore?"

He took her hand in his. "Stay calm for me."

That didn't sound good. That didn't sound good at all. She sat upright, her demon going stiff as a board. "What happened?"

His thumb circled her palm. "We were attacked at the park."

She froze. "What?"

"Whoever wants you dead struck again."

Feeling the blood drain from her face, she asked, "Is everyone okay? Why the hell don't I remember?"

"Everyone is fine," he assured her, cool and steady. "*You* weren't, though. Someone psychically struck your brain. You were unconscious, not to mention hemorrhaging. That's why you don't remember. But you're all right now. Maddox healed you."

Piper frowned as she tried sifting through her memories of the park. The last thing she could recall was talking with Levi near the see-saw ride. "Did you see who attacked us?"

His mouth tightened. "No. He concealed himself somehow."

She dragged in a breath and wiped a hand over her mouth, pulling a face when little brown flakes came away. Dried blood. Fabulous. "What exactly happened? I need to know how it all went down."

Standing, he tugged on the hand he still held. "Come. I'll tell you everything while you wash your face and brush your teeth, because I can see you want to. Fair?"

Piper stood. "That'll work."

She probably shouldn't have let him keep possession of her hand, but she was tired and freaked out—he was solid and steady and everything she needed right then.

In her private bathroom, she crossed to the vanity and said, "Start talking."

Propping his hip against the wall, he folded his arms and gave her a rundown of what happened while she cleaned herself up.

Her stomach rolled when he very vaguely mentioned he'd been injured. "I need to thank Maddox for healing us both. Just how badly were you hurt?"

He shrugged. "I've had worse."

She dumped the blood-stained face cloth in the hamper. "You've also showered and changed—you weren't wearing those clothes earlier." She narrowed her eyes. "I know you. So I know you wouldn't have easily left my side while I was sleeping. Not even to wash up. That tells me you don't want me to know exactly how many wounds you had or how bad they were."

"It's not important."

"It's important to me."

He pushed away from the wall, took a step toward her, and gathered her face in his hands. "The wounds are all healed. Every last one of them. Don't dwell on what he did, baby."

Whoa, *baby*?

"He doesn't deserve to have that power."

Just as the people around her didn't deserve to get caught up in all this bullshit. "I should have said no when Harper invited me to the park."

"No, you shouldn't have. You're not at fault for what happened today."

"But I *am* aware that someone wants me dead. I shouldn't have agreed to go on a group outing. I put them at risk."

Levi lowered his hands to her shoulders, pinning her gaze with his. "You didn't do anything. You're living your life. Which is exactly what you should be doing. *He's* the only one in the wrong here."

"Maybe, but I need to take more precautions. No more group outings, for starters. No more paying visits to my parents or anyone else. I can't go back to the studio for a while either." Hopefully Harper and Raini wouldn't fire her for taking time off. As for staying here . . . she couldn't do that either. Not anymore. "I should also move out—"

"No," he said, his grip on her shoulders tightening.

"I need to hole up somewhere."

"Do you really think I'd be good with you being on your own when you most need protection?"

"*I'm* not allowed to protect *you*? Leaving is the only way I can."

"You're not going anywhere," he told her, his voice low but firm. "I get that the attack shook you up. I can understand if you don't feel so safe with me anymore, considering you were dying and I didn't even notice—"

"What?" Frowning, she shook her head. "I don't feel unsafe with you. I'd say you were kind of caught up in what was happening around you, so it's not surprising that you didn't notice I was bleeding."

"You're eager to get away from me."

"Because I don't want you to be hurt again."

"This complex is secure. He can't penetrate it. That's *why* he struck in public." Levi tugged her close, swiping his thumbs over her collarbones. "Listen to me. *You're safe here.* Has it occurred to you that he'd hoped to have this effect on you? That he wanted to make you isolate yourself so that it'd be easier for him to nab you?"

Actually, no, that hadn't occurred to her. It should have. Dammit, she was smarter than this. "God, I hate him."

"He will be caught and dealt with, Piper. Then that sick feeling in your stomach will go, things can get back to normal, and we can find you another place to live. Preferably an apartment in this building."

Piper's insides seized. Celeste's past words echoed in her mind. *"Oh, and you're wrong if you think he'll let you return to your house. He'll want you living somewhere in his building so he can monitor your day-to-day activities."*

Piper stepped back, making his hands slip away from her.

His brows dipped. "What? What did I say?"

"You can't take over my life, Levi."

A look of genuine befuddlement fell over his face. "I'm not trying to take over."

"You want me to move out of my house."

He shrugged. "I thought you might not feel comfortable living there when you know he once squirted come all over the rear wall. If you're going to relocate, I'd rather you moved somewhere I know you'll be safe. This place is practically impenetrable. It's also close to the Underground, and you have friends here as well as me. It seemed like a good choice."

Her hackles lowered at the sincerity in his voice. "I can't say whether or not I'll want to relocate. Not until I go back to my house. But I wouldn't want to move to this complex. I don't think it'd be good for us to live virtually on top of each other. Anchors generally don't live too close together. It's better that way. For obvious reasons."

His eyes searched hers as he closed the distance she'd put between them. "You've been avoiding me. Avoiding being alone with me." Sighing, he rested his forehead against hers. "I miss it," he added softly.

She felt her brows flit together. "What?"

"The ease we had." He paused. "I miss a lot of things. Miss you."

She swallowed, cursing her stomach for fluttering. "You see me every day."

"There's a difference between being around someone and truly having their company. You and I might have gotten off to a shaky start, but we got past that. Things were going good. We were friends. Then it all got derailed." Raising his head, he palmed one side of her neck. "I want her back."

"Who?"

"My Piper." He gently squeezed her throat. "I want her back."

She averted her gaze. "Things will get back to the way they were in the beginning. It's obviously gonna take a little more time." From the corner of her eye, she saw him tilt his head.

"You forgot your ears."

She looked at him. "Sorry?"

"You forgot to clean them. There are flecks of dry blood in this one. You'll probably have them in your other ear."

Inwardly groaning, she grabbed the pot of earbuds.

"Let me." He took one of the buds, wet it with water from the tap, and then very gently wiped away the blood. And she let him. Because right then, he seemed so damn lonely. A feeling she understood, since she'd been wracked with it since the distance between them first appeared.

She ignored that her nerve-endings were enjoying his touch and closeness a little too much. Ignored that her hormones were all stirred up and ready to roll. Ignored how unbearably conscious she was of his close proximity and richly masculine scent.

Finally done, he chucked the used buds into the small trash can.

"Thanks." Piper's brow pinched as she stared into his eyes. There was a dark, tortured look in them. "What's wrong?"

He exhaled heavily. "I can't stop seeing it. That moment when you went limp against me . . . and I had no clue you could die."

"I'm okay, thanks to you and Maddox. He might have been the one to heal me, but you were the one who shielded me and then got me the help I needed. As you yourself once said . . . as anchors go, you're not half-bad." Her lips twitched at the memory. It was of a time when things were easier. A time when she'd been hopeful that they could be good friends.

A time when she'd had no idea that having him inside her just once would damn her to hell and back.

"So long as you don't wish your anchor was someone else," he said.

She frowned. "I would never wish that." It would be so much easier on them both if they'd been paired with others, but she could never long for that.

"Good. Neither would I. Now come here, I need to hold you for a minute."

His arms settled around her as he moved closer. With his warm chest pressing against the side of her face and his chin resting on the top of her head, she felt safe and snug and cared for.

"You can't die," he said, the words like crushed rock.

"It's not in my plans."

"I can't lose you. But sometimes I feel like I already have."

An ache lanced through her chest. "You haven't."

Maybe it wasn't wise but Piper closed her eyes and sank fully into the hug, slipping her arms around his waist. This man had curled his body over her unconscious form. Had solidly taken hit after hit after hit in shielding her. Had gotten her the help she needed when he realized she'd been seriously hurt. It was safe to say she would be dead right now if it wasn't for Levi.

He swept his hand up her back and began massaging her nape. She almost moaned aloud. Those fingers were all too clever. They knew what they were doing in *other places* too. Something she *really* shouldn't be thinking about. But it was difficult to be around Levi and not think sexual thoughts—they constantly flitted through her mind, unbidden.

As if he knew . . . or as if he was having some X-rated thoughts of his own . . . his cock began to thicken against her. Piper opened her eyes, unsure what to do. She didn't want to draw attention to it, though she doubted he'd be embarrassed or anything. She also couldn't exactly ignore that he was getting hard.

Her body certainly wasn't ignoring it. Nope. It was

responding in turn. Her pulse was speeding up, her nipples were tightening, and lots of very sensitive places were getting all tingly and achy. Which, yeah, could be a lot to do with how she kept remembering how good it felt to have that long, thick cock inside her.

He slowly trailed his mouth down the side of her face and over to her ear. "Sometimes, I wake up in the night and reach for you. Then I remember I don't have all of you anymore."

She'd done that a time or two. Woke. Rolled toward the other side of the bed. Found it empty. And felt like she'd been punched in the gut when reality smacked her.

"You don't know how many nights I almost came to your room, feeling like I'd go insane if I didn't have you," he added, his voice dropping an octave. "Instead, I jacked off. And I saw you in my head the whole time."

She squeezed her eyes shut. She'd often gotten herself off thinking of him. She wouldn't tell him that, though. The situation was too precarious while sexual hunger had turned the air static, leaving them both balancing on a ledge. Piper had the distinct feeling that any explicit confessions from her would send them both hurtling off it.

"Levi—"

"I know, I'll let you go." He tightened his arms around her for a moment but then pulled back, staring down at her through eyes that had darkened with need. "Rest. Call if you need me."

He took a step back. And another. And another. All that space between them . . . she hated it. Every inch of it.

His gaze dropped to her pebbled nipples, flaring with something feral. His eyes slowly roamed lower, and lower, and lower. Then they moved up, and up, and up before settling on her mouth.

It was a full-on eye-fuck, pure and simple. One that made her pulse jump, her stomach twist, her mouth dry up, and her brain short-circuit. The whole thing was impossibly nerve-wracking.

Without thought, she nervously licked her lips. His eyes lifted to pin her own—dark, dilated, gleaming, carnally cold. Whatever he saw in her gaze made a low growl rumble in his chest.

His hunger seemed to sweep out and clash violently with hers. The air tautened. Her body sang. The room temperature seemed to rise unbearably.

She wasn't sure who moved first, but they collided. Their mouths locked. Their tongues tangled. Their hands grabbed and squeezed.

Piper moaned as he ground his cock against her. The needs of her body completely drowned out her thoughts. That was good. She didn't want to think. Didn't want to care what was smart or unwise.

She just wanted him.

He tore his mouth free with a growl. "Fuck, I've got to have you."

There was pulling and shoving and yanking as they stripped off each other's clothes. Or removed some, anyway. Neither seemed to have the patience to wait until the other was fully naked. She still had on her bra when he lifted her, turned, and propped her on the vanity. *Well.*

Deliciously shirtless with his fly open, he gripped the underside of her thighs and roughly dragged her to the edge of the vanity. His eyes lowered to her brands as he dipped a finger inside her. His gaze snapped back to her face. "Wet," he bit out, pressing his mouth to hers. Then he shoved his finger deep. "Very wet."

Piper frowned as he withdrew his finger, but her complaints died on her tongue when he wasted no time in lining up the thick head of his cock to her pussy. Oh, yes. She wrapped her legs around his hips and squeezed tight—a silent demand for him *to get inside her.*

Levi bit down on her neck and slammed home, burying his long, fat shaft balls-deep in her pussy.

Her lips parted as she heaved in a breath. Fucking *hell* she'd forgotten how the first thrust always burned just a little. No other man had ever made her feel so full.

Pulling back his hips, he licked up her throat and bit her earlobe hard enough to make her wince. He hadn't been lying that time he told her he liked to bite. "You feel so fucking good." He drove his full length inside her once again.

She hissed. "More."

"Yeah, more." He fucked her hard. Like he hadn't seen her in years. It was rough and wild and everything her body craved.

He slammed *so deep* each time. Grunted. Growled. Snarled. All that animalistic, aggressive sexuality twisted her stomach.

"You have no idea how fucking hot it is to see those brands on your skin," said Levi, unsurprised by the guttural quality to his voice when he was caught in the tight grip of a haunting, elemental need. "I shouldn't like them. They shouldn't make my cock hard, but they do." Every damn time.

Levi purposely dug his fingertips into the brand on her inner thigh as he took her. Fuck, he'd missed this. Her taste, her moans, her nails clawing his back, the tight, hot clasp of her pussy. He'd never craved anything the way he did her. Never wanted someone so badly they invaded his dreams or popped into his thoughts too many times a day.

Nothing other than a clear 'no' from her could have made him walk out the door. He'd needed to be in her so badly he felt it everywhere. It was an ache in his chest, a throb in his veins, an itch beneath his skin.

She palmed the back of his head, scratching with her nails. "Faster, Levi."

He gripped her thighs tighter and upped his pace, savagely ramming into her. His demon all but prowled within him, wanting its turn, but it made no move to take over. It instead egged him on just as she did.

"Play with your clit. Yeah, good fucking girl." He watched her finger rub, press, and roll her clit; felt as her inner walls squeezed, spasmed, and clamped down on his cock. "You always make me come so hard. Do it for me now, baby."

She whimpered, her pussy getting hotter and tighter. Then it happened. Her back snapped straight, her head fell back, and a scream tore out of her throat.

Groaning as her pussy clutched and rippled around his cock, he drilled into her harder, pounding and pounding and pounding. And then he was gone. He buried his face in her neck as he blew his load inside her, wishing it would stay there.

Levi closed his eyes, fighting for breath. He'd missed this as well; missed the peace that fell over him each time he had her. It wasn't simply a chemical contentment. It was emotional, and it ran bone-deep.

His entity settled, pleased. Levi then realized why his demon hadn't surfaced. It had wanted the moment to be about her and Levi; wanted them to reconnect; wanted them to feel that there was no going back.

She dropped her forehead to his shoulder. "Why do we do this to ourselves?"

He stroked her back and kissed her head. The answer was simple, really. "We don't know how to stop."

Sitting in Knox's home office the next morning, Levi sighed. "It has to be either Sefton or Jasper."

"They both have alibis," said Knox, sinking back in the chair behind the U-shaped executive desk. "The same alibi, actually."

"Lester?"

Knox nodded. "He claims the three of them watched a game together."

"We've already agreed that he'd lie to protect them."

"But we can't prove that he did."

Levi silently swore. He wanted to have good news to pass on to Piper. Something that would vanquish the fear in her eyes.

She'd allowed him to lie with her during the night as she slept. She'd still been off with the fairies when Knox telepathed him an hour ago. Levi hadn't woken her. Instead, he'd left her a note to say he'd be back soon and to contact him if she needed anything.

"Are you sure it was wise to rule out Piper's ex?"

"I don't consider him a viable suspect, but I have people watching him." So far, Kelvin had done nothing out of the ordinary. Also . . . "They confirmed that he was at a friend's house during the time of the recent attack."

"So there's no need for us to question him."

"No." Sighing, Levi looked off to the side and stared, unseeing, at the three abstract art canvases of mechanical clockwork on the gray wall. "The fucker who's after Piper isn't going to be happy until she's dead. And that can't happen."

"It won't," Knox vowed. "Keep doing what you've already been doing—make it difficult for anyone to reach her. That's our best chance of ensuring he makes a mistake."

Hearing a child's squeal of delight come from somewhere in the mansion, Levi asked, "How's Asher?"

"His usual self," Knox replied. "He was unsettled yesterday, but he bounced back fairly fast. Don't forget he's been through his own share of scary situations."

"Plus, there's plenty of imp in him, even if he's not one." Very little bothered them for long.

Knox gave him an unimpressed look. "Yes. That." He tilted his head, studying Levi closely. "You seem different today. Less tense. Yet more troubled."

Exhaling heavily, Levi rubbed at his face. "I screwed up. With Piper, I mean."

"By starting to sleep with her, or by stopping?"

"The latter. I can't let her go, Knox." And it was about fucking time Levi acknowledged it. "But I don't know how to keep her."

Knox met his gaze steadily. "You were never going to let her go. You simply hadn't made your peace with it until now."

Yeah, that about summed the situation up. What bothered Levi was that . . . "I make a shit partner. I hold back. Stay detached. Don't look to build anything with anyone. Throw all of myself into my work and nothing into my . . . hell, I don't think you could even call them relationships. They were barely even flings."

"You've been a shit partner to others. But I don't believe you're incapable of being a good one. You just have to *want* to be. You never really did in the past."

"I should have. I was selfish."

"Yes. And no." Knox stood. "You put your work life first in the past, yes. But you didn't feel compelled not to, because you didn't connect with those women you bedded. You've always struggled to form attachments."

Levi felt his brow crease. "That's more my demon."

"No, you're just as bad for that." Knox skirted the desk. "Harper made me read a lot of parenting books with her. She was worried that, given she has a poor relationship with her mother, she would struggle to bond with her own child. It's important for children to experience loving bonds of some sort when very young—particularly a parent–child bond. Important for not only their brain development but also their emotional development.

"You didn't have a bond with your mother. You lost her. Going by all you learned after leaving Ramsbrook, you also had no bond with your aunt." Knox leaned back against the desk. "Ever heard of reactive attachment disorder?"

"No."

"I remember reading about children who, due to their parents not meeting their needs for one reason or another, developed reactive attachment disorder. The symptoms made me think of how you were as a child—withdrawn, defiant, distrustful, easily angered, avoided touch, showed no fear of strangers, sought no affection from anyone. You'd never had a real sense of family—"

"I formed my own at Ramsbrook."

"You *collected* us. Me. Keenan. Tanner. Larkin. You didn't initially connect with us on any level. It took time for you to do that. But, Levi, you already have a bond with Piper. And I don't simply mean the psi-mate link. You formed a connection with her while getting to know her and building the foundations for an anchor relationship. In other words, you got past what, for you, is the hard part. Now you just need to keep her."

The man made it sound so simple, but . . . "I don't know if I'll manage it in the long run."

"Why? You didn't sabotage the familial bonds you've formed with me and the other sentinels."

"But none of you are negatively affected by how much or how long I work," Levi pointed out.

"True. However, you're only as busy as you are because you *choose* to be. I'm not saying you escape into work. Nor am I saying you're a workaholic. You're a doer. A man who likes to fill up his time doing productive things. You've become so used to it that you haven't realized how much you've needlessly taken on. And until now, you've never had a reason to be bothered by it, so you've never thought much on it or done anything about it. There are many people you could delegate to, Levi. Many responsibilities you don't *need* to personally take on. Shed some of them."

"What, like no longer be your bodyguard?"

"Both Tanner and Keenan are bodyguards as well as sentinels. Tanner watches over Harper. Keenan guards Asher. They still make time for their mates. Granted, they're not as busy escorting their charges around as you are escorting me. But that doesn't mean you can't still have a meaningful relationship with someone. Especially if said someone understands and respects your commitment to your positions. From what Larkin told me, Piper certainly does." Knox twisted his mouth. "How would your demon feel about keeping her?"

Levi puffed out a breath. "It branded her. Twice. With the death ballad."

His lips twitching, the Prime lifted his brows. "I see. Well, that says everything."

"I don't know if it'll be easy to convince her to take a chance on me."

"I suppose you'll soon find out."

# CHAPTER EIGHTEEN

On the screen of Piper's cell, Olive folded her arms and threw her a dirty look as she said, "I don't see how we can come back from this."

Sinking more fully into the sofa, Piper sighed. "I'm sorry."

Her friend snorted. "No, you're not."

"Okay, fine, I don't regret not telling you. But I *am* sorry that you're upset by it."

"Are you? Are you really?" Another snort.

"I didn't want to worry you. Plus, you were on vacation; I didn't want to spoil it. I chose to wait to tell you until you got back—I thought it would be over by now."

Olive's sour expression softened slightly. "I get it, but I would rather you'd told me."

Piper lifted her shoulders. "There was nothing you could have done. You would only have gotten all stressed about it. Hell, you're stressing right now."

"My BFF—who has some *serious* making-up to do—is in

danger. Of course I'm stressing." Olive unfolded her arms. "I want to come see you."

Piper shook her head. "No. Not until this is over. I don't want any more people getting pulled into this. You'd say the same to me if it was the other way around."

"Pfft. I'm not quite that selfless."

Piper smiled. "Liar."

"*You're* the liar."

"I didn't tell tales, I simply didn't—"

"Lying by omission counts. You didn't even tell me that you and Levi formed the anchor bond *or* that—more interestingly—you did some rolling around in his bed."

"You had to see why I wasn't in a hurry to talk about the latter."

Olive leaned forward, wagging her finger in an accusatory fashion. "You mean you knew I'd tell you that you were playing a dangerous game by sleeping with him, and you didn't want to hear it."

"Yeah, that's pretty much what I mean. Maybe the whole agreement thing was stupid, but I don't think we would have left it at a one-night stand in any case. I don't have that much self-control, and he never seemed all that interested in exercising any."

"Hence what happened last night." Olive poked the inside of her cheek with her tongue. "It's a good sign that he asked to stay with you rather than heading off to his own bed."

"I'm trying to not read anything into it. I mean, he might have wanted to stay with me, but he acted as if what happened in the bathroom . . . hadn't. He didn't speak of it."

"Neither did you."

Piper pulled a face. "I didn't want to hear him say that it hadn't changed anything." Because she couldn't help but hope that it had. There was no point pretending otherwise. She was tired of lying to herself. Tired of blocking out her wants and feelings. It hadn't exactly gotten her anywhere good, had it?

"What makes you so sure he would've said that?"

"I wasn't *sure* he would. I was scared he would. I wanted to work out where his head was at before I brought it up."

"Maybe he was doing the same with you."

Maybe. But maybe not . . . and that was what stayed her hand last night.

If he hadn't been her anchor, Piper might not have been so hesitant to take a chance, put her emotions on the line, and declare that she wanted more from him than friendship. But this wasn't a man she could part ways from if he didn't feel the same. She'd always have Levi in her life. And if he didn't return her feelings, the knowledge would always sit between them, possibly tainting their anchor relationship.

Plus, she knew he'd hate to hurt her. She knew it would pain him to say they didn't want the same things. She didn't want to put him in that position.

So, all in all, it had seemed wiser to keep a lid on everything unless or until she felt they were on the same page. The problem was . . . "I couldn't sense how he felt about it. He'll be back soon, and I don't know what to expect. I don't know whether I should act normal. I don't know if I'll be able to keep my demon from bitch-slapping him if he proclaims that last night was a mistake."

"The entity still wants him, then?"

"It wants *all* of him. It's formed a minor attachment to him." Which was absolutely nothing to be blasé about. "How he acts this morning will either break it or strengthen it."

"What about you? What do you want?"

Piper drew in a long breath. "Something I very much doubt

he'll ever offer." A full-on relationship. Not one that was shallow, short, or casual. Something that was real and true. But Levi . . . he didn't do 'serious' or 'long-term.' So, well, she was pretty much fucked.

Hearing the key turn in the front door lock, Piper tensed. Her pulse kicking up, she quickly said her goodbyes to Olive and ended the call.

Levi stalked into the living room, all smolder and animal grace, his face a mask of frustration. She didn't get the feeling that the emotion was directed at her; no, the source of it had to be whatever he'd learned from his meeting with Knox. Or perhaps, more to the point, what he *hadn't* learned.

Ignoring how her feminine parts perked up at the gorgeous sight of him, she said, "I take it you have no good news to impart."

A muscle in his cheek ticked. "Lester alibied both Sefton and Jasper."

"You think he lied," she sensed. As it happened, she suspected the same.

"I do. I simply can't prove it." His gaze roamed over her face, drinking in every detail. "You look better. You slept well?"

"I did." Better than she had in a while, and she suspected it might have had something to do with Levi being at her side. "You?"

"I didn't sleep. Wasn't tired."

She tipped her head to the side. "Then what did you do?"

"Watched over you. Read a book on my phone. Listened to a podcast. Watched over you some more."

A slight ache built in her throat. "You didn't need to stay with me."

He stared at her for a long moment and then scratched the side of his jaw. "We need to talk."

Something about the way he said it made her feel defensive. She pushed to her feet in case she needed to make a sharp exit to save him from her demon's wrath. "If you're going to tell me that I shouldn't read anything into what happened last night—"

"That's not what I'm going to say."

Her hackles went down. "Oh. Okay." Trying not to be *too* hopeful, she asked, "So what's up?"

He crossed to her, each step fluid and purposeful. Then he was all up in her space. Like *right up* in it. Close enough that she felt the warmth of his body heat.

"I suggest," he began, toying with a lock of her hair, "we form a new agreement."

And all her hopes died in an instant. Simply crashed and burned. Her demon narrowed its eyes, not pleased by his suggestion but not ruling out that he would crush its own hopes. Piper, on the other hand, didn't have its optimism.

Her heart heavy, she sighed. "Levi—"

"Hear me out."

"There's really no point. I'm not going to agree to whatever you have in mind," she stated firmly, her voice edged with annoyance. It would have hurt to hear him declare that he wanted them to simply be friends, but to hear him actually suggest yet another 'agreement' that essentially allowed him to have his cake and eat it hurt her more.

"Maybe you won't." He lightly cupped the side of her face. "But I have to ask. I need to know if you would have said yes."

The lines of determination etched into his face made her inwardly curse. He wasn't going to back down, and she was too disheartened to argue with him. She wanted to get the whole thing over with so she could go lick her emotional wounds in privacy. "Fine." She folded her arms, her clipped tone indicating that she was merely humoring him.

His hand still palming her face, he brushed his thumb over her mouth. "I propose we stop fighting ourselves on what we want. It's pointless. It's maddening. And it's hurting us both. I say we agree to accept that we'll *never* be platonic anchors and go ahead and fucking embrace it."

"Yeah? For how long?"

He gave her a look of amused affection, as if the answer should be obvious and he found it cute that she was clueless. He dipped his head so their mouths were mere inches apart. "Indefinitely, baby," he replied, his voice low and soft.

Her world stopped. Her heart sped up. Her thoughts scattered.

She wasn't sure how long she stared at him, completely lost for words, but she eventually asked, "You . . . you mean that?"

"I mean it." He danced his fingertips down one side of her face. "I'll do what I can to ease my workload. I know you wouldn't ask that of me, but I'll be doing it anyway. Not only for you, but for me too. I want to free up time so I can be where I most want to be—with you."

It was hard to grasp what he was saying. To process it. To believe it. To *allow* herself to believe it. But Levi was telling the truth—she saw it in his eyes, heard it in his voice. So did her demon. The entity relaxed, satisfied. "You really are serious about this."

"Deadly."

"And you're not high or anything?"

His lips quirked. "No, not high." He smoothed his hands up her arms. "I know my past history with relationships isn't great. The truth is I was pretty blasé about them. They were more like a diversion. I didn't think I'd ever want to claim a mate, but then you came into my world and made yourself the most important thing in it. That would have been the case even if you weren't my anchor, because you're quite simply *you*." He brushed her hair away from her face. "There's no going back for me. Even if you turn me down, I'll still always want everything from you. There'll never be any changing that. But I don't think you want that to change. I think you want all that I want. Am I wrong?"

She swallowed. "No."

His gaze flared with warmth. "Then let's not make this more complicated than it has to be. We've already hemmed and hawed rather than taking the jump we should have took well before now. Let's not do that anymore."

She licked her lips. "I'm good with not wasting more time."

He palmed her neck with both hands. "Then this is how things are going to be from now on. You're mine. I'm yours. Not merely as anchors, but as mates. This is permanent, exclusive, and as serious as serious can get." His eyes bore into hers, searching. "Can we agree on that?"

"Yes. I prefer this agreement over the last one you came up with." She'd expected to see triumph in his eyes. Instead, it was relief.

"Thank Christ." He drew her close and curled his arms around her. His mouth quickly found hers. The kiss wasn't hard or wild. It also wasn't sweet or slow. It was hot, deep, and filled with promise . . . like they were sealing a deal. "I thought I might have to spend hours convincing you to give us a shot at making it work."

"Like you, I don't see the point in hemming and hawing any longer. I've already learned that only being your friend sucks. I wasn't happy. And I missed you. It felt like there was this . . . hole in our dynamic, in what we'd built."

"I know what you mean. For me, something was missing. And you'd slammed that wall up between us, and I didn't know how to get it down."

She winced. "I had to put the wall there. I only meant to do it for a little while. Just until I could think of you without wanting to ride you like a pony." She smiled at his snort. "Hell, I was so desperate to turn off all I felt for you that I even clung to some of the bullshit Celeste spouted at the studio."

He raised a brow. "Are you going to finally tell me about it? People do that in relationships, you know," he said, oh so reasonable. "Share important things."

"Is that so?" She had a feeling he'd throw those words at her whenever she had even the smallest secret.

"Yes, it very much is."

Piper heaved a sigh. "All right, I'll tell you. But you won't like it."

"I've already concluded that." He backed up to the sofa, pulling her with him, and then sat. He patted his thighs and hummed in approval when she straddled him. "Go on."

Piper fiddled with the collar of his tee. "I'll admit, a lot of what she said to me rang true. For, like, half an hour. I dismissed most of what she said after I gave it real thought. But a few things stuck with me. Or I *wanted* them to be true because I needed some help keeping you at an emotional distance. I told myself that she might have meant to cause trouble but that that didn't mean she was wrong about everything."

Fighting a smile at her babbling, Levi gave her hip a gentle, encouraging squeeze. "What did she say? Tell me."

He forced himself to remain silent as Piper relayed the conversation, feeling his anger build with each word she spoke. By the time she was done, he was honestly surprised his blood pressure wasn't soaring through the roof. "That bitch. I would never have used sex to make you form the anchor bond. You know that, don't you?"

"I do. I was miserable enough to give the idea some consideration, but only for a few minutes."

He rubbed her thighs, despising that she'd been so down—especially when it meant she'd also been so vulnerable that she'd been easy prey for someone like Celeste. "What parts did you let yourself believe for longer than a few minutes?"

"That it's your anchor you see when you look at me, not me as a person. I guess I did feel like a possession to you at times."

"Baby." He drew her closer and pressed a soft kiss to her mouth. "I'm sorry if I made you feel that way. In the beginning, I suppose I did add you to my collection of people. But not coldly. Bonding with others isn't my specialty. I'm like my demon in that respect. But I formed one with you as time went on, and it's not fucking going anywhere."

"Like I'd let it."

He felt his mouth hitch up. "What other bits of crap did you entertain as possible truths?" he asked without judgment. He wasn't upset with her for buying any of it. She'd been hurting, and Celeste knew how to play people.

"That you'd try to control my life as far as possible."

"Ah, that's why you thought I was taking over when I suggested you move to this building." He combed his fingers through her hair. "Would I *like* to take over your life and make certain your every need is answered? Sure. Would I do that to you? No. Not unless you were down with that. Which I know you never would be." His demon found it a shame, really. "I might push sometimes, but I figure you can keep me in line."

"And I figure you'll make an effort to *not* push, although I'm sure that's wishful thinking on my part. You'll be unreasonable on the off-chance that you can get away with it."

His chuckle was wolfish even to his own ears. "Probably." He swept his hand up her back, loving that he was free to touch her as much as he liked whenever he liked. "Anything else 'ring true' for you back then?"

"That you'd gotten beneath my skin and made me feel owned on purpose so I wouldn't be free of you."

"There's probably some truth in that, actually. I didn't consciously aim to do it but, yeah, I did want to leave some mark on you that went beyond us being anchors."

She slanted her head. "What about your demon?" she asked a little shyly. "I mean, will it be good with us being in a relationship?"

The entity snorted at what it perceived to be a preposterous question. "If it could, my demon would stamp itself on your very bones." He nodded when she blinked in surprise. "It has never wanted to let you go. How does your entity feel about all this?"

"At the moment, it's all 'well it's about time.' It kind of finds us ridiculous for only getting to this point now."

"My demon is of pretty much the same opinion."

"I suppose it's good that they're on the same page."

"Yeah." He ghosted his fingertips over her lower lip. "And now that you and me are as well, it's all fucking perfect."

Levi took her mouth in a soft, slow, drugging kiss. He wasn't sure what caused his control to snap, but he was soon eating at her mouth like he'd never get enough.

In a matter of minutes, he had her flat on her back on the sofa and was ragging off her jeans and panties. He impatiently unbuttoned his fly, settled between her thighs and—after a minimal amount of foreplay—he angled her hips just right. "My anchor. My mate. My everything." He thrust deep inside her. Took her hard and fast, every drive of his cock blatantly possessive.

She came fast, her orgasm sweeping him under. It was as he exploded inside her that the temperature dropped as her demon surged forward. It shoved a hand beneath his tee and slapped it on his chest. The flesh beneath its hand quickly began to burn like a mother, telling him he was being branded.

His demon smiled, smug.

Soon enough, the pain faded and her entity finally lowered its hand. Its dark gaze empty, it gave an unapologetic shrug and said, "Turnabout is fair play. Hurt her, and I will destroy you."

His own demon chuckled at that, finding the entity delightful.

Piper's eyes returned to normal as she resurfaced. "Well that took me by surprise." She lifted his tee, and her lips parted slightly. "Oh."

Oh? He glanced down and felt his brows lift. Right above his heart was a very distinctive anchor, its rope forming the shape of an infinity symbol behind it.

He got the message loud and clear. Her demon was letting him know that Piper now had a solid claim to his heart as well as his psyche. That wasn't a claim he had any intention of ever fighting.

# CHAPTER NINETEEN

Shifting nervously on the chic leather seating a week later, Piper wished she could be as excited as everyone else in the VIP box. Ordinarily, she would have eagerly accepted Harper's invitation to join her at the hellhorse racing stadium. Piper was a big fan of the sport. But, worried there'd be a repeat of what happened at the amusement park, she'd turned down Harper's offer. Three times, in fact. Certain she would be safe here, Levi had eventually talked Piper into changing her mind, assuring her that they'd take every precaution necessary.

He'd wanted her to have a break from being surrounded by the same four walls. It turned out that she didn't mentally deal very well with remaining indoors. She'd been as edgy and restless as a damn junkie over the past week.

Not that she'd only had Levi's company during that time. Khloë's twin brother, Ciaran, had teleported the girls to the apartment occasionally. Also, Devon and Larkin often came to say hi after work. Harper and Raini regularly called too.

Basically, they'd all done their best to ensure that Piper didn't feel alone or without support. She adored them for it.

They'd all been delighted on hearing that she and Levi had "gotten their acts together," in Larkin's words. Knox and the other sentinels seemed equally pleased, particularly that Levi was no longer alone.

She'd been worried that her mom and Joe would react badly, given they were well aware that Celeste would blow a fuse. But after Piper gave the couple the news when they came over for dinner, Whitney had grinned at her mate and said, "You owe me fifty dollars. Pay up." He'd only smiled and rolled his eyes.

Apparently her mother had sensed that something was brewing between Piper and Levi and, feeling that her daughter was 'easy to love,' had been sure he'd fall hard for her. Joe hadn't been so certain it would happen, given that Levi appeared to avoid serious relationships, but he hadn't been upset to be wrong.

Neither Whitney nor Joe had mentioned the inevitable fact that Celeste would lose her mind, but they all knew it to be true. Joe probably broke the news to his daughter before she had the chance to learn of it through the grapevine. Whatever the case, the banshee would be aware of it by now. Still, she hadn't contacted either Piper or Levi to rip them a new one. Maybe she'd finally decided to heed Levi's warnings. Stranger things had happened.

Hearing a low chuckle, Piper glanced at him. Sitting beside her on the incredibly chic and comfortable seats while munching on a hotdog, he was watching in amusement as Raini argued with her father, Lachlan. The male imp was a blast, much like the brother he'd brought along, Bram.

Piper had been to the stadium several times, but she'd never before watched a race from the luxury of a VIP box. She'd be enjoying the experience a lot more if she wasn't so worried that danger would strike again. Especially since Asher was here.

Silently cursing the fucker who'd apparently decided her life should be forfeit, Piper inhaled deeply and then blew out a breath.

Done with his hotdog, Levi put his lips to her ear. "Relax, all is good."

"Yeah, *for now.*" Piper rolled her shoulders. "I shouldn't have let you talk me into this."

He hooked his arm around her neck. "I get why you're worried, but no one who isn't part of our circle knows you're here. The glass wall is tinted. No one outside can see you. Ciaran teleported us into the VIP box, so no one saw you enter. He'll also teleport us back to my place, so you won't have to worry that anyone will spot you leaving."

"Someone could barge right in and—"

"The door is locked. Vin and Mason are manning it from the outside. The waiter delivered the food before we came, and he won't be called back inside until we're gone. The only person we'll be letting in the room is Teague, and you're not in view of the door so you won't be seen by anyone out there when the door opens." He brushed her earlobe with his nose. "I wouldn't have brought you here if I thought you wouldn't be safe. You know that."

She sighed. "I do know that. I just worry for everyone here."

"They worry for you, which is—"

A short crackle through the intercom preceded an announcement that the next race would soon begin. Piper glanced out of the glass wall in front of her to see if the hellhorses had yet filed outside. The rows of high-powered floodlights beamed through the air, lighting up the dirt track, obstacles, fake grass, and the spectators standing near the fence adjacent to the track. No hellhorses as yet, though.

One of the widescreen wall-mounted TVs listed the various demons who'd be racing. Khloë's anchor, Teague, was among them. His stallion was favorite to win, as per usual. Undefeated, it was believed to be the fastest of its kind. Having seen it compete many times, Piper would have to agree with that assessment.

Khloë was currently pouring drinks at the minibar. The imp seemed a little jittery, most likely nervous for her anchor. Who wouldn't be? Hellhorse racing was no easy sport. It was intense. Gruesome. Inhumane. Which was why her demon liked it so much.

The races were positively nerve-wracking to watch. The obstacles were *brutal.* The eight-foot high stone walls and hedges had ditches either side of them. Those ditches contained everything from bubbling hot lava to writhing masses of venomous snakes. Blood was always spilled, and injuries could be seriously severe.

One might ask why hellhorses would put themselves through that. Well, they weren't docile like full-blooded horses, and they could never be described as prey animals. They were wild. Volatile. Bad-tempered. Uber aggressive. Some might even say psychotic.

Demons loved to gamble, so there was no shortage of spectators. Fortunately for them, there was no shortage of seats. People could choose from the picnic area, cafeteria, tiered grandstand, and VIP boxes.

"That's it, I'm done," Raini burst out. "This conversation is *over.*"

Lachlan threw up his arms. "Do you always have to make a fuss about nothing?"

Raini frowned. "There's nothing fussy about me telling you not to steal the TV from the wall."

"No one will even notice it's gone," said Lachlan.

"You said that about Uncle Dan's coffin. Oddly enough, the people working at the funeral home noticed that his corpse was no longer in a coffin."

Lachlan frowned. "He would have wanted me to have it."

"Dear God, why?"

"These are hard times we live in. A man has to make his money somehow."

"By stealing from dead people?"

"What difference did it make to him? He was a goner. And it wasn't like he was getting buried."

"Actually, it *was*. They instead cremated him."

"He would have liked going out in a blaze of fire."

Raini shook her head. "I don't know why I ever expect you to have an 'oh yeah, that was unfair of me' moment. It's not like I'm not aware you have *zero* ethics."

"From what I've observed, they get in people's way."

"But they stop us from doing seriously unwise things. Like shooting your own brother in the head with a nail gun."

Lachlan shrugged. "We all agreed he had a screw loose. I did him a favor by giving him another one."

"No. No, you really didn't."

Again, an announcement came over the intercom. Cheers and whistles rang out as twenty hellhorses padded onto the track with their heads held high. All muscle and grace, they halted near the start line, lined up side by side.

It was easy to tell Teague's stallion from the others due to the scar that slashed across its neck. Unlike some of the others, his steed wasn't nervously twitching its inward-turned ear tips, trotting on the spot, or swishing its long, high-carried tail. It stood tall and proud and still, utterly calm and confident.

Staring out of the wall of glass, Asher opened and closed his fist, that adorable face creased in frustration.

Piper glanced at Harper, who was in the process of pocketing her cell phone. "What is the little man doing?"

"I think he's trying to pyroport a hellhorse to himself," replied the sphinx. "Let's all take a moment to be thankful that they're too big for him to move."

Piper snickered. She couldn't blame him for wanting one. They were magnificent. Truly. They were packed with pure, sleek muscle and boasted long powerful legs. Their elegantly arched necks, dark lush manes, and metallic black coat added to their regal air. Not even their all-black, wide-set eyes took away from how breathtakingly beautiful they were.

The steeds below repeatedly tried annoying their competitors by snapping their teeth, peeling back their lips, or puffing smoke out of their nostrils. Teague's stallion ignored them. Others? Not so much. Hence the neighing and body-slamming.

Asher huffed. "Gossake," he snapped—his attempt at saying 'for God's sake,' she'd learned. He stomped over to Harper. "Mommy, I wants one. *Pwease*."

Harper's expression gentled. "I'm sorry, baby, you can't buy hellhorses. They're not toys or pets."

Pouting, he leaned against his father's leg. Knox, in deep conversation with Tanner, briefly reached down to ruffle his son's dark, silky hair.

A champagne flute in hand, Khloë turned to Harper. "You know, Teague's demon will let Asher ride—"

"No," said Harper.

Khloë's brow furrowed. "Why not? The beast wouldn't hurt Asher."

The sphinx folded her arms. "The answer's still no."

"But the little guy would love it."

"I am not sticking my son on the back of a hellhorse. They're insane."

"You were riding rodeo bulls when you were like, what, four? Maybe even younger."

Piper felt her brows lift, though she probably shouldn't be surprised. Imps did all kinds of risky shit. Harper was raised by them.

"But not hellhorses," the sphinx pointed out. "That's a whole other ball game."

Letting out an annoyed sigh, Khloë shook her head. "They get such a bad rap, if you ask me. Everyone calls them wild and vicious. Pure lies."

Just then, one steed on the track bit deep into the neck of another.

Levi looked at Khloë. "Not vicious, huh?"

She grimaced. "It's just a little love bite."

Devon snorted, nibbling on a carrot stick she'd swiped from the buffet of finger-foods. "Face it, they're nuts. Ooh, seems like the race is about to start."

Like Piper and Levi, some gathered near the glass wall. Others remained in their seats. Maddox, Hector, Lachlan, and Bram opted to observe from the private balcony. They opened the sliding glass door—letting in the scents of horses, dirt, and concession food—and then closed it behind them.

Moments later, a tense silence fell. The hellhorses stilled. Piper held her breath.

A horn blared.

The steeds bolted over the start line and raced across the track so fast their legs were a blur. They didn't bother to remain in their own individual lanes. They ran as a herd, leaving clouds of dust in their wake.

Some put on impressive bursts of speed, jockeying for first

place instantly. Others, like Teague's stallion, moved fast but steadily and fell into the middle of the herd.

Piper loved the sound of their hooves thundering along the dirt track. She didn't pay much attention to the commentary that came over the loudspeaker. Her only interest was Teague's steed—who she'd been quick to put her money on.

Khloë repeatedly cheered on the stallion, bouncing on the spot in what seemed to be both excitement and restlessness.

"They're almost at the first hurdle," said Raini, her hands splayed on the sides of her face. "Here's where the race is gonna get hard to watch."

She was not wrong. The wall . . . shit, it had blades sticking out of its surface. Teague's steed pushed off its hindlegs and jumped like a boss, all but soaring over the obstacle. One of its competitors didn't leap high enough, scraping its belly on the blades and promptly falling into a ditch of red-hot spikes.

Devon flinched. "The amount of sadism involved in this sport is plain unnecessary."

None of the other hellhorses stopped to check on the fallen steed. They forged on ahead and soon arrived at the next hurdle. Most cleared it smoothly. Piper winced as one steed landed wrong, causing its foreleg to crumple. It collapsed to the ground but managed to avoid the ditch of broken glass shards.

The remaining hellhorses rocketed across the oval track and through a pool of flaming water. Well, ouch. They galloped from one horrendous hurdle to another. Some steeds cleared them. Others didn't and subsequently fell into pitiless ditches.

"Okay, we got fourteen hellhorses left," said Keenan.

One abruptly swung its head and breathed fire on the steed beside it, who flinched away and knocked into another hellhorse . . . who subsequently bashed into another . . . who inadvertently shoved its neighbor into a fence. The latter steed lost its momentum and wasn't able to gather itself in time to make the next jump. It fell right into a ditch of boiling water.

Piper hunched up her shoulders. "Oh, f—" Remembering Asher's presence, she edited herself. "Fudge."

Vicious as they were, the beasts bit and body-slammed their competitors as they ran. The biggest fan of such dirty tricks sped up enough to bite the ass of the competitor in front. That competitor whinnied in shock and pain, too distracted to time its jump right . . . and so the poor thing tumbled into a ditch of flames. Another tripped as it landed and went down hard, almost taking Teague's stallion with it. But his steed skillfully skirted around the fallen beast, thank God.

The fire-breathing asshole was a real problem—setting alight tails and manes, and burning the legs of whatever hellhorse was in front of it at the time. Which was stupid, really, because constantly exhaling flames took up strength that could be spent on, you know, *running*. But you could never count on a hellhorse to do the expected, so . . .

The racing steeds flew across the track, their coats covered in a fine sheen of sweat. It was clear that some were beginning to tire. They fell behind little by little. Others inched forward as they ran, including Teague's steed.

Piper tensed as she noticed they were now speeding toward a hedge that kept randomly bursting into flames. "Oh, hell."

They jumped. Some went unscathed, but not all. Squeals came from those who got hit by the flames, and Teague's steed was one of them.

Khloë went stiff. "No, no, no, no."

Piper puffed out a breath of relief when it didn't tumble into a ditch but instead ran on, steam shimmering off its coat.

Khloë dabbed at her face as if to cool it. "Nerves. Shot. Nerves. Shot. God, he's covered in wounds."

Yes, there were slices, bites, burns, and small puncture wounds from the thorny hedges.

"The other steeds are in no better shape," said Piper.

Fire-breather was a *mess.* And it right then decided to burn the flank of Teague's steed. *Son of a bitch.*

"I am *sick* of that . . . goober," Devon growled.

Apparently she wasn't alone in that, because the hellhorses either side of said goober body-slammed it in unison. Its pace faltered, and it went down on one foreleg. In doing so, it tripped up another, taking them both out of the race.

Khloë grinned. "And the fire-breathing A-hole goes down."

"Only eight left," said Keenan, splaying his hand on his mate's back.

Rocking back and forth on her heels, Raini made a sound of dread. "The final part of the track is always the worst."

It was. The hurdles were closer together, the ditches were often wider, and the jumps could sometimes be higher.

The steeds upped the dirty-trick ante to distract each other—sinking teeth into coats, bashing each other's bodies, puffing out smoke to obstruct the vision of others. But none of those tricks worked today. Every beast surged on.

There were more hedges. More walls. More ditches. More injuries. More falling hellhorses.

Soon, only five remained in the race. And all five were fast approaching the second to last hurdle. They began to *seriously* pick up the pace, their hooves thudding on the track harder and faster than before.

Teague's stallion put on a burst of speed just before it jumped the next hurdle and cleared the ditch, landing right into second place. The steed it had just overtaken tried catching up but couldn't.

"That's it, you got this." Her joined hands pressed against

her mouth, Khloë shifted from one foot to another. "Come on, come on, come on."

A hand to her throat, Harper said, "Okay, one more to go. Just one."

Which might have been reassuring if the hurdle wasn't an absolute fucker. Snakes writhed along the wall, hyped up somehow—maybe on pheromones or something. They hissed at each other and pitched their heads forward threateningly.

Khloë slapped a hand over her eyes. "No, I can't watch. I can't." But she spread her fingers and peeked out at the track.

As the hellhorses closed in on the hurdle, the spectators' voices and cheers rose in volume. The commentator's voice came sharp and fast and edged with urgency.

Teague's stallion edged more and more forward as it reached the obstacle. It leaped high, clearing the wall in one smooth jump and narrowly escaped being bit by a snake . . . and landed into first place. Then it was galloping even faster than before. The others tried catching up, but they had no chance. It had left them in the dust.

"That's it, that's it, that's it, don't fall, don't fall, don't—Yes!" Khloë jumped up and down as Teague's hellhorse zipped over the finish line. "It won!"

Keenan hugged her, smiling. "I don't know why you're ever surprised."

Applause rang out across the stadium. There were no doubt a few curses and boos as well, but the cheering was so loud and wild it drowned them out.

Beaming, Khloë snickered as Teague's hellhorse tossed its head in a very arrogant gesture while smoothly coming to a halt. "Cocky fu—fiend." She sagged. "I am so glad that's over. Now I need to go pee. My bladder can't take this kind of stress."

As the imp and Keenan left for the restroom, Piper and Levi returned to their seats.

"I really will never know why even crazy creatures would put themselves through that," Piper told him. "Devon's right, it's sadistic. Who actually seeks out pain?"

"I can't say shit about it," said Levi. "I fight in the combat ring often enough. Haven't since I found you, though."

"I watched you fight a few times." She wasn't about to admit it right there, but she'd had quite a sexually primal reaction to observing him let loose like that.

"I know. I saw you." He settled his hand on her thigh. "I always saw you. And I always wanted to haul you out of your seat, throw you over my shoulder, and take you home with me."

"How very caveman of you. I might have been down with that. What? Why are you smiling like that?"

He gave a slight shake of the head. "No reason."

She narrowed her eyes. "I'm not sure I believe you."

"I wouldn't believe me either."

"Tell me what's going through your head."

"Nah. I'd rather do this." Levi planted a kiss on her mouth. "Yeah, needed that." Before her, he'd never been big on kissing. He'd never really understood the appeal in it. For him, it had been more of a step in a dance. A means to an end. But he fucking *loved* taking her mouth. Loved tasting it, biting it, consuming it, seeing it stretched around his cock.

Shit, he needed to get those thoughts out of his head before he started getting hard right here in front of God and everyone.

"You two are so cute together," said Devon, grinning. "So, who's moving in with who after the danger is over? I'm guessing you don't intend to live apart."

"I agreed to move into Levi's apartment," said Piper.

He'd thought she might take a while to agree, but she'd been pretty easygoing about it. He suspected that he'd been right in thinking she wouldn't feel the same way about her house after what occurred there.

"Solid choice," said Devon. "It's a good building. Totally secure. And I'll be nearby . . . which means I can run to you with the baby when he or she won't stop crying, because I'll have *no* idea what I'm doing."

Tanner curled his arm around Devon's shoulders. "You'll be fine."

"Not if Khloë's right," she said.

"Not if I'm right about what?" asked the imp as she re-entered the box with Keenan behind her.

"Khloë said the baby might not like me if it's a hellhound," Devon told her mate. "Your kind considers mine prey. She could be right."

Khloë waved her hand. "I was messing with you. Whether it's a hellpup or hellkitten, it will adore you. It'll just adore me more." She frowned when Devon stared at her in silence. "What? Everybody does."

The hellcat looked at Keenan. "I don't know how you deal with her."

Khloë sniffed. "I don't know how you still haven't taken a shit. I mean, that's just unhealthy at this point."

"*Khloë.*"

Keenan tugged gently on the imp's hair. "Stop riling her up."

Her eyes smiling, Khloë pouted. "But it makes me so happy."

Devon rested a protective hand on her swollen belly. "You're stressing out me and Mistletoe over here."

Tanner's brows snapped together. "Wait, Mistletoe?"

Devon shrugged. "It's a nice girl's name. I'm trying it out to see if it works for me. I still like Axis for a boy."

Tanner slashed a hand through the air. "No kid of mine will be called Axis *or* Mistletoe."

"Why do you keep rejecting all my suggestions?"

"Because they're fucking bizarre *at best*."

Khloë chuckled. "I already have my daughter's name picked out." She paused. "Belladonna."

A line dented Tanner's brow. "As in deadly nightshade?"

"It's a *way* better plant than Mistletoe," Khloë stated. "Totally badass."

Tanner slid his gaze to Keenan. "You're down with your kid being named Belladonna?"

Keenan lifted one shoulder. "I really don't see the point in investing any time or energy in discussing the matter. She'll have changed her mind by tomorrow."

"What would *you* name the baby if given the choice?" Khloë asked Tanner. "Personally, I recommend you call it Mildred after my aunt if it's a girl."

Devon's eyelid twitched. "You don't have an Aunt Mildred, she doesn't exist."

Khloë's lips flattened. "If she heard you say that, she'd—"

"Cry fictional tears?" Devon suggested.

Folding her arms, Khloë shook her head. "I can't believe you don't remember her."

Piper leaned into Levi, and then her voice flowed into his head. *Is Mildred real?*

*I truly have no idea*, Levi replied. He turned his head as the door to the VIP box opened. Teague strode inside, tall and well-built, much like his demon.

Khloë's face lit up. "About time you got here."

"Hey there, gorgeous." He bent and pressed a kiss to her head then tipped his chin at the incubus beside her. "Keenan."

There was a time when the sentinel might have merely

grunted in return, but he and Teague had grown to like each other.

"Congratulations on your win," Keenan said to him.

The others all passed on their congratulations, including Levi. He then added, "This is Piper, my anchor and mate. Piper, this is Khloë's anchor, Teague."

She smiled at him. "I've heard a lot about you from Khloë."

"Right back at you," said Teague. He looked about to say more, but then a small body clamped around his leg.

"I wanna ride," Asher announced.

Teague arched his brows. "You want a ride?"

The little boy nodded. "Uh-huh."

Teague lifted Asher and set the kid on his shoulders. "How's that?"

"No, want *horsey.*" But Asher was giggling as he said it, because Teague was puffing smoke out of his nostrils just as his demon could.

*Isn't that smoke noxious?* Piper asked.

Levi cast her a quick glance. *Only if it pours out of his hellhorse's nostrils, and only if the demon wants it to be noxious.*

Called away by Lachlan, Teague stalked off with Asher.

Levi soon found himself deep in conversation with Tanner about an upcoming hellhound race when Piper's voice again floated into his mind. *Teague looks at Larkin a lot,* she said.

Levi looked their way only to see Teague—now with Asher no longer on his shoulders—standing a few feet in front of the harpy with his gaze locked firmly on her. *She pretends not to notice most of the time. But sometimes . . .*

*Sometimes, what?*

"Keep staring at me and I'll throw you off that fucking balcony," Larkin conversationally said to the hellhorse.

Teague's mouth curved. "Promise?"

Sighing tiredly, Larkin pointed at the opposite side of the room. “Go stand over there.”

“I like it here,” said Teague. “It has a pretty view. Dangerous but oh so pretty.”

Her lips firmed. “You think you’re charming, don’t you?”

“I’m sensing you’d disagree. That hurts. I thought we were friends.”

Larkin frowned. “I hurled chips of hell-ice at your face the last time I saw you.”

He smiled again. “I know, I’ve got them in a jar at home. Took me an hour to pluck them all out of my skin.”

“You . . . A jar? You have them in a jar?”

“I like mementos.”

She stared at him. “Your thought processes just aren’t normal. Khloë, Seabiscuit needs you for something.”

Teague chuckled. “You giving me a pet name only deepens our frien—”

“I got him.” Khloë linked her arm through his and began leading him away. She leaned into him and muttered, “Remember your oath.”

He grunted, the amusement slipping out of his expression.

Piper tensed. *What oath?*

Levi glanced at her. *You realize you don’t have to whisper when you talk to me telepathically, right? No one else can hear you.* He winced as she pinched his thigh.

*What. Oath?*

*I have no idea, I was wondering the same thing.* It might be something that explained why Teague—a man not known for hesitating when he wanted something—hadn’t ever made a move on Larkin when he very clearly had a thing for her.

Once more clinging to his father’s leg, Asher tapped it hard. “Daddy!”

Knox looked down. “What?”

Asher smiled. “Sniff up.” He giggled like a loon when Knox’s face scrunched up in distaste. “I farted.”

“Ah, the Wallis blood is strong in this one,” said Levi.

Knox met his gaze. “Don’t I know it.”

# CHAPTER TWENTY

Swiping his ringing cell from the kitchen counter the following evening, Levi saw Keenan's name flashing on the screen. He answered, "Yeah?"

"You ought to know that Celeste spent last night and all of today in a cell," said the incubus.

Levi blinked. "What? Why?"

"She caused a massive scene at the Xpress bar while utterly shitfaced. Threw glasses, upturned tables, spat at the bouncers, screamed like . . . well, a banshee."

"Jesus." One-handed this time, Levi went back to stacking the dishwasher. "Losing her shit to that extent in public isn't usually her style."

"When Vin and Mason brought her in, they said she ranted about you and Piper the whole time. She hates that you two are mated."

"Not a shock." Levi exhaled heavily. "She's been quiet recently, but I figured she'd do something stupid at some point."

"It would seem she's done bottling up her feelings." Keenan paused. "The main reason I'm calling is that when Vin informed her once again that she would not be allowed to call her father, she claimed to know who's been initiating the attacks on Piper."

Levi paused in reaching for a dishwasher tablet from the cupboard. "Did she now?"

"Yes. But she also said that she'll only talk to you about it."

He felt his nostrils flare. "That fucking woman." He grabbed a tablet and roughly placed it into the dispenser.

"It's unlikely that she knows anything. She's probably just playing games out of spite. It's what she does. Still, she's adamant that she has information you'll want to hear. Vin questioned her repeatedly, but she refused to cough up anything."

Grinding his teeth, Levi shoved the dishwasher door closed. There was a beep, and then the cycle started. "I doubt she'd be so stubborn if Knox was there."

"He won't be back from his business trip until tomorrow morning. I could ask him to pyroport back here and deal with the matter, but I only do that in cases of emergency. Celeste is not one. It's important we erase the danger to Piper but, as I said before, I'm not convinced Celeste knows anything."

"Neither am I, so don't bother Knox with this."

"I'm happy to question her myself and press her into changing her mind about only speaking with you. I can make her talk, no problem. It's up to you."

Levi didn't doubt that Keenan could change her mind. The incubus was good at making others part with information. But . . . "I'll hear her out." Or, more to the point, he'd use it as an opportunity to get a few things across to her.

"You sure?"

"Positive. I'll be there in about twenty-five minutes, depending on traffic." Levi rang off, pocketed his phone, and made his way through the apartment toward the main bathroom.

Since making things official, he and Piper had come up with an agreement—if she cooked, he cleaned up afterwards, and vice versa. So after they ate the dinner she cooked, he'd sent her off to take a bath while he lived up to his half of the bargain. He'd planned to join her in the tub at some point. He'd have to save it for another time, thanks to goddamn Celeste.

Entering the bathroom, Levi felt his mouth curve at the sight he found. "I didn't realize you were such a fan of bubbles."

"Things got a little out of control," she said, leaning back against the tub, her head barely visible.

"How so?"

"I used the bubble bath that Khloë gave me because she doesn't like the smell of mangos. It doesn't say on the bottle to use it sparingly." Her brow wrinkled. "Everything okay? You're smiling, but I can tell that something's up."

Liking that she was so very in tune with him, Levi crouched beside the tub and brushed aside some bubbles as he said, "Keenan called me. Apparently Celeste made a fool out of herself in the Underground last night while blitzed." He relayed the details that Keenan gave him.

Piper's lips parted. "Seriously? That's dramatic even for her."

"She was detained by Vin and Mason. She's still in a cell now." Levi dipped his hand into the water to cup her knee. "She claims she knows who's after you."

Piper sat up straight, gaping. "She claims *what*?"

"It's what she told Vin. She also said she'll part with the information, but that she'll only share it with me."

Piper's face scrunched up. "Bull*shit*. She doesn't know anything. Either she's playing a game because she's pissed about being locked up, or she's thinking she can bargain for freedom if she pretends to have information that you'll want." Piper's brow pinched when he said nothing. "Wait, you don't believe her, do you?"

"Not at all."

"But you still intend to talk to her," Piper sensed. "Why? On the off-chance that she's breaking habits and *actually* telling the truth for a change? You'll be wasting your time. If she knew who wanted me dead, she wouldn't tell you because then she'd also have to explain why she hadn't mentioned it sooner. Celeste doesn't fear much, but she's terrified of Knox. He'd be beyond furious with her for holding back something like this. She wouldn't want to suffer his wrath."

"I agree it's highly likely that she knows nothing, but I need to talk to her face to face."

Piper's eyes searched his own. "Ah, I get it. You're not really interested in hearing what she has to say, you know she'll only reel off a bunch of lies. You're going to see her because you want to confront her over what she said to me at the studio."

See, his girl was totally in tune with him. "I always planned to. I held off because you and I have more important things going on right now. I was planning to confront her once all the shit surrounding you has blown over. However, after how she behaved last night, she needs dealing with. Keenan could handle it, sure. But since the other things she needs to answer for all concern you, I might as well be the one who handles the matter."

"Tell me honestly. Did you only hold off on confronting her this long because things are hectic at the moment, or were you purposely giving her time to do something stupid and add to her infractions so that her overall punishment would be more than a slap on the wrist?"

His demon grinned, liking how easily she saw through Levi. "Would I really be that ruthless, baby?"

"Absolutely."

He pressed a soft kiss to her mouth. "True."

"She's not worth your time, Levi."

"The conversation I'm about to have with her is long overdue. She tried to make you doubt me. She tried to come between us. She made you *hurt*. I can't ignore any of that. I won't."

"I shouldn't have let her get into my head. I knew better."

"It's not on you, it's on her. I want her to receive the message that she does *not* get to fuck with you. I warned her, but it made no difference. And no minor punishment will make much difference either."

"So you gave her the chance to dig a deeper hole for herself."

"I did. And she fell head first into that trap." Just as he and his demon had counted on. "Hearing that you and I claimed each other as mates no doubt knocked her over the edge."

"Probably. She was furious enough when she learned we were anchors."

Levi sank his free hand into the water and linked his fingers through hers. "She's going to kick up more of a fuss if I don't nip this right in the bud. It needs to be handled in a way that discourages her from causing more problems. I know you're used to her playing these games and causing petty drama. But that's what pisses me off. You should never have had to get used to it."

Piper nibbled on her lower lip. "She's not going to be leaving that cell any time today, is she?" It wasn't really a question.

"No. She needs to pay for all she did. And she will. But I intend to have a chat with her first. Her reign of pettiness ends now." It had to. Piper had enough on her plate. He wasn't going to let Celeste add to it. Nor would he allow her to be a future problem for his mate.

"When are you leaving?"

"Now. I'll be back in about an hour and a half. Maybe less."

She sighed. "Okay."

Underwater, he gave her hand a little squeeze. "I was originally going to get in that tub with you. I'll save that for next time." He kissed her again, stood, and wiped his hands on the small towel. "See you soon. Love you, baby." He turned and headed for the door, smiling at her squawk of surprise.

"Wait, *what*?" she called after him.

"Enjoy your bath," he said.

She spluttered. "You can't blurt out something like that and then swan out of here!"

But he did exactly that, chuckling to himself as a string of loud curses followed him out of the room.

Exiting his apartment, he told Enzo and Dez that he'd be back soon and then headed out. Not long later, he was pulling up outside the prison's front entrance. The building not only had many complicated security measures in place, it was safeguarded by a myriad of spells that ensured no one could teleport inside or out. Moreover, every individual spell was covered with a protective spell to prevent anyone from unraveling them.

Waiting for Levi outside, Keenan pushed away from the wall he'd been leaning against. "Hey. How's Piper?"

"Probably annoyed with me," replied Levi.

"Why does that make you smile?"

"I wanted her to be thinking about something other than Celeste while I was gone. I'd say I achieved that. Now tell me exactly what went down at the Xpress bar last night."

Gesturing for him to follow, Keenan pushed open the front door as he explained, "The bartender said she came alone and sat at the bar knocking back shot after shot, blowing off any man who came near her but otherwise not saying much of anything to anyone."

"It's unusual for Celeste to send men away," said Levi as they crossed the reception area and bypassed the security desk. "She usually relishes such attention."

"Not last night she didn't." Reaching the door that would lead to the first floor of cells—all of which were reserved for people who wouldn't be confined long-term—Keenan punched the security code into the keypad on the wall. "Midway through yet another drink, it was like she quite simply snapped."

There was a loud buzz, and then Keenan pulled open the door. They both stepped through it but neither proceeded down the corridor as he went on, "She started screaming. She grabbed glasses and threw them at the wall, the floor, even at people's faces. She knocked over the nearest tables, slung a stool at someone, and even tossed coasters and bowls of complimentary nuts at the guys who tried calming her down.

"The bouncers came to remove her. She spat and swore and yelled at them as they hauled her out of the bar. She was still acting like a loon when Vin and Mason arrived to detain her."

Levi's demon shook its head in disgust. "Essentially, she had a tantrum."

"Essentially. She's not in the least bit sheepish or remorseful. In fact, she's outraged that her demands to be freed have been ignored."

Levi frowned. "She *does* remember what she did, right?"

"Actually, she claims she doesn't remember a thing." Keenan snorted in skepticism. "Also, she believes that none of it counts because she was drunk."

Levi let out a heavy exhale. "Unreal."

"She's used to people—namely her father—making excuses for her behavior and letting her get away with shit to compensate for her mother leaving. Which is probably why she's demanding she be allowed to call him. That demand has so far been ignored." Keenan twisted his mouth. "You still want to talk to her?"

Levi nodded. "It has to be done."

He and Keenan walked side by side as they headed toward the rows of cells. As they neared another security desk, they tipped their chin at the guard stood behind it.

"Evening," said Omar, rounding the desk. He pressed a button, a buzzer sounded, and the iron door in front of Levi and Keenan then slid open.

Holding back a grimace as the scents of bleach, iron, mildew, and sweat greeted him, Levi followed Keenan along the corridor of cells.

The incubus stopped outside a particular one and telepathically said, *It would appear she's had another tantrum.*

Glancing through the iron bars, Levi inwardly sighed. There was fluff everywhere, courtesy of the torn pillow that had been slung across the small space. The mattress cover had been yanked off and shredded—there were ribbons of it everywhere. The chair that was usually tucked under the steel table lay on its side at the other end of the cell. Also, there were a few fresh dents in the metal locker, making him wonder if she'd bashed it using the chair.

Celeste was leaning against the rear cement wall, her arms wrapped around her body. She looked, well, hung-over. Her eyes were bloodshot, her makeup was smeared, her face was puffy, and her hair was a bird's nest.

"Hello, Levi," she said, her voice croaky—probably courtesy of the screaming and yelling she'd done. "I wasn't sure they'd really contact you."

Levi folded his arms. "You claimed to have information about the person who's targeting Piper. Of course they contacted me."

Her mouth pinched, Celeste smoothed her hands down her

wrinkled dress. "I'm sure you find it rather amusing to see me in a cell."

"A cell you clearly didn't much like." He eyed the damage and flicked up his brow. "Yet another tantrum?"

Her eyes blazed, and her cheeks flushed. "You can be such a condescending bas—"

"I don't care. Let's hear this information you have."

Her brow creased. "What, you want us to talk here?"

"Why not?"

"Because it's a *cell*."

"And you're in it for a reason."

Her nostrils flaring, she scraped back her messy hair. "I can see why I was kept here overnight, but there's no need to detain me any longer. I'm quite sober now, and I'm no danger to myself or others."

Given how self-destructive she could be . . . "You've been a danger to yourself for as long as I've known you, but that's off the subject. Now, who's after Piper?"

Celeste inched up her chin. "Let me out of here and I'll tell you."

Sighing, Levi turned to Keenan. "She has nothing. I'm done." He stalked away, calling her bluff.

High heels clacked along the cement floor and then . . . "It's Sefton!"

Levi slowly spun on his heel.

Her hands curled around the iron bars, Celeste stated, "Sefton's the one who attacked Piper."

Pulling on her sweats, Piper silently cursed. What kind of person told a woman that they loved her and then just walked right on out of the room?

The kind that liked to mess with people. That was who.

The thing was . . . Levi generally didn't seem to take much pleasure in poking at others. He bantered and teased as much as the next person, sure, but fuck with people's heads? That wasn't something he made a habit of doing, and blurting out I love yous wasn't something people often did as a joke. But why say it and then leave? Why chuckle as he left? Why not give her a chance to respond?

She'd been obsessing over the whole thing since the moment he exited the bathroom. Her demon believed he'd been sincere, and it was rather pleased. Not that it was all that moved by the apparent declaration—it didn't feel or value love. But the entity wanted him tied to them; wanted him so committed to them that he wouldn't go anywhere.

She wanted to believe her demon was right to be so certain. She wanted it to be true that he cared for her so much. Because the truth was that Piper loved him right back.

There'd been some bumps in the road they'd taken to get to where they were now, but the rough journey had been worth it. *He* was worth it. And if it turned out he'd been yanking her chain, she'd verbally rail his ass. Her demon would probably bite said ass instead.

Well, she'd question him when he got home. Which should be soon. It wouldn't take him long to deliver his warning to Celeste.

Finally dressed, Piper sank onto the edge of the bed. She still couldn't quite believe that her stepsister had caused such a major public scene. Especially in the Underground. That was kind of like taking a shit in Knox and Harper's backyard. Then again, banshees weren't exactly known for having impressive self-control. Add in copious amounts of alcohol and a furious state of mind . . . yeah, that was a bad combination.

It could have been a cry for Levi's attention—maybe

conscious, maybe subconscious. If so, it had been a successful move. To an extent, anyway. It hadn't only earned her Levi's attention. No, in blowing a fuse in such a spectacular fashion she'd put herself on the shit list of a seriously merciless Prime. Knox wasn't known for his leniency.

Having heard some of the stories of just what sort of punishments the male demon liked to dish out, Piper felt sorry for Celeste. Kind of. Well . . . only a little, to be truthful. It was hard to truly feel bad for someone who'd invested a lot of energy in pissing her off over the years and would have come between her and Levi if she could have.

Really, the person Piper felt most sorry for was Joe. It would pain him to know that his daughter was not only locked up in a cell but also due a harsh punishment. He'd tried so hard over the years to save her from herself, and Piper knew he felt that he'd failed Celeste. In reality, Celeste had failed herself.

Standing, Piper crossed to the dresser and retrieved both her hairbrush and cell. As she dragged the brush through her damp hair, she pressed the button on the side of her phone to light up the screen so she could check the time. Levi hadn't been gone long. He should be back some—

A knock at the front door made her brow wrinkle. It definitely wasn't Levi. He wouldn't need to knock.

She set the cell back on the dresser, padded through the apartment, and then glanced through the door's peephole. *Dez.* Piper opened the door. "Hi," she said with a half-smile.

A tall figure slid behind him. One she recognized. She frowned. Why was he—

A force *punched* into her mind just as he snapped Dez's neck. Snapped it. Like it was a mere twig.

*Oh, fuck.*

She wanted to lob an orb of hellfire in this bastard's face.

Wanted to slam the door shut and lock it. Wanted to call out to Levi. But she couldn't move—not physically, not psychically. He'd effortlessly seized control of her in an instant, and no amount of struggling from her enraged demon had any effect.

Piper's heart began to pound in her chest as panic raced through her. This man . . . he was the person who'd killed Diem and Emma, the man who'd come close to killing Missy. More, he was the son of a bitch who murdered Levi's aunt and made him an orphan.

"Hello, Piper. I was hoping you'd be home. I understand that Levi isn't here right now. I'd say that's a shame, but I was hoping we could talk in private, if that's okay with you."

Her panic amped up as she found herself stepping back and opening the door wider in invitation. *Shit, shit, shit.*

"Thank you," he said with a placid smile, crossing the threshold and then literally dumping Dez's dead body on the floor.

Horror filling her, she dropped her gaze to the Force member, wondering if Enzo had suffered the same fate.

Her visitor closed the door, still smiling, the image of friendliness. "Sorry to barge in on you like this. I appreciate you taking the time to talk with me." The weirdo actually spoke as if she had willingly invited him inside, as if she'd had any choice in the matter. "Let's go into the living room, shall we?"

# CHAPTER TWENTY-ONE

"Sefton, you say?" Levi strode back to Celeste's cell. "And how is it you know this?"

She pulled a face. "It's obvious, isn't it? He blames her for the torture he endured. He wants her to pay, but he's not eager to endure *another* punishment, so he won't confront her. Instead, he comes across as contrite and fearful, and he lets his brother do lots of smack talk so that people look more at Jasper. Really, *Sefton's* the one after Piper."

"What proof do you have that it's him?"

Stretching out her arms, Celeste raised her shoulders. "Why would I need proof when, like I said, it's obvious?"

Levi felt his face harden. Just as he'd suspected . . . "You didn't really have anything to tell me. You didn't even spout that lie in the simple hope of getting yourself out of this cell, or you'd have tried making a deal with Vin. You asked for me to come here, because this was about getting my attention."

Her eyelids flickered.

"You wanted to make me come to you. And you think it makes you smart that it worked. You think it means you have power over me. That's where you're wrong. Because I didn't come here for *you*. I came here for Piper. She's what matters to me."

Red spots stained her cheeks as she sneered. "And, what, you think I'm jealous? You think I truly meant it when I said I wanted you back?"

"Oh, I think both those things, yes. Whether or not you were truthful when you told her I have some hold over you I don't know or care. But I am certain that you'd have me back if you could. Not for the right reason, though. It's not really about me, even if you do feel something for me. It's about Piper. About *hurting* Piper. It's one of your favorite pastimes, from what I've observed. And I made it clear to you that I wouldn't allow that to continue, didn't I?"

"What goes on between me and my stepsister is none of your business."

"You could not be more wrong. Everything to do with Piper is my business. Always will be. So you're going to have to get over this issue you have with seeing her happy."

"Happy with you, you mean." Celeste's hands locked into fists that were so tight her knuckles whitened. "She took my father from me. That should have been enough for her. But no. She wanted *you*. I saw that six years ago."

"And you liked that you had something she wanted, did you?"

"What was even better was that you didn't watch her when you thought I wasn't looking. My other boyfriends all did. Some even flirted with her. She acted like it made her uncomfortable, but I knew she loved it. You, though . . . I was so sure you had no interest in her. So sure she'd never have you. But then *bam*, you were back on the scene and giving her everything I ever wanted from you. Why, Levi? You could have had any woman.

They pretty much throw themselves at you. Why did you have to pick *her*?"

"Because she's Piper. It's as simple as that."

Celeste scoffed. "Don't give me that shit. You didn't want a damn thing to do with her until you realized she was your anchor. She never had your attention until then."

"Wrong. I've wanted her since the moment I met her."

The banshee stiffened. "You lie."

"No. That's the God's honest truth."

Pain and bitterness rippled across her face. "I'd say you didn't want her *that* much if you stayed with me . . . but you didn't really stay with me, did you? I felt you pull away after I introduced you to my family. I thought you just got spooked because I wanted you to officially meet them, but it wasn't that at all, was it? You pulled back from me because of her, didn't you?" She barked a humorless laugh that dripped with self-pity. "I should have seen it. Tell me what's so special about her, because I just don't see it."

"Celeste—"

"You think she's good and pure and kind? Really? Then how come she doesn't care that she's the reason her stepsister's mother hasn't come back?"

"I'd ask if you truly stupidly believe Piper's to blame for that, but I don't give a moose's last shit. I'm not here to give you a therapy session. I'm here to make a few things clear to you." Levi took a step toward the cell. "I warned you to let her be."

"And I did."

"You went to Urban Ink. You tried filling her head with all kinds of crap. You wanted to drive a wedge between me and her."

Flicking her hand in a dismissive gesture, Celeste gave him a look that called him dramatic. "I said some not-so-nice things, but it's not like we argued or anything. I didn't raise my voice. I didn't touch her. I didn't threaten her or refuse to leave. If you were that bothered about it, you'd have come pounding your fist on my front door."

"That's what you thought would happen. It's maybe even what you wanted to happen. But I gave you no reaction, and indifference is the one thing you hate. So I'll bet you were already furious before you even heard that she and I claimed each other as mates."

"You don't even know her!" Celeste burst out. "How can you commit yourself to a stranger?"

"It's *you* who doesn't know her. You don't want to. You've made her into an evil villain in your head because it suits you. The only person you're a victim of is *you*. You're the cause of every bit of drama in your life. *You* create it. *You* sustain it. *You* dial it up when you feel like it, just as you did at the bar. You went too far last night, Celeste."

She snorted. "Whatever I did can't have been *that* bad."

"You're really going to play the 'amnesia' card?"

"It's true, I don't remember."

"Well then, let me refresh your memory. There was the destruction of property, causing a disturbance, attempted assault, and *actual* assault."

She sharply leaned back. "I didn't lay a finger on anyone. I wouldn't have. No way."

"You threw glasses, bowls, and even a stool at people. You might not have touched those individuals with your hands, but you sure as hell still harmed them. Then there was the part where you spat at the bouncers. That's classed as assault.

"You can bet your ass that Knox is going to be *pissed*. Don't forget he and Harper own the Underground—if you disrespect the place, you disrespect them. You didn't even stop at causing damage to the bar, no, you continued down that route by tearing up the cell. Do you really think he'll take that well? Because I'm thinking no."

As if it finally registered just how badly she'd messed up, the bluster bled from her system. "I-I was drunk."

"Doesn't matter. You'll still pay. For *all* of it, Celeste. Not just what happened at the bar or what you did to the cell, but for what you said to Piper."

"I made mistakes—"

"Understatement."

"—but I don't deserve to be held here." She licked her lips. "I'll apologize to Piper, Knox, and the bouncers. I'll pay for the damage at the bar."

"Yes, you'll do both those things. *Once* Knox has decided and exacted your punishment."

Her face drained of color. "I want to talk to my father, I—"

"You can talk to him all you want once you've been released from here. Which, I'm happy to say, won't be for a while."

"You can't keep me here!" she yelled, panic edging her voice.

"Hmm, looks like we're managing it just fine." Levi's demon surged to the surface and took over. "You did not listen to his warnings," it said. "Perhaps you will listen to mine. If you do not wish to befriend Piper, that is your choice. But you will not provoke her. You will not play mind games with her. You will not attempt to hurt her. And if you have any sense, you will also cease trying to get his attention. If you do it again, it will not be *he* who comes to you. It will be me. I can—and will—hurt you in ways you cannot imagine. I will think nothing of it. Are we clear on that?"

Her eyes wide, she gave a jerky nod.

The demon withdrew, and Levi cast her one last look of warning. He and Keenan then walked away.

Once they were on the other side of the sliding

mechanical door, Keenan asked, "Do you think Piper will ask us to free Celeste?"

"No," replied Levi, nodding at Omar as they passed the security desk. "I already explained that Celeste would be facing punishment. Piper's got a big heart, but even she sees that the woman needs a wake-up call."

"I hope you're right," began Keenan, "because I wouldn't want something like this to cause friction between you and Piper. We can't let this shit slide."

"She won't try appealing for leniency on Celeste's behalf. Joe might, and I wouldn't blame him. Celeste is his daughter. But I don't think he'd expect his pleas to get him anywhere."

"It's got to be hard to watch your kid mess up their life. You'd blame yourself, wouldn't you? You'd feel like you went wrong somewhere and that the fault lies with you. I think that's part of why Joe defends her so much. It's like . . ." Keenan trailed off as Omar began humming behind them.

Recognizing that tune, Levi tensed. Both he and Keenan slowly turned to face Omar, who was staring down at his phone. The man was definitely not their killer, considering Levi had never had a problem recalling his name or appearance. But the guard had heard that song somewhere, and just maybe he'd heard it recently.

Keenan exchanged a look with Levi, and they then casually made their way toward the guard. "Hey, Omar," said the incubus. "What's that song you're humming?"

Omar's brows met. "Don't actually know what it's called. The tune got stuck in my head."

"Yeah?" asked Keenan. "Where'd you hear it?"

"Janelle is always either singing or humming it."

"Janelle?" Levi echoed.

"Yeah, she said her man often sings it. It's one of his favorite tunes." Omar's frown deepened. "Can't for the life of me remember his name."

Neither could Levi. He remembered seeing the man with Janelle in her front yard when Levi went to Diem's place after she was murdered. He even remembered speaking to the guy. But Levi couldn't recall his name or picture his face.

His heartbeat kicking up, he looked at Keenan, who was staring at him with his lips parted. "Fuck," they both said at once.

"We have to get to Janelle's place now," added Levi.

Her heart still thumping hard and fast in her chest, Piper had no choice but to walk ahead of Clyde as they made their way into the living room. Everything in her bristled, balked, and recoiled at her actions, but there seemed to be no way to take back control of herself.

It was like she was a prisoner inside her own mind. A mere presence that had been forced into a corner, where it had no say or influence. She couldn't crawl out of that corner . . . as if a large weight held her there. Her demon couldn't help, because it was trapped inside her.

No matter how much Piper psychically shoved at that weight, she couldn't get it to budge. No matter how hard her demon fought her supremacy, it couldn't surface. Even its scream of rage was trapped, much like the multiple curses that Piper wanted to sling at this sicko. Again, she tried telepathically reaching out for aid. Again, she failed.

Hot tears of frustration stung her eyes. Typically, anyone who entered the mind of a nightmare would find themselves facing their very own nightmare . . . unless they themselves were of the same breed. Clyde was clearly the same kind of demon as Piper. Worse, he was a fucking nutjob who'd murdered countless women, and she was currently defenseless against him.

Her heart bashed against her ribcage. Her face heated. Her palms grew hot. She tried again to shove off that psychic weight holding her in a corner, straining so hard her temples began to ache.

Nothing. It didn't work.

As much as she wished Levi would return, she also feared that he would. Clyde could be here to kill him. Or maybe to kill her. Or maybe both. She had no clue, and she had no way to do anything about the situation.

As they sat on the sofa, Clyde gave her an apologetic smile. "Sorry, I know Janelle introduced us but it's easy for names to slip out of our minds. I'm Clyde. Clyde Quincy."

Like Piper gave a shit. But she felt an amiable smile shape her lips, heard the words, "I'm Piper Winslow" flow from her mouth.

"Yes, I remember," he said . . . as if she'd spoken of her own accord. He really seemed to have convinced himself that this was a two-way conversation.

Jesus, this fucker was a total fruit loop.

She'd already known that, of course, after seeing Missy's experience for herself. But this here and now was different—so much more intense and frightening. Because there was always a small degree of separation for Piper when she walked through another person's memories. Now there was none.

"Pretty name," he told her, wearing a friendly yet creepy smile that sent chills fluttering down her spine.

"Thank you," she said, her tone ever so pleasant. God, she wanted to scream.

He inclined his head and then glanced around the room. "Nice place. Very Levi. I don't know him well, but I feel as if I do. You may or may not know that he and I are already acquainted. He was only an infant back then, but we connected. Babies do that. They bond with their carers."

Anger lashed her insides. He considered himself a *carer* of the children he used as props when playing happy families? Seriously?

"The person Levi's become . . . He's a good man, by all accounts. But you'll know that better than most, won't you? It's good to see him settled and happy. I'm proud of him."

He had no *right* to feel any pride in Levi. They were nothing to each other, no matter what this weirdo wanted to believe.

"I've always liked children," Clyde went on. "Not in a perverse way. I'm not a monster."

She would have gaped if she could have. He'd taken God knew how many lives over the years. He might not have harmed any children but he'd made them motherless. And he might not have *physically* tortured the women he killed, but this—taking their free will, forcing them to do his bidding, rendering them into a state of pure terror and helplessness—was a whole other form of torture.

Those women wouldn't have only feared for their own lives, they'd have feared for the lives of the children under their care. And he hadn't given a single flying, measly fuck. Similarly, he didn't give two shits how Piper felt right now. So, yeah, he was a monster all right.

"I simply prefer their company to that of adults," he added. "Children are uncomplicated. They don't have agendas. They don't play games. They're accepting and eager to approve of the people they meet. I like to be around them, which is why—no matter where I've lived over the years—I've often visited local parks."

She inwardly snorted. He didn't go to parks to observe children. No, those places were his hunting grounds. He went there looking for single mothers. Piper would have said as much if she could have spoken.

Just then, Levi's mind touched hers. *I'll be a little longer than I first thought*, he told her, all business. *Call me if you need me.*

She pushed against the mental weight trapping her, desperate to reach him, but nothing happened. And she heard herself telepathically reply, *No worries, see you soon.*

Her heart sank and her ribs tightened to the point that it hurt to breathe.

"It seems we'll have more time to talk than I initially expected," said Clyde. "Excellent. You know, Levi was such a cute kid. Not that his aunt appreciated him whatsoever. Moira was a horrid woman. Very bitter. She wasn't gentle with him at all. Didn't play with him or kiss him or cuddle him. She often left him in his crib to cry. Or she'd leave him home alone."

For Clyde to know all of that, he must have observed them for days.

"I didn't initially realize she wasn't his mother. Not until I first came to her home and entered her mind. That was a mistake on my part. I considered instantly backing off, but being inside her head and seeing what a mess it was . . . I thought I could change that she resented having to take care of him. I thought I could help rid her of all that bitterness. Parenting and juggling responsibilities can be hard, especially if you have no one to help. I wanted to give her that assistance and support. I thought maybe we could all be a family." His brow pinched. "That didn't work out as I'd hoped."

He was a plain psycho for thinking differently.

"She didn't want to be a better person. She didn't want to accept the help I offered, nor was she grateful for it. She wouldn't open her heart to me even a little. Sadly, Moira wasn't what I was looking for. And there was no way I could leave poor Levi with such a cold, uncaring woman, so I took him to the local home for demonic children. Ending her life was a kindness, really. It gave her peace she never would have found while alive."

It chilled Piper how he could rationalize his actions in such a way. The man really saw no wrong in anything he did.

"I couldn't believe it when I first saw him again as an adult. I recognized his energy signature straight away. It was sad that he didn't remember me . . . but nobody ever does. You already know that, though, don't you? You've already guessed who I am."

She felt a *push* for an honest answer. "Yes."

"I'm going to allow you to talk freely—only aloud, not telepathically. But if you try to scream, I will cut you off."

Excitement bubbled in her blood. She wouldn't scream now—the walls were soundproof, so it would do her no good. But if Levi came strolling into the apartment, she'd be able to yell out a warning.

"There. Now you can speak."

She blinked, surprised that she didn't feel any different than she had before. The mental weight trapping her hadn't lifted or anything. She experimentally tried to speak, and out popped her question. "Why are you here?"

"I have an . . . understanding with another member of your lair. The very one who has caused you so much trouble lately."

Her gut tightened. Wait, what?

"Not nice of me, I know. Levi will no doubt be furious."

That weirdly seemed to please him. "Why would you do that?"

"I needed to get into this building. Needed to get to *you*. Because unless I'm a lethal threat to the one person he cares about, Levi will *never* kill me. He'll instead lock me up somewhere and have me tortured for centuries. I would have simply taken over the mind of a resident and had them bring me inside, but measures were taken to ensure such a thing couldn't happen. The demons in the security office see every visitor via the cameras. They only permit entrance to people on the pre-approved list. I'm not on it. I needed an 'inside man' to distract them and allow me to enter."

"If you want to die, why not end your own life?"

"My demon would never permit it. It's very angry. It hasn't had a chance to make any sort of mark on the world. No one remembers it. No one cares for it. Demons aren't built to be alone. It's why we come in pairs. Maybe our anchor would have remembered us. We never found her. We looked and looked, but it came to nothing."

"Surely you could still have a relationship with someone. Like you do with Janelle. You'd just explain that they won't remember you clearly when you're apart."

He shook his head. "Oh, it works that way at first, yes. But part of my curse is that the longer you know a person and the more time you spend with them, the quicker they forget you when you're apart. Eventually, it's no longer a case of them merely forgetting your name and appearance. They forget you were ever around. It gets to a point where they don't recognize you anymore. They see you, but they don't know you. They don't trust you. They can't love you because they have no clue who you are. Imagine Levi always looking at you like you're a stranger. Imagine having to constantly try and fail to convince him that you're his mate. He'd brand you crazy. He'd order you to stay away. He'd begin relationships with others because he'd feel no love or loyalty toward you."

Her heart hurt merely imagining it. It would be a form of hell. "Who cursed you?"

"A witch. A woman who once claimed to love me. They say there's a fine line between love and hate. It's true. I . . . I cheated on Beth. With her sister. It wasn't planned. I loved Kathryn, who loved me in turn. In a moment of weakness, we acted on it. I don't know if Beth wanted to believe her sister would never be party to such a thing, or if she simply wished to smear my name, but she falsely accused me of taking Kathryn against her will. As if I'd ever do something so utterly horrific."

Well, Piper wasn't so certain he hadn't. The man believed his own lies, seemed able to justify anything he did to himself, and blamed everyone else for his actions. Could he have convinced himself that Kathryn loved him? Could he have ignored her objections, telling himself they weren't real? Could he have taken her will using his gift and forced her to go along with what he wanted, all the while convincing himself that she was willing? Yes. Yes, Piper believed he could have done any of those things.

"More, Beth ensured that her sister and I couldn't be together. She came between us out of pure spite by ensuring that Kathryn would forget me—eventually, she didn't only forget my appearance but my very existence. She called me crazy when I insisted we loved each other. And then her parents hid her from me, so I didn't even have a chance to convince her of the truth."

"What happened to Beth?"

"She killed herself, tired of suffering the same curse. And me . . . I'm ready to leave this world, too. I've tried to undo the curse but nothing has ever worked. It's time for me to make it end. And you're going to help me do that."

Inside, she went utterly still. "What?"

"I don't want to see any harm befall you. You seem like a very nice young lady. And anything that hurt you would hurt Levi—pain isn't something I'd ordinarily want for him. But he needs the right motivation to take me down. I've done everything to get his attention. He's too focused on you. I want it to be *him* who puts an end to this for me; I want us to come full circle. But like I said, he'd prefer to imprison me. You and I both know that he'll only end my life if he's insane with grief and rage. And that means his mate must die."

Her heartbeat stuttered. "You won't need to go *that* far."

"I don't intend to. At least not *personally*. Someone else will be doing that. I'll simply take the blame for it." He paused as a rhythmic knock came at the door. "Ah, here they are now. I'll let them in."

The moment Clyde left the room, she resumed her mental fight to free herself of his control. Fought so hard tears once more stung her eyes. But nothing—

The newcomer came into view, and Piper felt her stomach drop. "No."

"Yes, actually," he said.

A cold burn sharply sliced across her cheek, cutting through skin. She felt blood pool to the surface of the wound. *Smelled* it.

The bastard smiled.

In the front passenger seat of Keenan's car, Levi telepathically reached out to Knox. *Janelle's partner is the one who's been killing single mothers. Keenan and I are on our way to her place now.*

The incubus was driving at top speed.

Knox cursed. *I need a few moments to wrap up this meeting. Larkin and I will meet you at Janelle's house shortly.*

Levi then gave Tanner a telepathic heads-up, assuring the hellhound that he should stay home with Devon, who wasn't feeling well.

Mere minutes later, Keenan pulled up outside Janelle's house so abruptly the tires screeched. "Only her car's in the driveway," he pointed out.

They leaped out of the vehicle and rushed to the front door. Their knocks went ignored, as did the call Keenan made to her cell phone.

Levi telekinetically blasted the door lock and then pushed

his way inside with Keenan close behind him. The moment he stepped into Janelle's living room, Levi knew . . . "She's dead." Her body wasn't in sight, and her soul hadn't lingered. But emotional echoes of her death pulsed wildly through the air.

Devastation. Terror. Helplessness.

Keenan swore and raked a hand through his hair.

Fire roared to life a few feet away. The flames quickly died, revealing Knox and Larkin.

"She's dead," Levi told them.

Knox clenched his jaw. "Let's find her body."

It was Keenan who uncovered Janelle's corpse. She'd been dumped in a bedroom closet, her neck broken.

"She's been dead a few days," said Levi.

"There's no X on her forehead," Larkin commented.

"She wasn't what the other women were to him," Knox pointed out. "He'd wanted to be close to the lair. Close to you, Levi. Janelle was a mere tool he'd used. A tool he apparently decided he no longer needed."

"How could she have had a relationship with a guy she didn't properly remember when they were away from each other?" asked Keenan.

Levi twisted his mouth. "He might have fed her some spiel about why she wouldn't remember him. A sob story of some kind that would make her feel sorry for him. Janelle was the type to guard a person's secrets if she cared for them. But she would have at some point learned that the man who kept Missy captive couldn't be remembered, and then Janelle would have suspected her partner."

Keenan frowned. "And yet, she didn't tell us."

"He's probably been controlling her ever since," Levi mused.

Keenan's brows lifted. "Never thought of that. Why do you think he killed her?"

"Going by the lack of male anger in the air, it wasn't a case of him losing his temper," replied Levi. "There's determination, resolve, and regret."

Knox hummed. "He'd decided he didn't need her anymore, so he disposed of her despite that he didn't feel good about it. But why?"

"It would suggest he's chosen another single mother," said Larkin. "He probably can't control both her and Janelle at the same time."

Knox nodded. "I want every member of the Force who's monitoring the home of a single mother to go inside her house and check things out."

"I'm on it." Keenan whipped out his cell phone. "They might not necessarily know if the woman is being controlled."

"Missy said she cried," said Knox. "I would say they'll see in the mother's eyes if something is wrong."

Keenan crossed to the corner of the room to take the call.

Levi looked down at Janelle's body and then glanced around. "Where's her cell? If we're lucky, she'll have taken pictures of her and her partner. She may even have his number logged in her phone. We could track him that way."

"It's here." Larkin nabbed it from the nightstand and pressed a button at the side of the phone, causing the screen to light up. A picture of a smiling couple stared back at them. "That's him. Clyde. His name is Clyde Quincy. I *know* it now that I'm looking at him. He's a nightmare, like Piper."

"We need his number," Knox reminded the harpy.

"I'll need Janette's fingerprint to unlock the phone." Larkin bent down and very gently placed Janelle's thumb on the cell's screen. "Done." She scrolled through the contact log. "Yep, got his number."

"Get tracking his cell," said Knox.

"I'll need my laptop for that," Larkin told him.

"Then let's get to your apartment." Knox sighed at Janelle's body. "I'll have someone come here and take care of her body." The Prime pyroported them all to Larkin's apartment.

They waited impatiently while she used her computer software to track the male nightmare, her fingers flying over the laptop keys. Levi had already forgotten the bastard's name and face again—both felt *just* out of his reach.

Report after report came in from members of the Force who'd checked in on the single mothers. All said the coast was clear.

Keenan rubbed at his nape. "He could have gone after two sisters again, although I doubt it. Last time, he deemed it a mistake. Maybe he picked a single mother outside of our lair instead. Or it could be that he simply hasn't made his move yet."

"There's no saying he's hunting anyone," said Levi.

Larkin cursed, her body going still. "He's here."

Knox's brows snapped together. "What?"

"He's in this building somewhere," she replied.

Levi blinked. "That's impossible."

"Not according to the tracking software," she said. "He found some way to get past the security measures."

Levi shook his head. "There'd be no point in him even doing that. No single mothers live here. There's no one he could possibly want . . ." Levi trailed off, his gut filling with dread as a thought occurred to him. "He could have come here to see me. If he did, if he's at my place right now, he has Piper."

# CHAPTER TWENTY-TWO

Her injured cheek throbbing, Piper stared at the newcomer in shock. Even her demon was stunned. They'd never considered him a suspect. Not once.

An icy burn sliced through her brow this time. A hiss of pain whistled out of her. And he loved that—she saw it in his eyes.

"Just a little ability I bought," said Enzo. "They call it a psychic scalpel. Takes a lot of concentration to use—I'm not yet accustomed to wielding it—so it isn't much good in a fight. But it will certainly be of much use here and now."

"It was you all this time?" Piper asked, her voice unintentionally quiet. "You tried to kill me?"

"Over and over," he easily confirmed.

Her thought processes faltered as she struggled to understand. "But . . . why? I never did a damn thing to you." She barely knew him. And she'd never once pinned a crime on him using her gift.

"It was never about you, Piper," he said. "Levi made that assumption. A mistake on his part. Though I suppose it was natural for him to conclude that you were the true target. Really, you were the weapon I needed. He hurts when you hurt."

She blinked. "This is about Levi? But . . . you work under him, you—"

"Respect him? Obey him? Show him loyalty?" Enzo pursed his lips. "Of course it seems that way. I've spent many years convincing him and everyone else of that. Not that I drew this out for the fun of it. I'd have struck at him years ago if there'd been a *real* way to hurt him."

The psychic scalpel once more sliced her face. She ground her teeth, biting back a cry. He'd get no more sounds of pain from her. None. "Why? I don't understand."

"You weren't part of the lair when my brother was alive. Gian was a good kid. He struggled socially and never really found his own tribe. He was too shy to approach girls, so . . . he'd take pictures of them from afar. Not of them changing clothes or anything. Just pictures. It was harmless, really."

Uh, no, *not* really.

"He started posting the photos to the girls. I would have advised against that if I'd known, but I hadn't. There was no need for the girls to freak out the way they did."

Actually, *yeah* there was every reason to freak. Piper sure would have done if someone was taking pictures of her without her knowledge or consent. Posting them seemed like a progression. A taunt, even. It would no doubt have escalated further.

"They reported it." Enzo rolled his eyes, implying the girls had been dramatic. "A couple of them saw Gian from a distance. They weren't sure if it was him or me—we looked a lot alike. Anyway, Levi came to the house, did a little search, and he sure as shit found plenty of photos. I took the blame. Said it was me. Gian was too frozen by fear to say a word."

Or simply happy to let someone else suffer his punishment.

Piper had no fondness for Celeste, but she still wouldn't have tossed false blame at the woman's feet. Yet, Gian had let his brother throw himself under the damn bus. Not very 'brotherly.'

A cold burn slowly carved its way across her forehead. It hurt like a *mother.* Piper felt tears pool in her eyes. She blinked them back, refusing to shed them.

"I was always in trouble back then, so Levi found it easy to believe it was me," Enzo continued. "He took me to the prison at Knox's request. I asked Levi to have someone keep a watch on Gian while I was gone. You see, our father was a piece of shit. Griff beat on me and Gian whenever he fucking pleased. I used to protect my brother, but I couldn't do that from prison, could I? Now, ask me if Levi kept a watch on him."

Her mouth dry, she swallowed. "Did Levi keep a watch on him?"

"No, he didn't." A muscle in Enzo's cheek ticked. "So he had no clue that my father took a bat to Gian. I knew. Gian was telepathically *screaming* for me to help him. I couldn't do shit. See for yourself." He gripped her hand painfully hard and tossed a look at Clyde. "Make her use her gift to access that memory."

And then Piper wasn't in the living room anymore. She was in a dull, cramped, shadowy cell that reeked of sweat, mildew, iron, and blood both old and new. Chained to a cold wall, she could see cages hanging from the ceiling outside the cell. Could see torturous equipment such as the Judas chair and the iron maiden. Knox's Chamber, she guessed.

Whimpering people hung limply in the manacles attached to the walls. Another lay on a bed of spikes, weeping. Someone out of sight cried out as a whip cracked through the air and slapped flesh.

A voice edged with pain and panic blasted into her—no, into

Enzo's—mind . . . *Fuck, E, help me! Where are you? He's lost it, he's going to kill me.*

Swamped by terror and rage, she/Enzo called out, *Get out of the house, G! Fucking run. I can't get to you.* But the words only bounced around her/his mind, because the cuffs prevented whoever they shackled from telepathing outsiders.

Again and again, Gian called for his brother. Again and again, she/Enzo tried and failed to urge him to run while also begging the guards in the Chamber for help, but no one paid her/him any attention. Powerlessness crawled through her/his veins—

Piper snapped out of Enzo's memory, shuddering out a breath.

His eyes blazing, his jaw hard, he said, "All the time I was chained to that wall, I could hear my brother calling for me, but I couldn't respond. Gian must have thought I didn't care. You're helpless right now, just as I was then. You want to cry out to a person important to you, just as I did that night. But there's nothing you can do. It's enough to make a person murderous, isn't it?"

Hell, yeah. She wasn't gonna say that, though.

Pain *blazed* along her upper chest, throbbing like a bitch, as the scalpel sliced her yet again. Her demon snapped its teeth, raring to retaliate, infuriated that it couldn't.

"So your father killed Gian?" It was more of a guess than a question.

"No," replied Enzo, surprising her. "Gian killed him later that night."

Well she hadn't seen that coming.

"Neighbors reported screaming. Levi showed up. Gian told him it was self-defense and that our father attacked a second time that day. Levi said Griff's soul told him a different story. Pure bullshit, I'm telling you."

"You're saying Levi lied?" Doubtful. Highly fucking doubtful.

"I'm saying he wouldn't *listen*. He put more weight into Griff's words than in Gian's. My brother telepathed me, terrified. Said he couldn't make Levi hear him. Said the reaper was going to bring him to the prison, and Gian . . . he killed himself right there in our kitchen. Grabbed a knife and slit his own throat."

She inhaled sharply. And then she choked on a cry as pain *scratched* across her own throat like a razor-sharp claw.

"Don't worry," said Enzo. "The cut's not deep enough to make you bleed out. It's just a little graze."

*Just a little graze?* Oh, she officially hated this motherfucker.

"I tried talking Gian out of suiciding, but he wasn't able to hear one single telepathic word I said. Maybe if he had, he wouldn't have killed himself. I'll never know." Enzo swallowed thickly. "We had plans. Big plans. We were going to start afresh, switch lairs, head to New Zealand, and find our extended relatives. I just needed to get enough cash together first. Levi robbed us of that future; of my brother's future."

She almost flinched as the scalpel sliced her shoulder, tearing through her tee.

"More, Levi made me break my promise to Gian. I *swore* I'd always protect my brother. I didn't. Because Levi simply couldn't overlook a couple of goddamn stupid pictures. Or if he'd just looked out for Gian like I asked, things would have ended differently, but no. Levi didn't fucking bother, just as he didn't listen to or believe Gian—no, he believed the soul of a drunk who beat his own kids."

"So this is about payback."

"Oh, yeah. And it's been a long time coming. I needed to wait until Levi had someone worth losing. He had Knox and the sentinels, but that wasn't the same. It had to be someone he *needed*. So I waited. And I worked hard to gain a position in the Force, to earn people's trust—especially Levi's. And oh, how amusing it's been to be trusted and respected by someone who has no idea you hate them so much." Enzo smirked. "He even trusts me with your safety."

Levi would be pissed at himself for it when he learned the truth. She'd have to ensure he didn't rake himself over the coals for it. Which she *would*. She wasn't going to die here at the hands of these two assholes—oh, Clyde might not be physically touching her but he was figuratively holding her down so that Enzo could do what he pleased. And now she sported God knew how many cuts, all of which stung and pulsed like a bitch.

"When Levi found you, damn, the timing was perfect," said Enzo. "Sefton had just been released from prison, and he and Jasper were making nuisances of themselves. They're both responsible for the vandalism, by the way. It made them great scapegoats. It was easy for everyone to conclude that the attacks were an escalation."

Another burning slice—this time over her thigh, cutting through the denim of her jeans. Inwardly cursing, Piper again struggled against the mental weight cornering her. But, again, she failed to free herself.

"I had so many opportunities to kill you. But I wanted him to live in fear for a while. Just like me and my brother did as kids. Then I heard what our new, friendly neighborhood killer could do." Enzo tipped his head in Clyde's direction. "I knew he'd be able to control you so that you'd be as helpless as I wanted you to be while I hurt you. It was just a matter of unmasking him. I did that when I went to check on one of the single moms and happened to catch a glimpse of him watching her from the shadows. He ran, but not fast enough. He and I then made a deal. I'll kill you, and he'll take the blame.

"Shall I tell you what's about to happen? The moment we

hear the key turn in the lock, I'll slit your throat with my psychic scalpel—yes, you'll suffer the exact same deadly wound that Gian did. Clyde here will grab you, Levi will find you bleeding out in his arms . . . and then he'll avenge you. And me? I'll play the fighting-for-consciousness hostage; act like Clyde tried to kill me but failed. No one will ever know any different."

Dread churned in her belly . . . because it would be so easy for that plan to pay off.

"I'm sure you think you'll survive this; that Levi will come rescue you. Oh, he'll be here soon enough—Keenan telepathically called out to me a few times. I ignored him, since I'm feigning unconsciousness. But he'll inform Levi, who'll panic and rush right home." Enzo looked at Clyde. "Has he reached out to her?"

"Not in a while," replied Clyde.

"Hmm, he must not want to take the chance that whoever has her will hear him. Especially if he suspects *you* have her. He might not yet know who you are, but he'll know what you can do."

Clyde nodded. "It means he'll be ready for me."

"But he won't move fast enough. Won't stop my scalpel from doing its job." Anticipation lit Enzo's gaze as he refocused it on her. "I will so very much enjoy what's coming. Killing Levi would be more satisfying, but I want him to feel the agony of grief like I did when Gian died. I want him to feel the shame, the guilt, the pain. Even better, the breaking of the anchor bond will make him eventually turn rogue. Then he'll be hunted and executed by the people he calls friends—he might even kill some of them in his own defense. I can think of no worse fate for him."

Neither could she.

"After years of working under Levi, running his errands,

being loyal to him, treating him with a respect he didn't deserve, I've *earned* the right to avenge Gian this way. It's the least I can do for him. I let him down. If I bring him justice, maybe he'll find the peace he deserves. He's owed that."

Her demon hissed, not at all fooled. Nor was Piper. "Are you sure you're doing this for Gian? Seems to me like you're doing it for you."

Enzo's face tightened. "It matters not, really. The end result will be the same. You'll be dead. Levi will be destroyed. Gian will be avenged. And I'll be fucking delighted. Now . . . how about we have a little fun while we wait for your mate to arrive?"

Panic swallowed Levi whole. No. No, no, no, no, his woman was *not* being held hostage by a fucking serial killer. She wasn't.

The mere thought made Levi's demon lose its shit.

Before Levi could even think to act, Knox snapped his hand around Levi's arm and barked out, "Don't. Don't reach out to her. If the nightmare is with her and has hold of her mind, he will hear you."

Urgency pounding through him, he clenched his fists. "I have to get to her."

"You do," said Larkin, crossing to him. "And we will. All of us. But we have to be smart about it."

"I can't connect with Dez telepathically," began Keenan, "which means he's likely dead. Enzo isn't answering me, but I *can* touch his mind, so he's probably merely unconscious."

And if the guards had been taken out, it stood to reason that the killer was to blame; stood to reason that the bastard was in Levi's apartment *with Piper.* Forced to accept that, Levi squeezed his eyes shut as he said, "Fuck, he really does have her."

He strived to lock down his emotions. Failed. He couldn't get a handle on them, no matter how hard he tried. Especially while his demon was blowing a fuse inside him—roaring, pacing, lashing out.

Knox turned to Keenan. "Go to the stairwell. Poke your head into the hall and see if you can see the guards. Enzo might be unconscious, but he's probably been left for dead. The odds are that our boy moved both he and Dez out of sight, but maybe not. Maybe we can get to Enzo in time."

The incubus nodded and hurried out of the apartment.

Cricking his neck, Levi ground his teeth. "I telepathed Piper earlier, when I realized I'd need to head to Janelle's place. I told her I'd take longer than I expected. She replied, 'No worries, see you soon.'" Levi had thought it strange that she'd given him such a breezy response, because she'd been annoyed with him when he left the apartment, but he hadn't been concerned. "That could have been *him*, couldn't it?"

Knox sighed. "If he had hold of her mind at that time, then yes, it will have been him."

Levi felt his nostrils flare. "Motherfucker." He clenched and unclenched his fists as he began to stalk back and forth.

"We have to be smart about this," Knox cautioned. "You can't go barging into your apartment. He told Missy that he wants to die, remember?"

"I'll be happy to fucking oblige him."

"But you won't do it, because you want him captured and tortured—we all do. He'll see that. And a man who feels he has nothing to live for can do some crazy shit. He'd rather die than be detained, and I doubt he'd think anything of taking Piper down with him. He enjoys hurting people, whether he allows himself to see that or not."

"But why her?" Levi flexed his fingers. "Why harm *her*?"

"I don't know," said Knox, lifting his shoulders. "Maybe he has it in his head that she's not good for you, just as he had it in his head that your aunt was no good. Or maybe he doesn't intend to harm her, maybe he went there to see you and is just waiting for you to return. We can't be sure yet. But we can be certain of one thing: if we don't handle this delicately, Piper could be hurt as a result. Either by him or by his demon."

Knowing his Prime was right, Levi took a long breath and fought to calm the emotional storm swirling inside him. He couldn't lie, it didn't help much—not while he was brimming with panic, dread, and fury. He took one deep breath after another, until the emotions no longer beat at his good sense. "So now what?"

"I pyroport us inside your apartment. We listen. Get a feel for where they are and exactly what's happening. But we have to be *very* careful to remain undetected. No sudden movements, no rushing to her rescue. He has hold of her mind. He could force her to slit her own wrists. Let's not give him the chance to do it."

Bile rising in his throat, Levi's stomach did a slow roll at the thought. He snapped his mouth shut and gave a curt nod. Their boy wouldn't see this plan coming, because he'd have no clue that Knox could pyroport—few people did.

Keenan re-entered the apartment, his face hard. "Neither Dez nor Enzo are in the hall outside your front door, Levi. I don't see any sign of them."

*Fuck.* Urgency still riding him, Levi fisted his hands. "We have to move now."

"What room is furthest from the entrance of your apartment?" asked Knox. "We don't want anyone hearing us enter."

And pyroporting wasn't exactly a quiet process. "The gym," replied Levi.

Flames erupted around the four of them. When the fire died away, they were stood in the middle of Levi's gym. He tilted his head, reaching out with his senses. He couldn't hear any voices from there.

*We take it slow,* said Knox, speaking on a telepathic channel that reached out to each of the sentinels at once.

Adrenaline pumping through him as fast as the heart pounding in his chest, Levi took the lead as they stealthily left the gym and padded through the apartment, passing room after room. Muffled voices soon reached him. When those voices became clearer, Levi halted.

*Is that* Enzo *who's ranting?* asked Keenan, taking the question right from Levi's mouth. *Shit, it is.*

Levi resumed walking, listening as Enzo talked of Sefton and Jasper making good scapegoats and then . . . "I had so many opportunities to kill you," the traitorous piece of shit told her.

Levi felt his face morph into a snarl.

*Wait,* began Larkin, *Enzo's the one who's been after her?*

*It's all about Gian, apparently.* Levi didn't give a sliver of a fuck what the guy's motive was. He only cared that the bastard pay in every way imaginable.

He was just thinking that maybe Enzo was alone in the apartment with Piper, but then the asshole said, "Clyde here will grab you."

Larkin cursed. *Why would the nightmare be willing to take responsibility for her murder?*

Levi's jaw hardened. *There won't be a murder.* His heart clenched when he heard Piper's voice as she called Enzo on his bullshit. Apparently the nightmare was allowing her to talk.

Just as Levi halted near the entrance of the living area, he heard Enzo say, "It matters not, really. The end result will be the same. You'll be dead. Levi will be destroyed. Gian will be avenged. And I'll be fucking delighted. Now . . . how about we have a little fun while we wait for your mate to arrive?"

Knox's hand clamped on Levi's shoulder. *Not yet.*

"What does that mean?" asked the nightmare.

"It means I want her to physically suffer a little, since I can't put Levi through such pain," said Enzo. "You know, Piper . . . Handily, wielding a psychic scalpel wasn't the only ability I purchased. I also got myself a nifty little ability that will ensure you suffer maximum pain in mere seconds."

"You make a habit of buying gifts?" asked Piper. "Like the ability to conceal your appearance?"

"Actually, I developed that ability as a teenager. It's mine. But the gift of causing brain bleeds? That was purchased. I've since lost it. But, as I said, I've bought others. And one in particular is *really* going to hurt you."

"Fine, get to it," said Piper. "But don't fool yourself into thinking you're anything other than a fucking coward."

"Say what now?"

"You only attack when you can't be seen or when, as in this case, someone is pinning your target still for you. You say you want to let Levi live so he can suffer after my death, but you know what? I think it's more that you don't have the goddamn balls to go up against him, so you waited for him to have someone *weaker* than him in his life who you felt you could take on."

"To be fair," began the male nightmare, "I was wondering the same thing, Enzo. You've spent many years lying to yourself. It's quite sad."

A snort. "This is coming from a man who has *no* sense of self-awareness and feeds himself all sorts of lies?" asked Enzo.

"I know exactly who I am. We all lie to ourselves occasionally, but it is not something I make a habit of."

"No, you just live in a reality of your own making."

*What's our next move?* asked Larkin as the two men continued to argue.

*I can't dive into the nightmare's mind and try to overtake it due to what he is,* began Knox, *so that option's out. I also can't hijack Enzo's mind—he has tough mental barriers.*

Levi licked his front teeth. *I have a plan. It'll only work if we act fast. And I mean* fast.

Knox's eyes sharpened. *Tell me.*

Even as Piper kept the two arguing assholes in sight, she again strained to shove off the mental weight, concentrating so hard she wouldn't be surprised if she burst a blood vessel in her eye or something. But it did no good. The weight didn't budge in the slightest.

Still, she didn't give up. She kept fighting, feeling sweat dot her upper lip and bead her forehead, making the cut there sting like a mother. Her demon egged her on, a mass of fury and resentment. If this didn't—

Telekinetic power rippled through the doorway and crashed into Clyde's skull, sending his head whipping to the side. A mere millisecond later, flaming walls burst to life around her and a hand gripped her arm. The fire eased away, and she realized she was now in the master bedroom with Knox.

Taking in her wounds, Knox growled. "Does he still have hold of your mind?"

"Yes," she replied, inwardly frowning as she heard sounds of a minor battle coming from within the apartment. "Where's Levi?"

"Dealing with the problem at hand." Knox turned to Keenan. "Hold her here." With that, he disappeared in a roar of fire.

Keenan locked his arms around her from behind, careful not to touch any of her injuries. "Sorry, Piper, but we can't chance that you won't be forced to hurt yourself by the bastard controlling you."

"He wants Levi to kill him," she said.

"That isn't your mate's intention."

"Then, yeah, we should worry about what will happen if . . . God, what's the asshole's name again?"

# CHAPTER TWENTY-THREE

The very moment flames surrounded Piper, Levi came out of hiding and pitched an orb of hellfire at Enzo while Larkin blasted the nightmare—Clyde, he remembered—with hell-ice.

Shock plastering his face, Enzo ducked with a muffled oath and then winked out of view, concealing himself. The flaming orb instead whacked the doorjamb, charring the paint.

Spitting a curse, Levi fisted his hands. He caught a glimpse of Dez's limp body near the front door and had to force aside the anger that tried sweeping through him. Aware via his peripheral vision that Clyde and Larkin were trading blows, Levi went to conjure—

A crackling hot orb whooshed through the air, heading right for him. He telepathically batted it away with a flick of his hand and then blindly hurled a series of hellfire orbs—all of which halted midair and then came *sailing back at him.*

*The fuck?*

Surprised, Levi jerked to the side, but one orb's crackling

heat grazed his temple. The others crashed into the wall, and a mirror fell to the floor. Enzo had obviously purchased the ability to repel.

Fire burst into existence as Knox returned. Moments later, he was gone again, taking Clyde with him as planned.

As Larkin joined Levi in attempting to thrash an invisible Enzo with orbs of hellfire, Levi touched Keenan's mind and asked, *You have Piper? She's okay?*

*I've got her,* the incubus assured him. *She has a few cuts but she's otherwise fine.*

*I'll cover the front door.* Larkin took up position there, her wings spread to block the exit, as she and Levi continued to attack Enzo as a team, careful not to accidentally strike each other.

Levi remained in the mouth of the hallway, blocking Enzo's path to not only the fire escape but to Piper. Of course, Enzo wouldn't know that Knox had transferred her to a room within the apartment. But if he tried making a mad dash for the fire escape, he might well stumble upon her.

Enzo's shots repeatedly came from various angles as he evidently moved from spot to spot. That, together with his ability to repel anything aimed his way, made him a hell of a difficult target. The occasional grunt of pain rang out as an orb or telekinetic wave or chips of hell-ice hit their mark, but there weren't enough grunts for Levi's liking.

An orb slammed into his solar plexus, knocking the breath from Levi's lungs. Another punched his upper thigh hard enough that his leg trembled. His demon rumbled an animalistic snarl, bombarding him with sadistic images of the torturous ways it wanted Enzo to suffer.

Gritting his teeth as his skin burned, prickled, and tightened, Levi lashed out with one hard blast of telekinesis after another. Meanwhile, his blood boiled as betrayal swirled in his gut. Enzo . . .

Shit, this was a man Levi had trusted, respected, invited into his home, and more importantly entrusted with the safety of his mate. The whole time, Enzo had meant to fuck him over in the worst way—by taking from him the only person Levi had ever loved.

So many times Enzo had smiled at her, laughed with her, watched her back . . . and all the while he'd meant to one day kill her. As such, Levi would feel no devastation in having to end Enzo's life. No, this male would suffer dearly, and there'd be nothing quick about it. First, Levi needed to detain the little fucker. Which would be a whole lot easier if Enzo was visible.

Levi couldn't rely on his other senses to track Enzo. It was impossible to listen out for the sound of footsteps when the apartment was like a goddamn warzone. He could only track the location from which orbs came zooming toward him, but it often seemed that Enzo moved at an enhanced speed straight after striking.

More flames erupted from the floor as Knox returned. Wasting no time in joining the fight, the Prime said, *Clyde is now shackled in a cell.*

Good. The cuffs would ensure that the nightmare couldn't use his gifts, which meant Piper would now be free of his mental hold.

Pinning his full attention on Enzo—or, at least, on the bastard's general direction—Levi struck hard. Larkin and Knox did the same.

Their surroundings took a large brunt of the attack. Orbs scorched the furniture and charred the walls. Framed paintings dropped to the hardwood floor with shatters of glass. A telekinetic hit sent the TV toppling backwards off the unit. Chips of hell-ice embedded themselves in the coffee table and pinged off the fireplace.

Nothing about the battle was easy. Even with three against

one, it was a struggle to take out Enzo. Not simply because it wasn't hard for the little shit to dodge blows but because he could repel them. Hell, Levi spent as much time evading his own hellfire orbs as he did Enzo's. The same went for Knox and Larkin. Enzo didn't really *have* to attack them. By repelling their blows, he was using their own gifts against them.

Still, other than to duck or weave, Levi didn't pause or ease back. He kept up the pressure, as did the others. It paid off to some degree, going by the grunts of pain, snarls of anger, and curses of frustration that occasionally burst out of Enzo.

Levi telekinetically swept up the floor lamp and sent it sailing in the direction in which he suspected Enzo stood. There was a *clang* followed by a distinct grunt that made Levi's demon bare its teeth in a feral grin.

He telekinetically lobbed more objects in that direction, but the others harmlessly fell to the floor. Levi swerved as an orb came at him from the left, but he didn't move fast enough. The flaming ball punched his stomach, sending pain rippling through his ribs.

Inwardly cursing Enzo to hell and back, Levi sent out telekinetic slaps and punches. Some landed, some hit the wall, others rebounded back at him. He couldn't hold back a flinch when a hellfire orb crashed into an injury on his chest. *I am so done with this fucking shit*, he growled.

*He's showing no signs of tiring or backing down*, said Larkin, a note of pain in her voice. Her face and wings covered in burns, she sent more black chips of hell-ice darting through the air like bullets. *I'd say he's ready to die here.*

*He knows we'll hunt him for the rest of his days if he escapes*, Knox pointed out as a stream of hellfire poured out of his palm but hit only the wall.

*He'll still bolt if he gets the chance*, said Levi. An orb abruptly slammed into his face, narrowly missing his fucking eye. He grunted when his injured thigh was slammed by a second orb. He telepathically deflected a third, knocking it off course and sending it crashing into the wall.

The adrenaline pumping through his system dimmed the pain, but not quite enough. Not now that his body sported so many blistering burns.

Larkin flapped her wings. A cold breeze sailed at where Enzo had *likely* stood but seemed to hit nothing. More flaming orbs were blindly lobbed by Knox. Another hail of black chips zipped through the air. Yet more telekinetic blows blasted outwards from Levi's palm. But nothing collided with an unseen figure, nor was anything repelled.

Levi's nape prickled with unease. *Down*, he told both Knox and Larkin. Trusting them to duck low, he sent out a telekinetic wave that shimmered through the air like a heatwave. No grunts, no growls, no sounds of anyone hitting the floor.

Levi's stomach knotted. Could Enzo have somehow moved past them? Past *Levi*? It should have been impossible, but panic gripped Levi all the same.

His demon urging him to check on Piper, Levi telepathically—

A finger jabbed his side.

Pain crashed into his head first and then rocketed through his entire system. It was an agony he'd never before felt. It seemed to fry every synapse, sharply zap every nerve-ending, and overload . . . *everything*. His eyes felt like they'd explode. His skull felt like it would split apart. His heart felt like it would violently burst and shatter his ribcage.

The pain was so bad it turned his stomach. Almost retching, he dropped to one knee, every breath he took hurting his throat and lungs. Even as a guttural cry of sheer agony tore out of him, he sent out another wave of telekinetic energy.

There was a loud thud followed by a pained curse, and then he heard footfalls fleeing further into the apartment. His vision graying with the pain, Levi urged himself to fucking *pursue* ... but his legs almost went out from under him when he tried to stand.

Hands clamped around his upper arms. "You've got to get up," said Larkin as Knox raced past them. "Now, Levi. *Up*."

Her nerves wracked by fear and dread, Piper restlessly paced up and down in front of the bed, her demon equally hyper-edgy. Even as she knew that Levi, Knox, and Larkin could take out Enzo without her aid, she hated not being part of the battle. It galled her to sit it out. But she hadn't objected. It would be stupid, given she wasn't at her best right now. Expending so much psychic energy fruitlessly fighting the hold that ... whatever his name was ... had on her mind had left her woozy.

Still, having no idea how the battle was going made it hard to stay put. She wished she could at least *see* what was happening. Hearing the sounds of complete chaos didn't help in the slightest. "You have to go out there, Keenan."

"The others have this," he assured her, leaning casually against the wall, though anyone could see he didn't want to be holed up in here anymore than she did.

"But Enzo can conceal himself, and he bought a gift he seemed eager to use that could cause a lot of pain," she said.

He gave her a stubborn look. "I promised Levi I'd ensure you stayed here. He was terrified that you'd be killed, so his head was already a mess before the battle even started. If you go out there, you'll distract him—he can't deal with that right now. And you admitted you're not feeling at your best."

She exhaled heavily and halted in front of him. "I didn't say *I* should go out there. Yeah, my pride is suffering here, but I'm not going to let that lead me to make dumb decisions. I'll stay right here. *You*, however, could go out there."

His brows snapped together. "What? No way. I'm staying."

"Did you promise Levi you would?"

Keenan hesitated. "No, but I said I'd ensure you didn't leave this room."

"And I won't, I swear. Help them, Keenan. Enzo obviously isn't making this easy or it'd be over by now. He's fought often enough with you guys to know *how* you fight. He's exploiting that. After all Enzo's responsible for, I'd say Levi might just use the death touch. I want to save him from that, because I know he'll never forgive himself. Except I can't do that *personally*. I'm asking you to do it for me. To do it *for him*. Please, Keenan, I'll—"

An animal sound of pain ripped through the air.

The bottom fell out of Piper's stomach as horror punched through her. "Levi." Without thought, she raced to the door, yanked it open, and stumbled out into the hallway . . . just as footfalls came toward her. There was no one in sight, but she knew . . . *Enzo*.

Piper didn't bother hitting him with hellfire. Instead, she yanked up her tee, exposing her stomach. She could only assume that Enzo's eyes landed on the death ballad brand, because footfalls stumbled to a halt and then a male humming filled the air. His body flickered into view like a faulty light bulb. His dazed eyes were locked on the music score, and he didn't seem to sense Knox coming up behind him.

She jumped as Enzo slammed face first to the floor. He was somehow flipped onto his back, and then his hands and feet were pinned in place. It was only then Piper remembered that Knox had psychic hands.

Her only concern for her mate, she dropped her tee back in

place and was about to shrug past her Prime when she noticed Levi and Larkin prowling down the hallway. Relief fluttered through Piper. Both demons looked a little worse for wear. Okay, a *lot* worse for wear, but they were alive and in one piece—that was what mattered.

Levi's gaze raked over her, thoroughly scrutinizing her from head to toe. *In a minute, I'm gonna kiss the breath from your lungs. Right now, I'm going to deal with this piece of shit here.*

She had no objections to any of that.

Twisting his mouth, Levi glared down at a still-humming Enzo. "Let's snap him out of his daze, shall we?" He crouched down and briefly touched Enzo's leg.

The humming abruptly stopped, and awareness bled into the male's eyes. He blinked a few times, taking in the scene. Pure fright lit his gaze, and his entire body tensed. He jerked upward—or tried. Knox's psychic hands held him down, but that didn't stop the idiot from writhing and squirming so intensely his face reddened.

Piper felt a smile curve her mouth. "Doesn't feel so good to be helpless like that, does it?"

Enzo bent his head back and tossed her a sneer even as he continued to struggle.

"I can't tell if he really thinks he'll get free or if he's just trying to entertain us a little," said Levi, a taunting note in his voice.

Panting, Enzo stilled. "I should have killed you when you were on your knees just then."

"One knee," said Levi, sounding remarkably calm. "And yes, you should've. Not that you would have managed it. If I hadn't taken you out, Knox or Larkin would have."

Enzo barked a laugh. "Not even *three* of you could kill me while working as a team."

Levi, Knox, and the other two sentinels exchanged looks, and then all four were chuckling.

Enzo scowled. "What the fuck is so fucking funny?"

Smiling, Keenan scratched his temple. "You really have no idea what you were up against just now, do you? If they wanted you dead, you'd be dead."

"You didn't see how hard they struggled to get a few licks in," said Enzo. "I had them chasing their own asses."

"No, they were taking care *not* to kill you," said Keenan. "See, we all agreed it would be more enjoyable to make you suffer for many months on end—hell, maybe even years. Centuries would be my choice."

Piper's demon all but cackled as the blood drained from Enzo's face.

"It should have occurred to you before," Levi told him. "Or had you honestly convinced yourself that you had a real shot at defeating us?"

"I ran *rings* around you," Enzo snarled.

"Oh, you fought pretty well. Using gifts you *purchased*, so that doesn't make you powerful. If you hadn't been able to repel what came at you or moved at what appeared to be supersonic speed, you wouldn't have lasted anywhere near as long as you did. And if it hadn't been for that other ability you bought, you wouldn't have gotten past me."

"You couldn't even hold Piper captive without help," Larkin taunted. "You weren't prepared to hurt her unless she was powerless to retaliate." The harpy let out a sound of pure disgust. "You're *nothing*."

"You're also wrong about Gian," Levi told him. "He killed your father in cold blood, not self-defense. Which I would have thought you already knew, given you have access to the lair's reports."

Enzo's face flushed. "It was a cover-up. My brother—"

"Wasn't right in the goddamn head," Levi finished. "Not even as a small kid. Your mother was scared of him. You claim you were his protector, but it wasn't really your father you saw as the main threat to Gian. No, you wanted to protect your brother from himself. You knew he could easily do something that would land him in the Chamber. I'll bet you even suspected he'd kill your father if given the chance."

His lips clamped shut, Enzo shook his head wildly.

"You want to blame me for his downfall because you either can't handle or simply refuse to face the truth of who and what Gian was. The reality is that you *never* could have helped him. No one could have."

"He was a kid!"

"He was twenty-four years old. He took pictures of teenage girls," Levi added, his voice growing colder. "He used to hang around outside their school. He kept offering them rides in his car."

"And you twisted all that to make him seem like a sexual predator in the making."

To Piper, it sounded like that was *exactly* what Gian was.

"He tried to pin your father's murder on you," said Levi.

Enzo froze.

"Gian claimed you telepathically talked him into it all the way from your cell in the Chamber," Levi went on. "He said you threatened him; that he feared you; that he only went near those girls because he'd seen you follow them around and that he was 'looking out' for them."

"You lie," Enzo ground out.

"No, no lies. I never told you before now because I didn't see the sense when it would only hurt you. Now, well, I couldn't give a whisper of a fuck if you're hurting. In fact, the thought does nothing but please me."

*Did Gian really do that?* Piper asked, unsure if her mate was just dishing out some emotional torture.

*Oh, he did it.* Levi began to circle Enzo. "I knew he was bullshitting me, of course. For one thing, he wouldn't have heard a single telepathic word you spoke while you were chained up. For another thing, I examined the death scene, I felt what he felt as he killed your father. There was no fear or panic. There wasn't much of anything. A little excitement. A little triumph. Mostly curiosity. As if he wanted to know how it'd feel to take a life."

Swallowing, Enzo again shook his head. "Gian wasn't like that."

"Sure he was. Your father's soul only confirmed all I suspected—Gian struck while he was sleeping. Your brother didn't kill himself because I wouldn't listen to him. He simply didn't want to face punishment. He smiled at me before he slit his own throat, Enzo. In his mind, he was outwitting me."

"You're lying! It's all fucking lies!"

Keenan looked close to rolling his eyes. "No wonder he and what's-his-name came together and made a deal. They're so alike with their insistence on only seeing what they want to see." He glanced down at Enzo. "Well, the pair of you went and *fucked up*."

"I regret nothing." Enzo flicked Piper a look. "I might not have ended her life, but I hurt her plenty over the past few months," he taunted Levi. "I even almost killed her with that blow to the brain. She lived in fear—"

"You think you can piss me off enough to make me kill you?" Levi shook his head with a snicker. "I'm not so easy to manipulate, and you're not as smart as you think you are."

Enzo began to shake. "I'm not going back to that Chamber."

Levi's eyes bled to black as his demon took control. "Oh yes, you are. And you will stay there for a very long time. I will be a most regular visitor. I have had months to think up some . . . interesting plans for our time together. I think you will find them creative, albeit agonizing. Just to give you a little sample of what will soon come . . ." The demon hovered its hand above Enzo's chest.

The asshole bucked with a hoarse cry, his hands fisting, his face creasing with pain. It seemed to go on and on and on, but then the entity lowered its arm.

Enzo sagged, breathing heavily, his eyes wet with unshed tears.

"He'll be ready and waiting for you," Knox told Levi's demon. Flames then spurted out of the floor and surrounded both Enzo and the Prime. Mere seconds later, the two males were gone.

Levi's demon stalked to Piper, its black eyes drinking her in. "I loathe seeing you injured, little nightmare." It gently grasped her jaw and turned her head this way and that as it examined her face. "Every single one of those wounds will be revisited on him."

"Don't forget to rub chili in them," she said.

Humor glimmered in its eyes. "That I can do." It then retreated, and Levi's gunmetal gray gaze once more locked on her.

He carefully drew her close, mindful of her injuries. He didn't say a word. He didn't have to. She saw everything there in his eyes—his relief that she was alive, his anger that she was wounded and might have been killed, the lingering echoes of whatever panic he felt at knowing she was in danger. Considering that was a two-way street, Piper wondered if he saw the same emotions in her eyes.

"Are you okay?" she asked. "I know he hurt you bad, I heard you—"

"Shh, I'm fine." Levi dabbed a reassuring kiss to her mouth. "It wasn't a physical injury he gave me. It was phantom pain.

Hurt like a fucker, though." He smoothed a hand up her back. "Tell me exactly what happened from start to finish."

Piper inhaled deeply. "Well, Dez knocked on the front door . . ." Once she'd relayed the entire story, she added, "How did you find out that Enzo was the one who wanted me dead?"

"I didn't. Not until Knox pyroported us inside the apartment."

And what a nifty ability that was.

"I thought that only the nightmare was holding you hostage. We worked out that he was the killer when a guard at the prison hummed that damn song he loved and claimed Janelle's partner often sang it."

"Oh. I thought maybe Celeste really *had* known who'd targeted me."

Levi snorted. "She didn't have a single useful thing to say. I'll tell you all about that conversation later. First, there's something I need to do."

Piper frowned. "What?"

"Head to the Chamber."

"Wait, why?"

"I need to see for myself that the two bastards who wanted you dead are contained, baby. I trust that Knox saw to that, but I need to *know* it. I have to be sure that they can't get to you again. Plus, my demon's not going to settle until it has visual proof of that. I won't be long. Keenan and Larkin will be right here with you." He glanced at the harpy. "You'll stay with her?"

"Of course," replied Larkin. "If you guys want to sleep in my spare bedroom tonight, feel free to do so. It's gonna take a while to clean this place up. The damage in the living room is . . . *wow*."

"Thanks, Lark."

As Knox returned to his side in a burst of flames, Levi pressed a kiss to Piper's forehead and then said, "I'll be back soon."

# CHAPTER TWENTY-FOUR

After Knox pyroported Levi to the Chamber, they walked side by side along the row of cells, only slowing their pace as they approached the one that contained Enzo.

The moment the shithead spotted them through the iron bars, he began struggling to free himself from the shackles. "Let me out!" he yelled, anger and fear warring for supremacy in his manic eyes. "I want *out*!"

Knox sighed. "No one cares, so you might as well settle down."

Having nothing more to say to Enzo than he'd already said earlier, Levi didn't stop at the cell. He continued onto the next one, which now homed Moira's killer—and would do so for a while. The bastard had a *lot* of sins to answer for.

So many lives had been taken by him. So many children had been robbed of their mothers and then dumped at orphanages. Levi knew from experience that those places weren't all hearts and rainbows. Heaven only knew what had become of those kids.

Hanging in chains, Clyde lifted his head. Despite his current situation, he nonetheless gifted Levi with an amiable smile. "I knew you'd come," he said, seeming rather satisfied about it. He didn't even look at Knox. He was utterly focused on Levi.

"You have questions," Clyde assumed. No, *hoped*. He wanted attention. Company. Conversation. Maybe that had always been part of his personality, or maybe it was a result of the curse that had plagued him for so long and made him feel so very alone.

"Not really," said Levi, going for bored and disinterested, knowing it would push the asshole's buttons. "It's not like I could trust that your answers would be at all factual. Not when you lie to yourself as if it's your job and believe only what you want to believe."

Clyde frowned. "No, that would be Enzo."

"You're kindred spirits for sure."

"He was never anything but a tool I needed. You and me, though . . . we have a connection."

Both Levi and his demon bristled. "No, we don't," said Levi, still feigning boredom. "You tell yourself that because you need to feel connected to someone. You tried forcing your victims to bond with you. Didn't work so well, did it?"

"That was on them. I only wanted to love them. They wouldn't let me. Your aunt was most resistant. But you made the time I spent with her worthwhile." Clyde's mouth kicked up. "Such a beautiful little boy you were. So much potential. She would have squashed that."

"She might have tried. But that wasn't a reason for her to die."

"You were better off without her," said Clyde.

Levi felt his jaw harden. "That wasn't for you to decide. You played God with her, just as you did the other women. You weren't looking for love, you were looking for submission."

"No, I—"

"You wanted them to psychologically crumble so they'd be under your control without any effort on your part. It never worked though, did it? Know why?" Levi took a step closer to the cell. "It was because of the children. The women held out because they couldn't emotionally abandon their children.

"My aunt might not have loved me or even wanted me, but she loved my mother—that was the only reason she kept me, and it would have been the reason she didn't submit the way you wanted. In other words, you've been fucking yourself over right from the start, and you never once saw it."

Clyde swallowed. "You're wrong about me."

"No, I'm not. I see you, even if you don't. The woman who cursed you saw you too, didn't she? I believe her name was Beth." Piper had relayed the whole sordid tale.

"She saw my love for her sister as a betrayal."

Levi wasn't so sure Clyde had loved her or anyone else. The emotion eluded some people. Levi got the feeling that the man in front of him was one of those people.

"We can't always help who we love, can we?" asked Clyde. "Take you and Celeste. She loved you. It wasn't your fault that you didn't feel the same, but she held you responsible anyway. It also wasn't your fault that you fell for Piper—nor was it a bad thing—but Celeste resents you for that just the same."

"Not enough to curse both herself and me in such a grave way. And you know, considering just how far Beth went to punish you and *exactly* what a sick fuck you are, I actually think you truly were guilty of the crime she accused you of. After all, you've taken the lives of many women over the years and you're not one bit remorseful about it. I doubt that sexually assaulting a woman would be much to you."

"She *asked* me to make love to her."

"Maybe. But the question is . . . did she say those words voluntarily, or did you *make* her say them? Personally, I think it was the latter."

The nightmare's eyes flickered. Yeah, he'd been in her mind, ruling her actions. *Fucker.*

Clyde's expression tightened. "You shouldn't be so hard on me. I *saved* you. Your aunt would have ruined you. You can't say you don't like your life as it is. You can't say you don't owe me for the happiness you have now. Like it or not, we *are* connected."

"You're nothing to me," Levi stated firmly. "And I don't owe you shit except the beating of your fucking life for what you did to my mate."

"I didn't hurt her. I didn't even touch her."

"You stole her free will. You ensured she was helpless while another caused her physical harm, which means you're just as responsible for any injuries she suffered. And so you will suffer worse. There isn't one person who can claim you don't have it coming." Levi gave him a dismissive look and then walked away.

"Wait, we're not done talking!"

Levi didn't glance over his shoulder as he replied, "I'll be back when I'm in the mood to play with you."

"Don't you want to hear how many women there were? Don't you want—"

"Not interested."

"There are things you should hear that . . . *Come back!*"

Once they were out of hearing range, Knox said, "He really does hate being alone, doesn't he?"

"My guess is he's also thinking he can bargain his way out of the Chamber by offering up details about his crimes," said Levi.

"Well he'd be wrong to think so."

Indeed. But Levi would certainly wring as much information out of him as he could, since there might be people who would like to know what happened to their mothers. For now . . . "I have to get back to Piper."

Leaving her hadn't been easy when the fear he'd felt for her earlier still rattled in his bones. But, as he'd told her, both he and his demon had needed to *see* that the threats to her were properly contained. "Take me to Larkin's apartment, not mine. Piper and I are sleeping there tonight. We can't stay at our place while it looks like a warzone."

"Don't be surprised if Piper receives some visitors," said Knox.

"Visitors?"

The Prime pyroported them to Larkin's living room. Both she and Piper sat on the sofa while Keenan lounged on the armchair. They weren't alone. Devon and Tanner were present. And it wasn't long before Maddox, Raini, and Hector appeared. Knox then collected Harper, materializing moments before Ciaran teleported Khloë into the apartment.

Levi couldn't say he was happy to have so many people there when his mate was clearly tired, but since Maddox healed both Piper and Levi—the latter at her insistence—he couldn't really complain. Much.

"I can't believe it all went on while I was in the building none the wiser," said a pale Devon while her mate rubbed her back.

Khloë blew out a breath. "My demon *really* wants to kick Enzo's ass, and I'd be totally down with that." She lifted a brow at Knox, her hands clasped. "Any chance we can make that happen?"

The Prime pursed his lips. "I don't see why not."

Khloë pumped her fist. "Awesome."

It was an hour or so before all but Larkin left. Once more thanking the harpy for letting them stay at her apartment, Piper allowed Levi to lead her to the spare bedroom. As much as she appreciated that so many had showed up to check on them, she couldn't deny that it was a relief to be alone with him.

Dog tired and still a little shaky from all that happened, she wanted nothing more than to slide into bed with her mate; wanted to feel him pressed against her, safe and well and fully healed. But first . . . "I was thinking of taking a shower."

Her wounds might be healed, but dry blood still smeared her skin and stained her clothes—items which would need to be trashed, because they were all torn and would only make her think of what happened tonight. More, they'd make her think of what *could* have happened tonight if things had gone down differently. "Care to join me?"

He hummed. "Sounds good to me. Quick warning, I'll end up eating you out."

She blinked. "Well I do hope so."

His mouth curved. "Good."

She tried returning the favor after he made her come, but he resisted, claiming he wanted to explode inside her pussy tonight, not down her throat or all over her hand. But instead of taking her against the tiled wall, he ushered her out of the shower, intent on fucking her in bed. Having no objections to that, she didn't dawdle.

In bed, he didn't instantly put any moves on her. He only drew her close as he brushed her hair away from her face. "How are you feeling?"

Piper smoothed her hand over his solid shoulder. "Not too tired to get royally fucked, if that's where this conversation is heading. And I'm otherwise fine. You?"

"I'm better now that we're alone." He flicked her nose with his. "I'm not in the mood to share you."

She snorted. "Let's be fair, you're never truly in the mood to do that."

The corner of his lips hiked up. "True. I like having you all to myself. My demon likes having all your attention." He raked his gaze over her face, and his mini smile faded. "I'm usually good at locking down my emotions so I can get a job done. But when I realized the killer probably had you, I mentally lost it."

"That man is a fucking psycho." Even *thinking* about him made a chill run down her spine. "And he doesn't even seem to know it. I mean, what is up with that?"

"Crazy people often don't know they're crazy. Khloë seems to be the only exception to that rule." Sobering, Levi gave her a serious look. "He'll suffer hard, Piper. And for a very long time. As will Enzo." His jaw tightened. "I trusted that fucker. I trusted him *with you*."

Piper slipped her hand up to his neck. "He'd never given you a reason why you couldn't. So all that guilt I can see you're feeling . . . it's senseless. He spent years cultivating the image of a reformed criminal. You gave him a second chance. Lots of people did. That was the right thing to do. *He's* the one who was in the wrong."

Levi only grunted, guilt still plastered all over his face.

"I didn't once suspect him of being the person who wanted me dead," said Piper. "Not even for a millisecond. Do you blame me for that?"

Levi's head drew back as his brow pinched. "What? Of course not."

"Then you shouldn't blame yourself either."

He sighed. "It's easier said than done."

"I know." She began massaging his nape. "How's your demon?"

His eyes going half-mast as her fingers kneaded and glided, he replied, "Now that it's calmer and more settled . . . it's actually kind of smug."

She double-blinked, her hand pausing its movements. “Smug?”

“The way the entity sees it, the death ballad brand ‘saved the day.’”

She rolled her eyes. “Enzo would have been taken down with or without the ballad.”

“Of that I have no doubt. But my demon still intends to take the credit.”

“Of course it does,” she said dryly, resuming the massage.

He groaned. “Feels good.” His hand squeezed her hip. “How’s your demon doing?”

“It’s sort of sulking right now.”

“Why?”

“It didn’t get to kill anyone.”

He snorted. “I see.”

“It might not be so annoyed if *I’d* gotten to kill either Frick or Frack—it’s often content to live vicariously through me.”

“Will the entity feel better if I buy it lots and lots of diamonds?”

Piper found it almost pathetic that her demon’s mood immediately switched to gleeful. Like all such entities, it liked pretty, shiny things. “To my disgust, yes. Yes, it really will.”

“Diamonds it is.” His mouth curving, he rested his forehead against hers. “I fucking love you, you know.”

Warmth bloomed inside her. “So you didn’t only say it earlier to mess with me?”

“I’d never give you those words unless I meant them.”

“Good.” She kissed him sweetly, softly. “Because I love you.”

His smile kicked up a notch. “My demon feels you should also love the death ballad brand, but we’re gonna ignore that.”

“Yes. Let’s. Now, hello, why isn’t your dick in me?”

A chuckle eased out of him. “No patience.” He rolled her

onto her back, humming again as she wrapped her legs around him. "It's going to be rough."

"Just when I think I couldn't love you more . . ."

# CHAPTER TWENTY-FIVE

*Two months later*

"My God, she is such the cutest." Khloë smiled down at the baby in her arms. "I want to eat her."

"No, no eating," bossed Asher, hurrying over to the sofa.

Khloë chuckled. "I was just kidding, little man. No eating Anaïs, I promise."

He narrowed his eyes, apparently unconvinced.

"My boy already knows better than to take the word of an imp," said Harper.

Larkin snickered. "Like it's not something you make him recite as if it's a mantra."

"Well it's pure truth," Harper defended.

Piper would really have to agree with that. So it didn't surprise her that Asher, who had enough Wallis in him to know his mother was right, watched Khloë closely as she cooed over Anaïs.

He seemed to have appointed himself as the hellpup's protector—probably because, for him, it was the norm for people to have a personal bodyguard. Although his protectiveness was utterly adorable, they were all a little worried that he'd start pyroporting Anaïs into his arms whenever he pleased.

Piper exchanged an amused look with Levi, who stood off to the side with Knox. They all often turned up at Devon and Tanner's after work to check in on the new parents and Anaïs. Larkin was temporarily taking over for Tanner as Harper's bodyguard, since Levi had been reinstated as Knox's bodyguard and was once more a fully active sentinel.

Levi had done as promised and cut back on his hours, only working however long he needed to. Not that she'd expected any different, given he was fully committed to their relationship and—by his own admission—didn't like being away from Piper for long.

It was crazy how much her life had changed in such a short period of time. In addition to finding herself with a bunch of new friends—including Ella and Mia, who she'd finally met a month ago and clicked with instantly—she'd switched jobs, sold her house, and found herself with both an anchor *and* a mate.

A mate who'd slipped a black diamond ring on her finger a week ago.

It had shocked the shit out of her. Demons didn't do such a thing lightly since, for them, a black diamond ring was a symbol of the ultimate commitment. So she'd been certain to make sure *he* wore one, too. Her demon was rather smug about the whole thing.

Sitting beside Khloë, Piper gazed down at the baby, her mouth curving. Only two weeks old, Anaïs was spoiled rotten. An endless amount of people from both their lair and Devon's old lair had dropped by to visit, bearing numerous gifts. Raini in particular regularly went on shopping sprees and came back with clothes and toys. Hence why Khloë often accused her of jockeying for the position of best aunt—a position that Khloë felt should be *hers*.

Tanner tended to shoo everyone off fairly quickly, wanting Devon to get her rest. He was a super-proud father, and he'd allegedly been a terrific birthing partner . . . albeit a little bossy and impatient, as if pushing out a child should be simple enough. Still, Devon only tried to kill him twice.

Levi's mind stroked over Piper's. *You ready to leave?*

*Just give me one minute.* Smoothing her fingers over the pink blanket wrapped around Anaïs, Piper said, "I wanna have a hold."

Khloë cast her an annoyed look. "Not yet."

"You're hogging her," Piper complained.

"I don't care."

Levi smiled as his mate crossed her eyes. The most tolerant of the females, Piper seemed to have more patience for Khloë than the others, which he and Tanner outright admired.

Asher giggled. "Koey's a meanie."

Piper nodded, her lips curling. "She's a total meanie."

"Among other things," grumbled Tanner, shooting the imp a narrow-eyed look. Well Khloë *had* been driving him and Devon nuts, put-out that they wouldn't let the imp take Anaïs home for overnight stays so she and the baby could 'bond without interference.'

Tanner seemed a little terrified at the idea of his child bonding too closely with a woman who appeared to have made it her life's vocation to irritate as many people as possible on a daily basis.

Anaïs stirred, making a fussy sound, but then settled again.

"Aw, she snuffled," said Khloë. "Like a little piglet."

Tanner's eyelid twitched. "No, *not* like a piglet."

"Like a big, bad hellpup," said Khloë with an eyeroll. "Better?"

Tanner grunted and crossed to the sofa. "Hand her over to me."

The imp frowned. "Why?"

"She's my daughter. I don't need a reason."

"Can I have a teensy, weensy hold first?" Piper begged him. "Please? I'm leaving in, like, five minutes."

Tanner took Anaïs from a whining Khloë and carefully settled her in Piper's arms.

Piper grinned. "Yay, thank you." Cuddling the hellpup close, she nuzzled her soft dark hair. The sight made Levi's chest squeeze.

"Where are you heading off to?" Khloë asked her.

"The Underground," Piper replied. "Levi's fighting in the combat circle tonight. Larkin and I will be among the spectators."

"Ooh, I'm so there," said Khloë.

"Yes, *please* take her with you," Tanner said to Piper. "I need a break."

Khloë frowned at him. "What's that supposed to mean?"

Devon made a speculative sound. "I think it might have something to do with how you keep waking Anaïs to play with her—despite us reminding you over and over to *never* wake a sleeping baby—and then scrambling out of here when you can't get her to stop bawling. Oh, and there's the whole you drawing a you-know-what on Tanner's face while he was napping."

Khloë huffed. "I'm never gonna understand what you all have against baby hippos."

"It wasn't a—" Devon cut herself off and took a deep breath. "You know what, I'm not going to let you get me all worked up. I'm not. I'm going to stay calm. Serene. Placid—"

"Constipated."

"*Khloë*."

"Oh, I'm sorry, did the log finally leave the clogged pipe after all?"

Devon's face flushed. "Stop it."

"Wait, it hasn't? Damn. I was hoping the right pooportunity would come along for you."

A hiss slid through the hellcat's teeth. "Woman, stop."

Khloë wagged her finger. "Now, now, Miss Hissy, there's no need to get all constipangry."

"*And* it's time we left." Keenan hauled the imp off the sofa, ignoring her chuckles. "Come on, let's leave them in peace before someone throttles you."

"Yes, take her," Devon urged, baring her teeth. "*Take. Her.*"

Feeling his lips quirk, Levi looked down at his mate. "Now are you ready?"

"Yup." Piper stood, nuzzling Anaïs once more, and then handed the baby to Tanner. "Thank you for letting me come visit. Again."

Once goodbyes had been exchanged, everyone left the new parents and their hellpup alone. Levi drove Piper and Larkin to the Underground while Khloë and Keenan followed in their own vehicle.

Arriving at the combat circle, Levi didn't do his usual thing and immediately go backstage to ready himself for his upcoming duel. Instead, he escorted Piper and the others to one of the front spectator rows. The place was filling up fast, since the first fight would soon begin.

Levi gave her a quick kiss. "You good here?"

"Sure."

"Stay with Larkin at all times."

Watching her mate walk away, Piper rolled her eyes. The

cloud of lethal danger that had once hovered over her might be a thing of the past, but he remained as protective as ever. Not that he shouldn't. The demon world featured a lot of brutality, and there was always a possibility that people might strike at him through her . . . much like Enzo had done.

The entire lair had taken Enzo's betrayal hard. Levi still stupidly condemned himself for trusting the Force member with her safety, no matter what Piper said. He also paid the shithead regular visits at the Chamber, as did Dez's family, to punish the two males they held responsible for Dez's death.

Jasper and Sefton were more than adequately punished for the vandalism to Piper's home and car. They'd kept a low profile ever since. Celeste, too, had kept her head down since experiencing whatever punishment Knox had dished out. Piper hoped it would stay that way. *Hoped*.

"Right," began Keenan, "who wants drinks or food from the concession stand?" Once he'd taken orders, he headed off with Khloë. They returned relatively fast and handed out their purchases.

Piper happily took her popcorn. "Thank you." Spotting a familiar face coming to join them, she smiled. "Oh, hey, Jolene."

The grandmother of both Harper and Khloë—a woman who also happened to be a badass Prime who very few demons cared to tangle with—returned her smile. "Piper, always a pleasure. You remember my daughter."

Piper nodded and waved at the woman. "Hi, Martina."

"Hey, sweetie," she said.

Both women settled themselves near Khloë just as the imp looked up from her phone and turned to Larkin. "Did you *really* shoot chips of hell-ice at Teague's ass?"

The harpy gave an indifferent shrug. "He deserved it."

Khloë only snickered.

Piper had asked the imp what 'oath' she'd been referring to that day at the racing stadium. Khloë had openly told her how she'd made Teague promise not to get involved with any of her friends because, in her words, he was a total player.

While Piper understood why the imp would extract such a vow from him, she felt it was a real bummer for Larkin and Teague. The chemistry between them was insanely off the charts, and Piper had the feeling they'd suit in more than a sexual sense.

Levi himself had said that if anyone could handle Larkin's demon, it would be Teague. "*Her entity's level of crazy would be nothing to him*," Levi had added. "*Hell, he and his demon are psychotic enough to like it*."

So, yeah, it was a shame.

Another male materialized, dressed in a ratty-assed tee, faded jeans, and a plain red cap. He was munching on popcorn and *reeked* of weed.

Piper recognized him straight off, since she'd been at Harper and Knox's place a few times when he abruptly showed up. It was none other than Lucifer, the devil himself. Or Lou, as he preferred to be called.

He had a soft spot for Asher, referring to the little boy as his nephew. Which was why neither Harper, Knox, nor the sentinels had much patience for Lou. Then again, the obsessive, psychopathic man-child wasn't popular with anyone but his satanic cult 'followers,' which seemed to suit him just fine since he was highly antisocial.

His nose wrinkled at the sight of Larkin's slush puppy. "I don't know how anyone can drink that stuff."

The harpy's brow creased. "I don't know how anyone can be you and not *loathe* themselves, and yet . . ."

Lou smiled. "God, you're so rude and bitchy. I like it."

Larkin gave a quick shake of the head. She had a knack for handling him. Basically, she treated him like a spoiled child who shouldn't be either seen *or* heard. And he appeared to find it entertaining.

"What brings you to the combat circle?" Piper asked him.

"The siren songs that are screams of sheer unsufferable agony," Lou deadpanned.

Piper licked the inside of her lower lip. "All right."

Jolene peered down the row. "Hello, Lou."

His upper lip peeled back as he stared at the female Prime, who he had absolutely no tolerance for. He cut his gaze to Keenan. "I still have *no* idea how you could mate a Wallis imp. I mean, what were you thinking? Or were you simply *not* thinking?"

Keenan sighed. "You really need to let it go. And maybe also go find another seat."

Lou let out an indignant sound. "Excuse me, I am sitting with my friends."

Jolene frowned. "What friends?"

"Lauren and Pippa," he replied, smug.

Larkin exhaled heavily. "They're not our names."

"Yes, well, I prefer to have pet names for the people in my life," said Lou. "What is wrong with that?"

Larkin lifted a hand. "If you must sit here, don't talk. The mere sound of your voice offends me."

Lou grinned. "Best. Bitch. *Ever.*"

Staring at him, Martina shook her head. "Not many people actually bother me, but I truly struggle to deal with you."

"There's a support group you can join," Lou told her. "They have meetings every Sunday at a chapel on Piss Off Street near You Suck Balls park."

Khloë frowned. "Sorry, where?"

Piper snorted.

Cheers rang out as the umpire made his way into the center of the dome, microphone in hand. He called out the first two contestants—both of whom were female—and the duel soon began.

Piper spent a lot of time flinching and wincing. When it came to the combat circle, it was a case of, 'Anything goes.' So there were a lot of dirty moves, snapping of bones, and somewhat sadistic torment—which her demon thoroughly enjoyed witnessing. For Piper, however, it wasn't always so easy to watch. The only blessing was that neither contestant actually died. Because yeah, that happened occasionally.

Duel after duel took place. Some were over fast, others were dragged out. Some fighters left the dome conscious, others were knocked clean out.

Her nerves were rubbed raw by the time Levi entered the circle. His eyes were cold, his face was blank, and he fairly radiated self-assurance and determination. He didn't look her way. He was utterly focused on his opponent—a guy by the name of Cisco.

Piper took a moment to study Cisco. He was taller. Broader. Carried himself with confidence. She'd seen him fight before. He was a damn good brawler and boasted a few offensive abilities, so he wouldn't make this easy for Levi. Her reaper *would* win, though. He'd never lost a fight. Not once.

Then again, neither had Cisco.

The umpire exited the circle, a bell rang loud . . . and then the two males were moving. Fast. Explosive. Savage.

Fists flew, slamming into noses, jaws, temples, and ribs. Feet snapped out, ramming into knees or thighs. Power rippled around the space as crackling orbs, telekinetic energy, waves of despair, and balls of hellfire sailed through the air.

Like her demon, the crowd was *loving* it. They yelled, booed, or egged on the fighters.

Piper was somewhat torn. On the one hand, watching Levi fight—seeing all that power, strength, and pure viciousness he exhibited—flustered her feminine parts. Seriously, she should probably light a candle in penance for getting off on this so much. But on the other hand, it was impossible not to worry for him. Especially when such duels had been known to result in death.

And so, on the edge of her seat, Piper splayed her hands on either side of her face. Every hit he took made her stomach twist. Her comfort? Levi was *more* than holding his own and had very few injuries.

Winces echoed around the dome as a telekinetic blast sent Cisco crashing into the wall. He'd no sooner scraped himself off the floor than a hellfire orb smashed into his face so hard his head snapped back.

"Well damn," said Lou with a cruel chuckle. "Levi's on form tonight."

He was. He really—

She jolted as her mate took a crackling ball of whatever-the-fuck-it-was to the solar plexus. It knocked the breath from his lungs and sent him stumbling back a step. "*Jesus Christ.*"

Lou nudged her. "Oh don't bring *him* into this."

Ignoring that, Piper watched as Levi retaliated fast, telekinetically swiping Cisco off the ground and bashing him into the ceiling. *Well, ow.*

To his credit, Cisco recovered quickly. More punches and kicks were exchanged. More blows of power were traded. More bruises, cuts, and burns were caused.

Biting her thumbnail, Piper watched as a telekinetic hit slammed Cisco against the wall. Then Levi was there, hovering his hand near his opponent's abdomen. Cisco doubled over, guttural cries of pain escaping him. She could guess what ability her mate was utilizing right then, and she wasn't the least bit surprised when Cisco threw in the towel.

Piper and her group were instantly on their feet, cheering and clapping. They weren't the only ones. Many spectators even chanted his name, though Levi paid no heed to it. Nor did he cockily pace around the circle, smiling at the crowd. He . . . well, he made a beeline for Piper. He wrapped his hand around the back of her neck and kissed her hard, robbing her of breath. She melted into him, unable to do anything else.

He snatched her off her feet, tossed her over his shoulder, and strode toward the vaulted steps.

"Hey!" she yelled. "What the fuck?"

He ignored her, descending the stairs that took them backstage.

Oh, she was so gonna rip him a new one.

Inside a private room, he set her on her feet and backed her into the wall as his mouth once more crashed down on hers. It seemed like she wasn't the only one who got all stirred up by the fight. His tongue licked into her mouth as a hand collared her throat. Her breath hitched, her nipples tightened, her lower stomach clenched . . . and her control became a thing of the past.

Later. She'd rip him a new one later.

He kissed her like he needed her to breathe. Like she was his only source of oxygen. His tongue delved deep as he plundered her mouth and swallowed her every breath.

No one had ever made her feel the way Levi did—so *wanted*, so needed, so fucking possessed. It was exhilarating and intoxicating for both Piper and her demon.

*

Feeling like his entire body *pounded* with the need to be inside her, Levi broke the kiss long enough for them to whip off each other's tees. Then he was again feasting on her mouth, lapping up her taste. Once more keeping a dominant grip on her throat with one hand, he used his other hand to stroke and explore and again lay claim to what would always be his.

Images flickered through his mind—all sent to him by his demon. The entity wanted her helpless. Wanted her to only be able to take what they gave.

Liking the idea, Levi used power alone to cuff her wrists and pin them high above her head. She gasped into his mouth. He swallowed the sound, grinding against her, his cock heavy and throbbing.

She kissed him harder, moaning in what could only be described as feminine demand. He softly slid his fingers into her hair, gently kneading her scalp . . . just as he bit her lip hard and tightened his hold on her throat, knowing the dual sensation of gentle and rough pushed her buttons.

Sure enough, her pupils dilated and her breath snagged in her throat. "Levi."

"Need to be in you right fucking now," he said, his hands dropping to her waistband. He only took the time to free one leg from her jeans and panties before tearing open his own fly. He cupped her pussy, his fingers probing. Hot slickness coated his fingers, and a growl crawled up his throat. "Already wet." Just how he liked her.

Piper's heart jumped as he gripped her ass and lifted her like she weighed nothing. The power shackling her wrists didn't release her, it kept her pinned to the wall, pulsing and flexing. Which her demon totally dug. The blunt head of his cock bumped her folds and—

He slammed her down on his cock. Buried his full length

inside her in one ruthless, unapologetic move that told her she was his to do with what he wished. And then he was fucking her. He didn't thrust. He planted her on his cock over and over, using her brutally even as he looked at her like nothing else mattered.

It was wild. It was savage. It was carnal. And she absolutely drowned in it all.

A rush of cold swept over her skin as his eyes bled to black. "All fucking ours," said the demon. Just like Levi had done, it bounced her up and down on its cock. But the demon was rougher, more impersonal . . . as if she was a mere sex toy it was using to get itself off.

Soon Levi was back, feverishly impaling her on his shaft. But the demon surfaced again shortly afterwards, dialing up the level of sexual aggressiveness once more.

On and on it went, winding her tighter and tighter and tighter until she couldn't take anymore. Her release struck her like a white-hot bolt of lightning and thundered through her. It was a storm that wrenched a scream from her throat and scattered her thoughts so completely she was barely aware of Levi locking his cock deep in her body as he exploded.

Once their orgasms had finally subsided, she nuzzled his neck. "Congrats on your win."

He pressed a kiss to her head and released her wrists. "Thank you, baby."

She lifted her gaze to his. "Still, that whole throwing me over your shoulder thing—"

"You liked it."

"I did not."

He smiled. "Liar. You simply feel compelled to whine because you think you shouldn't have liked it."

"Um, excuse me, I do not whine or—"

"*And* you liked watching me fight. I reckon you were wet before I even touched you. Am I wrong?" He raked his teeth over her lower lip. "Tell me the truth, I dare you."

She sniffed, planting her hands on his shoulders. "I can admit that watching you fight is kind of like foreplay. But it's also nerve-wracking at the same time. I don't like seeing you hurt."

"But you were wet all the same, weren't you?"

She tossed him a haughty look. "Are we done here? Because I'm ready to leave."

Feeling a chuckle rumble out of him, Levi threaded his fingers through her hair, drinking in the sight of her, pure male possession filling him from head to toe. "Do something for me."

She narrowed her eyes. "The last time you said that, you slid a ring on my finger and asked that I never take it off."

And she'd agreed on the condition that he'd wear a matching one. Like he'd ever have objected. His demon was still unbelievably smug that she'd claimed them. "I need you to do something a little different this time."

"What?" she asked, wary.

"Take my surname." He palmed the side of her face. "I know it's not always done. I know you might not think it necessary. But we'll be starting a family at some point." The more he saw her cuddling and fussing over Anaïs, the more he imagined her with *their* baby. "I want us to have the same surname when we do." He held his breath as he awaited her answer.

A little smile curled one side of her mouth. "Sounds reasonable," she said, sliding her hand over the Pied Piper tattoo on his upper arm that she'd given him weeks ago. "I'm all about being reasonable."

A contented sigh slipped out of him. He gave her a soft, lazy kiss. "Thank you. Love you, baby."

"Love you right back. Always will."

"Promise?"

"Yes."

He swept his hand down her body to cup her hip. "And you promise to never do something stupid like try to leave me?"

"I do."

"And you promise to never remove that diamond ring?"

"Absolutely."

"And you promise to always obey me in all matters regarding your safety?"

She gave him a solemn nod. "I swear it on my hamster's grave."

Levi felt his lips flatten. "Your hamster. Right."

"I'm not fond of that tone."

"On a serious note, did you ever have any pets at all?"

"Sure I did. Including my hamster. His name was Wotsit. He was killed by Mom's cat. Super tragic."

"Your mom doesn't have any cats. Never did."

"Now that's not true."

"I call bullshit, baby."

Piper gaped. "I can't believe you don't—"

Levi cut her off with a hard kiss. "Woman, you're a menace. But you're *my* menace. One who, I must add, never owned a hamster in her life."

"I did too!"

# ACKNOWLEDGEMENTS

I have to say a super huge thank you to my family—your encouragement, support, and patience means everything to me.

I want to also thank my PA, Melissa, without whom I would be lost—woman, you are *the shit*.

Thank you also to the team at Piatkus, especially my editor Anna Boatman. You're all so amazing and supportive and oh my God I love the cover so thank you!

Last but certainly not least, a mega thanks to all my readers, you're all fabulous. I hope you enjoyed REAPER . . . and yes, Larkin and Teague's story will in fact be next.

Take care,
S :)